Molly's Song

Molly's Song by Lee Hutch

This is a work of historical fiction. While based upon historical events, any similarity to any person, circumstance or event is purely coincidental and related to the efforts of the author to portray the characters in historically accurate representations.

Cover image: Vintage silver print by William I. Goldman, taken at Sallie Shearer's brothel, Reading, PA

Cover and interior design by Jacqueline Cook

ISBN: 978-1-7366203-2-8 (Paperback)
ISBN: 978-1-7366203-3-5 (e-book)

10 9 8 7 6 5 4 3 2 1

BISAC Subject Headings:
FIC014000 FICTION / Historical / General
FIC014060 FICTION / Historical / Civil War Era
FIC044000 FICTION / Women

Address all correspondence to:
Fireship Press, LLC
P.O. Box 68412
Tucson, AZ 85737

Visit our website at:
www.fireshippress.com

For my friend and comrade Robert E. York
Gone but not forgotten.

And For Clare.

Molly's Song

Lee Hutch

Chapter One

"Don't you know there's a terrible war in America?"

Molly O'Sullivan fingered the Saint Michael's medal she wore around her neck. As she brushed her red curls over her shoulder, she asked, "And what does that have to do with me, Sean O'Hanlon? Are the Americans after sending girls off to fight for them?"

"Well … I … no," Sean said. "But Father Byrne says that we should avoid going to America or they'll force us into the army."

"It's precious little you have for brains, Sean," Molly said. "Father Byrne said young *men* should avoid going. And I'm not a young man now, am I?"

Sean looked down at the ground and stuck his hands in his pockets.

"Now that we've fixed that," Molly said, "maybe you'd dance with me? It's my wake we're having tonight. Or have you forgotten?"

Young people of all ages were gathered around the center of the crossroads, all of them barefoot in the light of the moon as the adults stood around sipping poteen from jugs they passed back and forth to ward off the late November chill. The air smelled of damp grass and stale alcohol as the air echoed with the laughter and jokes of the youths. Off to the side, by himself, Father Byrne watched over the activities with a frown on his face. Molly smiled at him but received a shake of the head in return. *Doesn't he think I'm—what was it he said?—incorri-something. He told me there weren't never any saints with the red hair. Surely that is a lie.*

A trio of musicians struck up a lively reel, using the glow of torches to aid them. Molly grabbed Sean's hand and led him over to where the young people had divided themselves into groups of four couples each. Molly turned to face Sean, putting her left hand on his right shoulder as he slipped his around her slender waist.

"I hope you've gotten better since the last time I danced with you," Molly said.

"We are about to find out," Sean said.

Molly and Sean followed the other three couples as they danced in a circle, each couple spinning around as they moved. Her head whirled as the couples separated and made a line. She tapped her hand on her thigh in time with music as she went through a series of turns, ending up back with Sean to start the circle again. Music and laughter filled the air around her. *Takes the mind off the journey, it does*, Molly thought as the music faded to a close. The older people who had stood around watching, perhaps with thoughts of their own childhood, clapped and one shouted, "Show us a dance, Molly!'

"And why would I do that, Martin Fitzgerald?" Molly asked as she put her hands on her hips and faced the man.

"Oh, come on with it, Molly," another man said. "This might be our last chance to watch ye dance."

"They're right," Sean said.

"Fine, then," Molly said, "but only one song."

Someone produced a wooden broom and placed it on the ground. Molly stood beside it and gathered up her skirt in her hands, the glow of the moon reflecting off her pale white calves. She nodded to the musicians, and they took up another tune. The crowd clapped in time with the music, or as close as they could get, given the amount of poteen consumed, as Molly danced around the broom, her bare feet never straying too far off the ground as she artfully moved back and forth from heel to toe. Sweat trickled down the back of her neck and she laughed as she moved.

When the music ended, Molly bent down and put her hands on her knees to catch her breath as the crowd whistled and cheered. Sean walked over and took her arm.

"Come on," he said. "Let's sit down so you can catch your wind."

He led Molly over to a felled log that lay alongside the road.

"Is it true that the lord himself is sending you?" Sean asked as they settled down next to one another.

"It is," Molly said.

Four months earlier, Lord Sanderson had summoned Molly and her mother to meet him in the study of the big house that sat in the middle of the estate. Large bookcases filled with leather-bound volumes stretched from the floor to the ceiling. The lord sat behind a massive wooden desk, a blue halo of smoke from his pipe hovering above his head. Molly had spent the first part of the day bent over a large cast iron pot in the center of the one-room hut she shared with her mother as Mrs. O'Sullivan ensured that Molly's hair and face were clean, or rather, clean enough, before she put on the only dress she owned that didn't have patches. Lord Sanderson did not rise when they entered the room.

"You wanted to see us, my lord?" Mrs. O'Sullivan asked as she gave a slight bow. When Molly did not do likewise, she reached over and tugged on her sleeve until she did.

"Yes, Bridget. Though I expected you here twenty minutes ago."

"Me ma's name ain't Bridget," Molly said. "It's—"

She fell silent when her mother elbowed her in the ribs.

"Yes, well, I wanted to extend to you an offer," Lord Sanderson said. "One that I think you'll approve."

The sound of his aristocratic English accent grated on Molly's nerves, and she bit her lower lip to avoid a frown.

"Yes, my lord?" Mrs. O'Sullivan asked.

"I know that you are widow and your eldest son came to a tragic end. However, he did do a great service for my family. Or rather for my son."

"Your lordship was kind enough to take us in during the hunger," Mrs. O'Sullivan said, "and the cottage you gave us in the village after my Jimmy went off with the young Captain to fight in the wars. Kind of you to let us keep it after he … died. I'd expect nothing else from you, sir."

The sin of despair is what the Father called it, Molly thought bitterly. *Had the war sickness, Jimmy did. And the church refusing to bury him in the consecrated ground. Bastards. Seven years in the British Army, and they turn their back on him.*

Molly did not know the true story of what happened in the Crimea, but it was rumored that Jimmy saved Captain Sanderson's life. Molly had been six and her brother Jimmy, fifteen, when they arrived on the estate looking for work in 1850. *Dirty and starving we were,* Molly thought. *With me da and the little ones dead during the hunger. All me ma could think to do was go beg for work, but all the estates turned us down till we got here. Acted like he was doing us a great favor, he did. Just like now. Maybe he was. Maybe he is.*

"There's no future in Ireland for the young," Lord Sanderson said. "As backwards and ignorant country as I've ever seen. Full of savages. Uprisings every decade it seems. Why my forefathers ever decided to settle here is beyond me, though I suppose they did bring you the gift of civilization. Yet your people killed my grandfather during one of your rebellions."

Molly shuddered as she thought of the massive portrait of Lord Sanderson's grandfather that dominated the great hall. *Got scary eyes, he does,* Molly thought. *Like he's after getting you in a dark corner and trying to put his hand up your skirt. Just like young Henry Sanderson.*

She snapped back to attention in time to hear Lord Sanderson say, "And that's why I propose to send your daughter to America."

"America?" Molly exclaimed. "Why?"

"Mrs. O'Sullivan," Lord Sanderson said, "your daughter must learn to show proper deference to her betters. Did I not have this same conversation with you when I told you why she'd not be allowed to work in the nursery again?"

"You did, my lord," Mrs. O'Sullivan said. "And she's sorry for that."

I am not, thought Molly. When they first arrived on the estate, Molly was too young to work in the house, but when she turned twelve, she started in the kitchen as a scullery maid. Two years ago, just after her sixteenth birthday, Molly was offered a position in the nursery, caring for the children of Lord Sanderson's three married daughters, but she'd only lasted six months there. She wasn't sorry for talking back to Lord Sanderson the morning she was sacked, but she missed the orderly days and the tidy nursery. And the laughter of the children.

"Yes, well, nevertheless, that is my offer," Lord Sanderson said.

"Generous of you, my lord," Mrs. O'Sullivan said.

"Consider it a reward for your loyal service and the great service your son provided to Queen and country. Captain Sanderson still speaks of him on occasion in his letters. A brave man. Pity he committed self-murder. But it is God's place to judge, not mine."

"Yes, my lord," Mrs. O'Sullivan whispered, her eyes focused on the floor.

It ain't a reward, Molly thought. *It's me he wants gone. Wasn't it just last week that young Henry Sanderson with the roaming hands saw me in the village and tried to … touch me? Thinks he owns me like his da owns all this land. The lord is afraid I'll fall for a baby and his boy will be stuck with a bastard child. And last week wasn't the first time. Henry's been after trying to touch me or kiss me ever since I was thirteen. But last week was the first time I slapped him. And lucky he is that Martin Fitzgerald happened by, or else I'd have pulled his aristocratic nose off and fed it to him.*

"Have you any relatives in America? I know it is common among the Irish."

"I have a brother in New York, my lord," Mrs. O'Sullivan said. "Been there for many years. He and his family, I mean."

"Do you have their address?"

"A letter came from them last year."

"Why don't you write to them and see if you can send Molly over?"

Mrs. O'Sullivan looked down at the floor.

"Oh … I see," Lord Sanderson said. "You can't read. Can you,

Molly?"

"I can make out my name," Molly said as she lifted her chin and looked Lord Sanderson in the eye, "and I know some numbers. Father Byrne taught me."

"Forgive me," Lord Sanderson said, "but how did you read the letter?"

"The Father read it to me," Mrs. O'Sullivan said.

"Yes, well, I suppose papist priests do have their uses," Lord Sanderson said. "Why don't you have him write a letter to them asking permission to send Molly over then?"

"I will."

"What if they say no?" Molly asked.

"And still she asks questions," Lord Sanderson said with a sigh as he looked at Mrs. O'Sullivan. Then his gazed turned to Molly. "But to answer your question, we'll find somewhere else to send you in that event. London, perhaps."

"And you're paying for it?" Molly asked.

"A loan to your mother," he said. "She can pay me back as time permits. No interest. But it's a chance for you to get more out of life than you would here."

"We accept, my lord," Mrs. O'Sullivan said before Molly could respond. Lord Sanderson dismissed them with a nod of his head. The older woman took her daughter's hand and dragged her from the room. As soon as they got outside the house, she grabbed Molly's shoulders and shook her.

"Are you daft, child?" she exclaimed. "He's our landlord and my employer. You can't sass gentlemen like that!"

Molly squared her shoulders. "Ain't none of them English lords better than me. They sit there in their big houses looking down on us like we're some kind of animals. But it's our country. Not theirs."

"It's theirs now," Mrs. O'Sullivan said. "But if you don't learn to control your mouth, you'll come to grief."

Molly ran away from her mother. She crossed through the green fields and headed in the direction of Knockma Hill. Mud clung to her shoes as she made her way up a path lined with moss-covered rocks, pausing several times to catch her breath. When she reached the summit, Molly looked out over the landscape—it was like she could see all of Ireland from here. The ivy-covered ruins of Castle Hackett were visible at the base of the hill and beyond them, the green fields seemed to go on forever. As a child, Molly's mother told her that fairies lurked in the woods nearby, ready to steal away children who did not behave. *If that's true, then they would've taken me long ago*, Molly thought. According to legends passed down for generations, Maeve, Queen of Connaught, was buried on the summit of the hill, her body placed in the grave in a standing position and facing her enemies in Ulster, though some insisted she was actually buried up in Sligo. Molly remembered the first time she climbed the hill, as a child. Her brother Jimmy brought her, a few months before he took the King's Shilling. *If Queen Maeve were still here*, she thought as she sat down upon a rock, *we'd own all of this ourselves as we used to. Would she want to go to America? Or would she want to stay here? The mere thought of a journey across the ocean made Molly's heart flutter and her stomach cramp. Ireland is my home, not America. But Lord Sanderson is right. There's no future for me here. And me ma is eager to pack me off too.*

As she gazed over the land, watered by the blood of its inhabitants over centuries, Molly sang softly to herself, an old tune called "Siúil a Rún" she'd learned from her grandfather. In times or doubt or trouble, the hill beckoned to her, telling her an hour spent on its crest might solve whatever problem she faced. *Sure, there'll be nothing like this for me in America.*

The sun cast long shadows on the ground as Molly walked the two kilometers back to the hut she shared with her mother. Tired, and covered in sweat, Molly dropped into a wooden chair in the corner and watched as her mother stirred a stew boiling in a kettle over the fireplace.

"Off to the hill again, were you?" her mother asked without looking up.

"I was," Molly said.

"You are a dreamer, Molly," her mother said. "I think America will suit you."

"I don't know," Molly said. "'Tis a long journey. I've never been on an ocean before."

"Eighteen is young for such a journey alone, but you'll be fine. Tomorrow I'll see the father about writing the letter. You're hardly the first from this country to go to America."

"But how will you pay the lord back?" Molly asked. "He said it was a loan, did he not?"

"Don't you worry your head about that. I'm old and will die long before the debt is paid."

"I wish you wouldn't talk like that. There's plenty of life left in you. But you'll be all alone when I go. Could you not come with me?"

"I've no desire to start over in a new country. And he offered to pay your way, not mine. So, it is here I'll stay and when I die, they'll bury me next to your father and the little ones. It's no other way I'd have it."

Sure, hasn't she put a husband and three children in the ground in Galway, Molly thought, *but ever since me da and me young brothers died during the hunger, she's acted as though I don't exist. She cares more for dead than the living, even more once Jimmy done what he did. If I go, then she can grieve them all like she wants. I'm only in the way. I miss Da. He loved me, at least.* She smiled as she thought of the nights when she'd sit in his lap in front of the fire as he told her the legends old Ireland and sang to her the songs passed down from one generation to another.

It took a few months for the letter to be delivered and a reply received. When it finally came, the short note indicated that Molly was welcome to come over, provided she secured employment upon arrival and assisted with the household finances and chores. Molly figured a job would not be difficult to obtain in a place as large as people said New York was. Lord Sanderson secured passage on a ship leaving Cork and the coach fare for her mother to travel with her as far as the docks. As was the custom, the village held a wake for Molly the night before she left. They called it an American wake. *Aye, it may as well be a funeral*, Molly thought, *for when people leave for America, they never come back*. She shivered and moved closer to Sean on the log.

"Will you miss me, Molly?" Sean asked.

"I'll miss Belclare. And Knockma Hill," Molly said. "And maybe

I'll miss you."

Sean reached out and took her hand in the darkness.

"Maybe when the war is over, I'll come to America and find you."

"Sure, you will." Molly laughed as she withdrew her hand. "And I'm the Queen of England. Come on. Let's get back. It's getting late and I've a long journey down to Cork City tomorrow."

After a restless night with little sleep, Molly and her mother boarded a coach for Cork City.

As it jolted its way south, her mother lectured her on the need to take care of herself. "You must be careful, Molly. You've not seen much of the world beyond Belclare. There'll be more people in New York than you've ever seen in your life. It's a big city, they say. Be careful."

"I can take care of myself," Molly said, "Ain't I been fending off the young lord for years now? I'm sure I can handle a Yank what gets too fresh with me."

It took a few days to reach the port city. Molly did not have much time to take it all in. They spent the night before the ship sailed in a dingy boarding house above a saloon on the waterfront that catered to sailors. The sound of laughter, music, and a fight in the street kept them up all night, not that the lumpy mattress they shared would have provided much rest anyway. After breakfast the next morning, they made their way to the ship, though it would be a few hours before passengers were permitted to board.

Molly reached up and closed her hand around the Saint Michael's medal.

"I'll have them write you a letter to tell you I've arrived safely," Molly promised.

"Try to learn to write yourself," Mrs. O'Sullivan said. "It'll be of use to you where you are going. Unlike here."

"I will."

Molly looked over the other passengers waiting to embark. Most were families, clad in little more than rags. The adults clutched meager belongings to their chests as they watched their skinny children, barefoot and dirty, playing along the water's edge. A group of young men kept themselves off to the side. A few looked sideways in Molly's direction, but she ignored them—she'd no need for a man's attention aboard the ship. She caught snatches of conversation around her, mostly excited discussion of what they expected to find in America—stories about tables piled high with food, money there for the taking, and no sickness or want. *It sounds like a paradise, it does. Like heaven come down to earth.*

Molly's mother asked one of the sailors nearby if any other single young women were making the trip, but the man shrugged and shook his head to indicate he did not understand.

"Do they not speak English on this ship?" she said when she turned back to Molly.

"I'm sure they do. But don't some sailors come from other places? Like the dago fishermen what came to Galway last year?"

"I think they were French," Mrs. O'Sullivan said. "But I hope for your sake, you can at least talk to some of the crew if you need."

"I don't think they care much about comfort," Molly said. "Remember the stories they told about the coffin ships going to America during the hunger?"

"It ended a long time ago, Molly. Things cannot be so bad as that now."

Molly studied the ship in front of her. Three masts rose from the deck, their sails splashed with the colors of many patches. A layer of peeling brown paint covered the hull. The whole ship seemed to sag against itself, as if the numerous trips across the Atlantic made it too tired to stand on its own. Likewise, the sailors in sight walked with slumped shoulders, as if they carried a heavy load on their backs. A man with a full brown beard, flecked with white, emerged onto the main deck and walked to the rail. He scowled as he studied the crowd of immigrants, then turned and barked rapid-fire orders to the crew on deck, who scurried to obey.

"A ship's captain on the ocean has greater authority than Queen Victoria herself," Mrs. O'Sullivan said. "Your brother Jimmy told me that once. After he came back from India. A long trip over the water, he said it was."

"Longer than America?" Molly asked. When Jimmy came home

from the Crimea, Molly hoped he might stay. *No, they had to ship him off to India,* she thought. *Did they not know he wasn't well anymore?*

"Yes, a lot longer."

"How long will it take to get to America?"

"A few weeks, I'd think."

"A few weeks ..." Molly repeated. *That seems like a long time to be on such a small boat. Out there among the waves and the wind in a boat what looks like its best days are long past. But the captain looks capable, not that I know what that means to a boat.*

"You'll be boarding soon," Mrs. O'Sullivan said. "Have you got your ticket?"

"In my bag," Molly said. "Should I get it out?"

"Best to have it in hand. They'll want to see it."

Molly knelt on the rough wooden dock and opened her suitcase. The ticket blew out and nearly disappeared over the edge of the dock, but she managed to snag it in mid-air.

"You must be more careful, Molly," her mother said. "If you'd lost that, I'd hate to see what Lord Sanderson would've done."

"I'm sure he could afford another," Molly said.

"That's not the point, child."

Her mother turned away and spoke a few words to a family standing next to her.

"My daughter Molly is traveling alone," she said. "Would you be kind enough to keep an eye on her? She'd be happy to help you with the children. Loves young ones, she does."

Molly looked at her mother, and then smiled at the boy and girl who peered at her from behind their mother's skirts.

"I'm Mary," their mother said, "and these two are Ellen and Thomas. We're down from Tuam. Headed for New York. My husband Joseph will be along directly."

"Aren't we almost neighbors then," Mrs. O'Sullivan said.

Molly walked over and knelt in front of the children. They studied her face with interest. She guessed the girl was around four and the boy near to six.

"My name's Molly," she said. "How are you?"

They buried their faces in their mother's skirt but did not cry.

"A bit shy, they are," Mary said. "But they'll warm up to you. By the time we get to New York, you'll be the best of friends."

"All passengers for the *Dublin Rose*," a uniformed man yelled through cupped hands, "the ship will now begin boarding. Have your ticket ready."

"I guess this is goodbye," Molly said as her heart accelerated in her chest.

"Take care of yourself, Molly," her mother said. "Go and make yourself a life there."

"I will," Molly said as a lump rose in her throat. *I'm saying goodbye to Ireland forever. I'll not see ma, or Queen Maeve again. Or maybe I'll return on the arm of a rich American and put even Lord Sanderson to shame.* She smiled at the thought.

"There's Joseph now," Mary said as she waved to her husband, a short, squat man with thick arms and an auburn beard. "Joseph, this is Molly. She's traveling alone and her mother asked if we'd keep an eye on her."

Joseph reached up and touched his hat in acknowledgment. Molly smiled and turned to her mother. They looked at one another in silence for a long moment. Finally, Mrs. O'Sullivan said, "Go on now, child. You don't want to be left behind."

Blinking away her own tears, Molly reached her free hand down for young Ellen who, to her surprise, took it and smiled up at her. They walked up the gangway behind Ellen's parents. She handed her ticket over to the sailor who stood watch and then stepped aboard the wooden deck of the ship. The line of passengers snaked its way down the deck toward a hatch that led below to their quarters. When she reached it, Molly looked back at the dock to try and give one final wave to her mother, but she had already vanished. *So, it's alone I am at last,* Molly thought as she ducked her head to walk below decks.

Chapter Two

By day five of the voyage, Molly had grown accustomed to the to pitch and roll of the ship, and the nausea which had seized her stomach like an icy hand subsided. After she finished nibbling on ship's biscuits and salted pork, the daily fare, she went topside to escape the reeking confines of the berth deck, bringing Ellen and Thomas with her. The night before, Molly overheard a few whispers from the darkness around her saying that the *Dublin Rose* was not meant to carry passengers, as it offered little in the way of accommodation other than one row of crude bunks with barely enough space for the children. The adults slept on the rough wooden deck. With only a few buckets to serve as toilets, it did not take long for the smell to burn itself into Molly's nose, even though the contents were dumped overboard twice daily.

Molly stood in between the children at the rail as they looked out over the water. *It goes on forever*, she thought. *Is there really land on the other side? Or are we fated to sail on for eternity?*

"Miss Molly!" Thomas exclaimed. "Let's walk around!"

"Take hold of my hand," Molly said. With Thomas on her right and Ellen on her left, she led them down the deck toward the bow. Young Thomas peppered the crew with questions as the men went about their work. Those who answered did so in gruff monosyllables, though they all managed a nod at Molly and a quick 'ma'am' as they touched a knuckle to their forehead. As she watched the men scramble up the rigging with all the dexterity and speed of acrobats, Molly wondered how they managed to not fall. *They've no fear of heights, to be sure, but how can they not lose their balance?*

An older sailor whom Molly took to be of some importance, as he shouted orders on behalf of the captain, told her the roughest part of the trip still lay ahead, and when they passed through it, passengers would not be permitted on deck.

"The sea's a cruel bitch, beggin' yer pardon, miss," he said. "We'd hate to lose ya overboard. Or have ya crack yer head takin' a fall."

"Is it really so dangerous?" she asked.

"There's parts of this ocean where they got waves as big as mountains. The *Rose* is a good ship, but she's old. We've spruced her up a bit over the years, but even the newest ships aren't a match for an ocean that's got riled up."

He went on to describe a passage around Cape Horn, complete with a graphic description of the wind and water which blew a man off the rigging and into the sea. By the time he was finished, the two children clutched Molly's legs, eyes wide, and her own face had gone as pale as the moon.

"And we'll be sailing through that soon? Molly asked.

The old sailor laughed and said, "No, miss! Why … that's all the way down off the tip of South America. Nowhere close to where we are going. But we've still the North Atlantic to sail through and it's bad enough at this time of year."

"You are scaring the children, sir," Molly said.

"Sorry, miss," the sailor said. "I didn't mean no harm by it."

"Come along, children," Molly said. "Let's let the nice man get back to work."

She led them away and found a spot to sit. Ellen climbed into her lap as Thomas sat next to her.

"Have you heard of Queen Maeve?" Molly asked them. Both children shook their heads. "Well, listen to Molly then. 'Tis a grand story."

She launched into the tale and before she realized it, an hour and then two passed as each child stopped her frequently to ask questions. *I should get them back to their mother*, Molly thought. *Though Lord knows I enjoy their company. They remind me of the wee ones in Lord Sanderson's nursery.*

She took their hands and led them below. In the dimly lit interior, Molly sensed something was wrong. Several of the passengers lay on their sides, hands clutching their stomachs, and the smell from the buckets even more nauseating than usual. She made her way over to Mary and knelt by her side. Beads of sweat stood out on her face. Her husband lay next to her in a similar condition.

It's the bloody flux, Molly thought. Like during the hunger. It comes on you quick, like the fog rolling in from Galway Bay.

"Are you poorly, Mary?" she asked as she wiped the sweat from the woman's brow.

"I am. I feel … weak."

"Are you thirsty?"

Mary nodded and Molly sent young Thomas to fetch a ladle of water from the bucket that hung from a peg nailed into the wooden bulkhead. He spilled a good measure of it as he tried to carry it back, but enough remained for Molly to pour some into Mary's mouth. Then she sent the boy back to bring some to his father.

"Sure, you'll be fine in a few days," Molly said. "You just need rest. Here, I've put your suitcase next to you in case you need it."

The woman groaned and wrapped her arms around her stomach.

"It feels like daggers are stabbing me insides," she said.

"Has anyone told the captain?" Molly asked.

"I don't know," Mary said.

Molly looked around the compartment. She estimated around a third or so of the passengers gave sign of sickness.

"I'll tell him," Molly said.

She took the children up with her to spare them the sight and smell of so many sick. Molly found the captain in his usual spot on the quarterdeck. He stood next to the helmsman at the wheel and shouted occasional directions to sailors on the main deck. She left the children near the hatch to the berthing deck so that they could not overhear the conversation. After a stern warning to not venture near the rail, Molly walked up the steps and approached the captain. He turned on her and roared, "What's the meaning of this? No passengers, especially no women, permitted on the quarterdeck!"

Molly ignored him as she walked in his direction, not stopping until she was only a few feet away.

"Be gone!" he yelled.

Molly blinked as spittle hit her face, put her hands on her hips, and said, "You've sickness below. The bloody flux from the looks of it. It's a doctor they're needing."

"This ship has no doctor," the captain said. "Do we look like HMS *Victory* to you?"

"Then we must return to Cork," Molly said. "They are very ill, sir."

"You come onto my quarterdeck and tell me what we must do?" the captain said. "You've some cheek on you, girl. I've seen the flux before. It'll kill you or you won't, and if it does, you'll be dead in five days anyway. By the time we reached Cork, it would have already done its work."

"But … sir—"

"Enough," the captain said. "Tell those not afflicted to come up on deck at once. The sick will remain below. That's all I can do. But if so much as one of you gets in the way of my crew, then I'll lock you all below decks until we reach New York. Understood?"

"Yes, sir," Molly said.

"Now get out of my sight."

When she returned to the children, she could see Thomas's hands pressed over his stomach. Molly knelt in front of him and put her hands on his shoulders.

"Does your stomach pain you?" she asked.

He nodded.

Jesus, Mary, and Joseph, she swore to herself. *Not the children too*!

"And you, Ellen?"

The little girl shook her head no. Molly told the girl to stand in place and not move an inch as she picked Thomas up and carried him to the ladder which led below. She relayed the captain's instructions, and some of the passengers headed for the main deck, eager to escape the confines of the berth deck.

"Mary," Molly said as she knelt by the woman's side, "young Thomas has taken ill too. But not Ellen."

Mary nodded.

"I'll lay him by you here and bring him some water," Molly said. "The captain wants those not sick to remain above. I'll keep Ellen with me."

"Thank you," Mary gasped.

"But I'll return to check on you all," Molly said. "Someone will need to bring you water and food, and I don't think the captain will let one of his men do it. He's a bastard, he is."

Two more passengers took ill during the night and were sent below. Molly made several trips down, leaving Ellen in the temporary care of a middle-aged woman from Clare. Some of the afflicted lay still, their blinking eyes giving the sign that they still lived. Others rolled around on the floor, moaning in agony as they held their stomachs and abdomens. The smell made Molly vomit more than once. Too sick to move, and the buckets overflowing anyway, most of the ill lacked the strength to move and simply went wherever they lay. She moved along the deck, giving each person a drink of water and pausing long enough to wipe their brows and tell them they would be well soon. From their eyes, Molly knew they did not believe her.

Don't they look like a person on their way to the gallows, she thought.

On deck, things were not much better. The smell rose from below and, though there was fresh air, it was not enough. Some of the healthy passengers pressed to go below to tend to family members, but the captain steadfastly refused to allow anyone other than Molly tend to them, lest more fall ill. The captain stood on the quarterdeck and turned away from the passengers, despite the entreaties and threats hurled his direction. When the sun went down, Molly noticed the captain, the older sailor who had spoken with her that afternoon, and several other members of the crew now went about their work with pistols stuck in their belts.

They'd shoot us down like dogs to keep us from tending the sick and bringing the sickness to the crew, she thought. *And then throw us overboard with the soiled buckets. Aye, we are nothing but shite to them anyways.*

That night, as moonlight reflected off the water, Ellen curled herself into Molly's side. Molly could feel her shaking and wrapped her with a blanket she had brought from below decks, but when that didn't help, she realized it was fear, not cold, behind it.

"Shhh," Molly said, "everything will be fine. You'll see. Would you like to hear a song?"

Ellen looked up at her and nodded through the glisten in her eyes. Molly sang the words to "Johnny Has Gone For a Soldier" softly, so as not to wake the passengers sprawled around her. By the time she finished the song, the girl was asleep. The next morning, when Molly made her way below decks, she discovered several people had died during the night. Mary and her husband lay facing one another, with young Thomas in between them. Molly knelt to wake them. Her hand shook as she placed it on Thomas's shoulder and gently shook him. The boy did not stir. Molly studied his chest and realized it wasn't moving. Neither was his father Joseph's.

"Jesus!" Molly exclaimed as a hand closed around her wrist. She took a breath to slow her heartbeat and looked down into Mary's pale face. Sweat trickled down her cheeks and she smelled like sour milk. Molly had to strain to hear her.

"I'm … dying …" Mary whispered.

"No," Molly said as she mopped the woman's brow with a cloth. "You'll be fit soon enough."

"No. Will … you …" Mary paused.

"Will I what?" Molly asked, she leaned in as close as she dared to hear the words.

"Will you … take … take … care of … Ellen?"

"I will, yes," Molly said. "You need to rest now."

Mary's breath left her in a long, ragged sigh and her eyes fixed on some distant faraway point.

"Damn," Molly swore as she wiped away a tear and crossed herself. *Imagine that*, she thought. *They leave Ireland only to die on this godforsaken boat in the middle of the ocean. Surely it would've been better for them to stay. Then young Ellen wouldn't be left an orphan.*

Molly rose and circulated among the sick to distribute water and some biscuits. She counted six dead and several others who would be in a matter of hours. After doing as much as she could for them, Molly went back to the main deck to speak with the captain.

"You've dead people below," she said. "Six that I saw. Including the family of the girl with me."

"We'll have to get rid of the bodies," the captain said. "It's a festering mess down there as it is. I can smell it all the way up here."

"Bury them at sea, you mean?"

The Captain looked out over the water and then turned toward her. "We haven't the time, nor do I have the inclination to halt the ship for such ceremonies."

"You mean to throw them overboard as if they are garbage?" Molly exclaimed. "Are you not a Christian man?"

"I am," the captain said, "but I'd wager the profits of this voyage that they ain't. Papists, most likely. Most of your kind are."

"Will you please say a few words over them, sir," Molly asked. "The other passengers would appreciate it."

"If I may, sir," the older sailor spoke up, "the folks are angry. They are mad about the sickness. Heard a couple of them saying this is a cursed ship. If they got family that died, maybe having a brief little service would help. Let 'em mourn their loss. If you don't mind my saying so, sir."

"Fine then, Babbins," the captain growled. "But I'll need two sailors to volunteer to sew them into hammocks. I won't order them to do it."

"I'll do it, sir," Babbins said.

Just before sunset, the entire crew along with the healthy passengers mustered on the main deck as sailors carried six white hammocks, five large and one small, and placed them alongside the rail. From his vantage point on the quarterdeck, the captain read a service from a thick, leather-bound book. Ellen held tightly to Molly's hand and watched the proceedings without a sound or a tear. Earlier, Molly had tried to explain to the child that her parents and her brother had to go away and would not return. The girl gave no indication she understood. When Molly finished, Ellen had simply asked, "Mama?"

Molly had turned away to hide her own tears from the girl. *At least when me da died, me ma was still there. Not that she was of much help. And what am I to do with young Ellen? Does she even know what's really happened? Surely, she has more family in Ireland, but how do I get her there? I cannot take care of her myself. I've no job waiting for me in New York. What will auntie say if I show up on her door with a child in tow? She'll think I was shamed and banished.*

After what seemed like an eternity of its own, the captain recited, "Then, we commit their bodies to the deep, to be turned into corruption, looking for the resurrection of the body, when the Sea shall give up her dead …"

As he continued to read, two sailors picked up the bodies, one at a time, and tossed them over the side. Molly flinched with every splash as they hit the water. The sound struck her ears like a cannon shot. She closed her eyes so as not to see the final body, that of young Thomas, tossed overboard, but Ellen watched it all.

After the captain pronounced a final "Amen," he turned to the crew and bawled, "Back to work. Let's get under away. We've wasted enough time as it is."

No other passengers fell ill, and no more succumbed to the sickness either. On the fifth morning after the outbreak, the Captain ordered the passengers to go below and scrub the berthing area. "I think it is safe for you to be down there," he said, "and even if it ain't, there'll be stormy weather soon enough, and you'll be down there regardless."

They spent the better part of a day on their knees, sopping up human waste and mopping the deck as thoroughly as they could. By the time they stopped, Molly's knees had almost worn through her skirt and her reddened hands ached. The odor wasn't completely gone, but the air was good enough to not induce gagging. On her first time below decks since the sickness began, Ellen went straight over to where her parents had been, near the bunk where Ellen and Thomas slept before the sickness.

"Mama?" she asked.

Molly reached down and grabbed the family's suitcase and took Ellen's hand.

"They've gone, Ellen," Molly explained. "They are … well, they've gone on a very long journey. You'll be with me now. At least for a while. Come on. Come with me."

Molly led her to a spot as far away as possible from where Ellen had last seen her parents. They sat down and Molly hesitated for a moment, and then opened the family suitcase. *I'm not robbing the dead,* she told herself. *There may be something here that Ellen needs.* The suitcase contained one change of clothes for each member of the family. Molly removed the dress for Ellen and put it in her own suitcase, then she caught sight of an item tucked away underneath the clothes. Pulling it out, she found it was a small doll.

Ellen grabbed the doll and hugged her, and Molly thought, *I told her we'd be together for a while, but it is for forever more likely. She's lost her family. I can't give her over to the care of strangers, though I'm a stranger to her myself. But how will I explain it to me auntie? I'll tell her the truth. But will she believe me? With my red curls and wee Ellen's straight black hair, no one would think her my own. Would they? She needs a mother just like I did. But me own mother had not a word of comfort to say to me when me da died or the little ones. Or when Jimmy done himself in. Alone with the sorrow, I was. And this poor girl has no one to help her either.*

After Ellen fell asleep, doll clutched in her arms, Molly grew restless. She wrapped herself in a shawl and wandered up on deck, careful to keep to the shadows to avoid detection and orders to return below. A sailor stood at the rail, gazing out over the water. Molly had seen him on a few previous occasions and noted his Scottish accent when he spoke to his shipmates. There, in the darkness, he began to sing. It was a song she'd not heard before. As she listened, she committed the lyrics and the melody to memory.

Maxwelton's braes are bonnie, when early fa's the dew
And it was there my Annie Laurie, gave me her promise true
Gave me her promise true, that ne'er forgot shall be
And for bonnie Annie Laurie, I'd lay me doon and dee

Molly closed her eyes as the man sang and wondered who he might be thinking of and what the girl must look like. She considered joining him, and trying to sing along, but decided not to intrude on his moment of solitude. *I feel like a thief standing here listening,* she thought, *with him not able to see me. But 'tis a fine song. Wouldn't me da have loved it?*

As a young girl, Molly would sit on her father's knee each night after supper and listen as he sang to her all of the songs he could remember. Her grandparents shared the mud-walled cabin with the rest of her family, and though they did not have command of the English language, they'd hum along with the melody and join in on the songs sung in Irish. As the sailor continued, Molly smiled at those fleeting childhood memories. *Sure, there was the famine at the time, but I was too young to know it. They kept it away from us. It wasn't until me grandparents took ill, and then me wee brothers that I knew something was wrong.*

She swallowed hard to drive the memories out of her mind as the sailor finished his song. Molly turned and slipped back down the ladder to the berth deck where she found Ellen asleep as she'd left her. Molly stretched out alongside her and took the child in her arms.

"Don't worry, wee girl," she whispered. "Molly will do her best to take care of you. I don't know how I will or even what to do, but I'll try. You have my word on that. I'll try."

Chapter Three

Every time Molly took the child up to the main deck, Ellen ran over to the rail over where the sailors had tossed the bodies of her family. She would stand there until Molly pulled her away. As the voyage neared the end of the second week, interactions between the passengers grew strained and the ship seemed to shrink in size. Quarrels broke out over mundane things, and despite the chill of the salt air, the berth deck remained stifling. Molly tried to spend as little time below as possible, and to keep Ellen away from the bickering adults, lest she be injured if an argument turned to fisticuffs. *It's our curse to turn to our fists to settle our differences,* Molly thought. *If we'd stop fighting each other long enough, we'd drive off the English in a week.*

"Might get a bit rough tonight, Miss Molly," the old sailor, Babbins, told her as she took her morning stroll around the deck. "Keep the little one close. And you might want to avoid the bunks as you could end up tossed onto the floor."

"How can you tell?" Molly asked. "There's not a cloud above us."

"I've been at sea for thirty years," Babbins said. "Spent twenty in the Royal Navy and the other ten on merchantmen. Been all over the world, I have. You spend that much time on the water, and you can smell a storm."

"What does it smell like?" Molly asked as she sniffed the air. All she could detect was the smell of saltwater and a whiff of sweat from the sailors.

"I don't know how to say it," Babbins said, "but my nose ain't never been wrong."

"Have you been to the city of New York?" Molly asked.

Babbins chuckled and said, "Dozens of times. We make this run on the *Rose* a few times a year. Know the waterfront like the back of my hand."

"Is it as big as they say?"

"Bigger. Hard to describe until you lay eyes on it. But you need to be careful. Lots of shady Yankees out to take advantage of the recently arrived."

"Oh," Molly said, "I've no need to worry about that. I've family waiting for me."

"All the same," Babbins said, "remember what I say."

The sky darkened in the late afternoon and the swells grew heavier. The wind moaned, then howled through the rigging. The Captain paced the quarterdeck and yelled orders to the crew, but the men went about their work with experienced hands and seemed to need no direction. It's a marvel to watch them, Molly thought. They move as one man. A gust of wind rattled the rigging as a large swell lifted the ship.

"Get below!" the captain screamed. "All passengers below! Damn your eyes! Can't you see it's a storm?"

"Why don't you damn your own eyes," Molly yelled back, but the wind swallowed her reply. Still, orders were orders, and she went below. Sailors came along and closed the hatches to keep water from getting inside. Molly mopped her brow as she struggled to breathe in the stale, stuffy air.

"We should've gotten more buckets," Molly said to Ellen as they watched a man vomit on himself. Several of the other passengers clutched wooden rosary beads in their hands and muttered prayers in a mix of English and Irish.

"There's nothing to be afraid of," Molly said as much to herself as to Ellen. "This is a fine ship what's seen many storms."

Molly pulled the girl closer to her as they sat with their backs against the bulkhead. The ship creaked and groaned with each swell. The wind howled like the banshees of Ireland. She shivered as she thought of what it must look like on deck. *But the sailors have been through it before, not like us what have to stay down here.*

Ellen squealed as two rats scurried by, headed aft.

"Just frightened, they are," Molly said. "They mean you no harm."

The ship shuddered violently and listed to port as a thunderous wave broke over the deck. Water ran down into the berth deck and sloshed back and forth, mixing with the passengers' own emissions. Molly heard the captain's voice over the sound of the storm. *He sounds frightened,* she thought. *It must be terrible up there if he is.*

"We've come all this way only to drown," a man said. "It's a cursed ship we sail on."

"That is enough, sir," Molly said. "You are scaring the girl."

"I'll say what I want," the man replied. "This is no longer Ireland. I can speak my mind here."

"Aye, you can," Molly said, "and I can come over there and kick you up the hole for saying it."

"You wouldn't dare."

Molly held the man's gaze until he looked away. He said no more about the storm but groaned with each wave that hit the ship. *He's not wrong,* she thought. *It is as if the devil himself stalks those aboard. Me da always said the fishermen in Galway were a superstitious lot, more so than the ordinary Irishman. Are the sailors here the same?*

She hummed a song as Ellen clutched her leg with trembling arms. "I'll not let anything bad happen to you," Molly said. "You need not fear."

I say that to her when I can't keep the fear out of my own voice. We may be minutes away from eternity and I'll go to it with a lie on my lips. She crossed herself and hoped it would cover her should the ship be lost. Her own stomach churned with nausea as the seasickness she'd thought she'd left behind returned. She turned her head away from Ellen and vomited the meager meal she'd eaten earlier. It made her stomach feel better, but a lightheaded sensation gave her a pain in her head.

It's the bad air. That's the cause of it. It'll get worse until I can get out of here, she thought. *But to go up on deck now? Even if the captain would let me, it might be too dangerous. I'm suffocating down here though, but I can't take Ellen up there. Could I crack the hatch long enough to get some fresh air in?*

Molly felt as though an invisible weight had been pressed on her chest as she tried to breathe. Each inhale only made her dizzier, and so she decided to venture topside long enough to get a few quick breaths. That should tide her over until the storm passed. Molly looked around and found a couple seated across the cabin that did not appear too ill from the tempest outside. She rose, and keeping her feet spread wide for balance, made her way over to them.

"Would you please look after the child for a moment?" Molly asked. "I need to go up on deck, but only for a minute."

"It's too dangerous for that, girl," the man said. "Stay here."

"I can't," Molly said. "I must go up. I … I just must."

The woman took her husband's hand and said, "It's all right. She'll be right back. I'll sit with the child."

The woman extended her hand, and Molly helped pull her to her feet. The two made their way over to Ellen, who sat and stared at the deck beneath her. Molly knelt by her side and said, "This nice woman is going to look after you for a minute. I'll be right back. You won't hardly know I'm gone."

Ellen looked up at her and blinked but gave no indication that she understood.

"Go on," the woman said. "And hurry back."

Molly made her way to the ladder that led up to the main deck. It took a few minutes for her to work her way up to the hatch. She lifted it enough to peer out onto the deck. No sailors were nearby, so she opened it and scrambled out. The wind tore at her clothes like an invisible hand while the wind battered her eardrums. The *Dublin Rose* was putting up a valiant fight, but she rolled in the swells so far that her gunwales nearly touched the water. In a matter of moments, the spray from the waves soaked through Molly's clothes. She shivered in the chill. The dark clouds and driving rain made it difficult for her to make out much. *I should get below*, she thought. *A bad idea, this.* As she reached down to open the hatch, the ship pitched sideways and spilled her onto the deck.

Molly struggled to her feet. The captain appeared at the rail of the quarterdeck and yelled some unintelligible command to a sailor she could not see. She tried to lift the hatch, but the pressure exerted by the wind made it difficult. A sailor passed close enough to her to brush against her arm, but he took no notice of her. Molly banged on the hatch with her fist, hoping someone below would hear it and help push it open, but no one came to her aid. *I need someone from the crew*, she thought. *They can help. Even if it means a lecture for being on deck.*

As she made her way forward, Molly bumped into a stout rope tied the length of the ship. It had not been there when the passengers were sent below. She kept a tight hold on it as she walked.

"Jesus Christ!" the captain yelled. "Steady lads! *Hold fast!*"

Ahead of the ship, a wall of water rose out of the sea, almost as high as a mountain. Molly gasped. The ship rode the swell up but was shoved backwards as the wave broke. A wall of water slammed into her, knocking her off her feet. Shouts and yells echoed around her as the force of the water washed her across the deck. Her hands searched for something, anything, to grab ahold of, but the sting of the salt water forced her to keep her eyes closed. *I'm going over the side*, she realized. *I'll be drowned.*

With no way to stop her progress, Molly resigned herself to the inevitable until a hand closed around her arm and she jerked to a halt.

"I've got ya, Miss Molly," Babbins yelled.

The rough wooden deck rubbed against her back as she was dragged to safety.

"Are we sinking?" she asked as soon as she caught her breath.

"Not so long as the pumps hold," he said. "We've sent some men down to man them."

"That wave ..." Molly's voice faltered.

"Largest I've ever seen," Babbins said. "Nearly did us in. But we're still afloat."

"Thank ... thank you."

"No thanks needed," Babbins said. "We're shipmates—well, of a sort anyway. Best get you below and under some blankets. You'll catch your death up here."

Babbins half carried, half dragged her over to the hatch, heaved it open, and pushed her down the ladder. Below, the passengers lay in a jumbled heap on the floor, with arms and legs sticking out in every direction. Several moaned as they held bloody heads or bruised limbs in their hands.

"Ellen!" Molly exclaimed as she tried to sort through the human pile. She found her, scared but unhurt.

"It was a big wave what done that," Molly told her as they resumed their place on the floor. "But we're safe now, aren't we?"

The night stubbornly refused to yield to the dawn. The boat still creaked and shook with the waves. *I never thought a night would last an eternity*, Molly thought. *But it's as if this one will never end. Is every storm like this*?

Ellen fell asleep, with her head resting in Molly's lap. She stroked the child's hair and whispered, "We'll be in New York soon. God only knows what'll happen between now and then. But we can see it through."

"Will you be keeping the child?" a woman asked Molly from somewhere in the darkness.

"I will," Molly said. "What else can I do?"

"But you're just a girl yourself. How about you let us, my husband and I, have her. In just a few years, she'd be able to earn her keep."

"I'm not a girl," Molly snapped. "I have eighteen years. And I'll not give you the little one for you to treat as a personal servant. She's a child, for God's sake! Not a source of funds for your husband to spend on the drink."

The woman was quiet after that.

When the dawn finally came, the storm dissipated, and the passengers took in the sun on the main deck. The sea appeared flat and calm, as if the night had not happened. When Molly mentioned this to Babbins, he said, "The ocean has a short memory. She'll try to kill you one minute and give you a picture the next."

"I don't think I want to set foot on another ship in my life," Molly said. "Not after this trip."

"Ah, sure you will," Babbins said. "Who knows? You may not find New York to your liking and sail off to Hong Kong."

"If I don't find New York to my liking," Molly said, "they say America is a big country."

"It is that," Babbins said. "But you'll do fine in New York."

"Thank you," Molly said. "I do hope so."

With Ellen in tow, she took several turns around the deck. Some bits of rail were missing, and a few sails hung in tatters. Two of the sailors had their arms in slings, though they worked on as best they could. It reminded Molly of what the losers looked like after Sean and his mates took on the boys from another village. *We'll hardly be making a grand entrance*, she thought. *They may laugh us out of the harbor*!

The crew sighted wreckage in the distance, and the captain altered course to run up alongside it. A few wooden planks, a wooden barrel, and some pieces of rope bobbed up and down in the gentle swells.

"Can you make out a name on the wood?" the captain yelled.

"No, sir," one of the men answered, "and I don't see nobody around it neither."

Molly stared at the debris as the *Dublin Rose* pulled away. *That could have been us. Lost to the storm. Maybe there's no curse on this boat after all.*

By the end of the day, Molly caught sight of a flock of birds as they circled in the distance. The captain ordered the crew to take in the sails and drop anchor.

"Why do we stop?" she asked Babbins.

"We be only a few miles out," Babbins said. "But it's late in the day. The captain doesn't want to risk entering the harbor after dark. So, first thing in the morning, we'll head in and by early afternoon you can rest your feet on the soil of America."

"At last," Molly said with a smile.

"What? You don't like our company?" Babbins asked as he gave her a gap-toothed grin.

"Where are you bound next?" Molly asked.

"Charleston. That's down in the Carolinas. And then to Galveston. After that, I don't know."

"Do you have a family?'

"I do not," Babbins said. "Life at sea, well, it ain't kind to families. We spend so much time away. And as you have seen, it's a dangerous life. I'd not want to put a woman through months of waiting to see if I'll come home or not. It wouldn't be fair. Besides, there's plenty of whores ashore to keep me company."

Molly reddened and he hastily apologized. *How horrible that would be,* she thought. *Having to work in such a place catering to every man what comes in the door.*

Sleep avoided her that night, as her mind mulled over what sights she'd see the following morning. *Surely it cannot be as pretty as Galway,* she thought. *Will it be as crowded as everyone says? An adventure to be sure. Will it be like the first time I climbed Knockma Hill?*

Ellen slept beside her, seemingly oblivious to what tomorrow might bring while Molly fretted over all she didn't know. *How far from the docks to where me auntie lives? Will it be too far for Ellen to walk?*

When the ship got underway the next morning, Molly took her young charge as far forward as she could and strained to catch sight of land. She saw a few ships in the distance, headed towards the *Dublin Rose*. As one drew abreast, Molly waved to the men on deck. A few lifted a hand in return, but most ignored her. *Are they sailing into the same storm? If so, may the saints protect them.* After what seemed like an eternity, Molly saw a rough outline of land ahead.

"When we get closer," Babbins said as he appeared beside her, "you'll see two cities. New York will be to your left and Brooklyn to your right. And a whole forest of ships at the docks of each. A few years ago, the Americans opened a place to land immigrants like yourself. Called Castle Clinton. It's way down on the tip of the island. But since we are officially hauling cargo and not people, we'll off load at the docks. They ain't too particular on rules around here."

Molly leaned down and scooped Ellen into her arms, grunting with the effort it took to pick her up.

"Look, Ellen," she said as she pointed, "it's America just ahead. We'll be on land soon."

Ellen looked around and asked, "Where's Mama?"

"She's not here, child," Molly said. "I'm with you now. Can you say Molly?"

Ellen said no more, but she did point to a ship making its way out of the harbor. Molly could hear the slap of the waves against the hull and the cry of seagulls overhead. As Babbins predicted, she saw a forest of masts appear in the distance before she caught her first sight of land. The air smelled of salt, fish, and coal. Soon, she could see the individual ships and then the city stretched out before them.

Molly marveled at the size of the buildings. She had never seen anything higher than two stories, and that was Lord Sanderson's house. Here, buildings rose five or six stories into the air, jammed against one another as if for mutual support. Ships crowded around the docks as sailors and longshoreman scrambled over the decks. Two larger vessels had gun ports on two decks. *Navy ships, perhaps, off to fight in the American war*? The crew of the *Rose* moved with an extra bit of vigor as the end of the voyage drew near. Molly hoped they at least managed a night or two ashore.

I don't know if I could stand another week or two on board, she thought. The other passengers gathered on deck, holding onto what little luggage they brought with them. They murmured excitedly as the ship closed the distance to land. Some discussed their plans, or the relatives they hoped to find.

The docks swarmed with people, some sailors who moved with a bowlegged gait on land while other men sweated, despite the cold, as they unloaded or loaded cargo of all kinds. Molly's hands shook a bit as she considered walking into this great wilderness of wood and stone in search of her family's address. *No*, she told herself. *This ain't no time for you to get scared. You've a job ahead of you and wee Ellen is depending on you.*

"We'll do it, won't we," she said to Ellen. "Us two girls can take care of ourselves."

Chapter Four

Before she disembarked, Molly thanked Babbins for his kindness during the voyage, then took up her suitcase in her left hand and took hold of Ellen's hand with her right. "Don't let go of my hand, Ellen," she said. "Not for any reason." Ellen looked up at her and nodded. Molly took a deep breath before she led Ellen down the gangway. After two weeks on a ship, it took a few minutes for her legs to adjust to land. Molly heard several languages spoken, and unintelligible forms of English among the crowd around the docks.

Across the street, several young women leaned out of a second-floor window and shouted promises of lewd, not to mention creative, acts to the men in the vicinity. Molly thought to cover Ellen's ears, but with her other hand holding the suitcase, her only option was to increase her pace to get away.

"Don't pay them no mind," she said. *Are those the girls that Mr. Babbins was talking about? What drove them to such a place, the poor souls?*

Several boys yelled offers of employment or accommodations. *No doubt for a fee*, she thought. *Gombeen men, most likely.* Two men with bushy mustaches and double-breasted blue wool coats stood behind a table beneath a sign that said: SONS OF ERIN! ENLIST TODAY! CASH BONUS! CITIZENSHIP! They wore swords buckled over scarlet sashes. Another man in a more modest uniform with three stripes on his sleeves and pox scars on his face stood in front of the table and yelled the phrases on the sign for the benefit of those who could not read them. A few young men wandered over, and the sergeant launched into descriptions of valor, glory, and the need for brave men to face the foe. In short order, the men took up the pen to make their mark on the enlistment papers.

Just like me own brother enticed by those red-coated devils into the British Army, Molly thought. *Still a boy when he went away, but he came back with the cold eyes of a fish. If it's a war they have, it's Irish bodies they want.*

Molly ignored the shouts of the peddlers, and the profanity used by some of the sailors. She repeated the address over and over again in her mind to make sure she would not forget it. Number 22 Canal Street. Apartment 12. Molly searched for a friendly face to ask about directions. The teeming mass of humanity that swirled around her nearly made her dizzy. She had never seen so many people in one place. The air smelled of wood smoke, offal, and manure in the streets. No one took notice as two pigs trotted by except for Ellen, who pointed at them.

"Those are pigs," Molly said. "They say 'oink.' Can you say that?"

Ellen frowned and turned her face away. Molly shook her head and walked a short distance down the street. She encountered a police officer near an intersection. He wore a dark blue uniform with a copper badge pinned to his left breast. A leather belt held a scabbard for his locust-wood club, but the officer held it in his right hand and tapped it into his left palm. *I hope the peelers are more friendly here than in Ireland*, she thought as she walked toward him. During the hunger, it was the police along with land agents who had turned her family out of their home. The man stood a head taller than most of those around him, and people gave him a wide berth as they passed. He surveyed the street with narrowed green eyes perched over a nose that looked as if it had been broken more than once.

"Excuse me, sir," Molly said when she reached his side. "Could you please help me?"

"Fresh off the boat, are ya?" the officer asked as he stuck the club in its scabbard and tipped his cap.

Molly smiled when she heard his accent.

"You're from Cork," she said.

"I am," he replied and ran the back of his hand over his bushy brown mustache. "Most of us with the police are Irish. A few Germans. But mostly Irish. I'd place you from the west. Galway? Or is it Mayo?"

"Yes," Molly said. "I … we … just arrived today. I'm from Galway. A village called Belclare."

"You've a beautiful child there," the officer said as he reached a hand toward Ellen, who pulled away from him. "A bit shy, I see."

"Her parents and brother," Molly said. "They …"

The officer smiled at her kindly. "Say no more. Sure, didn't I lose me own father when we came over."

As he spoke, a woman strode up to him and planted a kiss on his cheek.

"When are ya gonna come pay me another visit, Frankie?" she called out over her shoulder as she walked away. His eyes followed the sway of her hips.

"When was that?" Molly asked.

"I'm sorry? What did you say?"

"I asked you when it was you came to America," Molly asked.

"Oh, it was, I don't know, '48 or '49. I was around ten. During the hunger, it was. Now, tell me, what did you need help with?"

"It's an address I'm after," Molly said. "Where me auntie and uncle live."

She recited the address and he thought for a moment, then gave her directions.

"It's a bit of a walk," he said. "Can you manage?"

"I can. And thank you for your kindness."

"If you find yourself in need of aid, just call around the 6th Precinct over on Franklin Street. I'm on loan to the 24th Precinct for a few days, but I'll be back on my own ground tomorrow. Ask for Officer Francis Lynch."

"I'm Molly O'Sullivan," she said, "and this is Ellen."

"I'd offer a hand, but I see yours are full. I'll say welcome to New York. 'Tis a fine city, if a bit rough. But take care. Make sure you go directly to your family's place. A friendly face what offers you help may turn out to be in league with the devil himself. You can't trust some of my fellow coppers either. Some are worse than the criminals we pursue. A city like this can gobble up a newcomer fast. So be careful."

"I'll keep that in mind, Officer Lynch."

"Frank, please."

"Frank," Molly said with a smile. "Maybe we'll see each other again."

"I hope so, Miss Molly."

He seems a good sort, Molly thought as she walked away. *It might be good to have a friend what knows the city like he does. But I wonder what the business with that … woman … was about. Does he go to the same places that Mr. Babbins spoke of?*

Ellen turned and pointed in the direction of the ship and said, "Mama."

"Shhh," Molly said as she squeezed the child's hand, "it's Molly who's got you now. I'll not let you come to harm. Can you say that? Can you say 'Molly'?"

Ellen looked away and said nothing. Molly sighed and continued to walk. *She'll come around. It's just the shock of it. Sure, don't I know what it's like to lose a parent myself.*

As she moved away from the waterfront, and deeper into the city, the buildings rose like the walls of a canyon around her. Men sold fruits and vegetables from carts. Dirty children lounged in alleyways, watching people pass with the cautious eyes of a feral cat. Bells rang in the distance.

Muck clung to her shoes as she walked. Manure, rotten vegetables, and garbage covered the streets. Some blocks had sidewalks, but others did not, forcing pedestrians to pick their way through the mire. A few wooden buildings had balconies, and Molly saw even more women shouting propositions to men on the street. *My God*, she thought, *is the whole city filled with fallen women? Ain't that what me ma would call them?*

Laughter and music spilled out of saloons so numerous it seemed as though every block held five or six of them. Two drunken men staggered out of one and began to grapple with one another in the street as a police officer watched from nearby with an amused expression on his face.

The others on the ship spoke of America as if it were heaven on earth, Molly thought. *But if this is heaven, the hell Father Byrne spoke of must be terrible indeed.*

Shouts of 'Make way!' rang out from behind her and Molly hurried out of the street, dragging Ellen behind her. She turned and saw a group of twelve men in red shirts, black pants, and leather helmets running down the street. They pulled a fire engine behind them. Boys ran alongside and shouted encouragement. The engine had handles in the front and back and a white tiger painted on the side. Molly watched as they disappeared around a corner, but most of the others on the street took little notice.

"Terrible battle in Virginia! Many casualties! The Irish Brigade in the midst of it!" a newsboy yelled on a street corner. A few men stopped and took a paper from the stack by his side and paid him.

So, they've a brigade of Irishmen, Molly thought. *Jimmy was in a regiment. The Connaught Rangers. A brigade must be bigger than that*, she decided. *I guess it is true about the war.*

Molly determined to ask what the war was about as soon as she got the chance. As she moved along, her suitcase got increasingly heavy and Ellen moved more slowly. Molly's own legs, back, and arms ached, so she found a bench and sat down. She pulled Ellen into her lap, not wanting to lose her in the street.

"We'll just rest here a bit, Ellen," she said. "Then we'll be along. I'm sure there'll be a nice warm bed for you to sleep in tonight. And for me too, I hope."

A man hurried across the street to where Molly sat, tipped his hat, and said, "Can I help you with something, miss?"

Remembering the words of Officer Lynch, Molly gave the man what she hoped was a polite smile and said, "I've no need of assistance, but thank you. We just stopped to rest for a moment."

"Are you sure?" the man insisted. "I'd be happy to carry your suitcase for you."

"I am," Molly said. "But thank you all the same."

"It would really be no bother."

"I said no," Molly said, her voice hard. "Now be off and leave us in peace."

"Irish bitch," the man murmured as he walked away.

"Pushy people, these Yankees," Molly said to Ellen. "Come on. We'd better keep going."

When she found Bowery Boulevard, Molly turned right and walked through a square. Two jugglers tossed pins back and forth from opposite sides of the street, the pins sailing above the heads of the passersby. A man and woman, barefoot and covered in dirt, wearing clothes full of holes, sang a song. Some people paused long enough to toss a bit of money in the man's hat, which lay upside down on the street in front of him. She noticed an ornate theater ahead on her left. Fronted by massive columns and flanked by a hotel, the building looked grander than anything she had ever seen. A man and woman walked down the front steps, dressed in clothes finer than Molly could even imagine. *Like a king and a queen, they are! Not even Lord Sanderson himself has clothes as fine as that! They'd be the envy of all of Ireland*, so they would.

"Wouldn't it be grand to see a play there, Ellen?" Molly asked. "But it no doubt costs a fortune to get inside."

She took a step back as a carriage rumbled by. The wheel hit a puddle and mud splashed on Molly's skirt. After two weeks aboard ship, the mud was the least of her problems. She hoped her aunt and uncle had access to a cast iron tub like the one her mother kept out back behind their cabin. *The girl could use a good wash too*, Molly thought as she eyed the streaks of dirt caked into Ellen's hair. *From the looks of these people, we are far from the dirtiest among them.*

Her stomach grumbled as they passed a house with the front door propped open and smoke drifting from the chimney. It smelled of boiled cabbage and beef. Molly would eat bits of shoe leather to avoid any more of what they had been fed on board the *Dublin Rose*. She froze, her stomach continuing to protest, as images of her childhood flashed through her mind. Her grandparents, laying side by side on the floor, and holding hands as they withered away for want of food while her father, covered with the red splotches of typhus, sweated on a rough pallet in the corner. The hunger pains sharp as she doubled over in agony. Wandering the roads with her mother and Jimmy in search of employment or sustenance. Children crawling on their hands and knees in the fields eating grass like wild beasts. The smell of death and rot inescapable.

"Miss?"

Molly blinked and saw a man in front of her.

"I'm sorry, what did you say?" she asked.

"Lost," the man said, "I asked if you were … you seem lost."

"I was," Molly said. "But I am no longer."

The man shook his head and walked away.

"I'm sorry, Ellen. Be grateful you were born after the years of sorrow. 'Tis a terrible thing to go about with all that in your head."

Most of the accents she heard around her were Irish, which gave her comfort. Every corner of Ireland was represented in the streets of New York. As Molly marveled at the buildings around her, she wondered what she might find at her relatives' place. She doubted their home would be too grand, as they had left Ireland with nothing more than the clothes they wore, unless, perhaps, they'd made some fortune in America. *No*, she thought. *They made no fortune. Surely if they did, they would have sent the money for me ma and I to come over together. And in more comfort than what I found on the ship.*

"I think maybe we'll be there soon," Molly said. "It can't be too much farther. Not if Officer Lynch is a man of truth, which I think he is."

Ellen continued to stare straight ahead without a word. *Maybe a bath and a hot meal will cheer her up*, Molly thought. *The poor girl. It's all too much for her to understand.*

Her pace quickened as she turned onto Canal Street. She studied the numbers on the buildings. *Close*, she thought. *Thank God!*

The numbers got smaller as she headed away from Bowery Boulevard, so she went in that direction. After five minutes, Molly found herself in front of a narrow three-story brick building. Four windows on each floor faced the street, and the number painted about the door matched the one in her memory. Boards covered the windows on the second floor. The glass on the top floor windows was missing, and streaks of soot stained the red bricks around them. Light shone through them courtesy of the collapsed ceiling. *What has happened? Have they closed the building? Have the families here all moved away?*

Through the open front door, Molly saw bits of charred wood and debris piled in the center of the hallway. Even from the street she could smell the odor of burnt wood, like the fireplace in her childhood home. *A fire*, she realized. *Jesus, Mary*, and *Joseph*! *There has been a fire. But are me auntie and uncle living somewhere else now? Where? How will I find them? What am I going to do?*

As she pondered what to do next, a woman's voice behind her said, "Looking for someone?"

Molly turned around and saw a white-haired woman with deep lines around her eyes standing with her hands on her hips.

"I am," Molly said. "My auntie and uncle live here. I think … I mean … they did live here … maybe. What happened?"

"A fire's what happened," the woman said. "Everyone got out alive. Except the family upstairs in Number 12. That window, right there. Got trapped and the lads in the fire department took their own sweet time getting here. Whole family roasted to death right in front of me. Husband. Wife. Four kids. Worst thing I ever saw. Watched them carry the bodies to the street after the fire was out. God rest their souls."

Molly felt her heart drop while it started to beat faster. *Maybe I remembered the wrong number*, she thought. *That's it, surely.*

"Please," Molly said, "could you take the child's hand for me for a moment? I need to get something out of my suitcase."

The woman reached out her hand and Ellen took it. The child did not make a sound as she looked around the street. Molly knelt and opened her suitcase. It took a minute for her to dig out the folded scrap of paper. She stood up. Her hands shook as she opened it. The number jumped off the page. Twelve. Not wanting to frighten the child, Molly put the paper back in the suitcase, closed it, and took hold of Ellen's hand again.

"You look like you've seen a ghost," the woman said. "What was on that paper?"

"It was … well … my family isn't here. That's all."

Molly had last seen her aunt and uncle when she was five years old. She had a vague recollection of them leaving the village in the midst of the hunger. Her uncle was quite a bit younger than his sister, Molly's mother, and he and his wife left Ireland shortly after they married. *I can't even remember their faces*, Molly realized, *and I know nothing of their children. All I know of them is what me ma told me, but even she hasn't seen them in over ten years.*

The woman stared at her for a minute and then said, "My sympathies for your loss. Fresh off the boat, aren't you?"

Molly nodded. She did not trust herself to say anything else.

"Have you another place you could stay the night?"

Molly mouthed the word no.

"Money?"

Molly shook her head.

"Take some advice from an old woman. Find somewhere you can get off the streets for the night. For the child's sake, if not your own. Someone will take pity on you, a girl alone with a child. It's just not safe for you to be out after dark."

"Where should I go?" Molly asked when she found her voice.

"If I were you," the woman said, "I'd head uptown. Less crime there, or so the papers say. There's a bad element in this city that preys on unfortunate or lost souls such as yours. So, give them a wide berth, or as wide as you can."

"Where is … uptown, did you say?"

The woman pointed her finger.

She considered walking back to the docks to find Babbins to ask if she might be permitted to spend the night aboard, and set off in the morning to find … *what? They'll be just as dead tomorrow as they are now. I'm in need of a plan,* she thought. *Am I to wander around until someone takes pity on me? Or approach a stranger for help and hope they ain't a bad sort?*

Ellen fidgeted alongside her.

"I know you're hungry, child," Molly said. "We'll see if we can find you something to eat soon. It will be all right. I promise."

"I'd offer to let you sleep at my place," the woman said, "but I don't exactly got one. I mostly stay in the alley over there."

Exhaustion tugged at Molly's eyelids and overpowered the hunger in her stomach.

"And you are sure this uptown place you spoke of is safer?" she asked.

"So they say."

"Thank you," Molly said. "That's where we'll go then."

She took a deep breath, squared her shoulders, and marched up the street.

Chapter Five

Molly's resolve crumbled four blocks later. She ducked onto a side street and sat down, using her suitcase as a seat. With Ellen balanced upon her knee, she considered her options. For a moment, Molly thought about going back to the docks and trying to find Officer Lynch to ask for guidance. *Surely, he might know a place where I could stay? No, that isn't his job. It's my mess and I'll have to be the one to fix it.*

A dog walked up and sniffed her leg, its ribs visible through tightened skin. The dog looked up, growled, and walked away. Molly leaned against the side of a wooden building and closed her eyes for a moment.

She jerked awake several minutes later, fearful that Ellen might have wandered off, but the girl was fast asleep in her arms. *She's more tired than she is hungry, as am I.*

Molly's stomach rumbled in disagreement. Darkness descended upon the streets, and long shadows blanketed the alley where she sat. Her hands ached from the cold. She had a woolen shawl in her suitcase, and she knelt to open it so that she could place it around Ellen's shoulders. *It was December when we turned up at Lord Sanderson's estate too*, she thought. *We'd walked the better part of two days to get there. All of us cold, dirty, tired, and hungry just as young Ellen and I am now.* She smiled as she recalled being ushered into the kitchen, where the heat from the stove warmed them as they ate a bowl of soup. She shook her head and straightened. *Now is no time for memories. We must keep going.*

With nowhere else to go, Molly retraced her steps and headed back for the docks. *Though what I expect to find there, I don't know*, she thought.

As she passed back in front of the Bowery Theater, Molly stopped long enough to listen to a group of men and women gathered on the steps singing Christmas carols. Dressed in black, the men in top hats and the women in bonnets, their songs told of merry gentlemen and holy nights. Though unfamiliar to her, the songs brought Molly some comfort.

When her father and brothers were alive, there was no money to buy presents for the children. In the weeks leading up to Christmas, Molly would open her eyes in the middle of the night and find him hunched over the table carving toy soldiers for her brothers or a wooden doll for her. Later, when her mother secured work as a domestic for Lord Sanderson, she managed to bring home some food from the kitchen Christmas night after the lord and his family had gone to bed. Cookies, cake, and usually a bit of meat. Molly would pace back and forth in their cottage waiting for night to fall and her mother to arrive so that she could attack the food.

The following morning, her mother usually had at least part of the day off, and she took Molly to mass to celebrate Saint Stephen's Day. Later that day, in something the priest dismissed as pagan nonsense, they celebrated Wren Day. Boys from the villages banded together and appointed their captain, who wore a cape and a straw hat. He led them off to hunt a wren. If they encountered boys from another village, they battled one another with fists and feet until one group retreated. Once they secured their prey, the boys attached it to a pole and, with the accompaniment of musicians, strawboys, and assorted other costumed characters, they paraded through the village singing songs and asking for donations. Should they raise enough money, the boys hosted a dance in January. Each year, Father Byrne threatened the participants with the fires of hell, or a long stay in purgatory, but his entreaties fell on deaf ears.

Saint Patrick made us Catholic, but he let us stay Irish. That's what me ma always said. Molly smiled as she thought of Sean leading the boys last Christmas. *I wonder what he is doing this night. Does he miss me already? Or is he getting ready to lead the boys again this year?*

Soon, Molly found herself in the middle of a large crowd gathered in front of the singers. Men and women in all manner of dress surrounded her. Fancy gentlemen stood alongside people in tattered rags. They clapped at the end of each song.

After several carols, a man stepped out of the choir and said, "We shall now perform one last song. This one is for all of you who may have a loved one away this Christmas season, off fighting for the Union. May the Almighty protect them and bring them home safe and sound."

If the Almighty cared about their safety, why would there be a war, Molly wondered as she listened to a song about a maiden with golden hair named Aura Lea. The crowd drifted away before the song was over, and Molly moved along with them. Around her, talk swirled about the war and its progress.

"Let the Rebs go," one man said. "It ain't worth another life."

"Lincoln can't find a general what knows what he's doing," said a stocky Irishman. "That's why he's always after firing his generals once they go down and get another licking. If he was in charge of England, why, Ireland would be free in two weeks' time."

It must be going bad for their side, Molly thought. *Or else people wouldn't be complaining. I didn't hear angry words about the Irishmen what went to fight in the Crimea. Proud to serve, my brother was. And look what it got him.*

Another fire company rushed by, perhaps the same one as before, the men's eyes grim and determined, with exhaustion visible on their faces. As the sun set, a new cast of characters filled the streets. Ragged men with haunted eyes clustered in groups on the street corners, speaking in low, conspiratorial tones. Young girls, barefoot and dirty, hawked ears of hot corn. As she walked, Molly occasionally saw a gentleman approach one of the girls, hand her money, and then disappear into an alley, with no corn exchanged. *I wonder what that's about. Are they selling … themselves instead of corn*? Her stomach groaned with protest as she caught a whiff of the smell of hot corn and butter.

The sour smell of bad whiskey spilled out of the bars and the pores of the men on the streets. A few stumbled into Molly, muttered an apology, and staggered on. She saw several men passed out in the mud, though the few police officers around took no notice as they stepped over them and walked on. Back home, she had seen her share of men felled by the drink at the celebrations in her village. Some of the women sported bruises the morning after their husbands went on a spree. Her own father spoke ill of those in whom the drink released pugilistic desires.

"A man what can't handle his drink is no man at all," he said.

What am I looking for? Am I after a meal? A bed? People speak of America as if you can snatch money and food from the streets. All there for the taking. But I don't see nothing like that here. Maybe I got off the boat in the wrong country.

A group of sailors, navy men in white smocks with dark blue collars and cuffs that matched their blue wool trousers, stumbled by. The four men had their arms around one another for mutual balance, and they sang, badly, a bawdy tune about a maid in Amsterdam.

"Hey, Red," one of them called out as they passed by, "want a good time?"

"Shut up, Danny," one of his mates responded. "Can't you see she's got a child with her?"

"I ain't particular," Danny said.

Molly turned and walked away as Danny shouted lewd suggestions over his shoulder.

"Animals," she said to Ellen, who yawned sleepily.

"I know you are tired," Molly said. "We will find a place to sleep soon enough."

She considered going into a business and asking for help, but the only places open appeared to be saloons. *That's no place for a woman or a child.* Then she smiled. *A church! I'll find a church. Surely someone there can help.* She scanned the area around her, but the darkness and the buildings concealed any spires that she might otherwise see. I must ask someone, but who?

It was a difficult question for her to answer. Most of the men around were in various states of intoxication. The few women on the streets, in various stages of undress, were apparently … in the business of selling flesh. Finally, Molly saw a well-dressed woman, alone, walking up the street. Molly hurried over to her. She nearly stumbled in a hole but managed to keep her feet.

"Excuse me, ma'am," she said as she tried to adopt the deferential tone her mother took when speaking to Lord Sanderson, "could you help me? I've no place to go for the night and I am looking for a church."

"A Roman one from the looks of you," the woman said with a pronounced American accent. "You'll find one over on Mott Street, but I doubt they take in girls from the street such as yourself."

"What do you mean?" Molly asked. "I've only just arrived today."

"And where's your husband?"

"I've no husband," Molly said.

"Sent over by your family because of your sin," the woman said as she gestured toward Ellen. She turned and started to walk away.

"Wait, ma'am," Molly cried out, "it's not like that. Please. Can you tell me how to get to Mott Street at least?"

The woman ignored her. *Shite,* Molly swore. *All the arrogance of a landlord, that one had. Maybe I can ask a peeler for directions.*

She headed west, away from the docks. The buildings took on a much rougher appearance the deeper she got into the city. People shouted to one another. A cow walked by with no one to mind it. The smell of offal grew stronger. Molly shuddered as the buildings and the crowds made her feel for a moment like she could not breathe. She grew dizzy enough that she had to find a place to sit down. She sat her suitcase down and again used it as a stool as she pulled Ellen onto her lap. Despite the cold, sweat ran down her face and dripped onto Ellen's head as she held her. A wave of nausea swept over her. *It's just my nerves.*

I'll be fine. I need only to find Mott Street.

She continued on her quest as soon as she felt strong enough. Eventually, she came across a police officer and asked him for directions. He gave them in a gruff, monotone voice devoid of any human emotion. Molly thought back to Officer Lynch's warning, that not every officer was trustworthy, but she had no choice but to trust him and hope. She happily discovered Mott Street was a mere five-minute walk away, and soon she found herself outside of the Church of the Transfiguration at the corner of Mott and Park Street. Its brick façade and steeple rose high above the neighborhood. Molly walked over and tried the heavy wooden door. It was unlocked, so she slipped inside. Candles lit the interior, and she could see the altar with a large crucifix mounted to the wall behind it.

"Can I help you?"

Molly turned and saw a young priest walking towards her, a frown on his face.

"Please, Father," Molly said, "I arrived in town today and found my auntie and uncle dead from a fire. I've no other place to go for the night."

"We do not run a shelter here," the priest said, "but just down Park Street you'll find the Five Points House of Industry. They cater to wayward women. Perhaps you can find a place to sleep there, if you can put up with their Protestant ways."

"But I ain't a wayward woman, Father," Molly protested. "If it's the child you mean, her parents fell ill on the voyage and there was no one to see to her other than me."

"I see," the priest said, "but that doesn't change the fact that we do not allow people to sleep inside our church. If we did, half the drunks in the neighborhood would pass out in here each night and destroy the place. Surely you understand why I cannot make an exception in your case."

"And what am I to do, Father," Molly asked. "Not just for me, but for the child?"

"Remember the Psalm. I will lift up mine eyes to the hills from whence cometh my help."

"I didn't see no hills outside, Father."

"Look to the Lord. And you'll receive his help."

The priest walked over to the door, opened it, and beckoned her to leave.

"The Lord?" Molly asked over her shoulder as she walked outside into the night. "Surely it was him what got me into this mess in the first place."

She jumped as the door slammed behind her. *Bastard*, she swore. *For all their talk of Jesus helping the poor, when the poor show up on their doorstep, they turn us away like we was yesterday's garbage.*

Ellen began to cry. Molly leaned down and picked her up, using her hip to steady the child without dropping the suitcase in the other hand.

"Shhh," Molly said, "I've got you. I can carry you for a bit. We'll find something to eat here soon. I promise."

From where? A trash heap? But what else can I tell her? She walked away from the church and stopped at the door of the first place she saw that looked like a house. A light shone through the windows as she walked up to the door and knocked. After several minutes, the door opened and a middle-aged man with a sizable paunch and a graying beard said, "Yes? Can I help you?"

"Please, sir," Molly said. "I just arrived here today and learned my relatives are dead. Please? Could you maybe spare some food for us? Or at least for the child?"

"Who is that, Harold?" a woman's voice called out from inside. Molly caught the odor of food, and the smell, though pleasant, nearly made her vomit.

"It's just some paddy fresh off the boat that expects me to invite her and her spawn inside for supper."

"Please, sir," Molly begged.

"Your kind have overrun this country already. And yet you still show up on my doorstep wanting a handout. Why don't you go back to Ireland and get help from the English? That's right. They don't want you either. Just go."

He spat on her skirt and slammed the door. She turned away and kissed the top of Ellen's head before she put her back on the ground.

"There's bastards in every country, Ellen," she said. "Some just hide it better than others. At least he was honest about it."

She moved a few feet away from the door and stopped. *I won't beg again*, she said to herself. *Maybe if I … if I just left Ellen at the church, they'd have to take care of her. At least she'd be safe.* Children with eyes shrunken into their skulls and bellies swollen for want of food floated through her mind. *The children of the great hunger. And there I am, kneeling beside my own father's grave and wailing like a banshee and me ma had not a word of comfort for me. Too caught up in her own grief. Am I to leave young Ellen with no one to love her? No one to comfort her when she is scared?*

"No," she said so loudly several people turned to look at the disheveled redhead with a child in her arms. "I promised your mother I'd take care of you, and I must honor that. Whatever happens, it happens to both of us."

A man and woman walked toward her, approaching so rapidly that Molly took a step back in surprise.

"No, no," the man said as he held up his hand, "we've no desire to startle you!"

"Well, you did," Molly said.

"Are you in some distress, my dear?" the woman asked. "I mean no offense, but you look as though you are lost."

As she spoke, the man pushed his black bowler hat back on his head and adjusted the spectacles perched on his nose.

With Officer Lynch's words in her ears, Molly said, "I thank you, truly, but we are in no need of help."

"Come now, my dear girl," the man said, "Did I not just see you knock upon a door to inquire about food for yourself and your child?"

Molly frowned. *Is it that obvious that I need help? Of course, it is,* she thought. *I'm like a fish what gets dropped off on dry land and told to blend in with the cattle.*

"My name is Charles Ellsworth," the man said as he tipped his hat. "Of New Haven, Connecticut. I've resided in New York for the past several years. And this is my … fiancée, Susannah."

Susannah smiled through heavily painted lips. "A delight to meet you, miss …"

"Molly is my name. Molly O'Sullivan."

"And the little one?" Ellsworth asked.

"Ellen."

"A delightful child if I've ever seen one. She definitely favors her mother," Susannah said.

"Oh, she ain't *mine.* Not like that, anyway," Molly said. "Her parents, well, they died on the boat and she's for me to take care of now."

"Ah, a true Christian, you are!" Ellsworth exclaimed.

"It ain't that, sir," Molly said. "I made a promise."

"So, you are a woman of your word," he said. "How commendable!"

"Thank you, sir."

"You've the loveliest hair I think I've ever seen," Susannah said. "Look at mine! I can hardly manage to tame it on a good day."

"I doubt my hair looks that nice," Molly said. "I've been two weeks with no more than a quick scrub. We, Ellen and I, could use a good wash."

"Might I ask you a rather personal question?" Ellsworth looked at his fiancée then back to Molly.

"You can," Molly said.

"Well, for what reason are you wandering about the streets at this late hour? It's a bit dangerous for a pretty girl like you, especially when she's got a suitcase in one hand and a child in the other. Have you been walking the streets all day? Are you not exhausted?"

"I am," Molly whispered. *They must be safe to talk to*, she told herself. *He's got a woman with him. If he meant me any harm, he'd be alone. A nice couple, they seem.*

"Tell me what has happened to cause your distress?"

"It's …" Molly hesitated. "It's my relatives, sir. I was to go to them when I got off the boat, but I found their house burned and was told they were dead."

For the first time that day, Molly started to cry.

Chapter Six

"There, there," Susannah said. She held out her hand out toward Ellen. "I'll mind her while we walk."

Molly hesitated, then nodded to Ellen, who took the woman's hand.

"I'm sorry," she said. "I don't mean to cry. It's just that today has been … so …"

"I do believe we might be able to offer you some assistance," Ellsworth said.

They are safe, Molly told herself. They have to be.

"I would be grateful," Molly said. "Though I have no way to repay your kindness."

Ellsworth laughed as he reached down and took her suitcase.

"It wouldn't be assistance if we expected you to pay for it. Come on, I know a place where we can get you and the child some food."

Twenty minutes later, they sat in a dark corner of a saloon off Pell Street. The light of an oil lamp cast an eerie glow across the faces of her two benefactors, who sat across the table from Molly. She had Ellen in her lap and guided her hand, which held a spoon, into the soup bowl and up to her mouth. Sounds of card games and arguments filled the air around them. At a nearby table, four men argued over the best course of action for the Union Army to take in the field. Each man had his own plan for victory, and shouted it at the others, who shouted theirs in return. The bartender paced behind the bar as if he were a captain on the bridge of a ship, a revolver tucked in the front of his pants and a knife dangling from his belt. Assorted bottles of amber-colored liquid and wooden casks were stacked against the wall behind him. At the corner of the bar, a wooden keg with a hose on one end and a priming pump on the other provided a few seconds of brain-addling liquor for a nickel. The saloon smelled of cheap whiskey, unwashed bodies, and manure from the streets, which clung to the shoes of everyone inside.

"She's got a healthy appetite," Susannah said.

"After what passed as food on the ship," Molly said, "it's no wonder."

Ellen shook her head as Molly raised the spoon to her mouth.

"Are you finished, then?" Molly asked as she put the spoon back in the bowl.

"Why don't you come sit by me, Ellen, and let Miss Molly eat," Susannah offered.

Ellen slid out of Molly's lap and walked over to Susannah as Molly started to eat. A wave of protest rolled over her stomach as the first bit of soup went down. She waited for it to pass, and then she kept eating. Ellen began to nod off, and Susannah placed her in her lap. Soon, Ellen was asleep with her head on Susannah's chest.

Ellsworth produced a cigar from his coat pocket. "Do you mind if I . . ."

"No," Molly said, "I do not."

He struck a match on the table and held it to the end of his cigar. Ellsworth inhaled, and then blew a ring of smoke which drifted lazily above his head. As more alcohol flowed around them, the crowd in the saloon grew more boisterous. A fight broke out in one corner, and the two men fell on top of a table. It crashed to the floor, though the men seated at it managed to save their drinks. Molly flinched at the loud crack of a pistol shot. All conversation in the bar ceased. The bartender held the smoking gun in his hand. He gestured at the men on the floor, who paused their fight upon hearing the shot.

"Take it out to the street," he said.

One man stood up, extended his hand to the other, and helped him up. They walked outside with one another and, through the open door, Molly saw them resume their contest of strength.

"A funny place, New York," she said.

Ellsworth laughed. "You'll see so many strange sights here that soon enough you'll become immune to it," he said. "Give it a month or two and you'll be a seasoned New Yorker."

"I don't know," Molly said. "It's all so … new. I doubt I'll ever feel at home."

At the word home, a wave of emotion struck her with all the force of the wave aboard the Dublin Rose. Images of Knockma Hill, of her father sitting by the fire, and of Jimmy marching off to the wars raced through her mind. Molly bit her lip for a moment to force back the tears. *No, don't,* she told herself. *Don't let them see you cry again.*

"I'm sure everyone fresh off the boat feels the same way," Ellsworth said.

"Is the war as bad as I've heard?" Molly asked to change the subject. "It is talked about in Ireland."

"All wars are bad," Ellsworth said, "in their own way. It's not going well for our side. I won't lie and say it is. But we won a victory back in September down in Maryland. Well, it was sort of a victory. But President Lincoln issued a proclamation saying that the slaves in areas still in rebellion will be free on New Year's Day. Some folks here, primarily the Irish, aren't too happy about it."

Molly nodded. She knew little of the dynamics of the American states, but she had heard that wealthy people kept slaves in the Southern states where they labored to produce cotton for the textile mills of the northern states and also Great Britain. *I wonder if they live in grand estates like the landlords in Ireland. Except they've Africans to order around. They say there's no aristocracy here, at least not by birth. But don't the rich people here seem just like they do back home?*

"Would you like another bowl?" Susannah asked.

"If it ain't too much trouble," Molly said. "I hate to be a bother."

Charles raised his hand and snapped his fingers. The bartender appeared and placed a lukewarm bowl in front of her.

"It ain't hot," he said by way of apology.

"I'd eat it cold," Molly said.

Ellsworth and Susannah laughed. Molly noticed he had yet to pay the bartender for anything. *Maybe you settle your debt when you leave*, she thought. In a few minutes, Molly put away the entire bowl.

"I do thank you," she said. "I fear you might think me a cow."

"Not at all," Ellsworth said. "A pretty girl such as yourself needs to eat to keep her strength up."

Molly smiled and blushed. The bartender walked over and placed a measure of whiskey in front of her.

"Drink that," Ellsworth said. "It'll help with the nerves."

Molly started to protest. "I've never—"

"It won't hurt you," Susannah said.

Molly picked up the glass and slowly raised it to her lips. She took a tentative sip, the liquid burning a fiery trail down her throat and into her stomach. With the next drink, the warmth spread from her stomach to her toes. When she finished, Ellsworth signaled for another.

"Oh no, I couldn't," Molly said.

"One more won't kill you."

Molly giggled as she picked up the glass. Now, the warmth spread down her arms.

"Let's get down to business, shall we?" Ellsworth said. "Now, you've no place to stay and no prospect of employment, am I right?"

"You are," Molly said. "I'd hoped that me auntie or uncle might help me get a job. But now … now I don't know what I'll do."

"The main thing is for you to secure lodgings until such time as you find a job. You'll find it difficult, but not impossible to come by one. Have you any experience as a domestic? Plenty of Irish girls go to work for the rich families uptown. Sometimes the job comes with lodging as well. But without a reference it might be difficult to obtain a post."

"I can cook a little," Molly said. "And I can operate a broom, but me ma always said I was too headstrong for service work. It's my mouth, you see. Gets me into trouble."

Susannah laughed.

"I'm the same way myself," she said. "What did you do back in Ireland?"

"Oh, I was a scullery maid for a while on the estate where me ma worked," Molly said. "I wanted to work in the nursery with the children. They let me start helping out there when I was sixteen but then …"

"Come on," Susannah urged. "You can tell us. We are all friends here, right Charles?"

He nodded encouragingly and Molly said, "Well … it happened like this."

One spring day, Molly had gone up to the children's playroom on the second floor shortly after breakfast. After picking up a few errant toys, she sat down in a chair to wait for the governess, a middle-aged Scottish woman named Mrs. Cameron, to bring the children up to play. Gazing out the window at the countryside, lost in thoughts of Queen Maeve, Molly did not hear the door open.

"What is the meaning of this?" Lord Sanderson asked. "Who gave you leave to sit? Have you no work to do? And by God, girl, you will stand when I enter the room."

Molly's neck turned scarlet as she looked at Lord Sanderson and said, "And who gave you leave to sit on your own arse in my country and order me about? You ain't the King of Ireland!"

"Did you really?" Susannah asked.

"I did," Molly said. "And he sacked me for it and banned me from the house. If not for me brother Jimmy having just gotten home from India, he'd have probably sacked me ma too. I was the only girl. And me da always said that I was his favorite. He told me I didn't have to take no cheek from anyone. No matter how much money they had. He said that I had to stand up for myself or else the English and everyone else would walk over me like I was nothing."

"Ah, we've a Fenian on our hands, Susannah," Ellsworth said as he smiled at Molly. "No doubt you'll find your fortune here and then return to Ireland and lead an army to drive the English out. You Irish do tend to be a combative lot."

"It ain't like that at all, sir," Molly said. "But doesn't everyone want to be free?"

"And your father is back in Ireland?" Ellsworth asked.

"No," Molly whispered. "He died during the hunger. A year after me two younger brothers died. I was six. Sometimes I ..."

"Go on," Ellsworth urged.

"It's nothing," Molly said. Her earliest memories were of the years of hunger and sickness, but she also realized how hard her father had tried to shield them from the reality. *And what a reality it was,* she thought. *All of Galway starving and buzzards scattering bones over half of Connaught. And I didn't see Queen Victoria come hallooing about with food and medicine neither.*

"Maybe service work wouldn't suit her, Charles," Susannah said. "What do you think?"

"Here is what I can do for you," Ellsworth said. "I know a woman who owns a boarding house. It'll be a safe place for you and the child to sleep. I can pay for a week, maybe ten days in advance for you, and during that time you can find employment. If you like the boarding house, well, just stay on once you've found a job. I'm sure the woman who runs it wouldn't mind watching after young Ellen here while you look for work."

"Oh no," Molly said, "that's too much to ask of you. I won't turn down a night or two, but a week? That's too generous."

"Nonsense," Ellsworth said. "It's the proper thing to do under the circumstances. Forgive me for asking this, but it is important—are you literate?"

"Do you mean can I read letters?" Molly asked. "I can. Some anyway."

"You'll want to improve your skills," Ellsworth said. "Many of your people cannot read or write, and it proves a hindrance. A girl who can, why, that'll send you down the path to a wonderful future in this country. Isn't that right, Susannah? A wonderful future indeed. Isn't that what you want?"

"It is, I guess," Molly said. "But are you sure it's no trouble about the lodging? I do not want to impose on your kindness. A meal is one thing, but a week in a boarding house is quite another."

"Think of it as us doing it for the sake of young Ellen here," Susannah said as she stroked the girl's hair. "You don't want to see her sleeping in the streets, do you?"

"No, of course not," Molly said. "And on that basis, I have no choice but to accept your kind offer. I truly wish I could offer to repay you."

"I tell you what," Ellsworth said, "when you make your fortune here in New York, why, just help someone else in need and that will be repayment enough."

"I will," Molly promised.

After a ten-minute walk, they reached the two-story wood frame boarding house. It leaned a bit to the right, as a man who'd had too much to drink might walk. A sign just below the second-floor balcony promised cheap rent and weekly rates. A large middle-aged woman sat behind a counter just inside the door. Beyond the counter, a steep staircase led to the second floor. Paint peeled from the walls and collected in small piles along the baseboards.

"What have you brought me tonight?" the woman asked when the group walked in.

"Meet Molly O'Sullivan and young Ellen," Ellsworth said. "They are in need of lodging. A most tragic set of circumstances has landed them on your doorstep. How about a week? And if she needs a few more days, I'll cover that too. Does that suit?"

"It does," the woman said with a smile. "I'll show them up right away. Do stop by to see me again, Mr. Ellsworth. Goodnight, Susannah."

The woman took Molly's suitcase and led her up the stairs. *Did he not give her any money*, she wondered? *Maybe he'll leave it on the counter for her as he's on his way out. That must be it.* The second floor smelled of cheap tobacco, though Molly heard no sounds from behind the six doors, three on each side of the hallway. An open window at the end of the corridor let in the chill of the winter night.

"Don't you worry," the woman said. "There's plenty of warm blankets in the room. A bit itchy, perhaps, but they'll do."

She stopped in front of the last room on the right, the number six on the door, and produced a key. It stuck for a moment, and she had to give the door a shove with her hip to get it open.

"The lock sticks," she said as she sat the suitcase down inside the door, "and there's no way to lock it from the inside. I do apologize for that, but all our other rooms are occupied and so I've nowhere else to put you. But it's perfectly safe here. I keep a close eye on things. No one gets past the front desk that doesn't go through me."

The woman smiled and winked at Molly as she closed the door. The room was small, with enough space for a narrow bed, a small desk, and a chair. Two gray wool blankets with a few patches sewn onto them were folded at the foot of the bed. With no window, the air inside smelled stale. She helped Ellen sit on the bed and lit the oil lamp on the desk. Molly knelt by the bed and removed the girl's shoes and then tucked her under the blanket.

"Do you want to hear a song, Ellen?" Molly asked.

Ellen nodded her head in agreement, and Molly softly sang "The Peeler and the Goat" as she patted the child's head. As she finished, Molly noticed the child looking around the room. *The doll*, Molly realized. She went over to the suitcase and pulled the doll out.

"Here," Molly said. "Let's tuck her in with you."

Ellen smiled as she put her arm around the doll. Good, Molly thought. She smiled. That's a start at least.

"Things will be fine now," Molly said. "You just wait and see. I'll find work of some kind. We can get our own place. Just the two of us. Maybe we could even go visit that theater one day. It'll be grand."

Ellen was asleep by the time Molly finished speaking. She untied the leather laces on her own boots. The combination of exhaustion, the soup and whiskey in her stomach, and the newfound sense of hope she felt made it difficult to work her fingers. She considered undressing but decided to surrender to her body's demand for rest. Once she stretched out beside Ellen and her head hit the lumpy pillow, she was asleep in seconds.

She awoke when the doorknob rattled. The lamp had burned itself out while she slept and in the darkness, she could not see anything, though she felt Ellen's presence beside her. *Was I dreaming? That's what it was. A dream.*

As she closed her eyes and started to nod off again, the door was flung open. Heavy footsteps pounded against the floor. Molly jerked upright in her bed and yelled, "Who's there?" Two large dark shapes appeared beside the bed. One reached down and snatched the child, who awoke and wailed as the doll fell to the floor.

"What are you doing?" Molly demanded. She jumped out of bed. As one shape carried Ellen out of the door, the child screamed, "Molly!"

Molly took a step forward, but a heavy blow to her jaw knocked her backwards on to the bed. As she tried to push herself back up, a hand closed around her throat. She drew in a ragged breath as the cold fingers tightened their grip.

"Be quiet," a man's voice said, "or you'll never see the girl again."

Fight! You have to fight, her brain screamed as her hands clutched the wrist of the man as he pushed her back down on the bed. Molly groped for the man's face and sank her fingernails into the flesh of his cheek. As she raked them down his face, she felt the blood dampen her fingers. The man yelled and relaxed his grip. Molly bolted from the bed and made for the door. Arms seized her around the waist and lifted her in the air. She tried to scream, but her voice froze in her throat as she kicked her legs, trying to break the man's grip.

He flung her across the room, toward the bed. Her head struck the headboard with a thud. The shape of the man approached her again, but it felt like she was watching the events happen to someone else. A wave of dizziness struck her as she tried to rise. Molly saw the fist a split second before it crashed into her face. She sank back onto the bed as blackness enveloped her. As she sank into unconsciousness, Molly could hear the echo of Ellen screaming her name.

Chapter Seven

Dawn found Molly huddled in the corner, her dress torn to shreds. A trickle of blood ran down from her nose and dripped onto the floor. There were streaks of blood on the inside of her legs. Her head felt heavy, her mouth dry. Her brain seemed a tangled mess as one thought ran into another. *I'm … I'm … ruined*, she thought. *Why? What did I do? And Ellen! Did they … no, surely not. She's too young. Animals, they were. I … I … am I a fallen woman now? The kind me ma talks about. And Father Byrne at mass too. And what if I've a baby inside me? What will I do then? Oh Jesus! My dress! I can't go out on the street like this.*

When she heard the door rattle again, Molly shrank back into the wall and drew her legs up. She wrapped her arms around them, pulling them tightly into her body as she began to shake. Two young women entered the room, closing the door behind them. They were well dressed and moved with confidence and a touch of grace. One of them knelt in front of Molly and studied her for a minute.

"It's all right, Molly," she finally said. "We aren't here to hurt you.

My name's Katie and this is Liza."

She spoke with an Irish accent dulled by years in New York City. Katie's hair was as fair as Liza's was dark. She gave Molly a slight smile, then looked up at Liza and said, "She's a pretty one, Liza. She'll clean up nice. Give it time, and I bet the missus will have a new favorite."

Liza glared at Katie for a moment, then turned to Molly and said, "We are here to take you to your new home."

Unlike Katie, Liza sounded like the Americans Molly had met the day before.

"Come on," Katie said, "let me help you up. We'll get you to our place and you can have a nice, hot bath and maybe some food if you can manage it."

Molly looked at them and blinked, unable to say a word.

"You've been sold to a woman named Miss Cecilia," Katie added. "She's not a bad boss. Treats us fair, so long as you don't cross her. A pretty girl like you should be able to pay off your debt to her quick enough. After that, well, the sky's the limit."

Debt, Molly thought. *Pay off? What … what are they talking about? Where do they mean to take me? Am I to be a slave on a plantation? No … that can't be. They don't have slaves in New York. Do they? Do they have the child too?*

"Ellen," Molly whispered. "Where's Ellen?"

"Who?" Liza asked as she looked at Katie. "There's no one else here with you, girl."

"There's a doll on the floor," Katie said as she looked over her shoulder.

Katie stood up and reached out a hand. Molly hesitated for a moment and then took it. Katie pulled her to her feet while Liza draped a large, thick blanket over her shoulders. Before Molly could speak, the women each put an arm around her and tried to steer her toward the door, but Molly pulled away and snatched up the doll. Clutching it with both hands, she allowed herself to be led to the hallway.

"Why?" Molly asked, her voice low.

"Why?" Katie repeated. "Well, there's a constant demand for working girls in this town. People like Miss Cecilia recruit girls from out on the farms to come to town and work, and, barring that, well, let's just say you fell victim to another method of procurement."

When they reached the first floor, the woman from the night before still sat behind the counter. As Molly looked at her, the woman suddenly found the floor to be an interesting object of study. Outside the front door, a large, enclosed black carriage with thick velvet curtains over the windows and a gold *C* stenciled on the door waited for them. An elderly black man with gray hair sat in the driver's seat behind a team of fine, white horses that snorted and pawed the ground impatiently.

Molly tore away from the two women and raced down the street, oblivious to the stares of the crowds and the muck tugging at her bare feet. With no sense of a safe place, Molly headed in the general direction of the docks. Behind her, Katie and Liza's voices shouted threats as Molly dodged outstretched hands that tried to clutch her.

"I said, Come on. We ain't got all day!"

Molly blinked and found herself in front of the carriage again. *Did I get away? No. It was just a dream. Maybe that is what this is, all of it. Just a dream.*

Liza opened the door and got in first. She reached out and Katie gave Molly a slight shove toward Liza, who pulled her into the carriage. Once Katie climbed in and shut the door behind her, the carriage began to move. The interior smelled of cigar smoke, lilac water, and perfume. Molly clutched her stomach and hunched over.

"It isn't far from here," Katie said.

Ellen, she thought. *They took Ellen. The people seemed so nice. How was I to know? I should have listened to Officer Lynch. But we had nowhere else to go. Why did I not run from them? She looked up at the carriage door.*

"And just in case you might entertain a notion of running away," Liza said, as if she had read Molly's mind, "The last girl that tried that ended up getting knifed and thrown in the East River. No matter where you go, the missus will find you. Right, Katie?"

"Yeah," Katie grunted.

Molly closed her eyes and tried to think of home, of anything other than the dark shapes in the bedroom, the feel of a hand around her throat, and the sight of herself huddled in a corner of the room.

The carriage stopped in front of a white two story building with red trim around the windows. Katie and Liza ushered her into an alley and up the back stairs, which, Molly would learn, served as a discreet way for certain clients to slip out unnoticed lest their presence in a house of ill repute cause a scandal.

Katie pulled Molly into a room at the end of the hall. A middle-aged black maid bustled in and filled a large cast iron tub with hot water, while the two women helped Molly get undressed and climb in. Molly's hands did not want to work on their own and everyone around her moved several speeds slower than normal. She was only vaguely aware of Katie washing her hair for her as Liza watched from across the room, arms folded across her chest. *It's the first bath I've had since I left Ireland*, Molly thought. *I looked forward to this moment, but not like this. Dear God, not like this.*

"Here," Liza said as she flung a washcloth into the tub. "Make sure you get the blood off your face. Miss Cecilia don't like the sight of blood."

Molly winced and tears welled up in her eyes as she wiped her nose. Katie left the washroom and returned with a green dress, undergarments, and a corset.

"I think these will fit," she said. "They look about your size. Belinda, that's the cook she can alter them if need be."

Once they had put the clothes on her and fixed her hair, Liza led her downstairs. They passed through a parlor, down a hallway, and into a room just off the kitchen. It contained a wooden desk piled high with papers, two chairs, and a table. A woman who looked as though she was in her mid-thirties, perhaps older, sat behind the desk, focused on a piece of paper in front of her. She wore a dress of deep purple. When Molly and Liza walked in the room, she looked up and brushed a few stray blonde hairs back into place.

"New girl, Miss Cecilia," Liza said. "Her name is Molly."

"Welcome, Molly," Miss Cecilia said. "Please sit."

Molly could not move, as if her feet were rooted to the floor. Liza took over and steered her toward the chair and gently pushed her down into it.

"She's still in a bit of shock, I think," Liza said. "Hasn't said much. Either that or she's not the brightest. The Irish usually are dull-witted."

"Thank you, Liza. Please give my thanks to Katie as well. Run along. I'll summon you when I am finished here."

"Yes, ma'am," Liza said.

"So," Miss Cecilia said as she leaned back in her chair and folded her hands in her lap. "I must say my man did a fine job finding you. I think you'll do well here. Some men pay top dollar for a redheaded whore."

Molly stared at the floor, her brain unable to process Miss Cecilia's words.

"I run a clean house," she continued. "Most of our clients are well-off gentlemen from uptown or out of town. We only offer it straight. Nothing French. And my girls are clean. I'll have a doctor come around to give you a going over later today. Other than being a little on the thin side, you look healthy enough. You'll have a weekly amount due to me to cover the cost of your health check-ups, room and board, clothing, cosmetics, and meals. Belinda lays a fine spread and you'll soon put weight on. After that amount is paid, you get twenty-five percent of all transactions, paid to you weekly. I keep a ledger. Every last cent is accounted for."

She reached over and tapped a thick leather volume with her finger to emphasize her point.

"Your cut doesn't kick in until you've repaid me the funds I spent on obtaining you. That's one hundred dollars, plus the fifty-dollar bonus I paid for finding me a redheaded girl. I had one before, but the stupid thing let herself get pregnant. You can rest today, but you'll start working tomorrow evening. Understand?"

Molly raised her head and looked at Miss Cecilia. She opened her mouth to speak, but no words came.

"I asked if you understood," Miss Cecilia demanded.

"Yes," Molly whispered.

"Yes, what?"

"Yes … ma'am."

Miss Cecilia got up from behind the desk and walked over to

Molly. She stood close enough that Molly could smell her perfume, a heavy floral scent.

"If you've got designs on running away," she said, "I'd advise against it. You wouldn't get very far. I treat my girls fair, but buck me one time, and I'll sell you to one of my contacts and you'll be a dockside whore in an hour's time. You'll end up with the pox in your first year and it'll rot what brains you have. Think about that. Run away and I'll send my men after you. What they'll do when they catch you, well, it's best not to talk about that. Liza is like my second in command, so you do as she says."

She left Molly alone for a minute. *What's going on*? Molly wondered. *Why isn't my head working*? *And what happened to young Ellen*? A memory flashed through her mind. A dark shape by the bed. Hands reaching down to snatch the child. Ellen's scream. Molly closed her eyes and massaged her temples with her fingers to drive off the memory.

Liza walked into the room and said, "Come on. The missus says you can get some rest now."

She reached down and slipped her hand under Molly's arm and pulled her out of the chair. Miss Cecilia stood in the doorway and watched as Liza pushed Molly towards the hallway.

"Send for Dr. Howard," Miss Cecilia said. "And tell Belinda to send up some breakfast too. The usual precautions, Liza."

"Yes, ma'am."

When they reached the door, Molly pulled away from Liza's grasp and turned to face Miss Cecilia.

"Where's Ellen?"

"Who?" Miss Cecilia asked.

"She asked us about her back at the … the … boarding house too," Liza said.

"Ellen," Molly said. "The little girl I had with me."

"You had a baby?" Miss Cecilia asked.

"No, a little girl," Molly said, her voice barely audible. "Her family died on the boat."

"I know nothing about a child," Miss Cecilia said. "You must be confused. Liza, when the doctor gets here, ask him to administer a remedy to help her get some rest, would you?"

"I will, ma'am," Liza said as she tightened her grip on Molly's arm. She led Molly up the back stairs to a hallway lined with doors on either side. Midway down, Liza stopped and fished a key from her pocket. "This room will be yours. It locks from the outside, so don't be thinking about slipping out. And the window is nailed shut for now. Until you've earned the trust of the missus. And I doubt that will ever happen. Go on. In with you."

Liza placed her hand in the small of Molly's back and shoved her into the room. Molly winced as the door slammed shut behind her. The room contained a narrow bed, a nightstand with a ceramic washbasin, and a small table with a wooden chair. There was just enough room to navigate between the furnishings. She sat on the bed, trying to avoid the stain on the blanket.

It's like the gaol where me granda said his da was held after the ninety-eight, she thought. *But at least he knew he'd get out eventually.* Molly rose and walked over to the window. She frowned when she discovered it nailed shut as Liza said. Despite the circumstances, exhaustion tugged at her eyelids. Ignoring the stain this time, Molly collapsed onto the bed and tried in vain to sleep.

Dr. Howard arrived a few hours later. He was a young man, with spectacles and a goatee. When he entered her room, the doctor sat his black leather bag on the desk. The look he gave her alternated between sympathy and embarrassment.

"So, you must be the new girl," he said. "Molly I'm told your name is. I'm Dr. Howard and I provide services for Miss Cecilia. You'll see me each week, on Sunday mornings, for your check-up. Now, I was told that I need to give you an examination. Is that acceptable"

Molly did not answer him. Instead, she thought of the doctor whom her mother summoned as her father lay dying in the corner of the hut. "I can do nothing," the man had said, "and even if I had some cure for the typhus, I couldn't help you as you lack the means to pay." When he left, Molly wept by her father's side as her mother sat and stared at the wall.

"Yes, well, I know this is a delicate matter," Dr. Howard said, "but

I assure you that I am a professional and take no pleasure in my job. Or rather, I take no pleasure from examining patients. And that is what we are about here. I am a doctor and you are my patient. I mean you no harm. Would you prefer me to turn my back while you undress?"

When Molly did not reply, Dr. Howard got up and went to the door. He stuck his head out into the hallway and called to Katie, who came in the room with him.

"Could you help me?" he asked.

"Sure, doctor," Katie said. "When are you gonna come visit me on a day that ain't Sunday?"

The doctor stammered and turned red.

"I'm only joking, doctor," she said.

Katie helped Molly undress and stood by while the doctor checked her over. Molly closed her eyes, though she flinched at the touch of the doctor's hand. *Pretend*, she told herself. *Pretend you are somewhere else.* She thought of Knockma Hill and Queen Maeve, though it now seemed a lifetime ago that she last visited.

When he finished, the doctor dismissed Katie and turned to Molly. "Listen, Molly, I can give you some laudanum to help you sleep. But you should know that it is an easy thing to become attached to. If you aren't careful. Some of the girls who work here, they … well, they find that taking it daily helps make things more … more … tolerable. You need to be careful with it. Once Morpheus has you in his arms, he seldom lets you go. Understand?"

"I don't want no medicine, doctor," Molly whispered.

"Should you change your mind, just let me know during my weekly visit. Or, in an emergency, send Belinda over to my office and I can send some back with her."

"Yes, sir," Molly said.

Dr. Howard picked up his bag and then knelt in front of the bed. Molly drew away from him as he leaned close and whispered, "Look, I know the circumstances that have led you to this unfortunate place. You aren't the first to fall victim to a fancy man impostor who causes your ruin. I do not condone of such practices. I only seek to alleviate the sufferings of those so affected. If you're in need of a friend …"

His voice trailed off. After a few seconds, he stood and walked out of the room. Katie came in next with a tray of food, a huge pile of bacon and eggs alongside a mug of coffee and a glass of milk. Molly clutched her stomach as the smell, though pleasing, made her nauseous.

"Chamber pot's under the bed!" Katie said.

Molly rolled over onto her side and thrust a hand under the bed. It struck a ceramic object, and she yanked it out and emptied the contents of her stomach into it. Katie sat the tray on the desk and said, "I'll leave this in here for if you want it later. But don't let it get cold. Here, let me empty that for you. I'll bring it back."

Molly lay back and closed her eyes. Her mind drifted back to her last night in Belclare. She heard the music and the laughter, but it was as if she were watching herself from the outside as a heaviness settled upon her chest.

Chapter Eight

Molly looked out over the intersection of Mulberry and Bayard Street from her upstairs room. Sweat ran down between her shoulder blades as the hot June sun waged an unrelenting assault upon the city. Below her window, a newsboy shouted the latest headlines as men and women with slumped shoulders and stiff movements trudged by on their way to work. Two dogs panted in the scant shade provided by the building across the street from Miss Cecilia's while a policeman shouted at a drunk man stretched out on his back in a pile of muck.

At least I can open my window now, she thought. *Six months. Six months later and here I am. What would me ma say if she knew*? She reached under her bed and withdrew a small wooden box. Inside, Molly kept a mixture of coins and paper money, the savings she'd managed to accrue once she worked off her initial debt to Miss Cecilia. Each week, Molly had a tiny amount left after deductions and since her living expenses came out of her pay up front, she had little to spend it on. At Katie's urging, Molly had obtained a small knife in a leather scabbard, which she kept tucked into her right boot.

A month ago, Molly had entertained a client lately returned from California. He described the state as a veritable paradise; heaven on earth, he'd said. Since that night, Molly found herself dreaming of going there. Katie gave her a map and, from time to time, Molly would take it from under her bed and study the distance that she would need to travel. Though she did not fancy another trip across the ocean, it was the best way to get there according to Katie. Tickets were not cheap, and she knew she would also need some provisions for the journey, but by her reckoning, she would have enough saved up by the fall, at least enough to get her there and keep her fed on the way. However, despite satisfying her debt to Miss Cecilia, Molly knew the woman would not agree to let her go and would come up with other debts to hold her. *I'd like to see the figures in her ledger for myself,* Molly thought, *but I don't know enough about numbers. She could say anything she wanted, and I'd be none the wiser. It's a secret move I'll have to make,* she told herself. *But I must find what happened to Ellen first. If she's in the city, I can't leave without her.*

A knock on the door broke into her concentration.

"Come in," she said.

The door opened and Katie stuck her head in as Molly shoved the box under her bed.

"Coming downstairs?" Katie asked. "The missus is asking where you are."

"Tell her I'm on my way," Molly said as she crossed her legs to lace her boots. During the day, the women who worked at Miss Cecilia's typically wore a white chemise, white drawers that went down to mid-calf, a pair of stockings covering the calves, a corset, and boots. Molly had been shocked to discover the drawers were lacking a seam along the crotch, but Katie had explained that this way she could service a customer without having to remove her clothing. In the evenings, when the more well-heeled men came by, the women put on dresses.

Two men were sitting in the parlor. Both wore army uniforms. Though she did not know the exact rank insignia, the eagle on the shoulder boards of the older man looked more important than the single bar on the shoulder of the younger man. *He's barely older than me*, Molly thought.

The young man's face reddened when Molly and Katie walked downstairs, and he tried to keep himself from making eye contact. As usual, Daft Eddie sat at the piano, pounding out a Stephen Foster tune, though he switched to Beethoven or Mozart whenever the mood struck him. Molly squeezed his shoulder as she walked by and he looked up at her with a gap-toothed grin. A few years ago, he'd been kicked in the head by a horse, which left him a little brain addled, thus giving him his nickname. Even after the injury, he was said to be the finest piano player in the Five Points. Miss Cecilia lured him away from another madam by giving him a slight raise and a room to live in upstairs. A young servant girl named Sally entered from the kitchen with a tray of whiskey and cigars for the visitors as they lounged on a couch with red velvet cushions. Through the door that led into the parlor, Molly caught sight of one of the two Irish plug uglies Miss Cecilia employed as protection. His eyes darted back and forth and when he thought no one could see him, he produced a flask and took a long drink before he stuffed it back in his pocket. *It's the drink what got him and his partner fired from the peelers*, Molly thought. *That's what Katie said. Them two ain't worth what Miss Cecilia pays them, not that I know how much that is.*

"I'm Colonel Harrison," the older man said. "And this is my nephew, Lieutenant Harrison. He's never been with a woman before—have you, boy?"

The boy looked at the floor as his face flushed an even brighter shade of red.

"Our regiment is off to the front tomorrow," the Colonel continued, "and I'd hate for him to fall dead to a Rebel bullet never having known the true delights hidden beneath your drawers."

Poor boy, Molly thought. *He's damn near dead from the shame of it.*

She walked over to him and held out her hand. "My name's Molly," she said. He took her hand and she felt the moisture on his palm. "I'll take care of you, if you'd like."

"He would," the Colonel said as he stood up and put his arm

around Katie's shoulders. "We can rendezvous here afterwards."

"Come along, then," Molly said, tugging on his hand. The young man rose slowly. She kept a grip on his hand as she led him toward the stairs.

When they reached her room, Molly took in several deep breaths to steady her nerves. Though forced outwardly to exhibit the confidence of a professional woman of the town, inside the memory of that night in December tormented her. Her first night 'on duty,' Katie told her to just close her eyes and pretend she was elsewhere. *But that doesn't work, does it,* Molly thought. *It's the thought of getting away, finding Ellen, and going west what gets me through. Nothing else.*

Once the door closed behind them, Molly sat on the bed and faced the young man.

"So, you want to skin those clothes off, or do you want me to do it for you? That's no extra charge."

When he didn't answer, Molly got up and stepped towards him. She extended her arms to unbutton his coat. Young Lieutenant Harrison pulled away so quickly that he bumped into the wall. Molly sat back down on the bed.

"I'm sorry, Lieutenant," she said. "I didn't mean to startle you, truly. Go ahead and do it yourself."

"My name's Bartholomew. Bart," he said. "My father arranged the commission for me."

"Are you not proud to go off and fight?" Molly asked.

"No. I wanted to be a writer. A journalist. My father is doing this to punish me."

"The army, you mean?"

"Yes. Says it will make a man out of me."

"My brother was a soldier in the Crimea and India," Molly said. "Seems like a thousand years ago now, it does."

Jimmy … so proud he was of his red coat. He made a handsome soldier lad. Lord Sanderson himself even shook his hand and wished him luck. When the war ended and he got to come home for a bit, he had the haunted eyes. He didn't laugh or joke no more like he used to. Ma said he had a nervous disposition. When they were ordered to go off to India, Jimmy almost seemed happy to leave. And when he came home from that, well … he just wasn't Jimmy. Like someone else, he was.

"Would it … do you think … could we just, I don't know, talk," Bart said. "And then when we go downstairs you could act like we did the other, so my Uncle won't get mad?"

I don't know what the lad's more afraid of, me, the Rebs, or his Uncle, she thought. Molly smiled at him and said, "Why don't you sit down here next to me and we can talk about whatever you like?"

Bart smiled and followed her suggestion. He told Molly all about his desire to write, and she told him of some of her life in Ireland.

"Your hill, what's it called? Knockma? It sounds wonderful," he said.

"It is," Molly said. "I, well … this is my first summer away from Ireland. I miss the fields. I miss the green everywhere. And it don't get hot like this. Not in Galway. Or at least, it rarely does. The days are long, and sometimes, when the sun went down, we'd have a dance at the crossroads in the village."

She smiled as she thought of the music and laughter in the air.

It sounds like a lovely place," Bart said. "I might visit your Knockma Hill one day."

"I hope you do, Bart," she said. "You'll fall in love with it as I did, or my name ain't Molly O'Sullivan."

When it came time to return downstairs, Molly reached up and tousled his hair. He let her unbutton his coat and then button it up again, with one button off. Then she bent over and shook her own red curls before straightening up.

She winked at him and said, "Aye, this'll fool that uncle of yours."

Bart offered her his arm, which she took, and the two of them descended the stairs as if they were a king and queen. Colonel Harrison sat on the sofa with Katie in his lap. He looked at Molly but addressed his question to Bart.

"And how was it, boy?"

"Well …" Bart hesitated.

"Like a stallion your nephew is," Molly said as she patted his arm. "Damn near wore me out! You can be proud of this one, your honor."

"That's my boy!" exclaimed Colonel Harrison. "I suspected your father was wrong about you. That's why I agreed to let you come along with the regiment. Now, let's be off! We've an early start for Virginia in the morning."

Molly turned to face Bart. She put her hands on his shoulders and stood on her toes to give him a kiss on the cheek.

"Take care of yourself, Bart," she whispered in his ear. "You are a brave lad. No matter what anyone else may say."

The young man paused when he reached the door. He turned around and looked at Molly, who waved goodbye. Bart smiled and mouthed the words "thank you" before he walked out the door and into the arms of the war.

"What was that all about?" Katie asked as she walked up beside Molly.

"Oh, nothing," Molly said. "He was a nice boy."

"And he didn't want a screw neither, did he?"

"No," Molly said. "He didn't."

Katie walked back into the parlor. As Molly turned to follow her, she heard Miss Cecilia call her name from the office near the kitchen.

"Ma'am?" Molly asked as she walked into the room. She frowned when she saw Liza standing beside Miss Cecilia.

"Katie told me that you have a fine voice," Miss Cecilia said. "She hears you singing to yourself in your room at night."

"It ain't that nice, ma'am," Molly said.

Liza snorted and said, "You got that right. Sounds more like a goat."

Molly narrowed her eyes. *I'd rather sound like that than a strangled toad like you*, she thought. *Useless feck that you are.*

Miss Cecilia cleared her throat and said, "I believe tomorrow is your day off?"

Molly nodded as her stomach twisted into a knot. Each girl at Miss Cecilia's received one morning and one evening off a week; though they were supposed to be the same days each week, Miss Cecilia occasionally revoked the time off for people who angered her. *Is that what she's about to do to me?*

"What do you intend to do with the time?" Miss Cecilia asked.

"Well, ma'am," Molly said, "I wanted to go to Crown's Grocery. I've need of a new brush. Mine, well … it disappeared. I can't find it."

Liza looked away when Molly mentioned the brush. *Surely, she didn't take it*, Molly thought. *No, she did. A thief she is, on top of everything else.*

Miss Cecilia nodded and said, "I think we can let you go unaccompanied this time."

"But, Miss Cecilia!" Liza protested.

Miss Cecilia silenced her with a wave of the hand.

After her first four months at Miss Cecilia's, during which she ventured no further than the front door Molly had been permitted to take a brief stroll around the neighborhood once a week in the company of Katie, Liza, or one of the two plug uglies. Just enough to orient her to the neighborhood

"Thank you, ma'am," Molly said.

"I have a few items that I need you to pick up for me," Miss Cecilia said. "I'll give you a short list and some money in the morning, so see me before you leave."

"But that's my job," Liza said.

"It's a test, Liza," Miss Cecilia said. "It's been six months. We need to see how trustworthy she is now."

"I can tell you that she ain't," Liza said.

"I know I can be trusted with a hairbrush," Molly snapped. Liza flushed and looked away.

"Enough of this," Miss Cecilia said as she slammed her palm on the table. "I'll not have catfights in my establishment. Molly, remember, I know everyone in this neighborhood and everything that happens in it. If you try to run off tomorrow, it will go hard on you. My contacts will be watching your every step. Try to get away, and you'll be begging for death by the time my people finish with you. Understand?"

"I do," Molly said. "I'll not try to run off."

At least not tomorrow, she added silently.

Chapter Nine

The next morning, Molly took a bath before she left the house. Miss Cecilia insisted on cleanliness, and the girls took a bath once every three days, on a rotating schedule, a copy of which was affixed to the wall over the bathtub. Molly intended to keep an eye out for Ellen and, if possible, she wanted to ask a few questions to see if anyone knew something, anything, which could indicate where the child might be. Dressed in a green-and-white checkered day dress with a detachable white collar, Molly looked in her mirror as she pinned a dark green hat to her curls. *I feel like a prisoner what's gotten a reprieve*, she thought. *But I guess … I guess that's what I am.* Downstairs, she collected the list and some money from Miss Cecilia, along with a small basket to carry the items home in.

On a previous venture outside Miss Cecilia's, Katie pointed out the location of Crown's Grocery on Worth Street across from Paradise Square. Katie suggested that if Molly were allowed to go out alone in the future and she needed an item from the store, then she should go on a Monday or Tuesday morning. That's when Mrs. Crown wasn't behind the counter to comment on their wickedness when one of Miss Cecilia's girls entered. When Molly had asked Katie which streets were the safest, the young woman laughed and said, "They're all equally dangerous." From the sounds which reached her room after the sun went down—shouts, screams, and fire bells, always the fire bells—Molly did not doubt the truth of Katie's statement.

"Big cavalry fight in Virginia! Details inside! Lee's on the move!" yelled a newsboy across the street as Molly walked out of the house.

Always the war, Molly thought. *They talk about men dying in Virginia when there's people here dying in the streets of hunger or the consumption. It ain't no different than Ireland. The people what gots the money don't take the time to notice the rest of us.*

During the time she spent locked in her room, Molly had set about improving her ability to read. Miss Cecilia encouraged the young women who worked for her to read the papers, and even novels, so they might discuss them with clients inclined to do so. The only rule was to refrain from praising or criticizing the Lincoln Administration lest they alienate a client and lose a sale. When Molly asked for reading materials, Miss Cecilia furnished stacks of newspapers, mostly issues of the *New York World* and the *National Police Gazette*. Katie loaned her a copy of *Les Misérables*, but Molly found it hard to follow. As she read, Molly underlined words she did not know in pencil and asked the other girls, or on occasion Miss Cecilia, what they meant. When the weather cooperated, she liked to sit on the balcony and read aloud to practice her pronunciation. Before long, Molly felt as though she could read anything placed in front of her.

I did what I promised me ma, she thought as she dodged a muddy puddle in the middle of the street, *but that's the only thing I've done here that she'd be proud of. And I cannot write and tell her, because then I'd have to tell her the whole of it.* The air felt heavy after the overnight rain, as if a hot hand pressed down upon Molly's chest as she walked.

When she reached the intersection of Bayard and Baxter Streets, Molly saw a child with black hair and the same height as Ellen. She rushed over and grabbed the child's shoulder. The child let out a startled cry as Molly spun her around to find that it was not Ellen.

"I'm so sorry," Molly said as she scanned for an adult to whom the child might belong, "I thought you was someone else, I did. Where's your mother, child?"

The little girl pointed to a house on the corner, and Molly gave her a gentle nudge in that direction. "Run along home and get out of the street."

Distracted by the sudden flash of hope she'd felt when she spotted the girl, Molly turned the corner without looking and collided with a young man in a red shirt with a large number fourteen embroidered in black silk on the front.

"What in the hell?" the man exclaimed. When he saw it was a young woman who had run into him, he pulled his leather helmet from his head and tucked it under his arm. "I'm sorry, miss. The fault was mine."

"Lost in my own thoughts, I was," Molly said. "I should be more careful."

"I've not seen you around before," the young man said. "Are you new in town?"

"Not really," Molly said. "I, well … I haven't gotten out much since I've been here."

"I'm Patrick McMahon, late of County Tipperary and currently of Hibernia Engine Company No. 14 on Elizabeth Street. At your service, miss …"

"Molly," she said, "Molly O'Sullivan. I gathered you was a fireman from your outfit."

"Ah, sure it is a uniform, not an outfit?"

Molly laughed and agreed with him. Patrick wasn't much taller than Molly, with dark hair and eyes. *Sure, you could pick him out as being Irish from the other side of the ocean*, Molly thought.

"May I ask where you are bound this fine morning?" he asked.

"I'm off to Crown's Grocery," Molly said. "And I've a desire to stretch me legs a bit."

"I know this is forward of me to ask, but might I accompany you?"

"Why?" Molly asked. "Afraid I'll catch on fire?"

"Not at all," Patrick replied. "It pains me to see such a lovely girl walking through these dirty streets alone. Especially one from the old country."

"I don't think that's such a good idea, Mr. McMahon," Molly said. "It isn't a thing to do with you, truly. But I'm not someone you want to be strolling around in public with. You've my word to take for that."

"You can call me Patrick, or Paddy, like everyone else, and am I not the one to decide who I wanna stroll with? It don't bother me at all."

He seems like a nice lad, Molly thought, *with an important job to do. But I'm … I'm … a whore. That's what I am, and it would tarnish the lad's reputation to be seen in public with me. Surely it would. But if has no problem with it …*

"Are ya sure?" Molly asked.

"Why shouldn't I be?" Patrick asked. "You talk as though you are a … wait, you're not a … are you … ?"

"I believe the polite term you are looking for is a fallen woman," Molly said. "Though I've heard others. Public woman. Slut. Whore. Or, if you lack imagination, the proper term is prostitute."

"Jesus Christ!" Patrick exclaimed. "No need to be vulgar, Miss Molly."

"The truth is often vulgar," Molly said. "And I do apologize for running into you. Now, I'll say good day."

She stepped around Patrick and continued down the street. He hurried after her and said, "Wait! Miss Molly! Wait! I said I'd walk with you and I will do it."

He stopped alongside her and offered her his arm. She hesitated for a moment, and then took it. Patrick smiled down at her and she smiled back. I almost feel like a proper lady, she thought. Almost.

As they walked, he told her about how his family came to America during the years of the hunger, when he was seven. His father and two siblings died, and his mother got off the boat with Patrick and his older brother Seamus and no means to support herself. The boys grew up on the streets and started as runners with the Hibernia Fire Company before achieving full membership in 1859.

"Seamus, the fecking fool, ran off to enlist with the 69th New York when the war started. Died at a place called Bull Run. I told him he had no business going off to fight for a country that spit on us when we got off the boat, but if there was a fight to be had, Seamus always wanted to be in it."

Molly had a sudden thought. "You say you grew up roaming the streets?" she asked.

"Aye," Patrick said. "Me ma died after we'd been here a few years and the fire company sort of took us in, but we spent our time getting into fights, stealing food, and causing trouble. You know, in a way it was almost fun."

"Are the streets not dangerous for children?"

"Oh, aye, they are," Patrick said. "That's why you gotta band together like for protection."

"Are there people that … steal children?"

Patrick stopped and looked at her.

"I've heard of it," he said. "Why do you ask?"

"When I arrived in New York, there was a child with me. Her family died of the bloody flux on the boat and I promised to take care of her. One night I was … accosted … and a man snatched her from my arms. I've not seen her since, though I haven't had much occasion to look."

"There's a dastardly trade in the city that involves young children, girls mostly, but not always," Patrick said. "Certain rich bastards like to have, uh … you know … with girls that ain't never done … you know."

"My God!" Molly exclaimed. "She's only four years old!"

"Oh, well," Patrick said. "The man what took her probably intends to keep her until she's around ten or so, then he'll sell her to one of the madams what specializes in that sort of thing."

"And why do the police not stop it?"

"It's some of the big wigs with the peelers what take advantage of it!" Patrick said. "It's all connected. You can't trust the police, not most of them, anyway."

"And is it safe to trust the fire department?"

"Likely it's not," Patrick said with a laugh. "We are all volunteers, you know. Though it has been rumored for a while now that the city intends to start a paid department like what they got in other big cities. The war kind of put a stop to the talk, but it's been hard on us. We're at about half strength since the fighting started, and we've gotten busier too."

"I've heard the bells," Molly said. "it seems as though they never stop ringing."

"We don't sleep much," Patrick admitted.

"But you say you are all volunteers, so does that mean you don't get paid?"

"It does," Patrick said.

"Then, forgive me for asking, but what do you do for money?" Molly asked.

"Our foreman, Captain Flaherty, runs a construction company. I do jobs for him. Plus, I sleep at the station anyway and so I've no need to rent a room anywhere. Each company elects its own officers. Captain Flaherty is good enough to give several of us jobs, so we give him our votes."

They reached the three-story wooden building which held Crown's Grocery. A mixed crowd of men and women milled around outside, where several baskets filled with goods for sale caught their attention. Molly followed Patrick down a short staircase to the entrance, a few feet below ground level. Inside, she had to duck to avoid various meat products which hung from hooks on the ceiling.

"God help us if this place ever catches on fire," Patrick said. "The Widow Crown runs a saloon upstairs too. It's always crowded here."

"I don't know where to start looking for anything," Molly said. "I'll be here all day and I don't have that much time."

"What is it you are after?" Patrick asked.

"I'm looking for a brush and some other items for … someone," Molly said. "I have a list."

"Oh, I, uh … I can't read," Patrick said. "Never had much cause to learn. Just read the list to me and I'll help you find the stuff."

Molly read him the list and, with Patrick to guide her, she located the items she needed. In addition to the brush, she also purchased an apple and a bottle of spring water for herself. He then cleared a path for her to reach the counter. Molly paid for her goods, which Mrs. Crown placed in the basket for her. Though she scowled at Molly, she did not say anything. As they left the grocery, Molly and Patrick's path took them in front of the Five Points House of Industry.

"What is that place?" Molly asked. "A priest once told me I could go there for help."

Patrick laughed.

"It's a mission full of prods. Sure, they'll take you in and give you a meal, and a place to sleep, but they'll make you renounce the Catholic church before they'll help. Just like them soupers what came to Ireland during the hunger. They said they'd feed us, but only if we turned our back on our own church."

A man in a black frock coat stood near the front door with a collection of pamphlets in his hand. He exhorted all passersby to learn the teachings of God, or at least what he said were the teachings of God.

"Repent!" he yelled. "Turn away from your Roman popery before it is too late! The fires of eternal damnation await all those who do not embrace the true Lord!"

Molly walked over to him and asked, "Is it true that you provide assistance to the needy in this place?"

"We do as we are commanded by our faith," the man said.

"To get the help, does a person have to join your church?"

"Why, naturally we provide religious instruction and all those who enter do eventually see the error of their false beliefs."

Molly stuck out her hand and said, "Can I have one of them papers?"

"Certainly!"

Molly nodded her thanks, took a few steps, and then called out over her shoulder, "Might need something to wipe me arse with later, and this will come in handy!"

Several people around began to clap and cheer; the missionary stammered as though seized by an unseen hand around his neck.

"You've a mouth on you," Patrick said. "But haven't I got one myself?"

"Me ma always said I was headstrong," Molly said, "and when you work in my … business, you pick up a thing or two."

"Have you ever thought of leaving?"

"Sometimes," Molly admitted.

Of course I have, she thought. *Every minute of every day. All the 'yes, Miss Cecilia' and 'no, Miss Cecilia.' And the fancy men what look down on us, yet they still spend their money. Sure, aren't the rich all like that? They turn up their noses at us, but they still want to feck us. Bastards.*

"Have you heard of a place called California, Patrick?"

"I have," he said. "It's out west somewhere. I've not been out of New York City other than Ireland and the boat what brung me here."

"I do think maybe one day I'd like to go and see it," Molly thought. "Do you ever think of leaving the city?"

"No, why?" Patrick shrugged. "I've got all I ever need here, so I do. I'll not leave unless the conscription gets me, and I have to join the army."

Conscription. Molly had heard a lot of that word over the past few months. During the spring, she read in the paper about how with enlistments low and casualties high, the government decided the best way to keep adequate manpower was to mandate military service unless a person paid $300 for a substitute. *The rich men sit on their fat arses getting richer and make the poor go fight for them*, she thought. *The same as at home. No one wants an Irishman around unless there's fighting to be done. And then it's here's a musket, Paddy. Go do your bit.*

"Are you afraid of it?" Molly asked.

"I ain't a coward," Patrick said. "My record with the fire department proves that. But I ain't stupid either. Why would I go off to fight in someone else's war? It ain't my fight. And it wasn't my brother's fight either. It must be easier to be a girl. Without these things to trouble you."

"Easier?" Molly asked. *I don't see you being outraged by a man in the middle of the night, having a child ripped from your arms, and then forced to sell yourself like you was a slice of beef*, she thought. *Women have never had it easy. But we're expected to endure it all without so much as a complaint.*

"I'm sorry," Patrick said. "I shouldn't have said that. See, my mouth runs away from me sometimes just as yours does. Curse of the Irish me ma always said. We tend to speak before we think."

"Didn't my own ma tell me the same," Molly said. "It gets me into plenty of trouble."

They stopped across the street from Miss Cecilia's. Molly looked over at the house and then back at Patrick. He opened his mouth to speak but stopped as though he were afraid of what he might say.

"Yes?" Molly asked.

"I was wondering if you might like to walk out with me sometime?"

"What? You mean like …" She paused.

"Aye," Patrick said. "It's nice to spend time with a young lady such as yourself."

"I cannot do that, Patrick. I'm a, well … a …"

"I know what you are!" Patrick said. "It doesn't make a difference to me."

"It does to me," Molly said. "I'm no longer suited for that. What would the lads at your company do if they found out you were out sparking with a whore? Throw you out on your Tipperary arse, they would."

"Don't say that word!" Patrick exclaimed.

"What word?" Molly asked with a sad smile. "Tipperary?"

"You know what I meant. Jesus!"

"I'd be happy to have you as a friend, Patrick. I truly would. Lord knows I've few enough of them as it is and none what live outside those four walls unless you count the doctor what comes to see us on Sundays. Just trust me on this. Please. It's for your own good."

Patrick stuck his hands in his pockets and turned away. He took a step, then stopped and called out over his shoulder, "I won't change my mind, Molly."

I hope you don't, she said to herself, and I hope I do. With my own reputation such as it is, I cannot let an innocent lad be dragged down into the mire. My world is a prison what ain't got no walls.

When she walked back inside the house with her purchases, Miss Cecilia met her at the door and said, "There's a few gentlemen in the parlor. Do go in and say hello."

"Do you mind if I bring this up to my room first, ma'am?" Molly asked as she kept the brush, apple, and spring water, but gave the basket with the rest of the items to Miss Cecilia. "I'll only be a minute."

"Go on," Miss Cecilia said.

When she got to her room, Molly sat at her desk and drank from her bottle of spring water as she ate the apple. She stalled for time by chewing as slowly as she could manage. Molly opened the window and chucked the apple core into the street when she finished. Then she attempted to get her hair to cooperate with the brush, to little avail.

I've no way out of this mess, she thought as she dragged the brush across her head with enough intensity to hurt. *And there's an innocent child out there somewhere suffering because I couldn't protect her like I said I would. God knows what outrages might be done to her.* She sighed in resignation and slammed the brush down on her desk. As she made her way down the stairs into the parlor, Molly saw two men seated on the sofa and one in a chair. They all clutched cigars in their hands; a haze of smoke obscured the ceiling. The men stood as she reached the foot of the stairs. She looked at them and forced a smile onto her face.

"Welcome, gentlemen," she said. "I do hope the day has been kind to you."

Chapter Ten

One morning in mid-June, Molly visited the pump behind the house to fill a pail to wash some of her clothing. She saw Liza deep in conversation with a girl. *She can't be more than fourteen*, Molly thought. *What is she talking to her about? Surely not working here*. She moved closer to listen to what Liza was saying.

"Why don't you just come in and talk to the missus? You'd like it here. Sure, the work can get kinda dull, but you've got the chance to make more money than you can make doing just about anything else."

The girl nodded, her eyes wide.

"And," Liza continued, "you'll get your meals and a roof over your head. We even have a doctor who comes round once a week to give you a check-up."

"And what kind of work is it?" the girl asked.

"We can talk about that inside," Liza said. "Come on. It's hot out here. Let's go in."

Liza reached out and took hold of the girl's arm. When she turned around, she saw Molly and frowned. Molly dropped the pail, put her hands on her hips and said, "And what are you about, Liza? Has the missus turned you into a recruiting sergeant likes the ones what wait by the docks to sign up poor Irish lads fresh off the boat?"

"This don't concern you, Molly," Liza said.

Molly looked at the girl and said, "Be off with you. Unless you want to make your living staring up at a ceiling, if you take my meaning."

The girl looked back and forth from Molly to Liza as if she was unsure of whom to believe.

"Go!" Molly shouted. The girl turned and fled without so much as a backward glance.

Liza marched over to Molly so quickly that Molly took two steps back, but Liza pressed in close enough for Molly to smell the whiskey on her breath.

"You owe me fifty dollars," Liza said. "The missus said she'd pay me if I brought in another girl, preferably a young one. I had her, God damn it! And then you have to show up and ruin it. You'll be paying me too. Bitch!"

"Would you want your own younger sister to work here?" Molly asked. "Or your daughter?"

"I wanted fifty dollars," Liza said. "And I'll get it too. Just you wait and see."

Molly pushed Liza out of the way and scooped up her pail. *She'll only find another girl*, Molly thought. *But at least I kept this one out. For a while anyway. If she lives on the streets, then she'll end up somewhere like this eventually. Either that or she'll find herself among the departed. Them what told me the streets weren't safe for young women after dark weren't telling lies, that's for certain.*

As she carried the pail upstairs, careful to not slosh any water on the floor, Molly walked by Katie. When she said good morning, Katie turned away and did not answer. *Wonder what that's all about*, Molly thought. She placed the pail in the room with the bathtub, where a line stretched from one end the room to another to hang damp clothes. Though outdoor clotheslines were common enough in the city, so too was the theft of clothing, which was why Miss Cecilia, who paid for the clothes worn by her girls, insisted that the girls be dried inside. Molly grabbed the washboard and placed it into the pail, then she retrieved some undergarments from her room. Pushing her sleeves up, Molly whistled the tune to "Follow Me Up to Carlow" as she brushed a bar of soap along each item, dunked it in the water, then scrubbed it on the board before dunking it back to rinse off the suds.

Once she'd hung the items to dry, Molly went downstairs. She kept an eye out for Liza, but she did not see her. In the parlor, Miss Cecilia stood talking to a burly police captain with a handlebar mustache. *Like Frank*, Molly thought. *I wonder if it is required to have one.* Standing next to the captain was a portly sergeant with a large scar across his cheek, who smiled at Molly when she entered the room.

"Molly," Miss Cecilia said, "have you met Captain Murphy?"

"No, ma'am," Molly said. She turned to Captain Murphy and gave an approximation of a curtsy. "Pleased to meet you, your honor."

"And this is Sergeant Daniels."

"Nice to meet you, sergeant."

"I'm glad things are well with you, madam," Captain Murphy said in a soft Irish accent.

"And you, sir," Miss Cecilia said. "Do come back and visit us sometime."

Molly watched as the captain lifted a finger to the brim of his cap in salute as Miss Cecilia produced a small coin bag and handed it to the sergeant, who passed it to the captain.

"Nice to meet you, Miss Molly," the sergeant said as the men made their way to the door.

"What was that about?" Molly asked once the men were gone.

"It's not your place to ask questions," Miss Cecilia said.

"Sorry, ma'am," Molly said.

Sure, isn't that the same thing Lord Sanderson said to me back in Ireland, Molly thought. *No one wants me to ask questions about nothing. Like life is one giant secret. I wonder if she pays them to keep the place open. Or does she pay them to do her bidding when she needs it. Like when one of her girls runs away and she sends her goons out after them. Ain't that what she said would happen to me if I tried to leave? And didn't Katie … or was it Liza … say a girl ran off and got killed? And the peelers will shed no tears over a dead prostitute. Will they?*

That evening, several men crowded into the parlor. Molly recognized Tobias O'Driscoll, one of the police officers on the local beat, but he wore civilian clothes on this night. Two men discussed the latest war news as they sipped their whiskey to the accompaniment of Daft Eddie on the piano.

"I'm telling you," the larger of the two men said, "the Conscription Act passed by the Lincolnites in the spring is an act of tyranny. Making men go off and fight against their will is the tool of a dictator. A dictator, I say!"

Molly moved across the room and slid her arm through the man's to distract him, lest there be trouble.

"And what would you have us do?" the other man asked. "Give in to the damn rebels?"

"Spoken like King George," the first man replied. "Have you not listened to the noise of the streets? If they try to force the issue and go so far as to draw names, there will be trouble in this city. The Irish will never stand for it! Allowing the rich to buy their way out with three hundred dollars was a mistake."

"Would you like to go upstairs, sir?" Molly asked.

The man waved her away with his hand. She retreated to the couch, where O'Driscoll sat watching the argument with an amused expression on his face. Molly looked around for Miss Cecilia but did not see her. Liza was upstairs with a customer and Katie sat alone in a chair, her eyes focused on the floor. *And where are the plug uglies what guard the door*, she wondered. *Probably drunk in the alley, good for nothing shites.*

"And I say that you are a coward," the second man said. "A coward who wishes to avoid serving his country in her time of need."

"And what are you doing to help the war effort, sir?" Molly asked. She cursed herself as soon as the words left her mouth.

The man spun on her and said, "By God! I'll not take lip from a whore!"

Molly flinched as he raised his hand to slap her, but before he could swing, the first man crashed a fist into the side of his head. The man staggered and then turned and tackled his adversary. The two rolled around on the floor, biting, gouging eyes, and kicking while Daft Eddie still played his tune. O'Driscoll stood up and stretched.

"I hate it when duty calls when I am not at work," he said to Molly. As he reached down to separate the combatants, the front door flew open and the plug uglies rushed in.

"Tobias O'Driscoll is it?" one of them yelled. "The man what got me sacked from the department. Stand and deliver, ye bastard!"

The two men pounced on O'Driscoll, who managed to fell one of them with a punch just as the other managed to wrap his legs up and take him to the ground. Doors upstairs opened and several customers ran down to see what the commotion was. A few joined in the fray. Molly shrank back against the wall, unsure of what to do.

"You! Red!" Tobias yelled. Molly looked down and saw that he now had the second of Miss Cecilia's men in a headlock, though the man kicked and twisted as he tried to break free. "Reach in my pocket and get my whistle. Then go outside and blow it. Loud! Come on! Do it!"

Molly knelt beside him and thrust her hand into his coat pocket. She felt the wooden whistle and attached string and she fished it out. With the commotion growing louder behind her, Molly ran out the front door and gave one loud blast on the whistle. Then another. And another. Within a minute or two, the sound of heavy footsteps echoed up the street and three uniformed policemen hurried toward her, their clubs in hand.

"In here," Molly said. "'Tis a fight that's started."

One of the officers grinned. "Excellent! Come on, lads! Let's go crack some heads."

The officers pushed by and entered the fray. Molly heard the sound of glass breaking and a few yelps of pain.

"What in the devil is going on in there?" Miss Cecilia walked up to Molly and took hold of her shoulders.

"A fight, Miss Cecilia," Molly said. "Some of the gentlemen. They got cross with one another and fell to fighting."

"I leave for an hour and this is what happens?" Miss Cecilia grabbed Molly's wrist and dragged her inside.

Bedlam ruled the parlor. O'Driscoll was on his feet trading punches with a man who must have come from upstairs. The plug ugly who he had knocked down earlier had managed to regain his feet and had one police officer's head locked beneath his beefy left arm while he used his right arm to fend off blows from another officer's club. Katie was nowhere in sight, but Liza and a few other girls watched from the stairs. Daft Eddie continued to play as if oblivious to the commotion.

Miss Cecilia slipped her fingers down the front of her dress and produced a small derringer from her bosom. Aiming at the ceiling, she pulled the trigger. Everyone froze as the shot echoed. Molly belatedly covered her ears, which were ringing from the sound.

"This is not some dockside whorehouse," Miss Cecilia said. "Nor is it some low dive in the Bowery. I permit no such behavior here. None. Kindly collect your things and vacate the premises. Any more such conduct will earn you a bullet."

She kept the pistol aimed into the parlor, but not at anyone in particular as the men went about the task of collecting their hats and coats.

"There will be no charges filed by anyone here tonight," she said to the officers.

"Yes, ma'am," they said as they filed out the door behind the customers.

"Liza, summon everyone to the parlor. I want to discuss this with all of you."

As the girls gathered in the room, Molly looked around for Katie but did not see her. Miss Cecilia noticed her absence as well and ordered Liza to go up and bring her down. A minute later, Liza returned and said, "She ain't here, Miss Cecilia."

"Who has seen her?" Miss Cecilia demanded.

"She was down here, ma'am," Molly said. "Then the donnybrook started, and I went out front. I don't know where she went after."

"I seen her," one of the other girls said. "When I heard the ruckus, I, me and my customer, I mean, went out into the hallway. I saw her coming out of Molly's room."

"My room?" Molly asked.

"Yeah, but I don't know where she went."

Why was she in my room, Molly asked herself. She rose and hurried up the stairs, as Miss Cecilia called after her to come back. When she got to her room, her heart sank when she saw her wooden box, open and empty, beside the bed. *How did she know? I never told her I had money. No … the other day. She came in and saw me putting it under the bed.* Molly swallowed hard to drive away the tears which sprang to her eyes.

"What is the meaning of this?" Miss Cecilia asked from the doorway to Molly's room.

"It's nothing, ma'am," Molly said. "It's just some money that's gone. I'd been saving it to buy a …"

Molly froze. *I can't tell her what I was after*, she thought.

"A what?" Miss Cecilia asked.

"Nothing important, ma'am," Molly said.

"Come here," Miss Cecilia ordered. Molly walked over to her, as slow as she could without appearing impertinent.

"I'll teach you to lie to me, you little bitch!" Miss Cecilia exclaimed as she landed a slap across Molly's face with such force that it knocked her into the wall. Her face felt as if a bee had buried a stinger in it. Something wet and sticky trickled from the corner of her mouth.

"I know what is going on here. Katie owed me money. You've been helping her hide it away so that she could run off. Liza! Bring me the ledger."

"Yes, ma'am," Liza called out from down the hallway.

When she returned, Miss Cecilia opened the leather volume and thrust it at Molly.

"Look! See this? Last August, the stupid slut let herself get pregnant. I loaned her the money to have a procedure done. But there were complications. She had to be under a doctor's care for a couple of months with no work. All on my tab. She owes me. And Liza told me before I left for the evening what transpired today after I specifically charged her with bringing me another girl. So, you owe Liza fifty dollars. I'll collect it on her behalf. And you'll also be working off what Katie owed me too. Understand?"

Molly worked her jaw as she tried to respond. All the while, Liza smiled triumphantly over Miss Cecilia's shoulder. *I'll never get out*, Molly realized. *I almost had enough to get away, at least partially, but now I'm stuck here forever. I'll never find Ellen. I'm doomed. I'm as cursed as the Dublin Rose was.*

"Have you forgotten you speak English?" Miss Cecilia asked. "I asked if you understood me."

"I do, ma'am," Molly said with a sigh. "I'll be working to pay you what you say Katie owes and what you promised to give Liza. But … could you tell me what the total sum is that I owe you?"

"No," Miss Cecilia said with a snort. "What would you know about math and figures? And I do not need to explain myself or my business to you. Not now. Not ever."

"Yes, ma'am," Molly said as she looked at the floor.

"Now, we've other customers to tend to that have just come in. Get yourself down there and start earning me money."

"I will, ma'am," Molly said. "Just give me a minute, please."

"Watch her, Liza," Miss Cecilia said.

Molly sat at her table and looked at her cheek in the small mirror she kept on her desk. An angry red splotch stood out against her pale skin. Molly powdered a bit of cosmetic over it to try and conceal it as best she could.

"I told you I'd get my money somehow," Liza said as Molly left the room.

Downstairs, three men gathered around Sally and took whiskey from her tray. Molly talked to one of them and they soon went up to her room. She had three other customers that night. After each, Liza barged into her room to seize any tip money left behind, though only two had given Molly anything.

As the first pale streaks of light in the east signaled the dawn of a new day, Molly sat at the small table and looked at herself in the mirror. She frowned as she focused on the dark circles beneath her eyes and the new lines on her face. *It's only been six months and I look as though I've aged five years,* she thought. *How will I look in another six months? Or year? And now … with all this money to pay back, I'll never get out. I don't even know the total I'm expected to pay.*

Molly flung herself across her narrow bed, unable to stop the tears. They ran down her cheeks and left a damp stain on the pillow.

Chapter Eleven

A few nights later, four gentlemen from New Orleans visited Miss Cecilia's. During the time she had worked there, Molly met several wealthy New Orleans businessmen in town to negotiate deals, usually involving the sale and transportation of cotton, which the federal government needed. Many a transaction took place under the watchful eye of Miss Cecilia. Molly wondered if she received a cut of each deal negotiated in her parlor. These four men spoke quietly with one another as Miss Cecilia hovered over them like a mother hen.

She's got her claws in everything, Molly thought. *I bet she gets a pile of gold each time the north wins a battle, as rare as that seems to be.*

Molly's ears picked up enough during her time at Miss Cecilia's to understand as many people thought the war bad as good. All of them agreed that it was good for business. Those steadfastly opposed to preserving the union or emancipating the slaves still sought government contracts for goods produced so cheaply they often wore out before they reached the men in the field. On more than one occasion, she heard men in the parlor openly boast of the ways they'd fleeced the War Department out of substantial sums of money. *It's like some of them think the war is being held for their own personal enrichment*, she thought. *And they expect the poor to go and die for it.* And now, arguments over the Conscription Act took precedence.

I don't understand what people are so worked up about, she thought as she watched the men talk. *Sure, it's unfair. But it's been done to us for centuries at home. Why expect any different here*? Molly remembered the broadside posted in the village that enticed her brother to go off to fight the Russians. *He said it was his duty, but duty to whom? Some fecking queen what sits over there in London while we starved to death. I don't see her losing sleep over it neither.*

The men seated in the parlor smoked their cigars and sipped brandy while Daft Eddie played a melody. Three of them were older, with expansive bellies that spoke of easy living, but the fourth, a young man with a scar along his jaw, did not join in the laughter as his eyes swept the room, never focusing on any person or object for longer than a few seconds. His right leg twitched. *Got the war sickness, he does*, Molly thought. *Poor lad. Like me own brother. I hope he don't go down that same road.*

"Why don't you sing something for the gentlemen, Molly?" Miss Cecilia suggested.

"Oh, I don't know," Molly said. "I ain't much for singing in front of people. Makes me nervous, it does."

"Please, Molly?" the young man asked, his first words of the night. Molly smiled at him and he nodded.

"For you, sir, I will," Molly said. She walked over to Daft Eddie and placed her hand on his shoulder. He looked up at her with a wide grin, his teeth almost as black as the gaps between them. She motioned for him to begin. As the notes from the piano filled the air, Molly began to sing.

Kathleen Mavourneen the gray dawn is breaking
The horn of the hunter is heard on the hill
The lark from his light wing the bright dew is shaking
Kathleen Mavourneen what slumbering still!

Molly closed her eyes and let her mind drift away, across the ocean, back to the cliffs of Galway and across the valleys to Belclare. She saw her grandparents in front of the hearth, her grandfather smoking his pipe while her grandmother stirred a pot over the fire. Her father sat in his chair in the corner, with young Molly upon his knee as he sang to her an Irish ballad. Her mother arranged some plates on a table in preparation for the evening meal. Outside, birds whistled as the sun went down. Then the image in her mind switched to Knockma Hill, where she sat and dreamed of being a great warrior like Queen Maeve. A tear ran down her face as the memories of her lost life vanished.

Oh, hast thou forgotten how soon we must sever
Oh, hast thou forgotten this day we must part
It might be for years and it might be forever
Oh, why art thou silent Kathleen Mavourneen?

She opened her eyes and smiled at the young man, who wiped the corner of his eye. The rest of the room, including Miss Cecilia, broke into applause. Molly squeezed Daft Eddie's shoulder and then gave a slight bow to the men in the room.

"Magnificent," the young man said. "You belong on a stage. I'd pay top dollar to hear you sing."

Molly cast a quick glance at Miss Cecilia and then said, "Oh, I'm not cut out for the stage. I've no desire to leave this fine place. A girl's got everything she needs here. A warm bed, fine clothes, food, and the company of fine gentlemen such as yourself."

She crossed the room and stood by the man's side.

"Does that song remind you of someone? A girl at home perhaps?"

"I had a fiancée before the war," the man confessed. "I joined up like everyone else when the war started. I was a cavalryman. A captain. But after Shiloh …"

"You were wounded there," Molly said.

He nodded. "I was. And captured. Spent months in a Yankee prison camp. I got paroled and exchanged home a few months ago. My fiancée, well, she didn't wait for me like she said she would."

"I'm sorry to hear that." Molly put her hand on the man's arm.

"I do mean that. My brother was in the army. Fought in Crimea and India. He, well, he was different when he came back."

The man shrugged.

"Seeing the elephant does that to a man, I reckon."

"I thought the cavalry rode horses, not elephants," Molly said.

The man smiled and said, "It's just an expression. It means a fellow has seen battle. Up close."

"Is New Orleans as nice as I've heard?" Molly asked.

The man's expression softened and he spent twenty minutes telling her of the grand houses in the city, the crowded docks, the music, and the French Quarter.

"There's mansions the likes of which put New York City to shame," he said. "And the food. What can I say about that? It's the best you'll find. There's always a party to be found. I assume you are Catholic, given your accent."

Molly nodded.

"Well, you ought to visit Saint Louis Cathedral. It's beautiful. A few years ago, maybe seven or eight, they dedicated a statue of General Jackson in the square next to it. It's a nice place to go for a stroll, but you ought to take in a mass there."

"I'd like to visit someday," Molly confessed. "If it's as nice as all that."

"You should. If you get a chance."

Liza got the attention of the room by relaying a story she had read in the *National Police Gazette*. A foul villain had snuck into a fancy bordello uptown and, while the women were downstairs, he gained entry into their sleeping quarters and began to gather up as many pantalets as possible. Caught in the act by the maid, the fiend hurled himself through a window and vaulted over the balcony rail to the street below where he hobbled away, leaving a trail of white garments behind him to the delight of bystanders while the prostitutes, alerted to the crime, ran to the balcony and turned the air behind him blue with their curses.

"The police are calling it the case of the Purloined Pantalets," Liza concluded. "I think they are spending more time on that case than on any other in recent memory."

"Why's that?" Molly asked.

"Think about it, Molly. If you are the officer who catches the man who stole the whores' drawers, then they'd no doubt be grateful, if you get my drift."

Molly had never seen a newspaper until she arrived in New York. They were filled with all manner of war news and gossip, but she liked the crime stories as they provided lurid details about every manner of criminal offense. *From reading them, you'd think the whole city was full of criminals. But didn't Officer Lynch—Frank—almost say as much himself?*

"Do you smell that?" Miss Cecilia asked, her eyes serious.

Everyone in the room looked around and Molly said, "Smell what, ma'am?"

"I smell smoke in the air. Liza, run upstairs and make sure there's no fire. Hurry."

Liza darted up the stairs and a minute later yelled down, "All clear up here, ma'am!"

Molly sniffed and noticed the smell for the first time. She stood up and walked over to the front door. She pushed it open. A tongue of flame shot out from the second-floor window of the building directly across the street. A column of smoke rose in the air.

"It's a fire, ma'am!" Molly called out over her shoulder. "Across the street."

The fire bells rang six times and paused, then four times and paused, and then fourteen times. Passersby in the street took up the cry, "Fire! Fire on Mulberry Street!" Their words echoed down every street and alleyway in the area and soon a crowd started to gather.

The flames grew thicker and the smoke heavier as the crowd waited for the arrival of the first fire engine. Within a couple of minutes, the men of Hibernia Engine 14 dragged their apparatus around the corner. Molly edged further out the door to see around the crowd. One man grabbed a roll of hose strapped to the back of the engine and stretched it towards a wooden hydrant on the corner. Her breath caught in her throat when she recognized Patrick as he attached a second hose to the engine and moved towards the building. The other men took up positions along the rails and began to furiously pump them up and down to draw in the water and push it out the nozzle. A beefy man several years older than the others in a white helmet and leather suspenders with a pair of gold eagles pinned to them yelled orders through a brass speaking trumpet.

More shouts heralded the arrival of Hook and Ladder Company 1 from Chambers Street. The men glistened with sweat in the hot evening air as they raised a ladder up to the window. Patrick shut down the nozzle and, with the hose over his shoulder, scrambled up the ladder to direct a stream of water inside. Another fireman moved up the ladder behind him and took up some of the slack from the hose. As thick, black smoke coiled over his head, Patrick swept the stream of water back and forth along the ceiling.

Molly's heart froze as she watched him step inside the window frame with his left leg, while he kept his right on the rung of the ladder. With his weight shifted to his front foot, Patrick continued his assault on the flames as four other firefighters raised a second ladder to the roof. With axes and picks, the men ran up the ladder as fast as some men might run on level ground.

Patrick looked over his shoulder with a grin so wide Molly saw it from across the street. He yelled, "I pushed her down the hallway. She's coming outta room down there."

The building belched a roll of smoke over Patrick's head. He laughed and shouted, "Come on, you bastard! That's the best you got?"

He nodded to the man behind him on the ladder and pulled himself through the open window. The second man followed him while another moved up to the top of the ladder and fed more hose into the window.

Molly held her breath for what seemed like an eternity until Patrick appeared at the window and leaned out. Soot streaked his nose and mouth.

"Think we got it! Send some boys up with some picks to open up the wall and ceiling."

"Come on down, Paddy," the man with the speaking trumpet yelled. "You've done your part."

Molly watched him climb down. The door to Miss Cecilia's opened and Belinda walked out with a large pail and a ladle. Molly turned to the ladle and asked, "May I?" Belinda nodded and Molly scooped up some water and made her way over to Patrick, dodging firemen and stepping over hoses as she did. As she reached him, Patrick coughed and spat a black glob onto the ground.

"Molly?" he rasped. "What brings you here?"

"I live across the street," she said. "Remember?"

Patrick took the ladle of water and drank half of it. He swished the water around in his mouth and spit it out. Molly noticed his spittle was as black as the lines under his nose. Patrick swallowed the remainder in the ladle and Molly returned it to Belinda.

"Thank you for that," Patrick said when Molly came back to him. "That one was snotty."

"What do you mean?" Molly asked.

"For every bit of smoke you breathe in, the same amount of black snot comes out the nose," he said. "I'll be coughing for a few days."

"'Twas very brave of you," Molly said.

Patrick shrugged and looked away as he said, "It's my job. Ain't nothing brave about it. A building burns and we put it out. Simple as that. I'm just glad there don't seem to be anyone inside."

He took off his helmet and wiped the sweat off his forehead. Behind him, men from Americus Number 6 took up the work of soaking all the remaining embers, lest they reignite the moment the firemen returned to their quarters.

"Those are Boss Tweed's boys," Patrick said.

"The man what runs Tammany Hall?"

"Aye, he started out as a fireman, you know," Patrick said.

"Who is the man what wears the white hat?" Molly asked. "The one yelling all the orders."

"That's Chief Engineer Decker," Patrick said. "He's in charge of the whole department. Manages to make most of the fires too. He's a good sort. I'm glad I ran into you though. I've a question to ask."

"What is it?" Molly silently hoped he would not ask her to call on her. *He's a nice lad. Reminds me of Jimmy in a way, but I'd not want to see him in a whorehouse.*

"Next week on the Fourth of July, I'm boxing against a Scotsman what works for the police. We're using Brennan's Saloon over on Centre Street. The fourth is sort of a holiday in America. Celebrates independence from the English. Want to come and watch?"

"I don't know." Molly hesitated. "It would depend on the time and if I can get off … work. Do they really celebrate independence from the English here? Wouldn't it be grand if we could do the same in Ireland some day?"

"We will," Patrick said. "The Fenians will see to that."

Fenians, Molly thought. *Isn't that what Mr. Ellsworth said I was*? Her stomach clenched when the thought of Ellsworth brought back memories of that night. Ellen's shrill scream of her name echoed inside her head. Molly closed her eyes and tried to will the memories to leave.

"It's at seven o'clock," Patrick said. "The fight, that is. The winner takes four hundred dollars and I can use that money to pay off the Enrollment Officer. They'll be drawing names soon, you know."

"I've heard," Molly said as she opened her eyes. "I wish you luck, Patrick. I truly do. But I don't know if I can come."

"But you'll try?"

Jesus, Molly thought, *I can't be giving the lad false hope. But it would be nice to get a few hours away, if the missus will let me. There's no law against me having a friend now is there*?

"I promise to try," Molly said.

Patrick reached out and patted her arm before he turned back to his work. Molly went back inside the house and out onto the balcony on the second floor. From there, she watched the reporters as they circulated among the crowd, notepads and pencils in hand, and the firemen as they packed up their gear. As Hibernia 14 left the scene, Patrick looked up from his place on the hauling lines and lifted a hand. Molly waved back.

Molly's hand closed around her Saint Michael's medal. *Keep them all safe. Defend them in battle.* As the crowd drifted away, Molly went back to the parlor. She expected to see the four gentlemen from New Orleans, but she found the room empty. After a few minutes, Miss

Cecilia, Liza, and a few of the other women came in from the street.

"Guess our gentlemen callers were pressed for time," Miss Cecilia said. "They left after the fire. We should have stayed inside and made our money while the fire burned, but damn me if they didn't want to go out there and watch it too."

"Maybe they'll come back, ma'am," Molly offered.

"Shut up," Miss Cecilia snapped. "I saw you there making eyes at one of the firemen. If that young man wants to talk to you, he's got to pay for his time. Just like if he wants a screw. Am I clear?"

"Yes, ma'am," Molly said.

From across the room, Liza smirked at Molly as Miss Cecilia walked out of the parlor.

Chapter Twelve

"Big fight in Pennsylvania! Lee defeated! Details inside!"

Molly leaned out of her window and saw a large crowd gathered around a newsboy. Men in the crowd thrust their money at him and snatched copies of the paper in return. In minutes, the boy stood there empty handed. *All the talk of a big battle in Pennsylvania the past few days,* Molly thought. *Must be over now. The city will really be ready to celebrate. Those that don't have the black bunting over their door frames for a dead relative, that is.*

Molly waited until the morning to ask Miss Cecilia's permission to attend the fight that evening. At breakfast, with the young women gathered around a table in the kitchen, Molly said, "Have you read of the big fight scheduled for tonight at Brennan's Saloon?"

"I have," Miss Cecilia said. "It's been in all the papers. The police department versus the fire department, they say. It should be a fine night. All the big wigs will be there, or so I'm told."

"I think"—Molly hesitated for a moment, then plunged ahead

with her plan—"I think there's money to be made."

"What do you mean?" Miss Cecilia put down her fork and looked at Molly.

"Well, ma'am, there'll be lots of gentlemen there what want to see the fight. After watching two men punch each other in the face for an hour or two, no doubt their blood will be up. It'll be a whore they want. If you were to let two of us go to the fight, say, Isabella and I, we could sort of mix with the crowd, like. And when the fight's over, we could bring some gentlemen back with us. There are other whorehouses closer to the saloon, and if it is a quick fix they are after, they won't come this far. But if we were there to guide them ..."

Miss Cecilia leaned back in her chair, a contemplative look on her face.

Please, Molly thought. Please say yes.

"For all your sass," Miss Cecilia said, "you do have a most uncharacteristic intelligence for your race. I do believe that's a fine idea. We won't get much trade here at that time of the evening. Everyone will be watching the fireworks or watching the fight, so it won't cost me any money. If you go and bring back, say, four gentlemen. Yes, that would work. But you'll take Liza with you instead of Isabella."

Molly frowned as Liza beamed at her from across the table.

"Why not?" Liza said. "It ain't like I've got big plans or anything. Might be fun, besides."

"Wear your best dresses, girls," Miss Cecilia said. "And I'll have you delivered in the carriage. Whatever gentlemen you bring back can ride with you, if they can fit. It's my house you'll be representing, so be on your best behavior."

"Of course, ma'am," Molly said, her enthusiasm diminished by the thought of who her partner would be. "We'll do you right."

"Do not disappoint me," Miss Cecilia warned.

As the day wore on, the crowds on the streets got larger and louder. People waved flags and sang songs, both American and Irish. Molly listened through her open window as she got ready for the night's event. *The Irish here sing of beating the English during the American war since we haven't done it in our own country yet*, she thought with a smile.

Imagine the songs when we drive them out of Ireland for good. We'll not stop singing for a hundred years or more. She began to hum "A Nation Once Again" to herself as she applied some cosmetic.

"Just a minute," Molly called over her shoulder when someone knocked on her door. After a final look in her mirror, she opened the door and saw Liza. Miss Cecilia provided each girl who worked in the house one ball gown for formal events. In the seven months she'd been there, Molly had not had cause to wear hers until this night. *It's the finest thing I've ever seen*, she thought. *But it ain't hardly mine, is it. Like everything here, even me, it belongs to the missus. And she'll take it out of my pay if I ruin it.*

"It's time," Liza said when Molly opened the door. "The coach is waiting."

Liza wore a dark blue gown with white lace trim while Molly wore green.

"I'm ready, I think," Molly said.

"This idea of yours better work," Liza said. "The last thing I need right now is for her to get cross with me."

"It will," Molly said.

They walked downstairs and received last-minute instructions from Miss Cecilia. When they went onto the steps, Molly saw the coach for the first time since the morning it brought her to the house. She caught a whiff of perfume and cigar smoke from inside. She froze as though her feet sprouted roots which held her in place. Darkness clouded her eyes as her heart raced. Her breath came in ragged gasps. Moisture dampened her palms. It was as though she had been transported back in time to that day. She watched Katie and Liza lead her to the carriage, wrapped in a blanket. Molly began to shake as she felt everything—the cold, the pain, the blood trickling down her thighs—all over again. *Ellen. They took Ellen. They took … everything.*

"Molly!"

She jumped as a hand grabbed her arm. Molly blinked her eyes and saw Liza beside her, a frown on her face.

"What in the hell is wrong with you?" Liza demanded. "It's your idea and yet here you are about to have a fit or something."

"I'm all right," Molly said. "I'm sorry. I don't know what came over me. For a moment I felt like I was … never mind. Let's go."

She took a few deep breaths to clear her head and then walked to the coach. The driver hopped down and helped each woman get inside, Molly first and then Liza.

"Don't go getting any ideas about how you're the favorite," Liza said once the door closed and they were alone. "Just because you came up with one good idea. I'm still Miss Cecilia's second, and you'd do well to remember that."

"I'm not likely to forget it with you always around to remind me, am I?"

"Any more from you and I'll tell Miss Cecilia."

Molly bit her lip and kept her mouth closed for the duration of the trip, though it took a tremendous effort.

A large crowd had surrounded Brennan's Saloon by the time they arrived. Men who could not afford tickets were crowded around the open windows to listen to shouted updates from spectators inside. Molly noticed two fire engines, Hibernia and Americus, alongside Hook and Ladder One, their crews preferring to bring their equipment to the fight so they might have a speedier response should bells interrupt the contest. A few police officers circled the edges of the crowd with an eye out for pickpockets or troublemakers. A large Irishman blocked the door. Liza slid up to him, put her hand on his chest and said, "Miss Cecilia sent us." The man nodded and stepped aside.

Most of the tables had been removed from the saloon. A large rope marked off the ring. Patrick stood off to one side, bare chested but with his suspenders still up, as the foreman from his fire company massaged his shoulders. His opponent, MacGregor, was a head taller, with considerably more bulk than Patrick had on his wiry frame. Matt Brennan, an enormous man with large black curls that hung over his face and made him look like a dog in need of a grooming, walked to the center of the ring and in a booming voice yelled, "Fighters! To me!"

As Molly and Liza separated and moved around the back of the crowd, Brennan shouted the instructions for the benefit of all present.

"London Prize Ring rules! A knockdown ends the round. You'll receive a thirty second rest if you are standing. If not, you get thirty seconds, plus eight more to regain your line. In between rounds, you may sit upon the knee of your second, but you must rise under your own power. No biting! No gouging! No knees or elbows to the balls! No head butting! Obey my orders at all times!"

The crowd buzzed with excitement. Men shouted bets and waved fistfuls of paper money in the air as they sloshed drinks on one another. Molly tried to stay back, out of Patrick's line of sight. *I want to be here, but I don't want to distract him*, she thought. *Maybe I'll get a chance to say hello once it is over.*

As Brennan shouted for the first round to begin, a hand grabbed Molly's elbow, causing her to jump. She turned to see who it was and saw a face, vaguely familiar, but she could not place it.

"It's Miss O'Sullivan, is it not?"

"Yes," she said. "I do believe you have the advantage of me, sir."

"Oh," the man laughed. "Aye, I'm not in uniform. It's Frank Lynch of the police. I'm a detective now, so no more uniform."

"Why, Mr. Lynch," Molly said, "this is quite a surprise. Here to watch the fight, I suppose?"

He leaned in close and whispered, "I can't say this out loud, but I hope that fireman beats the shite outta MacGregor. He's a fecking bastard, pardon my language. But what of you? A fan of pugilism as well?"

"No," Molly said, "I'm here … working, I guess you might say."

"Weren't you going to live with your family? And you're dressed too fancy to be a barmaid."

"I was, sir," Molly said. "But when I got to their apartment, it had burned. A woman on the street said they'd roasted inside. I had nowhere to go and …"

"I see," Frank said with a nod. "I recall you had a child with you when we last met. What became of her?"

Molly's eyes watered and she said, "Gone. Stolen out of my arms."

Frank frowned.

"We've a bit of that happening here, I'm sorry to say. Some men have no control over their appetites, I can tell you that much. Have you not been able to find her?"

"No," Molly said, "but I've not much time to look either. I, well … I'm not …"

"I understand," Frank said. "You're not the first to have such a thing happen to you, for sure. Maybe I could make some inquiries for you? I cannot promise you much, but you never know. I've an ear to the street and know enough vagrants to fill the Bowery Theater. Who knows? I might turn up something. If I do, where can I find you?"

"Miss Cecilia's," Molly whispered. She gave him all the information she knew about Ellen, but given the child's age and lack of communication, she doubted much, if anything, would come of it. Frank promised to get word to her no matter what he found, and she moved away.

The crowd roared, and she turned to the ring in time to see blood pouring from MacGregor's nose. The man reeled back for a moment, but regained his balance and stormed forward, raining blows on Patrick. The smaller man took a few steps back and tucked his face behind his guard, catching most of the punches on his arms. MacGregor tired quickly, and the rapidity of his punches slackened. Patrick took advantage of it to land a solid shot to the man's liver, followed by two quick punches to the jaw. MacGregor collapsed and the crowd roared with cheers or taunts, depending on who they backed. He soon regained his feet, and the fight resumed after the mandatory thirty second rest.

Molly circulated through the crowd, pausing long enough to speak to the more sober and affluent of the patrons. A simple whisper that Miss Cecilia's would be open after the fight with free drinks and a complimentary cigar was enough to gain a promise to stop by. *Get a bit of the drink in them*, Molly thought, *and they become easy to manipulate.*

MacGregor landed a vicious blow to Patrick's chin and the crowd gasped, but somehow, he managed to stay on his feet. The bigger man looked puzzled, and Patrick retaliated with another punch to the liver. The men circled one another, like two dogs in the street. The crowd exhorted both men to do their worst to one another. The air inside the saloon was stale with the odor of perspiration, alcohol, and smoke.

"Good evening, sir," Molly said to a well-dressed gentleman near the back of the crowd.

"Are you working?" he asked.

"I am," Molly said. "My name is Molly. From Miss Cecilia's place."

The man kept his eyes on the fight as he draped his arm around Molly's shoulders. She swallowed hard and managed a smile to mask the nausea which overtook her stomach. The man pulled her into his side, and he rested his hand upon her breast. Molly bit her bottom lip and tried to focus on the fight. She noticed Liza across the room in between two men. One of them whispered something to her and she laughed.

The two fighters moved toward the center of the ring. MacGregor had his back to where Molly stood. Patrick took a step to the side and for a moment, he locked eyes on Molly. His face registered surprise. Molly tried to step away from the man, but he simply squeezed harder with his arm and hand. Patrick frowned. He failed to see the massive fist MacGregor threw at his chin. It connected with a mighty crack. Patrick's head snapped sidewise, flinging blood and sweat onto Brennan. Molly tucked her head into the man's side. She heard Patrick's body hit the floor with a thud as the crowd howled.

"Fight's over," Brennan declared after a pause. "MacGregor of the 4th Precinct is the winner!"

Molly looked up in time to see Brennan raise MacGregor's arm in triumph. Through the crowd, she could see that Patrick was still on the floor as his second knelt by his side. Dr. Howard appeared and bent down to examine him. Soon, Molly saw the foreman help Patrick into a sitting position as the doctor looked at his chin and mouth; Patrick's blood dripped onto the floor.

Jesus, Molly swore. *He needed to win to get his money for the draft substitute. Had he not seen me, maybe he would have. Damn this country and damn this war! I've already Ellen on my conscience and now, if he goes off to get killed by the rebels, then it is my fault too.*

"Shall we?" the gentleman asked as he nodded toward the door.

"Aye," Molly said with a sigh. "We've a coach outside if you don't mind sharing with Liza."

"Certainly not," he said. "Come to think of it, I believe I'd enjoy the company of both of you tonight."

"I'm sorry, sir," Molly said, "but Miss Cecilia don't allow no two-fers. Against the house rules. But you can pay for each of us separate like, if you want."

"I just might," the man said.

On their way out, they picked up one more and so, with the two men with Liza, they'd managed the four Miss Cecilia demanded. Inside the coach, Molly and Liza sat facing one another, squeezed in between two men each. The coach jostled its way toward Miss Cecilia's. Molly closed her eyes and tried to steady herself as the men gave one another a blow by blow account of the fight they'd all watched.

At one point, Molly opened her eyes and saw Liza roll hers and shake her head at the men's talk. Soon, the talk turned to the war.

"The government's going to draw the first names one week from today," one man said. "Saturday the 11th. Don't know if there'll be trouble or not, but I think we can expect the paddies down here will show up to try and stop it. Being the ignorant gorillas that they are."

Sure, just talk about us like there ain't one sitting right here next to you that you plan on screwing in five minutes time, Molly thought. *Bastards. No doubt all four of them have paid their three hundred dollars in blood money so some poor man has to go fight on their behalf.*

Miss Cecilia met them at the door, all smiles, and soon the men had drinks and cigars in their hands. She suggested they all go up to the balcony to watch the fireworks. *I hope Patrick's all right*, Molly thought as she watched the bright explosions in the night sky. *Surely Dr. Howard will put him to rights if he isn't. A kind man, the doctor.*

Later that night, once the men were gone, Molly sat alone in her room and stared out the window. The streets were empty, except for the occasional drunk stumbling on his way home. Even the street walkers seemed to have taken the night off. *Odd behavior, that. Normally you'd expect to see more people about, despite the late hour.* She wondered if what the man said in the carriage was true. *Are people up to something? Do they mean to try and stop the draft? No, it's probably just idle boasting by a few drunken men in the saloons what's got people concerned. Nothing will happen.*

The fire bells rang off to the north in the Fourteenth Ward. Molly used her wash basin to clean her face and hands. She climbed into bed and tried to sleep, but the combination of heat and dreams made it difficult. Every time she closed her eyes, she felt a man's hand on her throat and heard the Ellen scream her name as another bore her out of the room. She felt the man's fist strike her face. Felt the blood. When the sun rose, Molly was still awake.

Chapter Thirteen

The day the enrollment officer drew the first names passed with little fanfare. The next morning, while waiting for Dr. Howard to make his rounds, Molly read a full account of it in the paper. The crowd treated it as something of a farce, and shouted jokes after the official announced each name. When it was over, they drifted away, and the city breathed a sigh of relief. Molly wasn't so sure. On Sunday, Dr. Howard told her that he'd heard rumblings of trouble in the streets all day.

"It's nothing like I've heard before," he said. "Up until now, people shouted their unhappiness with the conscription, but now they are talking in whispers. I admit that it frightens me."

"When do they start drawing names again?" Molly asked.

"Tomorrow morning. That's when the trouble, if there is to be any, will start."

"How is the boxer what got knocked senseless at the fight last week doing?" Molly asked.

Dr. Howard smiled and said, "He's fine. Back to work with the department as far as I know. What's your interest in him?" He looked up from the implements he was packing into his bag. "What's this? Is Molly O'Sullivan blushing?"

"He's only a friend of sorts," Molly protested. "We met on the street one day and again when the place across the street burned. Patrick was kind to me, that's all. And few people in this city have been. Other than yourself and a peeler named Frank Lynch. I'm glad to hear he's recovered."

"It's a cruel city in which to live," Dr. Howard said. "I know you've seen your share of cruelties, and in my practice, I see many more. That's why I fear the wrath stirred up by the draft. Casual cruelty for no reason other than general cussedness is the norm in New York City, so I can only imagine what it might be like when there is a purpose behind the violence."

"Can I ask you something, Doctor?"

"Of course."

"Do you know anything about people who take children?"

"Take them where?"

"That's what I don't know," Molly said. "When I got here, to New York, I mean, I had a young child with me. Named Ellen, she was. She wasn't really mine, not like that, but I was to care for her after her parents died during the crossing. The night that the … the night that I ended up … well, here eventually, someone came into the room and took her away."

"There is great evil in this city, Molly," Dr. Howard said. "I could only speculate as to what purpose the innocent was taken from you, and I think it better if I do not."

"But where could I find her?"

"She could be anywhere," Dr. Howard said.

"That's what I was afraid of, Doctor."

Trade was slow Sunday night. By eleven o'clock, there had been no visitors for several hours and Miss Cecilia sent the women to bed. Molly awoke from a nightmare shortly before dawn. She heard noises outside on the street and opened her window to have a look. Men and women in small groups streamed up Mulberry Street, headed uptown. One carried a sign that said NO DRAFT! They said nothing, their footsteps being the only sound to mark their passing. It sounded like an army on the march. *Hopefully they mean no trouble*, she thought, *but it don't look that way from here.*

The crowds increased in size and grew louder as the sun came up. Every few minutes, someone would shout, "No draft!" One large group moved along singing "We'll Hang Horace Greeley From a Sour Apple Tree." Men passed bottles among themselves, and Molly was surprised to see a number of women mixed in with them, shouting just as loud as the men. When she went downstairs for breakfast, Miss Cecilia assured them that any trouble would happen uptown, away from their neighborhood.

"Not even the Irish are stupid enough to burn down their own neighborhood," she said, "Right, Molly?"

"Yes, ma'am," Molly said as she poked at her eggs with a fork.

"Won't be much for us to do today," Liza said. "None of our type of visitors are going to venture down here with the paddies all worked up like they are. It could be dangerous. Those crowds will spot a three-hundred-dollar man from a mile away."

"We'll be safe here regardless," Miss Cecilia said, "but I wouldn't want to be a rich man or an abolitionist Republican in the city today."

The young women gathered in the parlor and listened to Daft Eddie on the piano and tried to ignore the increasing sounds of large crowds on the move outside. *They'll throw a few bricks*, Molly thought, *then the peelers will crack some heads and send them on their way*. The fire bells rang just after ten a.m. and continued almost unabated for two hours. Around noon, a beefy gentleman walked through the door.

"It's hell out there," he said. "Just came from uptown near the Enrollment Office. The men of the Black Joke fire company attacked the building and set fire to it. When other fire companies showed up to put it out, the crowd attacked them with bricks and stones. Finally, they yielded to let the men work, and turned on the police instead. There's pitched battles in the streets right now. I was lucky enough to escape with my skin intact. I saw them club a policeman to insensibility and then carve him up with knives right there in the middle of the street."

"You look in need of a drink," Miss Cecilia suggested, "and perhaps the company of one of my girls. They do wonders for distracting the mind ..."

"I'm sure of that," the man said as he focused on Molly. "I like this redheaded one here. Irish, are you?"

"I am, sir," Molly said.

"Then why aren't you outside with your own people?"

"I wasn't aware they was drafting women, sir," Molly said. "If they get around to that, maybe I will join them."

The man laughed as he swallowed two shots of whiskey in rapid succession. Contrary to Liza's prediction, several men entered the house saying they wanted to wait out the unrest. Most were businessmen who worked in the area and feared they might not make it home. *Sure, they leave their wives and children to the mercy of the mobs and go to a whorehouse for comfort,* Molly thought. As the men paired up with the young women, the first man stood and announced he was ready to go upstairs. Molly slowly got to her feet, extended her hand, and led him up.

Twenty minutes later, as the man got dressed, he said, "You'd be the first redheaded whore I've been with."

"Are you wanting a medal for it?" Molly asked. "Your time's up. Go on. Off with you."

"Maybe I want an encore," he said as he placed his hands on his hips for a moment and then hooked his thumbs into his suspenders.

Jesus, Mary, and Joseph, Molly thought, *this is just what I need. A flash man what thinks he can get seconds for free.* She knew three sharp knocks on the floor of her upstairs room would summon the protection, provided they were neither drunk nor off with the mobs. Her eyes shifted over to the wash basin on top of the small desk. *I could brain him with that,* she thought. The customer followed the direction of her eyes and stepped in front of her desk.

"Is there something in there you are wanting?" he asked. "I know how you whores love to secrete weapons about the place."

Molly frowned. "No," she said as she stood up, "but you'll be needing to go downstairs and talk to the missus if you want another go. We've men waiting and you'll have to go to the back of the line."

"I ain't waiting in no line again," he said. "Besides, it don't look like you could stop me from taking what I want anyway."

"I wouldn't be so sure of that," Molly said. "But I suppose if you are willing to pay for it, there's no need for you to go downstairs."

"That's more like it," the man said.

"Just let me take my shoes off," Molly said. She knelt and pretended to unlace her black leather boots. *Careful*, she said to herself as her hand crept towards the small knife sheathed in a scabbard sewn into the inside of her right boot. Her right hand closed on the handle as her left gave three knocks on the floor; she hoped they were loud enough to be heard above the sound of the piano in the parlor.

With surprising speed for his bulk, the man sprang forward and lifted her off the floor by her throat and then backhanded her across the face. She tumbled from his grasp and landed on the bed. Though her head rang from the blow, Molly had enough presence of mind to roll completely off the far side of the bed so when the man lunged after her, he landed on the empty mattress. When Molly got up, she clutched the knife in her hand.

"Get out, or I'll carve your balls off," she said to the man, her voice even.

With her left hand, she reached back and opened the door to her room. *For feck's sake*, she thought, *where's the boys what toss the riffraff out?* The man advanced on her, his arms outstretched as if he meant to throttle her. Molly backed into the hallway until she bumped into the wall. She cast her eyes towards the staircase, expecting to see help, but there was none. The sounds of piano music and laughter drifted up from the first floor. With sudden dread, Molly realized no one had heard her signal.

She turned and made for the stairs, but the man seized her from behind, his arm closing around her neck before she managed to take two steps. He lifted her off the ground and began to back into the room. Her vision blurred as his beefy arm cut off her windpipe. With as much strength as she could manage, Molly plunged the knife into the man's thigh. It sank into his flesh all the way to the handle and she felt his warm blood ooze from the wound. The man screamed in rage and pain, and then screamed louder when she twisted the knife and felt his muscle and tissue tear. She collapsed onto the floor as his arm relaxed, her lungs drawing in great mouthfuls of air. Her head cleared quickly, and she got back to her feet, wiping the blood from the blade across the leg of her dress.

"You Irish bitch!" the man roared as he staggered towards her.

Molly lunged for him, her blade poised to strike at his heart. The man leapt backwards and crashed into a table in the hallway, knocking a kerosene lamp to the floor. The lamp shattered, and burning fuel spread eagerly across the floor. The man got to his feet and staggered down the stairs yelling, "Fire!" Molly stood transfixed for a moment, watching the flames spread along the floor and up the wall, fed by the oils used to treat the wood. *Now I've gone and done it*, she thought.

Smoke gathered along the ceiling and started to drift down the hallway. From the sounds coming from the rooms along the hallway, she realized no one had yet smelled the smoke. Molly began to work her way down the corridor, pounding on doors to alert the girls and their customers. Doors flung open and men and women in various stages of undress tumbled out to see what the commotion was about.

"You gotta get out before you roast alive," she said, pointing down the hallway to the back staircase. Molly coughed as the smoke grew thicker and flames danced along the wall, reaching upwards towards the ceiling. She heard the fire bells ring again.

Molly ran to her room and grabbed a dress, then raced down the back hallway. Just before she reached the door, a hand grabbed her shoulder. She whirled around and saw Miss Cecilia.

"You!" Miss Cecilia rasped. "You think you can burn down my house?"

"We've got to get out, ma'am," Molly yelled. "Come on!"

Molly tried to pull away, and Miss Cecilia jerked her back around and slapped her. Molly stumbled into the wall. She shoved Miss Cecilia with both hands, causing the older woman to tumble backwards and fall. A piece of wood, from an overhead beam crashed to the floor. Embers landed on Miss Cecilia's dress and started to burn. Molly took a step towards her, and then noticed Liza through the smoke.

"Murder!" Liza yelled as she ran for the front staircase. "Murder!"

Molly paused long enough to see Miss Cecilia thrashing around on the floor as flames devoured her dress, then she turned and ran down the back staircase and ducked into an alley, where she put on her dress as quickly as she could. A lone fire company, not Hibernia, pulled up in front of the building. The men took to their work slowly, alert for any sign of danger, not from the building but from the crowd.

It must be bad to the north of us, Molly realized, *if even the firemen ain't excited by a fire*. She peeked out of the alley and saw a few of the girls gathered behind the fire engine. Though she couldn't hear their words, Molly saw Liza gesturing toward the building and toward the alley where Molly was standing.

"Look, there she is!" Liza yelled. "Quick! Get the police! Don't let her get away!"

Molly turned and ran through the alley, pushing a few street urchins out of her way. When a barefoot woman dressed in rags stepped into her path, Molly bowled her over. The woman launched a stream of profanities that trailed behind Molly as she crossed one street and found another alley. *Go north*, she thought. *Go north and blend in with the crowds. They won't be able to find you there.*

After a few minutes, Molly stopped to catch her breath. My hair. I have to cover it. Otherwise they'll notice me. She searched around and soon found a woman passed out drunk, or maybe dead, behind some empty boxes, a black bonnet on her head. The woman made no movement or sound as Molly leaned down and unfastened the knot, removed it, and then placed the bonnet on her own head. Her stomach recoiled from the odor of sour vomit and whiskey which clung to it. *Still, 'tis better to have it, smell and all, than to risk being discovered. But where am I to go? I've no money and no place to hide. It's like I've stepped off the boat all over again.*

She considered her options, but only until she heard a person shout, "Look! There!" Molly turned and saw a uniformed policeman walking towards her as he raised his whistle to his mouth.

For God's sake, she swore as she turned to run, *ain't they busy enough with the conscription mess right now?* Molly longed to walk over to the officer and explain that the fire was an accident, and that she hadn't meant for Miss Cecilia to catch on fire either. *It cannot be murder if you don't mean it, right?* With the authorities not in the mood to hear explanations for anything, Molly knew that her only chance was to try and avoid detection for as long as possible while she tried to formulate a way out of the city. Keeping to the alleys and the side streets, Molly tried to put as much distance between her and Miss Cecilia's as she could.

Eventually, she emerged onto Broadway, where a large crowd marched north. With a quick look to make sure no one was behind her, Molly darted into the crowd. No one took much notice of her, other than to nod hello. She moved with them as if she were being carried along by an ocean wave. Several waved signs denouncing the draft and the Lincoln administration. She caught whispers around her of what had taken place earlier that day. The Enrollment Office had burned, and several police officers had been killed. A small unit of soldiers had fired into the crowd and then were driven away, with a few being beaten to death with their own muskets. *Jesus, it is bad after all. It's like a war going on right here in the city.*

Large fires burned in the distance, so many that the fire bells no longer rang. There were no police officers or soldiers around. It was if the city belonged entirely to the mob. *No, the authorities are probably up north where the violence is*, she thought. *Not here where people just march and sing songs.* A fire company appeared and tried to force its way through the mob, but the crowd drove them back with bricks and paving stones. Rather than risk the destruction of their engine, the men turned around to look for a better route.

"Won't the whole city burn if they don't let the firemen go about their work?" Molly asked a man next to her.

"Who cares, miss?" he asked. "They are doing the bidding of the fat cats what run this city. Fuck 'em, and the coppers too."

Molly decided not to voice any other questions. They passed a few burned-out buildings and several bodies in the street, some in police uniforms.

"Look out!" yelled a man from a rooftop. "There's a flying wedge of coppers coming down. They mean to take you in the flank. Don't give the bastards an inch, you hear!"

The crowd roared with anger as several men waved clubs and others began to break up more paving stones from the surface of the street. Molly pushed her way to the back of the crowd and sought safety in a doorway, but there were few safe places in the city this day.

Chapter Fourteen

A group of police officers emerged from a nearby alley, and Molly shrank against the doorway as if she were burrowing into the earth. The police and the mob tore into one another with frenzied enthusiasm. Clubs rose and fell as the police gave ground grudgingly, but they kept their formation to protect one another. Shouts of anger and cries of pain filled the air as skulls cracked under the blows of police clubs. Men appeared on the roofs directly above the police officers. They hurled ceramic tiles which shattered as they hit the street, sending shrapnel in every direction. Molly flinched as a piece struck the wall near her head. She searched for a safe place to run, but rioters and police blocked every avenue of escape. Several police officers went down, as did a few members of the mob. Their formation broken, the police retreated down a side street, pursued by at least fifty howling men.

One officer tripped and fell. The crowd surrounded him. Molly covered her eyes as blows rained down upon the hapless man until he stopped moving. People moved on down the street, leaving a trail of broken bodies behind them. One patrolman and at least a dozen rioters lay sprawled on the pavement, their blood forming pools around them. A young man sat holding his bloody hands to his head. *He's hardly more than a boy*, Molly thought. She left the doorway and knelt by his side. She tore a strip from the bottom of her skirt and gently pulled the boy's hands away. An ugly wound ran along his scalp. Blood seeped out and ran down his face. Molly could see the white bone of his skull through the gap in his skin. She swallowed the bile that rose in her throat.

"Here," Molly said, "let me." She wrapped the makeshift bandage around his head and secured it with a knot.

"You've need of a doctor," Molly said. "Though I don't know where you'd find one today. I imagine they are quite busy."

The boy stared at the ground and said nothing. Molly stood and hurried down the street after the mob. *I've no desire to witness more of this*, she thought, *but I can't risk being by myself where I might be recognized.*

The smoke thickened as she moved north. *It's like the whole world's on fire*, she thought. *Or I'm no longer in the city and have now reached the devil's doorstep*. The stores were deserted. No street vendors shouted enticements. With no breeze, the smell of ash clung to the air and pressed down on her. When she turned a corner, the mob appeared again, as if she had stepped into another world.

They carried her along like an ocean current as they drifted further and further uptown. They shouted their feelings about the draft, Republicans, or both. Some men waved clubs, and Molly noticed knives in the hands of several women. *There's murder in their eyes*, Molly thought. *And who can stop them? The peelers are outnumbered. And there's no soldiers in sight.* She watched as several men scaled telegraph poles and cut the wires.

Eventually, the mob stopped outside the Bull's Head Hotel and demanded the management serve them free alcohol. The hotel employees refused, and the crowd soon produced torches, which they tossed through the windows. As flames devoured the hotel, two fire companies arrived. The mob parted and, for a moment, Molly figured they meant to let them go about their work. As soon as the firemen stretched a hose to the hydrant and tried to attack the flames, the mob fell upon the hoses with knives. The firemen fled as the mob upended the fire engine and began to smash it with picks, clubs, and axes. *Hell has let loose its demons upon the city*, Molly thought. *It's rage they feel for all they've endured both in Ireland and here, but that ain't the fault of innocent people they are attacking.*

"It's a black day for the city," said a voice beside Molly. She turned and saw a man dressed like a laborer, but cleaner. He held a notepad in his hand. "This is worse than the Dead Rabbits riot back in '57."

"The what?" Molly asked.

"The Dead Rabbits Riot. It was a two-day long fight between the Dead Rabbits and the Bowery Boys. They fought each other and the police. I'd thought that was the worst this city had to offer until today."

"I've seen nothing like it before," Molly confessed. She pointed to his notepad and asked, "You some kind of a writer?"

"A reporter," the man whispered. "I'm currently without portfolio but I hope to sell a few pieces to the newspapers this evening."

"Don't let anyone catch you with that notepad," Molly said. "They ain't exactly in the mood for talking to reporters, in case you haven't noticed."

She shoved her way into the middle of the sea of humanity to get away from the man. *That's the last thing I need on this day, a description of myself in the newspaper. I cannot risk them finding out what part of town I'm in, though I've not been this far uptown myself before.*

As she'd been carried along by the mob, Molly doubted she'd be able to find her way back to the 6th Ward without directions. *But I can't go back there. That's the first place they'll look for me. If not the peelers, then someone might recognize me. Dr. Howard might help, but that's the only person, besides Patrick, I could maybe depend on.*

As flames consumed the hotel, people in the mob clapped and cheered. One man jumped upon a wooden box and gave a short speech, but due to the noise, Molly did not hear a word he said. A man next to her said that he'd heard the army was sending in troops to fight them, while another said that was impossible as the telegraph wires had been cut and there was no way to get word out of the city. People argued with one another over where to go next as they milled around with no true sense of direction or purpose. Some insisted on heading back south to sack police headquarters. Others said the best course of action would be to destroy the buildings housing some of the city's many newspapers. A few argued for burning the houses of some of the wealthiest citizens in the city.

Finally, they began to drift away as a single unit, though to where Molly did not know. The NO DRAFT signs carried by the men at the head of the mob guided them. People began to laugh and sing again as they moved along, as if they'd not brought death or destruction at every stop along the way. *They are treating this like a giant picnic*, Molly thought. *Do they not know that, at some point, either the peelers or the army will put down their clubs and pick up muskets? Will they still be laughing when there's cannons aimed at them? I need to get away from them before worse happens. But I don't know where to go. Maybe I'll stay with them for a little while longer, then I'll strike out on my own.*

Around six o'clock, the mob halted outside the Colored Orphan Asylum on Fifth Avenue between 42nd and 43rd Streets. The massive building loomed over a fine garden, as green as anything in Ireland. *My God! Do they mean to harm the children?*

Molly watched as men went inside. They flung various pieces of furniture out of the windows. No children appeared, and Molly breathed a sigh of relief. *They must have got them to safety. A small miracle, that.*

Frustrated in their bid to catch the children, the mob set fire to the building. A few fire companies arrived shortly thereafter, led by the same man in the white helmet carrying a speaking trumpet that she'd seen at the fire across from Miss Cecilia's. *Chief Decker*, Molly remembered. *That's what Patrick said his name was.*

The firefighters halted at the edge of the mob. "Will you let us go to our work?" Chief Decker called out.

The mob turned and began to hurl insults at the firefighters. Decker turned to his men. "All right, boys. Are you with me?"

"We are," they yelled.

Molly watched as the firefighters waded into the mob. One fireman took off his leather helmet and bashed a man on the head while another used the flat of his axe to fell several others. Molly gasped as she caught sight of Patrick in the midst of the fray. *But this isn't his company*, she thought, *what's he doing way up here*?

The sheer size of the mob drove the firemen away, and they abandoned their engine and ladder and retreated to safety. A few minutes later, Chief Decker appeared alone. He walked to the front of the mob and tried to reason with them. Several men seized the chief and dragged him over to a tree. Someone produced a rope which was quickly fastened around his neck while the other was tossed over a tree branch.

Decker laughed and said, "Go ahead. You'll only stop my draft. Not yours."

Molly watched in amazement as the men in the crowd started to chuckle and then roar with laughter. They removed the rope and moved on. Several of the men took the time to pat the chief on the back as they passed him.

Once the mob dispersed, Molly approached the chief, who was busy studying the burning orphanage with a frown on his face.

"They got the children out, but it's too late for the building. A damn shame too. It was a fine place."

"You are very brave, sir," she said.

He turned and studied her for a moment.

"The streets aren't safe for women this day," he said. "You should run along home."

"Are they ever safe for women?" Molly asked as she put her hands on her hips. "Besides, I've something to ask you."

"Yes?"

"I'm looking for Patrick McMahon of the Hibernia Company in the 6th Ward. I saw him with you earlier. I need to talk to him."

"McMahon? Yes, he's with me. You'll find him a couple of blocks down. There's a fire in a drugstore, I think. We put together a mixed crew to come up here when we heard of what was happening. Thank God they got those poor children out in time."

"Yes, sir," Molly said. "'Tis a miracle, truly."

Molly turned and hurried in the direction Chief Decker indicated. She found two other engine companies spraying water on a fire to little effect. With all the men wearing the same red shirts and leather helmets, she had a hard time locating Patrick. She scanned the crowd, focusing on the company number on each man's shirt, until finally, she saw him. Molly waved. Patrick squinted at her for a moment, and then turned back to his work.

He don't recognize me with this bonnet, she realized. Molly ripped it off and yelled, "Patrick! It's me!"

His face registered surprise. Patrick motioned for another man to take his spot on the hose line. He hurried over to her and said, "Molly! What in hell's name are you doing way up here?"

"I could ask you the same," Molly said.

"Ah, well, that's easy enough to answer. We got called out earlier today when they attacked the Enrollment Office. Several fires came in after that and we got set upon by a crowd of banshees. They drove us off and destroyed our engine, damn them. So, we split up to help the companies what still have equipment to use. But why are you here?"

"I need to talk to you, Patrick." Molly grabbed his arm and led him several steps away. "Today, at Miss Cecilia's, a man attacked me. I was only defending myself, but he knocked over a lantern and started a fire."

"Why would you be in trouble for that?"

"No," Molly said, "there's more. When I was trying to get out, Miss Cecilia … she … grabbed me and hit me. I shoved her away and she fell down. Her dress caught fire and …"

"Jesus," Patrick swore. "They'll be after you for murder, Molly. Even if you didn't mean it. You know how it is. We don't get fair trials here, just like at home."

"All I could think of to do was run," Molly said. "And hide with the mob so no one will recognize me."

"I think the coppers have other stuff on their mind right now," Patrick said, "but I'd stay outta sight if I was you. Do you got somewhere to go?"

"No," Molly confessed. "I've no money and no way to find a place off the street to hide. It's like the day I got off the boat."

Memories came rushing back to her. The fatigue. The dull ache in the pit of her stomach. The rejection everywhere she turned. *And the night,* she thought. *That horrible night.* She swallowed hard to drive them out of her mind.

"I don't know what to tell you, Molly," Patrick said. "But you need to find somewhere safe to go. Anywhere. Let things blow over. Then maybe you can go talk to the peelers and tell them what happened. Surely, they'll be reasonable about it once they hear from you."

Sure, and I'm Old Abe himself, Molly thought. *Even Frank Lynch don't trust them, and he's one of their own.*

Patrick turned as the roof of the burning building collapsed, sending a shower of sparks into the air.

"I gotta get back to work," he said. "I'll try to come round when all this is over. I'm sure it will go in your favor, Molly."

"Be careful," Molly said.

"I would say the same to you," Patrick said. He smiled and rejoined his comrades as they battled the fire.

Molly put her bonnet back on and hurried away, lest another firefighter be able to identify her. Several blocks away, she happened upon a terrifying scene. A man and a woman, both black, swung from lamp poles, whether dying or dead Molly couldn't tell. The mob doused parts of their bodies with tar. A man stepped forward and touched a torch first to the man's body and then the woman's. As flames consumed the twitching bodies, men and women danced beneath them in the glowing light. Molly collapsed to her knees and vomited. She quickly looked up to see if anyone noticed her, but they were enticed with the sight of the bodies and paid her no mind. *Will this day ever end? Are we to carry on until there is no one left alive in the city?*

She scrambled to her feet and walked away, wiping her mouth with the back of her forearm. A crackle of gunfire several blocks away made her jump—a single shot at first, followed by a ragged volley, and then three more single pops. People streamed toward her from the direction of the shots. One shouted, "They're shooting us down like animals!" Molly wasn't sure who was doing the shooting; it could be the police, or the army, or even people shooting each other from the crowd. Molly got out of the way lest she be trampled. A rumble of thunder shook the ground. *Thunder, or a cannon?*

Molly turned a corner and saw several police officers taking turns beating a man with their clubs. None seemed to notice her as she walked by. A few men drifted past, broken arms clutched to their chests. On streets where confrontations took place earlier in the day, men and women busied themselves dragging the injured and dead away. Smashed windows and the burned facades of stores loomed over the streets. *It's an unusual mob what takes the time to remove its dead,* she thought. *Maybe they want to make it seem like there was no one what got hurt.*

As night descended upon the city, a hard rain started to fall. It drenched the fires, allowing the fire companies to retreat to their stations. It seemed to dampen the spirits of the mob as well, and the streets grew deserted except for a few police officers, whom Molly tried to avoid as best she could. In an alley somewhere east of Broadway, she found shelter underneath a wooden overhang behind a shop. She sat with her back to the door and drew her knees up to her chest. *At least it isn't cold,* she thought, *but I've had nothing to eat since breakfast. Tomorrow I'll have to find some food somewhere. With all the stores the mob damaged, surely there's one that I could go in and grab something out of.*

During the years of the famine, Molly sometimes wondered why her father or mother did not simply sneak into one of the estates and steal food. Apart from the obvious difficulty of infiltrating a large, guarded home, she came to realize that her parents did not believe desperate straits justified theft. *And look what it got me da,* she thought. *An early grave. I'll not starve myself for the sake of morality.*

A small party of soldiers passed by the entrance to the alley. Wounded men from the Invalid Corps, they shuffled rather than marched down the street. *If they aim to stop the mob, they'll need fitter men than that,* she thought.

As she sat there, too tired and scared to sleep, Molly considered all she had seen during the day. *I don't blame a man for not wanting to go off and die for the rich man what gets to stay at home, but how does burning down an orphanage and attacking the fire department put a stop to it? Will it not serve only to make the fancy men what run this city mad?*

She shrank back into the shadows as two men staggered past, too drunk to notice her. A few police whistles sounded in the distance.

An hour went by, and then two. Her exhaustion overcame her fear, and Molly felt herself starting to drift into sleep. Soon, her body relaxed, and she began to dream of California. Her mind portrayed it as a lush landscape, with green hills and valleys like those in Ireland. Everyone lived on large estates like Lord Sanderson's. Food covered every table, and clean water and cattle were yours for the taking. And the gold? It lay out in the open; all you needed to collect your fortune were two hands and a bucket to put it in. The weather never got too cold and never got too hot. The streets were like those of heaven. Molly was most disappointed when she opened her eyes later and found herself still in New York City.

Chapter Fifteen

The next morning, the mob appeared again, unfazed by the previous day's violence. More street battles broke out between rioters and the police. And here I am only wanting breakfast, Molly thought.

She found a group of women in the middle of looting a grocery. As Molly approached, she heard one woman say that her husband said the government was sending troops in to fight. Molly pushed her way inside, stepping over the door, which had been smashed down. Empty shelves greeted her as women argued and shouted at one another. When two began to shove one another in a dispute over a ham, a loaf of bread dropped to the floor. Molly lunged for it. She snatched the bread and dashed out of the store before anyone could stop her. Clutching her prize to her stomach, Molly walked several blocks south and east toward the river before she stopped to eat it.

With her mouth parched by lack of water and the smoke in the air from fires started that morning, she had a difficult time forcing the bread down. As she ate, Molly remembered the large breakfast spread

Belinda put out every morning at Miss Cecilia's. Bacon, eggs, pancakes, and coffee to wash it all down with. *It seems like all that was a million years ago, not just yesterday. How fast it all can change. And what now? I've food but I've nowhere to go.*

Molly drifted south, back toward the 6th Ward. She knew it was dangerous, but at the same time, with so many people uptown with the rampaging mobs, Molly decided it might be the safest place to hide out for a while and formulate a plan. She reached up and fingered the Saint Michael's medallion around her neck. *It's all I have left now,* she thought. *Everything else is gone. Even Ellen's doll. The only thing I had to remember her by. Burned up in the fire, it was. I should have gone back for it. No, then I'd have burned up too.*

It's food, shelter, and money that I need, she decided. *Or maybe money first to buy the others. But how to get it? Am I to walk up to another whorehouse and ask if they have need of a redheaded whore what might be wanted by the peelers?*

As she passed police headquarters on Mulberry Street an hour later, she saw a group of soldiers marching north. The soldiers were young, but their eyes spoke of horrors incomprehensible to those on the home front. Behind them, a flying squad of police officers— some bruised or with bandaged heads, all with exhausted faces—moved along, their clubs tapping out a beat on the pavement. She turned her back and waited for them to pass, lest one recognize her.

As soon as it was safe, Molly walked to Broadway. She froze when she heard someone shout her name. Expecting a phalanx of police officers, Molly breathed a sigh of relief when she turned and saw Frank.

"Molly," he said, as he took her arm and led her over to the doorway of a boarded-up shop, "what are you doing here?"

"I don't know," she confessed. "I ... I have nowhere to go. And you? Why aren't you off dealing with the mobs?"

"I should be. But it's you I was looking for. Have you not heard?" he asked.

"Heard what?"

"We, the police I mean, know what happened. The man you stabbed. He died last night. Thankfully for you, his family wants to avoid a scandal. They don't want it known he died after getting stabbed by a whore, begging your pardon, but I heard this morning from one of my contacts that they've made it known they'll pay someone to do you in. And then there's the matter of Miss Cecilia."

Molly nodded, cautious. *Should I be talking to him at all? It must be safe. He's not after arresting me. He'd have done it already if he was.*

"One of the other women in the house gave a statement at the 6th Precinct that said she saw you beat Miss Cecilia unconscious and leave her to the mercy of the flames."

"That's a lie!" Molly exclaimed. "It was an accident."

Frank held up his hands and said, "The less I know, the better. It will result in a charge of murder. I can assure you of that. Miss Cecilia has, or had, some very highly placed friends."

"And are you here to haul me away to the cells?"

"No," Frank said. "Formal charges haven't been processed yet. We've the riots to deal with first. And even if they had ..."

"You were the first kind person I met in this city," Molly said. "I wouldn't presume on what I hope is our friendship to get you to turn your back on your duties. You'd be given the sack and we'd both be on the streets."

"Have you anywhere to go?"

"I do not," Molly admitted. "I'm at a bit of a loss, honestly. I had some money saved, but one of the girls ran off with it. Katie."

"Here"—Frank thrust his hand in his pocket and withdrew some money—"it's not much, but it will get you off the streets for a couple of nights."

"Oh no, I couldn't," Molly said as she pushed the money away.

"Take it," Frank ordered. "You can pay me back later. I don't want to know where you are. That way I can deny it if anyone asks. But you really need to start thinking about getting out of the city. And fast. Don't worry about the police. We're easy enough to dodge and the riots will keep us busy for a few more days, at least. Watch your back, Molly. That man's family ... if they are willing to offer money for your scalp ... someone will take them up on it. And the police can't help you, because we want you for ourselves. Got any protection?"

"I had a knife," Molly said. "Not anymore."

Frank opened his coat and Molly caught the wooden grip of a revolver stuck in the front of his pants, "I would give you this, but it's a bit heavy for a girl of your size. Kicks like a mule too. Do you know how to shoot?"

"No," Molly said. "I've not had cause to learn."

"Knives are easier to come by anyway. Try and get one. Now here, take this."

He pressed the money into her hand, and Molly accepted it with a smile.

"I don't know how to thank you," she said.

"Don't thank me," Frank said, "just pay me back one day. Now get out of here. Find somewhere and get off the streets."

Molly hurried away. *Kind of him to help*, she thought. *But surely, he will expect something in return. No one helps a person like me unless he's got some hidden reason for it. I'd be a fool not to accept though*. She found a boarding house offering rooms by the week. The clerk barely looked up from the newspaper as he took most of her money and turned over the key. As she made her way up the narrow wooden staircase, her heartbeat accelerated. Her mind projected the image of herself walking up a similar staircase at the last boarding house she'd entered. With Ellen in her arms. And a room, and ruin, awaiting her at the top.

Molly stopped midway up and leaned against the wall. *I can't*, she thought. *I can't stay here. I'll go down and ask for my money back. No … I have to stay. I have to go on.*

Slowly, she lifted a foot to the next step. It took her five minutes to reach the top, but the visions cleared when she did. Molly found her room, midway down the hallway. It contained a bed, a nightstand with a wash basin, and nothing more, not even a chair. A single small window directly above the headboard of the bed looked out over a narrow alley where a group of dirty children lounged near the carcass of a dead cat. *That's my only way out if someone tries to get in*, she thought. *And it's a long drop.*

Molly looked at the door, then at the nightstand. The heavy nightstand scraped across the floor as Molly strained to move it into place in front of the door. A bit of water sloshed out of the washbasin and once she felt the door was secure, Molly cupped her hands and drank some of the dirty liquid. It tasted more like sweat than water, but she gulped it down all the same. *It's wet enough, and that's all that matters.*

It would be impossible to stay in the room indefinitely, Molly knew that much, but she felt it best not to venture outside again until nightfall. Before she climbed into bed, Molly raised the window to provide a last-ditch escape if needed. *If it is this or jail,* she thought, *I guess this is better. I'll not go down without a fight this time. I'll not let it happen again. If they send someone to kill me, they better send an army.*

She slept until an hour after sunset. Then she rose, closed the window, removed the nightstand, and left the room. A new clerk stood behind the counter. Molly asked him if he had any paper and an envelope. He pushed a piece of stationery over to her and rummaged behind the counter until he found an envelope.

"A pencil too?" Molly asked.

The clerk rolled his eyes and took the pencil from behind his ear and handed it to her.

"Thank you, sir," Molly said.

She bent over the paper and tried to consider what to write. She decided to list only her initials and the address of her boarding house, along with a request that the address be passed on to Patrick McMahon of Hibernia Engine Company 14. Molly sealed the note inside the envelope and addressed it Dr. Howard.

"Could you see that this gets delivered for me?" she asked.

The clerk shrugged and said, "This ain't the Metropolitan Hotel. We don't deliver mail for people."

"If I leave you some money, could you maybe find a boy to deliver it?"

"I guess," the clerk said. "Must be important to you to pay for it."

"It's just a note to a friend," Molly said. She gave the clerk a coin. He took it and stared at her until she added another and said, "And this is for your trouble."

"I'll get it done tonight," the clerk said.

Molly left the boarding house and searched for an open shop where she might buy a small amount of food. Fires still burned in the distance, and the glow created an eerie halo over the city. The streets were not as deserted as the night before, but nowhere near as many people milled about as on an ordinary night. She caught fragments of conversations around her, enough to know the mobs still roamed the streets and more people had died in street battles earlier in the day. The city and the army were slowly regaining control. Block by block, they were taking the city back from those bent on its destruction. *And Patrick and Frank in the thick of it*, she thought. *I hope they are careful. Or as careful as they can be under the circumstances.*

Molly finally located an open grocery and purchased a few apples, some more bread, and a bottle of spring water. She hated to spend the money on the water when she could get it for free from any pump in the city, but as the women in the neighborhood crowded around the pumps and exchanged gossip, they'd know she didn't belong in the area and ask questions. Molly gulped down half of the water right away and decided to save the rest for later. With the money gone, Molly realized she had not obtained any means of protection. *I'll just have to hope no one comes after me*, she thought. If the man who'd attacked her was truly dead, she doubted he managed to give any information other than her first name and description. As some prostitutes used the equivalent of stage names, Molly knew a name alone would not be of much help. *But I'll stand out because of my hair*, she thought. The irony of her hair, a source of pride, now being the very thing that might bring about her doom brought a brief smile to her face.

Later, in her room, Molly barricaded the door again and ate an apple and part of her loaf of bread. Though she felt like having all of it, Molly made sure to save enough for at least one more day, if not two. *I'll figure out a way to get more later, but I have to make this last as long as I can.*

In the light of the oil lamp mounted on the wall, Molly read over the headlines in the newspaper she'd picked up from the counter when she got back to the boarding house. In bold, angry type, the paper denounced the actions of the rioters while at the same time recounting lurid details of their every move. The government decided to suspend the draft until the city got things under control. *That'll make the people happy*, she thought. *But it won't stop them. It ain't so much the draft as it is the idea of the draft.*

The open window did little to ease the stuffy feeling inside the room; there was no breeze outside to relieve the city from the heat of the summer. In the alley beneath the window, Molly heard a street walker arguing with a man over payment for services rendered. She considered asking them to move along and find some other window to stand beneath but decided against it. This is New York City. Another couple will be along in ten minutes time.

With the city falling apart around her, Molly hoped Ellen was safe, wherever she might be. *As soon as I take care of my own problems, I'll have to take the time to find her, if it can be done. I doubt she's dead, but she is likely hidden away so well that not even the police could find her.*

With little else to do, Molly put out the lamp and tried to get some rest. She managed to make it an hour or so before the sensation of a hand around her neck jolted her awake. In the darkness, she flailed her arms at her unseen assailant as her lungs gasped for air. No matter how hard she struggled, Molly could not seem to free herself. A fist pounded on the wall and a voice shouted, "Hey! Be quiet in there! I'm trying to sleep!"

She rolled over and tumbled onto the floor. The sudden jolt woke her, and she looked around the room and blinked. *Was it a dream*? It took a few minutes for her legs to respond, but Molly stood up and walked over to the nightstand barricading the door. *It's still there. And the door is still locked.* She lit the lamp and peered underneath the bed. *No one here either. Sure, it all must have been a dream. But it felt so real. Like I was back in the … no, don't think about that now.*

Chapter Sixteen

Dawn broke over a city still reeling from the explosion of violence the previous few days. With no breeze, smoke clogged the air; the city baked, as though it was a cake in a giant oven. Molly rose and scrubbed her face and hands with lukewarm water from the pitcher on the nightstand, then she carefully moved it out of the way of the door. She sat back down on the unmade bed and ate what remained of the food she'd purchased the day before. *And what now, with the money and food gone? Am I to beg? And to get out of the city too? How am I to do that? And where to go?*

When she was eleven years old, Molly had asked her mother what would happen if the potato blight returned to Ireland. "Don't worry about that which you have no control over," Mrs. O'Sullivan said. "You'll sleep better at night that way." In a country ruled by a foreign government, it was perhaps the best course of action to take. Be silent. Draw no attention to yourself. Just quietly go about your business. *And doesn't that serve me well too in America? What I wouldn't give to climb*

Knockma Hill one more time. If only I had Queen Maeve to tell me what to do. Would she tell me to run or to stay and fight? She smiled at the image in her head of her younger self climbing the well-worn path up the hill, only to frown as an image of Ellen replaced the image of her. *Where is she now? And what is she doing? Is she scared? Is she waiting for me to come and find her? But what can I do to find her when the peelers are after throwing me in the cells?*

Sweat trickled down her face in the stuffy atmosphere of her room. Molly opened the window, but there was no breeze. The haze of smoke outside made the air taste foul. She coughed once and closed the window, preferring the stale odor of sweat to the that of burned wood. *I cannot bear to sit in here all day,* she thought, *but do I risk the dangers of the street?* She debated with herself for several minutes and decided to chance it outside. *If the police get me, or the man what's been sent to kill me,* she thought, *at least I'll die outside in the sun.*

"Any messages for me?" she asked the clerk downstairs.

"No," he replied. "Are you expecting any?"

"I don't know," Molly confessed. "I'll be out for the day if anyone delivers a note. Would you keep it for me if they do?"

"This is a hotel, not a post office."

Molly flashed a smile and said, "I'd be ever so grateful if you did me such a kind favor, sir. Grateful indeed."

"I guess I can take a message for you," the clerk said.

"Thank you." *If I learned anything at Miss Cecilia's,* Molly thought, *it's how to manipulate men with a smile. So easy to control, they are. Smile and bat your eyes and they melt in your hands like butter on a hot plate.*

Outside, people stood around in small groups as they talked with low voices, but there was no sign of the larger crowds from the previous two days. It was as if the riots sapped the strength of the masses and left them gasping for breath. Molly caught snatches of conversations, most of which centered on the number of dead, as high as a thousand some said. *They'll be saying ten thousand by the end of the day,* she thought as she made her way down the street. She wanted to put a bit of distance between herself and her lodgings so that in the event she was recognized, it would be easier to elude a pursuer and return to her room.

Molly saw four police officers approaching from the opposite direction, their stout clubs slapping rhythmically into their left palms as they swept the streets with narrow, weary eyes. She quickly turned and pretended to take great interest in a dress displayed in a shop window. *They are as nervous as I am*, she thought. *The week's events have them jumpy as all hell. No doubt they'll bash the head of the first man or woman who so much as spits in their direction. That's the norm of it for them though.*

A few brave, or perhaps foolhardy, souls ventured to shout insults at the policemen, but went no further. She breathed a sigh of relief as the officers moved up the street. *It's a good thing I've never had a photo taken of myself.*

A newsboy on the corner shouted gory headlines detailing the pitched battles fought in the streets the past few days. He allowed Molly to borrow a paper long enough to scan it, looking for news about the death of Miss Cecilia. She found it on the next-to-last page.

A FOUL MURDER!

SCARLET WOMAN SOUGHT IN THE DEATH OF BELOVED 6TH WARD RESIDENT

On Monday last, a woman of ill fame, late of Ireland and with the criminality common to her race, set fire to the premises of Miss Cecilia's, located on Mulberry Street in the 6th Ward. As smoke and flames ravaged the building, a fine example of our city's best sporting houses, the destruction hid another deed more hideous than the first. Once the fire was out, the police discovered the body of Miss Cecilia, a woman of considerable influence in the community, roasted to death in the confines of the establishment she ran for many years. An employee of said establishment told the police that as the place burned, she observed a certain other employee, a Molly O'Sullivan of Ireland, rain blows upon Miss Cecilia in a fiendish manner, leaving her wounded body prostrate on the floor at the mercy of the flames. The police were unable to give immediate pursuit to this villainous woman as the fire coincided with the outrageous and traitorous actions of certain residents of our city in opposition to the draft. At present, they are offering a $50 reward for any information leading to her capture.

Molly O'Sullivan is described as being around 5'2 or 5'3 and slight of frame with red hair and brown eyes. If you know of her whereabouts, please contact the 6th Precinct Headquarters on Franklin Street with all possible dispatch. Anyone capable of such a shocking outrage cannot be allowed to roam our streets to strike again when the next murderous rage overtakes her. Think of your own dear ones at home! Do you want them to sleep safely in their beds? Such a hideous creature as this needs a speedy trial and an even speedier trip to the gallows.

Molly handed the newspaper back to the boy and shook her head as she walked away. *They make me sound like I'm a cold-blooded murderer*, she thought, *and the whole thing was just an accident. It's Liza who told the lies. But why? I know she dislikes me, but enough to lie to the police?*

It made no sense, but Molly knew the damage had already been done. A group of firemen trudged up the street, without their engine. Black soot stained their faces. One man had a bloody bandage wrapped around his head; a sling supported another man's arm. They walked with a weariness that made them look decades older. All of them had a black number six embroidered on their shirt. *Boss Tweed's men*, Molly thought. *Ain't that what Patrick called them? Americus. That's their company name.*

"Excuse me, sirs," Molly said as they drew abreast of her, "Can you give me any news of the Hibernia company on Elizabeth Street?"

"Don't know much, miss," the fireman with the bandaged head said. "Heard they got into a bit of a scrap last night uptown somewhere. Mob went after them with brickbats and paving stones."

"Are any of them hurt?" Molly asked. "I have a friend with them, you see."

"A few of 'em were," the fireman said. "Heard one was killed too. Someone threw a brick down on him from a rooftop. Hit him in the head and split his skull. Least that's what I heard."

"Do you know his name?"

"Don't know nothing more than what I just told you, miss. Now if you'll excuse us. We need to catch up on about a week's worth of sleep."

Molly stepped aside to allow the men to pass. She felt sympathy for them, as she'd witnessed their attempts to save the city with her own eyes. *Is it better to die at the hands of your own people or far away on a battlefield at the hands of a stranger*, she wondered. For a moment, she considered making her way to Hibernia's station on Elizabeth Street, but dismissed the thought as soon as it came to her. *Too close to Miss Cecilia's. Someone would be sure to recognize me there. But somehow, I must find out about Patrick. I hope he's not among the injured.*

As she considered her next move, Molly noticed a man leaning against a building across the street with a hat pulled low over his face. Though he appeared to be looking down at the street, she noticed every so often he looked up at her and then quickly turned his eyes away. She felt a chill travel down her spine. *He's trying too hard to make it look like he's not after watching me*, she thought. *Is he a detective? Or a hired killer?*

She had no desire to find out which the man was, but she knew that to turn and run would only draw more attention. When a group of young women, domestic workers by the looks of them, walked by, Molly fell in alongside them. Out of her peripheral vision, she saw the man step away from the building and trail along from a discreet distance. *How did he recognize me? I'm covered in dirt and I've got my hair tucked up under a bonnet. Am I that noticeable or is he just acting on suspicion?*

"On your way to work?" one of the young women asked Molly.

"I am," Molly replied.

"Who do you work for?"

"Um," Molly hesitated, "well, you see, I'm not actually employed presently, but I am hoping to find work today. I'm very skilled with a needle. Perhaps I can find someone in need of a seamstress."

"I wish you luck."

"Thank you," Molly replied. She wanted to turn and see if the man was still following her, but she knew that would be too obvious. *Better I don't let on that I know he's there. Not yet anyway.*

Headed north, away from her room, Molly tried to plot a route that would allow her to make a wide circle back to the relative safety of the boarding house. After another few blocks, Molly suddenly stepped away from the group of young women and ducked into an alley. She darted past sleeping drunks and a group of orphaned children sprawled in a doorway, then turned down a second alley. Taking refuge behind a large stack of wooden crates, she paused and waited to see if the man would follow her. *He'll either come after me or wait for me to leave the alley. If it's me that he's after, that is.*

Several minutes passed and then she heard the footsteps.

Her heart pounded as she scanned the ground for something, anything, to use as a weapon. She settled upon a large rock and scooped it off the ground. The rough wood dug into her back as she pressed herself against the crates and waited, swallowing hard to try and calm herself. The man moved with slow, deliberate steps as if he were afraid she might hear him.

As the man moved past the crates, Molly caught sight of the knife blade in his hand. Her heartbeat accelerated, and she felt the moisture on her palms. Moving the rock from her right hand to her left, she rubbed her hand on her skirt to dry it. *He's not a peeler then*, she realized. *He means to kill me.*

The man took a few more steps, his eyes fixed on a point down the alley where shadows danced along the wooden walls.

It's now or I'll lose my chance!

She stepped behind him and brought the rock down on the base of the man's neck with all the force she could muster. He grunted and dropped the knife as his legs wobbled. She bashed him again for good measure, and he crumpled to the ground. Molly grabbed the knife and tucked it into her boot. As she turned to run, the man's hand shot out from under him and grabbed her ankle. She stomped on it twice with her other foot and then delivered a kick to his head. When his grip relaxed, she dashed back toward the street.

Molly did not stop running until she burst through the door of the boarding house. The clerk looked up, startled.

"Where's the fire?" he asked.

"No fire," Molly gasped. The word fire reminded her of Patrick. She shook her head to ward off the gloom that seized her. "I just realized I … forgot something in my room."

"Something important, I'd say."

Molly shrugged and said, "A bit, yes."

When she got to the room, Molly reached down and took the knife from her boot, tucking it under the pillow on the bed. She stood and paced the room as the minutes and then hours passed with glacial slowness. The heat increased as the day wore on. She felt red creep up her chest and into her face. Despite the smoky haze, Molly had to open the window in a vain attempt to coax even the smallest breeze into the room. After an eternity, the sun finally began to sink over the horizon as if exhausted from its brutal assault on the city. But the heat and the excitement and danger of the day made her weary, and soon Molly found herself sitting on the bed and fighting to stay awake.

What's a short nap? Surely Dr. Howard will knock when he gets here and that will wake me up, though I'm nowhere near presentable enough for guests. And that's if he even comes.

She closed her eyes, intending it to be for a few minutes, but when she jerked awake later, the room was dark. Molly froze on the bed and listened. Her ears caught the slight sound of footsteps, and then a hand rattled the doorknob. She leapt from the bed and grabbed the knife. Moving on the balls of her feet, Molly crept closer to the window.

"Who's there?" she asked in a loud whisper, but there was no answer.

"Dr. Howard?" she asked, louder this time. "Is that you?"

The doorknob stopped moving. For two minutes, the only sounds in the room came from the street through the open window and her heartbeat. *Maybe it's just my imagination*, she told herself. *I'm just jumpy from what happened earlier today and back … back then. It's nothing. I'm frightened over shadows, that's all.*

The door jolted inward with a sudden crash, though the nightstand kept it from opening completely. Molly screamed and took several steps back. She held the knife in front of her, with the tip pointed at the door. *Shite*, she swore. *I guess I didn't hit him hard enough after all.*

"Open up, God damn you!" a man's voice yelled, "Or I'll make sure it takes all night for you to die. You hear me? Open the fucking door!"

The door jolted again, opening further this time, as the man struck it with his foot. Molly only had a few seconds to consider her options. Despite the knife, she doubted she could hold her own against someone in such close quarters. That only left one thing. Molly walked over the window and lifted her leg to tuck the knife in her boot. She turned and lowered herself backwards, holding on to the ledge with her hands. After one more kick, the door shattered. A large man, bigger than the man from earlier in the day, swatted the furniture aside and looked around the room. When his eyes met Molly's, she released her hold on the window and dropped down into the street below.

Chapter Seventeen

Molly's knees buckled and she sprawled on the ground. She rolled to her right and sprang to her feet. Her assailant spewed profanity and threats from the window as Molly hurried down the street. In the darkness, she hoped to lose him in the maze of twisting alleyways and blackened corners. After what seemed like an hour, though it was really a matter of minutes, Molly collapsed in the doorway of a shop to catch her breath. She drew her knees up in front of her, resting her forehead against them as her lungs spasmed for want of air. *And what am I to do now? The bit of money's gone, and I can't go back to my room. I can't go to Dr. Howard. Someone might recognize me.*

Two pigs sauntered down the alley, pausing to snort curiously at Molly before they moved on. Once her breathing slowed, Molly stood up and walked along behind the pigs. When they stopped to fight over the carcass of a dead cat, Molly parted company with them. After the sudden terror of the night's attack started to wane, her eyelids began to droop with exhaustion. *Sure, I'm not cut out for the outlaw life. A terrible*

Fenian I'd make.

Near the back entrance to a dressmaker's shop, Molly found a few wooden crates and boxes. She arranged them in the shape of an *L* with the tip against the wall. Molly huddled behind the barrier and soon drifted into an uneasy sleep.

"Hey! What are you doing?"

Molly opened her eyes and blinked in the gray light of dawn. A man stood over her, hands on his hips and a frown on his face.

"You can't be sleeping back here," he said.

"And why not?" Molly asked as she got to her feet. The man's position blocked her only avenue of escape. Her eyes traveled down to her boot and the knife. "America is a free country, is it not?"

"America may be, but this alley ain't. You wanna sleep here, you gotta pay me for the privilege. You can pay me in coin or in trade, if you take my meaning."

"I'll just be on my way," Molly said as she stepped toward the man, intending to force her way past.

He put a hand on her chest and shoved her back.

"You owe me for one night," he said. "Settle your account, and then you can go on about your business."

Molly defaulted to the tone of voice she used in Miss Cecilia's parlor as she smiled at the man and said, "I do have some money, sir. I keep it tucked in my boot. You can have it all if you'd like."

The man grunted and watched her drop to one knee. Molly slowly raised the hem of her skirt, enough to expose several inches of her stockings. She felt the man's eyes traveling up her leg and slipped her right hand into her boot and took hold of the knife blade. *Don't stab him unless you have to*, she warned herself. *No need to attract even more attention from the peelers.*

In one fluid motion, Molly pulled the knife out as she rose to her feet. With her elbow tucked against her side, she moved the blade menacingly back and forth in front of her. Surprised, the man took several steps backwards as Molly advanced on him.

"Wait … wait!" the man said. "I meant you no harm! Look! You can go!"

"If I hear of you trying to take advantage of fallen women," Molly said, her voice gone flat and emotionless, "I'll hunt you down and carve out your liver. Understand? You wouldn't be the first man I've had to stick my blade in."

She feinted a slight lunge in his direction, and the man turned and fled. Molly laughed as she put the knife back in her boot. *Typical bully, all thunder and lightning until you threaten them.*

The morning brought more people into the streets, which provided some opportunity for her to blend in and escape detection, but at the same time, it brought more policemen out as well and increased the potential that someone might recognize her. With her stomach issuing a stern protest at the lack of food, Molly moved uptown, where she knew no one. She tried to keep against the buildings, only breaking away to cross intersections at as quick a pace as she could manage. Her heart froze each time she saw a police officer on patrol, but they paid her no mind. *Still*, she thought, *it'll only take one to come after me and then I've had it.*

The further uptown she traveled, the better the clothing she saw in the shop windows and on those around her. Even the streets smelled better than in the squalid 6th Ward. Her dirty and disheveled appearance drew looks of disgust from several women, who turned their noses up and made comments about someone not knowing their place in voices loud enough for to Molly to hear. Well-dressed men in waistcoats with gold watch chains tipped their hats or scowled at her, depending on their preference. *Fecking toffs*, she thought. *The lot of them wouldn't survive a night in the Five Points.* She smiled at the thought of men in fine clothing pursued down Mulberry Street by a swarm of b'hoys. *Ah, that would be a grand thing to see. I'd pay for the pleasure of watching it, if I had the money, of course.*

As the day wore on, Molly stopped and sat down on a bench to take stock of her situation and determine a plan for the evening. She considered presenting herself at another house of ill fame and offering her services but dismissed the idea as quickly as she'd thought of it. *The other madams all know Miss Cecilia, and even if they didn't like her, they'd turn me over to the police as quick as they could.*

To escape the city, she needed money. Attempting to find a job was out of the question, as any reputable employer would guess her previous line of work. *I won't stoop to lifting my skirts in an alley. Starvation is better.* Her stomach rumbled again to remind her of the real possibility that she might. *Or is it a life of crime I must turn to*? She smiled as she thought of herself in a highwayman's mask and brandishing a revolver. Her smile quickly turned to a frown as a group of men pushed past her.

"Watch where you're walking, you bastards," Molly called after them. One man turned and spit in her direction before he continued up the street.

A few gowns in a shop window caught Molly's eye and she drifted over to look at them. *Wouldn't I look like a grand lady in that one*, Molly thought as she looked at a purple gown. *Not that I'll ever be able to afford such a thing as that.*

A company of soldiers came down the street as Molly turned away from the window. Though their rifles looked well oiled, dust covered their leather belts and most of their blue coats and trousers bore patches. The crowds in the street parted to let the unit pass, and several people broke into applause and shouted huzzahs, though the soldiers loped along as if indifferent to the world around them. *Ah sure, the soldier boys are heroes to the fat cats what live up here. Protecting them from the rabble like me what comes from the 6th Ward.*

Molly turned and made her way east, towards the river. She moved with no sense of purpose as she did not have a destination in mind. Sweat ran down her back and dripped off the end of her nose as the sun continued its attack upon the city. With no money to purchase a drink, Molly kept an eye out for a pump. Finding one behind a restaurant that advertised oysters and fresh fish in the window, she removed her bonnet and leaned down as she pumped the lever with her right hand. Lukewarm water splashed over her red curls. She gulped a few mouthfuls and nearly spit it back out. The foul odor of the water matched the taste, but it was wet, and she forced herself to swallow it. *With my luck, I'll catch the flux from it*, Molly thought as she walked away. *That would solve my problem of no money and no lodgings.*

She spent another restless night in an alley, listening to the streetwalkers ply their trade as the sound of drunken shouting and the tolling of fire bells kept her from much rest. By the time the sun rose, she was even more tired than the day before and as wrathful as a rattlesnake. She felt weak, though she did not know if it was from lack of food or lack of sleep. *I've no choice*, she said to herself as she stood and stretched her back and arms. *Today I've got to find a way to get to Dr. Howard without the peelers spotting me. Or anyone else I know. And maybe I can find word of Patrick as well. Sure, it's a risk. But has my whole life not already been a risk? With a little luck, I'll manage to get down there and back unseen or at least unrecognized.*

Molly managed to make it to the intersection of Elizabeth and Canal Streets, just across from Hibernia's fire station, when her luck ran out.

"Hey! You! Stop!"

She turned and saw a heavyset policeman waddling in her direction. Sergeant Daniels! From Miss Cecilia's, Molly realized. Her eyes darted left and right, searching the faces around her to see if by chance one of them was the object of the officer's attention. None of them gave any indication of alarm. *Go*, she told herself. *Run.*

It took her a moment for her legs to obey the command. The policeman gave a loud blast on his whistle as Molly sprinted down Elizabeth Street. *I can lose him in Mulberry Bend*, she thought. *If I can get there.* She doubted the overweight policeman could keep up with her, but she knew others, alerted by his whistle, might block her path.

As she turned onto Bayard, she chanced a glance back over her shoulder. The officer huffed along behind her, shoving people out his way. Molly collided with an apple cart and sprawled atop the contents, which spilled into the street along with the man who pushed it.

"Look at what you've done!" he growled as people in the street pounced on the apples and snatched them up.

Molly got to her feet and shouted a quick apology over her shoulder as she hurried away. With the officer's curses ringing in her ears, she turned onto Mott Street and then into an alley which would take her across to Mulberry Street and the maze of narrow passages which offered her only chance at refuge. Another police officer stepped into her path. Molly twisted away as he tried to grab her. He swung his club in a great arc, aiming for her head, but she was already past him.

When she reached Mulberry Bend, Molly slowed her pace as drunk men and women lounged along the alley in various states of consciousness. A group of children, dirty and covered in scabs, sat in a circle on the ground. Molly knelt beside them.

"Can you help me?" she asked.

"With what?" one of them asked, his eyes narrow and guarded.

"It's the peelers after me," Molly said. "If you see one come this way, do you think you could slow him down?"

"Fucking booly-dogs," the boy said. He spat a glob of phlegm on the ground to punctuate his dislike of the police. "Aye, we'll do better than that. Ain't none of the bastards come very far in the Bend anyway. We'll just encourage 'em to go elsewhere."

"Thank you," Molly said. "I've only a smile to pay you with. I hope that's enough."

"Go on, miss," the boy said. "Leave it to us."

The buildings overhead all but blocked out the sun. Molly slowed her pace to a walk to allow her lungs to recover their wind. She felt dizzy, as though the ground moved rather than her feet. *It's the hunger I'm feeling*, she thought. *Like when I was a girl.* Images like photographs danced through her mind—her grandparents as they lay dead beside one another; her father, ravaged by fever and want of food; the line of bodies alongside the road to Galway City; and the sight of children, with swollen bellies and shrunken eyes. *Make it stop*, she told herself, hands pressed to her temples. *I don't want to think about that now.* She shivered despite the heat of the day. *It's a cursed people we are. Luck of the Irish, they say. Ah, but the only luck we have is the kind to make you wish you were among the departed.*

As she moved along, she passed a man in mid congress with a prostitute. The woman faced the wall with her skirt hiked to her waist. The man, who stood behind her, winked at Molly as she walked by. Her stomach growled and spasmed as if to encourage her to reconsider her decision to starve rather than reducing herself to soliciting customers in the streets. Every so often, Molly looked over her shoulder to see if anyone was following her, but she only saw shadows. *I'll be safe here until nightfall,* she thought, *then maybe I can find Dr. Howard.* She frowned when she considered that safety and Mulberry Bend were not commonly used in the same sentence.

Heavy with fatigue, Molly sank to the ground with her back to a wall, lest someone sneak up behind her. She drew her knees to her chest and wrapped her arms around them. *Maybe down here in the dark, no one will see me if they walk by. Just an hour or two, and then I'll be off.* She closed her eyes and rested her forehead upon her knees. The sounds of clinking bottles, laughter, and debauchery swirled around her. Her nose caught a whiff of smoke, though from a cookfire or a burning building, she could not tell. The sounds lulled her to sleep for a brief moment. When she opened her eyes, a large shadow loomed over her. Molly screamed, more in surprise than fear, as her hand reached for her knife. She rolled to her side and scrambled to her feet, knife held in front of her.

"Come on," she said, "if it's me you want, you'll have to pay the piper first."

The shape in the dark said nothing and Molly took a step forward.

"Get lost," she shouted. "I'll not hesitate to stick you."

"Shhh … keep your voice down, Molly," Frank said.

Chapter Eighteen

"You are a regular hellcat, Molly," Frank said. "Could you put the knife away now?"

"What's gotten into you?" Molly demanded as she knelt and tucked the knife in her boot. "Nearly scared the life out of me, you did. Do you make a habit of sneaking up on helpless girls in the dark?"

"You ain't exactly helpless. The officers what walk this beat all know you was spotted earlier today. Sergeant Daniels said he saw you disappear into Mulberry Bend. They plan to turn this place inside out come sunrise. That's why I came to find you. You can't stay here. Not unless you fancy being hauled off to the gaol in the morning. Why didn't you stay put inside somewhere? Jesus! Are you trying to get caught?"

"Someone tried to attack me in my room, but I got away," Molly said. That's how come I'm out here on the streets. But I spent the money you loaned me on a room and some food. It's gone now."

"I think I've found a way to get you out of the city. I'm afraid you won't like what it is," Frank said, "but it's the only chance you got."

Molly's heart leapt with anticipation, but she kept her voice calm. "And what would that be?"

"Not here," Frank said. "Come on. I know a place we can speak in private."

He grabbed her wrist and pulled her along. At first, she tried to protest, but fell silent when she realized that his chance, whatever it was, might be the only way for her to escape an early grave. Before they emerged onto Baxter Street, Frank tugged his hat low across his face and threw his arm around Molly's shoulders.

"Lean into me a bit," he said. "Like we're the worse for the drink."

She did as he requested, wrinkling her nose at the odor of cheap tobacco which rose from his coat. The two made their way down past the Grand Duke's Opera House to the narrow lane that ran between Pearl and Baxter Streets. Midway down the lane, Frank steered her around to the side of a wood frame house which leaned precariously to the left. He opened a door and motioned her to go in ahead of him. She stepped into the blackness. The musty smell reminded her of the stables at Lord Sanderson's estate. Frank lit an oil lamp. Shadows danced along the bare wooden walls. The small room contained a bed, two chairs, and a desk. There was only one door, the one which they had used to enter the room.

"Is this where you live?" she asked. "I thought the city paid you a wee bit better than that."

"Pay us better? Not likely," Frank said. "But I don't live here. At least not all the time. It's a room I rent under a different name. Makes my detective work easier sometimes. The department don't know I have it since I pay for it myself and leave it off my reports. You can have a seat on the bed if you'd like."

"I'll stand if it's all the same to you."

"Fine, now, hear me out and don't make your decision until I've a chance to tell you what I need to tell you."

"Enough with the suspense, Francis Lynch," Molly exclaimed. "Just say it and be done."

"I know a respectable woman of this city who is engaged in a bit of business on behalf of some enterprises in New Orleans. With it being an important port and with the ongoing war, well, they've need of certain services there. Do you follow?"

"Services?" Molly asked. "I ain't a blacksmith if that's what they are after."

"No, no," Frank said as he waved a hand. "They are in need of, shall we say, services of the flesh. My contact here in New York City is recruiting suitable ladies who are willing to go down there and work. They say the brothels in New Orleans are the finest in the world."

"You mean to send me off to whore in the Confederacy?"

"It's not the Confederacy anymore," Frank said. "We took it back in '62."

I wanted to be done with whoring, she thought. *And now I'm offered one way to escape the gallows or a knife blade, and it is to travel God knows how far to do the same thing I done here.*

"How would I pay to get there?" Molly asked. "I'll not take any more of your money."

"That's good because I have no more to give," Frank said with a smile. "But to answer your question, if you meet with my contact and she likes you, then your passage is free. Or rather, she covers it. You'll be given a letter of reference to present to a particular establishment in New Orleans when you arrive. It costs you nothing."

Nothing but your reputation, Molly thought, *but it ain't like I have a good one anyway*. She stayed silent for a few minutes and considered Frank's words. Molly knew that to remain in New York was out of the question, if she intended to stay alive. With the police after her, and a hired assassin on her trail, Molly understood her freedom could be measured in days, if not hours. *What's more important*, she asked herself, *my life or not having to service men in order to survive? It's the devil's own choice I have.*

"How long do I have to decide?" Molly asked.

"A few minutes," Frank said. "My contact has almost filled her quota and the ship sails tomorrow afternoon. If you are interested, I'll bring you to meet her straight away. Or rather, maybe you can go somewhere and get cleaned up first and then I'll take you to meet her."

"Go somewhere to get cleaned up?" Molly asked. "You mean like a horse trough? I've no money for a bath house."

"I know a Chinese woman what runs a laundry place around the corner. She owes me a couple of favors since I look the other way about the opium she sells out the back door. She's got a tub you could use and maybe she can clean your dress up a bit while you wash."

"Yes, well, I haven't exactly been staying at the Metropolitan Hotel."

Frank laughed as Molly's mind worked over her predicament. She frowned as Ellen's face flashed in her head.

"I can't go anywhere," she said. "I've got to find Ellen."

"I've got my boys out looking for her," Franks said.

"And what good would that do?" Molly snapped. "It's your people what got their fingers in every kind of sin this city has to offer. Tell me I'm wrong."

"You are not," Frank said as he shook his head. "I understand your need to find the child. I truly do. But you can't find her if you are swinging from the gallows or floating in the East River, can you? Why don't you let me keep my ear to the street, as it has been, and make your escape. If I find her, why, I can send her to you. If enough time passes, it'll be safe for you to come back to the city and take up the search once more, if need be."

"But I'd be abandoning the girl again," Molly said. She flinched as the image of a man carrying a screaming Ellen out of the room bored its way to the front of her brain. Her eyes watered, and she bit her lip to try and force the tears away.

Frank stepped close to her and put his hands on her shoulders. He squeezed them gently and gazed into her eyes.

"Listen to me, Molly," he said. "I know you feel responsible for what happened to her. And I know you mean to rescue her from wherever she is now. But if you stay here, you are going to come to a bad end. If that happens, there will be no one to find young Ellen. The only chance to save her is to save yourself first. As distasteful as it might be for you. That's the only way. I'm begging you, Molly. Please."

"And why do you care what happens to a whore like me?" Molly asked. "Do I strike your fancy or something?"

"Does it matter why?" Frank asked.

Molly shrugged and said, "I guess not. I will take your offer of help. Not that I have much of a choice. But I've one more question for you. Do you know the whereabouts of Patrick McMahon of the Hibernia Fire Company? I heard a rumor that someone from that company had been killed."

Frank turned away from Molly and pretended to wipe dust from his coat. "I've not heard anything about it. Sorry."

Damn, Molly thought. *So it is true. Another kind Irish boy dead. He was kinder to me than me own mother, and him only knowing me for a few months. Gone now.*

"Shall we go to the laundry then?" Molly asked once she regained her voice. "I fear I may lose my nerve otherwise."

"Yeah," Frank said. "Let's go."

An hour later, her dress and skin scrubbed clean and her red curls pinned atop her head, Molly made her way through the dark streets with Frank by her side. Neither spoke a word as they trudged uptown. When they reached the hotel, Frank held the door open but did not follow Molly inside.

"Aren't you coming with me?" she asked.

"No," Frank said. "Just go on up to room 24. Knock on the door and tell her that Frank Lynch sent you. And she'll get you squared away."

Molly frowned and said, "Fine. Thank you for helping me, Detective Lynch. I hope one day to be able to repay the kindness you've shown me."

"That won't be necessary. As soon as I find out anything, no matter how small, about young Ellen, I'll be in touch. And it's Frank, or have you forgotten?"

"How will you find me?" Molly asked.

"I'll get in touch with the missus and she can let me know where to send a telegram."

Molly stood there for a moment and tried to think of something, anything to say. *How do you thank the man what saves your life? There's no words to do that.*

With a slight shake of her head, she walked over to Frank and stood on her toes to give him a kiss on the cheek. As she walked away, she chanced a glance over her shoulder and saw him standing there with the fingertips of his right hand pressed to the spot where her lips had brushed his skin.

A well-dressed woman of indeterminate age answered the door to Room 24.

"Can I help you?" she asked.

Molly gave what she hoped was an acceptable curtsy and said, "My name is Molly O'Sullivan, ma'am. Frank Lynch sent me to see you. He said that, well, he said that you might be able to help me."

"With what?"

"To … to … secure a position in New Orleans, ma'am."

"Come in."

The woman introduced herself as Miss Alexandria Miles as she seated Molly in a chair and offered a drink of whiskey, which Molly refused.

"You do understand what type of work it is you'd be doing?"

"I do, ma'am," Molly said. "It's work I've done before."

"I assumed as much, you being a friend of Frank Lynch."

"What do you mean?" Molly asked.

"He's got an eye for the whores," Alexandria said. "His mother took to the work when they arrived in the city. He grew up around them. He knows every bordello in this city inside and out. But he's a kind man, for a policeman. Now, tell me your story."

Molly explained how she'd come to work in a house of ill fame, though she left out any mention of Ellen and of the circumstances which led to her being on the run. Alexandria listened, making sympathetic noises in all the right places that sounded a bit forced to Molly's ear, though her own voice sounded remote and detached, as if she were describing things that happened to someone else.

"Yours is a sad tale all too familiar to me," Alexandria said once Molly finished. "Girls arrive in the city thinking they can find happiness. Then someone comes along to take advantage of them. Why do you want to go to New Orleans?"

"I've heard it's a lovely city," Molly said truthfully.

"It is," Alexandria said. "Now tell me something, Molly. Do you have a talent for anything outside of the bedroom?"

"What do you mean?"

"Can you play the piano? Dance? Sing? Many of the houses in New Orleans offer entertainment beyond the horizontal variety."

"I can sing, ma'am," Molly admitted.

"Of course you can. Being Irish and all."

"Would you like me to sing something?" Molly offered.

"No," Alexandria said. "Stand up and take off your clothes."

"What?" Molly exclaimed. "Why?"

"I'll not send a girl to work down there without seeing exactly what she looks like. I've a reputation to protect. I vouch for only the cleanest, most attractive ones. It's not personal. Just business."

"If you insist," Molly said.

"I do."

Molly removed her dress. Miss Alexandria motioned for her to remove the rest. Molly took a deep breath and did as she was directed. She closed her eyes and told herself it would be over soon as Alexandria circled around her to examine her for scars or other marks. *I'm a human being, not an animal*, she thought. *There has to be another way to make it in this world. There has to be. And I'll find it or die in the attempt.*

Molly opened her mouth to expose her teeth when told to do so. Alexandria put her hand on Molly's chin, tilting her head, first to one side and then the other. Satisfied, she told Molly to put her clothes back on.

"You'll do fine in New Orleans," Alexandria said. "You're pretty enough. And have all your teeth. And you are young. Who knows? Maybe you'll snag yourself an army officer that will overlook your occupation and marry you. It's been known to happen."

"I don't think I've the makings of a wife for anyone," Molly said. "Not anymore."

Alexandria walked across the room and grabbed a key from a desk as Molly put her clothes back on.

"Room 28 will be yours for the night," she said. "It's just down the hall. Get yourself some sleep and I'll draft a letter of introduction for you. I have a place in mind where you'll fit in quite well. The owner is Madam Delacroix. Descended from the French nobility, or so she claims. Beautiful house. I think you'll like it there. Only the wealthiest clients are allowed in the door. Call on me in the morning and I'll give you the letter and your ticket to board the ship. It leaves in the early afternoon."

"Thank you, ma'am."

"Where's your luggage?"

"Ma'am?" Molly asked.

"Your suitcase. Don't you have a change of clothes or personal items?"

"No ma'am," Molly said as her heart fluttered. *Damn. Now she'll know I'm on the run for something. Why didn't I think of that*!

Alexandria studied her for a moment and said, "I see. Well, let me see what I can scrounge up. I'm sure I can find you at least one more dress and a change of undergarments. It wouldn't do to show up not looking your absolute best."

"I would appreciate that, ma'am," Molly said. "But I've no money to pay you for it."

"There's no need," Alexandria said. "I'll receive a healthy enough commission once you and the other girls arrive. It'll be more than enough to cover the cost of a few articles of clothing."

"You are too kind, ma'am," Molly said.

"No," Alexandria replied. "I'm a businesswoman. That is all. Now, I'll bid you good night."

Molly gasped when she lit the oil lamp in her hotel room. It was larger than any bedroom she'd ever seen. A large, soft bed with feather pillows took up part of the room, but it also contained a small sofa, a cushioned chair, and a table with a wash basin. A vase with flowers sat atop the desk and gave the room a pleasant smell, like a warm spring afternoon. *It's a room fit for the queen herself*, she thought as she sat down on the bed and bounced up and down for a minute. *Are the houses in New Orleans like this? It'd be easy to pretend you weren't a whore if I had a room like this of my own.*

She undressed quickly, excited by the prospect of a night's sleep in such surroundings. She fell asleep within minutes of her head touching the pillow.

Several hours later, Molly awoke with the feeling that a heavy hand was pressing down on her chest. She tried to move, tried to scream, but couldn't. Her heart pounded and she struggled to take air into her lungs. For what seemed like an eternity, she hovered on the edge of consciousness and the terrors within her own mind. Finally, her heart slowed to normal and she took a large gulp of air. *It was all just a dream*, she told herself. *Just a dream. That's all. Everything will be right in the morning*. She got out of bed and spent the rest of the night in the chair, where she hoped the ghosts from her first night in New York would not find her.

Chapter Nineteen

The ship, named the *Lady Anne*, was larger and more accommodating than the *Dublin Rose* had been. As she walked up the gangway, she cast a glance over her shoulder. Her eyes searched the faces in the crowd around the docks. *Is there an assassin waiting for me? Or the peelers come to haul me off to the cells?* Molly encountered nine other young women on board. A large, balding man who introduced himself as Morris said that he would be accompanying them on the voyage. He paired the girls up, and then led them to their staterooms. Molly found herself assigned to a room with a young German woman who introduced herself as Hannah.

"I come from the town of Munich," Hannah said as she placed her suitcase on one of the narrow beds. "It is in the south of Germany."

"I'm from Ireland," Molly said. "Are your parents in America too?"

"They are. We have a large family. I am eighteen and the oldest of eight children. My father said it was time for me to make my own way, and so I was sent to New York last year."

"What did you do when you got there?" Molly regretted the question as soon as she asked.

Hannah looked down and said, "I did what I had to do to survive."

"As did I," Molly said. "As did all of us, I reckon."

The routine on board the ship differed little from her previous experience at sea. Molly quickly regained her sea legs and the gentle rock of swells lulled her to sleep each night. She noticed Hannah did not sleep much. Sometimes at night, Molly awoke and saw her sitting on the floor, knees drawn up to her chest, as she stared off into the darkness as if looking for a life that no longer existed. She said even less than she slept. Other than the initial conversation, Molly found attempts to draw Hannah into talking resulted in single-word answers or outright silence. After a time, Molly gave up. The other girls proved far more talkative and held endless discussions about what they might find in New Orleans. All speculation, of course, for none had ever visited the city.

When Molly mentioned that she was headed to work for a Madam Delacroix, the other girls spoke up with the names of the establishments they were destined for. Except for two girls bound for a place on Royal Street, according to their letters of introduction, none of the others would be together once they arrived in the city.

The ship stopped in Key West to take on provisions and discharge a few passengers. The young women were not permitted to go ashore, but from the deck, Molly studied the houses and the bustle of the harbor. A large stone fort—called Fort Zachary Taylor, according to Morris—overlooked the town. Most of the men wore uniforms; in addition to the soldiers at the fort, there were soldiers from the two naval vessels in the harbor. In the afternoon, shortly before they got underway, an officer visited the ship and spoke with the captain. Molly overhead enough of the conversation to know that the navy wanted the *Lady Anne* to exercise caution in the Gulf of Mexico as there were rumors of a Confederate commerce raider prowling about somewhere between Havana and New Orleans.

"What is a commerce raider?" she asked Morris later that night.

"It's sort of like a pirate ship," he said.

Pirates, Molly thought as she made her way to her cabin. *I thought those days were over a long time ago. Sure, didn't we all hear the stories of Grace O'Malley growing up! A brave woman, she was, telling Queen Elizabeth herself to get bent.*

Molly found Hannah sitting on the edge of her bed with tears in her eyes.

"What's wrong, Hannah?" Molly said as she sat down and put her arm around the young woman's shoulder. "Are you ill?"

Hannah turned and buried her face in Molly's shoulder, as sobs racked her thin frame.

"Shhhh," Molly said as she stroked her hair. "It's all right. Everything will be all right." *Are you saying that for her or for you*, Molly asked herself.

Hannah looked up at her and said, "I do not think I can keep doing this. Not anymore. I never wanted to end up a …"

"I know," Molly said as her own eyes watered. "Neither did I. It just sort of happened. But think of it, Hannah. We're off to New Orleans and things must be better there. For they could surely not be worse."

"It can always be worse," Hannah said.

"Sure you ain't Irish?" Molly asked. "That's something me ma would say."

"But it is true," Hannah insisted.

"Don't think of it that way," Molly said as she wiped a tear from the girl's face. "You won't be doing this forever, you know. Some man will come along and fall in love with you and then this will all be like a bad dream and nothing more. You have to believe that."

But I don't believe it myself, Molly thought. *Sure, Frank Lynch helped me get away from New York, but it was to exchange whoring in New York for whoring in New Orleans. But at least I'm alive. There's a victory in that.*

"Listen now," Molly said. "Let me tell you of Queen Maeve and Knockma Hill back home. It's a grand story. You'll love it."

Hannah fell asleep before Molly finished the story. Gently, Molly eased her down on the bed, removed her shoes, and tucked her under the covers. She whispered, "Sleep well" before slipping out of the cabin.

On the main deck, she watched the crew go about their tasks. They laughed and joked with one another as they worked. No one shouted any commands, and the captain was nowhere in sight. *A happy ship, this*, she thought. *Unlike the tyrant what ran the Dublin Rose*. She smiled as she remembered the kindness of the old sailor, Babbins. *A nice man, that one. Very kind to wee Ellen.*

Her mind wandered back to that night aboard the *Dublin Rose* when she heard the young Scottish sailor sing. Without realizing it, Molly started to sing it herself.

Maxwellton's braes are bonnie when early fa's the dew
And it was there my Annie Laurie gave me her promise true
Gave me her promise true. Which ne'er forgot shall be
And it's for bonnie Annie Laurie, I'd lay me doon and dee

Several sailors, who had paused their work to listen, broke into whistles and applause when she finished. Molly blushed in the darkness and gave a slight bow. Several of the men insisted upon an encore, but Molly begged off, saying that she needed to save her voice for New Orleans.

"Miss Alexandria told me you said you could sing."

Molly jumped, startled by the words spoken from behind her. She turned and saw Morris smiling as he leaned on the ladder which led up to the quarterdeck.

"She wouldn't really know," Molly said. "I didn't sing nothing for her. Just told her I could sing."

"She's good at spotting a liar," Morris said. "She knew you were telling the truth. May I give you a bit of advice?"

"You may," Molly said.

"With a voice like that, there is no need for you to spend your best years working in some whorehouse, no matter how fancy. You could be on the stage, traveling the world and performing for the likes of kings and queens. Take some time when you get to the city to build up some money, and then make your way back to New York as soon as you can. I'd wager you'd be onstage at the Bowery Theater within two months' time. Why sing for free when there are people who would pay to hear it? And be privileged to do so."

"Kind of you to say so, sir," Molly said. "But I'd get too nervous in front of that many people. I'll stick to singing in the parlor. That I can handle."

"Just think about what I said," Morris said.

"I will keep it in mind, sir," Molly said. "I promise."

As she made her way back to her cabin, Molly considered the man's words. People judged actresses and singers to be little better than common prostitutes, so such a life would mean no great damage to her reputation. Perhaps the money might even be quite good. *Ah, but I made money at Miss Cecilia's too. And it was stolen away from me. No. I must take it a day at a time.*

The next morning, Molly overheard some of the crew say that the ship would be at the mouth of the Mississippi River that afternoon and would switch over to the boilers to propel them up the river to somewhere called "Pilot Town." After a night there, they'd travel upriver to the city itself. Around noon, a lookout spotted a sail on the horizon off the port bow. He reported it looked to be on a parallel course and would close with the *Lady Anne* soon.

An hour passed and the lookout yelled, "Looks like a single screw sloop. Flying British colors. Merchantman from the looks of her. Maybe low on coal. She's under sail, not steam."

Molly scanned the faces of the crew around her. None seemed to show any apparent concern. The rest of the girls crowded on deck to see the ship for themselves. The British ship backed its sails as it drew near, as if it meant to stop. When it reached hailing distance, a voice from onboard called out in an English accent, "This is the *Mary Elizabeth*. We're a week out of Vera Cruz bound for our home port of Liverpool. Have you any news of the war?"

The *Lady Anne* drew alongside the *Mary Elizabeth* and Molly heard the captain's voice answer, "We've got some newspapers from New York City. Not too old. Send over a boat and you can have them."

Out of the corner of her eye, Molly saw the British flag drop from the vessel's stern. She gasped as a red flag with a blue cross filled with white stars rose in its place. At the same time, hidden gun ports on board the *Mary Elizabeth* flew open as her crew ran out cannons.

"This is the Confederate States Ship *Indianola.* Stand fast or we'll give you a broadside!" a voice in a southern accent called out.

"We surrender," came the reply.

"Muster your crew on deck and stand by to receive a boat."

Several of the girls squealed with fear, but Morris tried to calm them, saying, "Southerners are gentlemen. They do not make war on women and children. You'll be safe. Calm down or go below where the rest of us don't have to listen to your wailing."

Molly searched for Hannah but did not see her. *Must still be in the cabin*, she thought as she watched a small boat travel the short distance between the two ships. The sailors at the oars wore all manner of dress, none of it military. A uniformed officer sat at the stern; his eyes fixed upon his prey. Some of the men around her muttered curses under their breath, but most seemed resigned to whatever fate Poseidon had in store for them.

The officer of the Confederate vessel appeared at the Jacob's ladder and stepped onto the deck. He saluted and said, "Lieutenant Owen Johnson. Executive Officer of the CSS *Indianola.* At your service, sir."

"Jefferson Putnam, master of the *Lady Anne*," the captain said.

Some of the Confederate sailors who had manned the oars now crowded onto the deck behind their officers. Cutlasses dangled from leather belts around their waists and most had a pistol tucked into their pants. When they saw the group of young women on deck, they elbowed one another and grinned. *Don't they look as though they haven't seen the inside of a bathtub since the Baby Jesus saw the inside of a manger*, Molly thought.

"Are you carrying cargo?" Lieutenant Johnson asked as he rested his left hand on the hilt of his sword. "Or just passengers?"

"We're in ballast as you can plainly see," Putnam said. "You should've waited until we left New Orleans. Then we'd have a hold full of sugar and rum for you vultures to plunder."

"We are most certainly not vultures, sir," Lieutenant Johnson said. "And I'd remind you to hold your tongue. Now, show me the logs and have some of your men point my boys in the direction of the hold. If you truly are carrying only passengers, then we'll let you go on about your business."

"This way," Putnam growled as he turned to lead the officer to the master's cabin.

Hannah burst up from below decks and rushed over to the port side of the ship. She raised a bare foot onto the rail.

"Hannah!" Molly exclaimed. "What are you doing?"

The girl looked back over her shoulder at the astonished faces of the crew of both ships, and the other young women, and yelled, "No man will touch me again!"

With that, she hurled herself into the ocean. The splash struck Molly's ears with the force of a thunderclap. For a moment, she was back on deck of the *Dublin Rose* as the dead passengers were tossed over one at a time. The screams of some of the other girls brought her back to the present.

"She's gone under," one of the *Lady Anne*'s sailors shouted. "Can't see her."

"Get below and check out the hold," the Confederate officer told his sailors. "This isn't our concern."

Molly caught a flash of fear in Putnam's eyes. *What is he about*, she wondered. *Is he hiding something there that'll get us set adrift? Imprisoned? Or worse? No doubt they'll find it. Unless … unless …*

She ran over to the same rail where Hannah had jumped and pulled herself up onto it, using the rigging to steady herself, as she'd seen the sailors aboard do.

"I'll jump too," she called out. "Don't come any closer. I'll do it. I'm serious!"

Molly watched over her shoulder as the Confederate officer froze mid step. He looked from his sailors to Molly and back again.

Molly lifted one foot and dangled it over the side of the ship.

"Don't move!" the officer shouted. "We will depart."

He turned to Captain Putnam and said, "Do you give me your word that you've nothing of a military nature in your hold?"

"Of course," Putnam said. "Like I told you. We are in ballast."

"Very well," the officer said. "I'll leave you to tend to this … whatever it is. Give her some laudanum if you have any. I do believe that girl is insane."

Molly stayed in that position, legs cramping, as the Confederate boarding party rowed back across to their own ship. She did not step down until the crew of both ships prepared to get under way again. When she stepped down, Morris hurried over to her and said, "You wouldn't really have done it, would you?"

"Of course not," Molly said. "But I think our captain has something he didn't want them to find. It was all of us I was thinking of. But come on, we must get them to search for Hannah. Surely there is still time to find her."

"There isn't," Putnam said as he walked up beside her. "When a person is intent on drowning, there's no finding them."

Molly turned to face him and asked, "What do you mean, sir?"

"Just that. But I do appreciate your actions. I think you saved the ship, Miss O'Sullivan."

"But please, sir," Molly begged. "We have to at least try to find her. Please!"

"I'm sorry," he replied

Morris walked over and gently took Molly's arm.

"She's gone, Molly," he said. "There's no finding her now."

That night, alone in her cabin, Molly opened Hannah's suitcase and sorted through the contents. Inside, Molly found a letter written by Hannah and addressed to her parents. She tucked it into her own suitcase and said aloud, "I'll mail it for you, Hannah."

Chapter Twenty

As she walked away from the ship, Molly turned and looked back one more time, waving to the other young women as they split up to go their separate ways. She thought of Hannah, and what terrors the girl must have had in her mind to compel her to jump into the sea. *We all have our demons,* she thought, *but some are more powerful than others. The poor girl. I understand what she did. The same as Jimmy done. For some, maybe those demons just get to be too much.*

As she walked along the docks, Molly caught snatches of conversation in English and several foreign tongues, and even Irish, which made her smile. She tasted the salt in the air mingled with the odors of fish and tobacco. The scenes reminded her of her arrival in New York City. The wet heat felt like a damp rag pressed around her mouth and nose, and each breath felt like steam burning her lungs. *I thought New York City was hot,* she thought, *but this feels like the depths of hell itself.*

Prior to disembarking, Morris had scrawled an address on Dauphine

Street onto a piece of paper and handed it to her along with directions on how to get there. She'd changed into the dress given to her by Alexandria so she'd look presentable to her new employer, but as sweat ran down her face and dripped off the end of her nose, Molly realized the futility of it as she trudged up Canal Street away from the river. Swarms of mosquitoes buzzed in the air, and she yelped as one bit her neck. *What kind of place is this with the heat and these infernal creatures what try and suck your blood? Maybe they should've let the Confederacy keep it. Or maybe that's why the rebels gave it up?*

Molly paused to study a statue of a man near the intersection of Canal and Royal Streets. She asked a passerby for the identity of the man in the statue.

"Henry Clay, I think," the man answered.

"Is he a hero or something?" Molly asked.

"No idea," the man said over his shoulder as he walked away.

Molly shrugged and continued her walk. She reached Dauphine Street and turned right. Her eyes searched for the house number. Morris had told her the house was halfway down the block. When she saw it, her mouth fell open and she could not stop herself from saying, "It's like a mansion!" The house rose three stories above the street, supported by black iron columns on the first floor and an iron railing along the second and third floor balconies. Painted a light pink, the house had dark green shutters beside most of the windows except the two windows on either side of the front door, which were covered instead by a thick red curtain on the inside. Ivy or moss, she was not sure which, wrapped around some of the iron and ran all the way up to the third floor. Piano music and laughter drifted through the open front door along with the smell of fresh bread and tobacco. *Oh, it's a grand place*, she thought. *Finer than anything I've ever seen, except maybe Lord Sanderson's estate.*

Following the instructions she'd been given, Molly did not enter the front door but ducked down a narrow alley, a mere six or so feet in width, and knocked on the side door used for servants and deliveries. She knocked and waited for a moment. The door opened and Molly found herself looking into the face of a small black girl around eight years old.

"You need something?" the girl asked.

"I am here to see Madam Delacroix," Molly said.

"She expecting you?"

"I ... well ... I don't know," Molly confessed. "I just arrived from New York. I have a letter of introduction to give her. Could you please tell her that?"

"I guess you can come on in," the girl said.

She stood aside and Molly stepped into a narrow hallway. The girl pushed passed her and pointed to a room up ahead.

"That's the office," she said. "You can wait in there. I'll go find the madam."

Molly entered the room and surveyed the contents: a desk piled high with papers, a narrow bookcase with thick leather volumes, and a table with chairs. Her mind flashed back to her first time in Miss Cecilia's office. *And yet here I am again*, she thought. *Of my own will this time, but am I really? My choices were death or prison. Not much of a choice, that.*

She shook her head to clear the images and tried to calm her nerves. After a few minutes, a middle-aged woman with graying hair walked in; her movements made it seem as though she glided across the floor.

"And who might you be?" she asked.

"My name's Molly O'Sullivan, ma'am," Molly said. "I have a letter of introduction from Miss Miles in New York City. She's the one what sent me here."

"Let's take a look at it then," the woman said. "I trust your voyage here was not too taxing?"

"No, ma'am," Molly said as she opened her suitcase and fished the envelope out.

Madam Delacroix accepted it without a word and studied it for a moment before placing it atop a stack of papers on the desk. "Says you've experience in our line of work. And you wish to work down here. Is that true?"

"It is, ma'am," Molly said. "'Tis a fine city you have, if a bit hot."

"I run a clean house," Madam Delacroix said. "You'll need a health certificate from an army surgeon before you start work. We cater to army and navy officers here. Most of them are gentlemen, or at least they act like it. Enlisted men are not permitted inside, nor is anyone who cannot pay the entry fee, which is separate from the cost of services. Understand?"

"I believe so, ma'am."

Madam Delacroix recited the house rules which were similar to those at Miss Cecilia's---the weekly doctor's check, the precautions against social diseases, and the work hours. When she finished, the madam asked Molly if she understood.

"I do, ma'am," Molly said.

"If you get pregnant," Madam Delacroix said, "I have a doctor who will discreetly take care of it for you, but it is a risky procedure at best. Most of our clients won't use a French letter. We will provide another preventative but try not to let yourself get with child."

"I won't, ma'am."

"Good. Each act has a set price. We don't allow anything too exotic here. You receive twenty-five percent of the fee from the customers you handle, less deductions for room and board, meals, and clothing. I only deduct a modest amount, as this is a very profitable establishment. And my books are open. You can look and see the deductions for yourself. They are the same for all my girls. Once you've been here a while and built up your own client base, you might be able to clear twenty dollars a week."

"Twenty dollars!" Molly exclaimed. "Why, that's … that's a lot of money!"

"Yes, well," Madam Delacroix said, "as I told you, this is a fine house. I do not keep anyone here against their will. All my girls came here of their own accord, just as you did. Should you decide to walk away, that is your right. All I ask is that you settle your account with me prior to leaving. But I won't stand in your way and I'll send no one after you. Should you have issues with a client, leave it to me to handle. I've friends on the city council, the police, and I dine with General Banks, the Union commander of the city, once a week. Should a client cause you trouble, rest assured that he will be dealt with. Now be honest with me, do you chase the dragon?"

"Chase the what?"

"Do you use opium, in any form?"

"Oh, no, ma'am," Molly said. "I've never touched it before. I did work with girls who took the laudanum all the time and I have no wish to end up like them."

"Good," Madam Delacroix said, "I do not allow it in my house except in the event of a medical issue of some sort, and then only if administered by a doctor. If you use tobacco, be warned that I do not allow my girls to smoke in front of customers, though you may smoke on your off time or in your room."

"I don't smoke, ma'am," Molly said.

Madam Delacroix picked up the letter and studied it again.

"This says you can sing," she said. "Is that true?"

"I can sing a bit, yes," Molly said.

"I'll get you set up with Daphne. She's one of my best girls. We'll get you cleaned up and changed. Then I'll send for one of the army surgeons to come and do your health inspection. Take a day or two to get acclimated to the city. Then you can start work. Do you have any questions for me?"

"Was the girl who opened the door a"—Molly leaned forward and whispered the next word as though it were an epithet—"a slave?"

"Jane? Why, no," Madam Delacroix said. "Her mother has been in my employ for many years. As has her father. A fine family. They are free persons of color. That's what we call them here. In New Orleans, you'll find some blacks are free and others slave. A mix, really."

"In New York City, we had some trouble because of the, I forget the word, the thing about the slaves. And the conscription."

"The Emancipation Proclamation," Madam Delacroix said. "Yes, well, it does not apply to areas under Union control, which this city and some of our parishes are, and so slaves are still kept in the city. I imagine when the war ends, so will slavery. Provided the Union is victorious, of course. It looks as though they will be. So, you saw unrest in New York?

"I did, ma'am," Molly said. "A terrible business. I wish to never see such sights again."

"Then we shall hope that no such calamity visits our fair city." Madam Delcroix picked up a bell on her desk and rang it. After a moment, Jane came into the room and Madam Delacroix said, "Jane, be a dear and take young Molly here upstairs. Introduce her to Daphne and tell Daphne I said to look after her. Molly can use Sarah's old room. Draw her a bath and then straighten up the room for her. Understand?"

"Yes, ma'am," Jane said. "Come with me, Miss Molly. I'll take care of you."

Molly followed her to the back staircase.

"There's three floors," Jane explained as they walked up the narrow wooden steps. "Third floor is for sleeping and second floor is for working. You get a room on each floor."

"That's very generous," Molly said as they reached the third floor.

The bedroom doors opened off a central hallway. Jane pointed to the one Molly was to occupy. Jane stopped outside the room next door and she knocked once on the door. After a minute, the door opened, and a cloud of cigar smoke drifted out into the hallway.

"Miss Daphne," Jane said. "The madam wanted me to tell you to take care of Miss Molly here while I draw her a bath and get her room cleaned up."

The door opened all the way. Daphne was a couple of inches taller than Molly, with brown hair and weary green eyes. She gave Molly a visual going over and then motioned for her to enter the room.

"Have a seat," Daphne said.

"Thank you," Molly replied as she lowered herself into a cushioned lounge chair.

"Irish?" Daphne asked.

"I am," Molly said. "But I've come here from New York."

"Welcome to the city," Daphne said. "I'm from Mobile, Alabama. I ran away from home when I was sixteen. Made my way here. One thing led to another and, well, here I am. What about you?"

"Something like that," Molly said. *Don't reveal too much*, she warned herself. *The less you say about why you are here, the better. There's no way to know if a person would turn you in if they found out the truth.*

Molly listened as Daphne gave her a rundown of the house rules and the expectations Madam Delacroix had of her employees. It sounded similar to the way Miss Cecilia operated her house, just without the ever-present sensation of living in a prison. Molly asked if it were true that girls were allowed to leave if they wanted. Daphne laughed before she replied.

"Sure, you can. But where will you go? There's nowhere else a gal can make this kind of money. You'd be on your own completely, since no man'll want to marry you after you've been whoring for years. There's a couple of girls here that left but most of them came back once they got hungry!"

"I know a little about hunger," Molly said, her voice low. "God help me, I do."

"The potato thing," Daphne said. "Heard about that. It's the reason why there's so many Irish in the city. They say New Orleans just plain filled up with your people fifteen years back. A lot of them, the men anyway, joined up to fight when the war started. Most of the men left in the city were too old or too young to be of much use to the Confederacy. You got brothers with the army?"

"No," Molly said. "I came over by myself. I had an older brother in the army, but it was the British Army."

"Got three brothers serving with General Lee," Daphne said with no small measure of pride. "They are with the 4th Alabama. Law's Brigade."

"You must be worried for them," Molly said. "I remember how scared I was when my brother marched off to fight in the Crimea."

Daphne shrugged. "I reckon they can take care of themselves."

"Is it hard though?" Molly asked. "With the … customers all being on the other side?"

"Not really," Daphne said. "I'd rather be paid in Yankee greenbacks than that worthless paper that passes as Confederate money."

"Do your brothers know what you … what your … occupation is?"

"Of course not," Daphne said. "I'm saving everything I can. Maybe one day I'll run my own house. I'll have so much money that they won't care how I made it."

And what would Jimmy say if he were alive and knew what I was about now, Molly wondered. *No. If he was alive, I wouldn't be here. He'd have given young Henry Sanderson a bloody nose and told him to keep his hands to himself. And he wouldn't have let me ma agree to send me to America. I'd still be there in Galway.*

Jane returned and told Molly that her bath was ready. She led Molly down the hallway to the last door. Inside, Molly found a cast iron tub filled with steaming water. Towels hung from hooks along the wall.

"Go ahead and get in, Miss Molly," Jane said. "I'll be back with some clean clothes for you once I finish fixing up your room. Supper will be at six o'clock. Downstairs. Take as much time in there as you want."

"Jane?" Molly asked, "if we are on the third floor, how do you empty the tub?"

"There's a hose that fastens underneath it, Miss Molly," Jane said. "I just connect it, stick the hose out the window, and open the drain. Anyone walking by can get a shower of their own if'n they want!"

Molly took off her clothes and lowered herself into the water. The heat eased her muscles as she slipped entirely beneath the surface to soak her hair. When she came up, Molly leaned back and closed her eyes. The heat lulled her to sleep for a few minutes. She awoke when she heard laughter in the hallway outside. After liberally applying the soap, she watched as the crusted dirt and sweat from her sea voyage vanished from her skin. Jane returned and placed her clothes on a table in the corner.

"Your room is ready," she said. "Go make yourself at home as soon as you finish washing."

"Thank you, Jane," Molly said.

Once the girl left, Molly got out of the tub and dried her freshly pink skin. She dressed quickly, in a dress finer than any she'd ever seen. *Miss Alexandria wasn't lying about this being a fancy place*, she thought. *But it's still a whorehouse. No matter what you dress it up as.*

Sobered by the thought, she walked out of the washroom and down the hall to her room. She paused outside for a minute, unsure about what she'd find inside. *Be brave*, she told herself. *You survived the streets of New York. There's nothing left that can hurt you.* She opened the door and walked into the room.

The bed was large enough for two people to sleep comfortably side by side. Next to the bed was a small nightstand with a ceramic wash basin and pitcher. There was a wooden desk and chair in the corner. The last piece of furniture was a chaise lounge as nice as the one in the parlor at Miss Cecilia's. Molly walked across the room and looked at the desk. There was a hairbrush and a handheld mirror on it. The mirror had two large cracks, one vertical and one diagonal. She opened the drawer and found a few ribbons and a small leather journal. *Does this belong to the girl who was here before*, Molly wondered as she picked it up. Someone had torn out half the pages and the ones left had no writing on them. *Odd that she'd leave and not take this with her*, Molly thought as she put it back in the drawer.

Chapter Twenty-One

Within a few months, Molly had settled into the easy rhythms of life in New Orleans. Life in the city moved at a leisurely pace compared to New York City, as though the oppressive heat and ever-present humidity sucked all the energy from the inhabitants and made them sluggish, like a man one drink away from intoxication. During her free time, Molly took to wandering the streets, pausing to marvel at the architecture and the strange sights and smells she encountered—the smell of fried fish, the swampy odor of the Mississippi River, and the ornate, brightly colored homes with wrought iron balconies. When she'd arrived in New York City, it matched what she thought an American city would be like, but New Orleans seemed foreign, exotic even. *Queen Maeve would like this place, I think. I almost feel at home here. Almost.*

On occasion, Daphne accompanied her, and the young woman filled Molly in on all the gossip at Madam Delacroix's. According to Daphne, Sarah left the house after finding out she was pregnant and refusing the services of a doctor.

"The missus was upset," Daphne said, "but she said that was Sarah's decision to make. She wasn't going to force her to do nothing she didn't want to."

"Where did Sarah go?" Molly asked. "There aren't many places that would take in a young woman with a child." And don't I know it, Molly thought as she remembered the priest on the night she arrived in New York. Look to the hills for help, he said. The bastard.

"Maybe back home." Daphne looked away. "But I don't know where that is. She could be lifting her skirts in the alley over there for all I know."

"Was she not using the … preventative … I think that's what Madam Delacroix called it?" Molly asked. She shuddered as she thought of the glass syringe in a wooden box inside the nightstand drawer in her room. Madam Delacroix required her girls to irrigate themselves with a mixture of water and lemon juice to rinse out semen after each customer. At her place in New York, pregnancies were left to chance. *At least we have something*, Molly thought. *But I swear on Saint Patrick's grave, using that afterwards is almost as bad as the … the … act itself.*

Daphne shrugged, and the two women turned back in the direction of Dauphine Street.

One afternoon in late October, Molly set out to purchase a new handheld mirror. On her way back to Madam Delacroix's, she dodged a couple of street performers entertaining some Union sailors with a juggling act. The performance ended on a sour note when a juggler misjudged a pin and it struck him on the head, knocking him to the ground. The sailors roared with laughter and applause as they tossed coins into a bucket. *Must think it was part of the act*, Molly thought with a smile. *With that loud a smack, I doubt it was planned.*

A well-dressed man in a black frock coat and a bowler lounged against the side of the building opposite the alley that led to the side entrance to the house. Molly glanced at him briefly, but he averted his eyes.

When she ducked into the side entrance to the house, Molly nearly tripped over Jane, who was kneeling on the floor scrubbing at a large, brown stain.

"I'm sorry, Jane," Molly said. "Didn't see you there."

"No bother," Jane said without looking up. "Oh, Miss Molly! There's a telegram came while you was out. Madam Delacroix said it was from New York. I stuck it on your pillow upstairs."

"New York?" Molly exclaimed. "Are you sure?"

"That's what she said, Miss Molly."

Molly said a quick thank you over her shoulder as she hurried up the back staircase to her third-floor room. Inside, she found a white envelope with her name and the address of the house penciled on the back flap. Her hands shook as she tore the envelope open and scanned the message. "Found info about child. Stop. Still in the city. Stop. More to follow by post. Stop. Frank." Tears sprang to her eyes as she pressed the message to her chest. *Please, Francis Lynch*, she thought. *If Ellen is still in the city, then he can surely get her! But then what? I can't hardly raise another family's child while living in a whorehouse. What would her poor departed mother think of that? But what else is there?*

A light knock on the door interrupted her thoughts.

"Come in," she said.

Daphne walked in and asked, "Good news from New York?"

"I think it is, yes," Molly said. "A peeler I knew there, the one what helped me get to New Orleans, sent word that he may have found the child I lost in the city."

"You had a child?" Daphne asked, eyes wide.

"Yes, I mean, no, I mean, not like that," Molly said. She told Daphne the general story of what happened, though she chose to omit the attack in the boarding house. Instead, Molly said she lost the child's hand in a crowd and was unable to find her.

"Sad story," Daphne said when Molly finished. "And you couldn't stay behind to try and find her yourself?"

"I looked for her for months," Molly said. "Then I had to leave the city and Detective Lynch said he'd keep after the case for me."

"Left in a hurry, did you?"

"I did," Molly said.

"Never mind about that," Daphne said. "Most of us are here 'cause we were running from something. We all got our secrets. Now, we got some gentlemen downstairs needing a bit of company."

"Do I have time to take a bath first?" Molly asked. "I'm sweating like a mule from walking to the shop. I don't think I'll ever get used to the heat here."

"A few extra minutes won't matter," Daphne said. "Give them some more time to drink. The more liquored up they are, the more money they'll spend on us. Ain't that a fact!"

After she'd washed and changed into a fresh dress, Molly made her way down to the parlor. A trio of naval officers clad in dark blue, double-breasted coats and white trousers, stood in a corner sipping brandy. Two of the men puffed furiously on cigars while the third held a cob pipe in his hand. A civilian sat on the coach next to an army officer. *A major*, Molly thought to herself when she saw his rank. *I know my army ranks now but not the navy ones*. Madam Delacroix watched over them from her chair in the corner.

"Ah, Molly," Madam Delacroix said, "you are just in time to entertain the gentlemen. I think a fine song would definitely be in order, don't you?"

"I don't know," Molly said.

"Please," the major said as he stood up, "it would mean quite a bit to us."

The naval officers nodded in agreement and Molly consented. She bent down to discuss a tune with the piano player. He nodded his head and she turned to face the men. She selected a bawdy tune she'd heard from sailors in New York. When the officers joined in on the last verse and chorus, she knew she'd made the right choice.

A rovin', a rovin' a rovin's been my ru-i-in
No more will I go rovin' with you fair maid

"Brava" the men exclaimed when the song ended. Molly smiled.

"Thank you, Molly," Madam Delacroix said. "That was … interesting. Fine singing. But perhaps something less … vulgar next time?"

"Oh, come now," the major said, "this is a bordello, is it not?"

"I run a respectable house, Major," Madam Delacroix replied. "If it is a waterfront whore you are looking for, the docks are that way. My girls are the finest in the city."

"They are indeed," one of the naval officers said as his eyes swept up and down Molly's body. He licked his lips and extended his hand to her. "Come over here by me."

"I do believe the army has priority on this matter," the major said after he caught the reaction on Molly's face. "After all, it's only by our authority that such establishments are allowed to remain open. I'm afraid you'll have to be entertained by one of the other lovely young daughters of Venus employed at this fine place."

The officer grunted his assent and the major walked over to Molly and stuck out his hand.

"My name is Major Warlow. Timothy Warlow. From Chicago."

He was only a few inches taller than her, though his uniform gave him the appearance of being much bigger. His black hair was combed back and held in place with a liberal amount of pomade. Like many of the army officers she had seen, Major Warlow also had a trimmed black goatee.

"I'm Molly, your honor," she said as she shook his hand. "Molly O'Sullivan. You know where I'm from by my accent."

"Indeed, I do!" Major Warlow said. "We've many sons and daughters of Hibernia in Chicago. Have you ever had cause to visit?"

"No sir," Molly said. "I come over to New York from Ireland and then from New York to New Orleans. It's all of the country I've seen."

"Well, now," Major Warlow replied, "you absolutely must visit the city as soon as you get a chance. Not nearly as hot and humid as this place. Though a fair town, I admit New Orleans does take some getting used to. Do you find it so as well?"

"It ain't Galway," Molly said. "That's for sure. But I like it well enough."

"Ah, a practical woman, I see. You find the good in your circumstances no matter what."

"I try, sir," Molly said. After all, she thought, what other choice do I have?

Major Warlow smiled at her and an awkward moment of silence ensued. *Does he not know how to ask a whore to go upstairs,* Molly wondered. *Surely, he does.*

Finally, Molly put her hand on his shoulder and whispered in his ear, "Would you be wanting to go upstairs?"

"Oh … no … not at all," the major said quickly.

Molly put on a pained expression and asked, "Do you not find me attractive, sir?"

"Of course I do," the major replied. "You are as pretty as a sunset over the plains."

"Why, thank you," Molly said. "I do believe that's the kindest thing any man has ever said about me. I guess you've a wife and babies at home, then."

"Not at all," the major said. "I am, I suppose you could say, without amorous commitment at the present time. From time to time, I get a little bit lonely. Perhaps a touch of the melancholia. My mother always said I was a bit of a sour apple. Whenever I've the sudden urge for female companionship, I try and visit a fine establishment such as this for the company, that's all. I find that women in your … forgive me … profession are quite a bit easier to talk to. Besides, we Yankees are not the least bit welcome in this town. Mothers lock up their eligible daughters as soon as they see us on the street."

"Afraid you'll go around outraging their daughters and freeing their slaves," Molly said. "That's be my guess."

"Young women need not fear officers of the Union," Major Warlow declared, "And as for the slaves, well, the war will settle that question soon enough."

"Do you think it will end soon, then?"

"Come," Major Warlow offered her his arm. "Let us sit and I will tell you all about how and when this infernal war will draw to a close and what new world we will face in the aftermath."

Molly took his arm. "You sure don't talk like anyone else I know. You use a lot of funny words. Why, you almost sound like Lord Sanderson back in Ireland! Just with an American accent."

"Ah, my dear girl," Major Warlow said as they sat down on the sofa, "that's because my mother was an English lady. Shall I tell you about her?"

Molly looked across the room, where Daphne stood next to one of the naval officers, his arm encircling her waist. She gave Molly a look somewhere between concern and anger.

What's she about, Molly wondered. *She's got her own gentlemen to tend to at the moment. She's no need to chase after the major.*

Molly turned to face him and lost herself in his story.

Chapter Twenty-Two

The letter from Frank arrived a month later. Molly opened the envelope with a mixture of excitement and fear. Frank informed her that he learned from one of his sources on the street that a certain prominent businessman in the city procured very young girls and passed them over to a woman who raised them to be high-end prostitutes. Once they came of age, the girls were sold to a madam who specialized in supplying young virgins for men who paid top dollar. *Jesus,* Molly swore. *Of all the evils in the world, this must be near the top.* He told her that he intended to find the location where the children were kept and asked her to be patient.

She froze as she read the last line.

"I must also tell you something of great importance," Frank had written. "There is a warrant out for your arrest in the city on the charges of arson and murder. Do not attempt to come back for any reason. You should be safe where you are, as other than me and A.M., no one knows where you have gone. But you risk the gallows if you come back.

I'll be in touch again soon."

Molly walked over to the desk in her room and held the edge of the letter over the flame of a candle. It caught fire right away, and Molly held it in her fingertips as flames licked their way up the page. *I've no cause to go back to New York City anyway*, she thought as she dropped the burning letter into an ashtray, *unless it was to get Ellen. But if Frank can do that for me, then maybe he could just send her to me.*

She frowned as she left the room and walked downstairs to the parlor. Daphne looked up from the newspaper when Molly entered the room.

"Paper says the war will be over soon," Daphne said. "That would be bad for business. How are we gonna make money once all the Yankee soldiers and sailors go back home?"

"I imagine we'll make it from the Confederate soldiers and sailors who will also come home," Molly said.

"They'll be too broke to pay for a meal, much less a whore," Daphne said. "Hell, when this war started, I was all for the Confederacy. But now? Now I'm for the side with the most money, and that'd be the Yankees. Much as it pains me to admit it."

Molly laughed. "Men are the same no matter what color their uniform," she said. "They all want the same things in life. Whiskey, women, a fine cigar, and a meal."

"Yeah?' Daphne asked. "And what do we want?"

Out, thought Molly. She decided not to say it aloud, and instead shrugged and said, "Hope for a better future, I think. One without a war."

"I reckon you're right," Daphne said.

"Daphne"—Molly hesitated for a moment—"do you ever think about what you'll do when you aren't doing … this for a living anymore?"

Daphne slapped her knee and laughed. "Why … that's …" Daphne's shoulders shook as she tried to talk. "That's the funniest thing I ever heard! Give up whoring? They don't give no pensions to retired whores. We'll work until we're used up and ugly as three-day old spit, and then they'll toss us out on the street to starve to death. Kind of like how folks said your people starved back in Ireland because of the potatoes."

Potatoes, Molly thought. *If only that were all it was.* As she and her mother had staggered through the Galway countryside during those lean years, they saw wagons full of food rumble past on more than one occasion, guarded by soldiers. When she asked her mother why they didn't stop the wagons and feed the human skeletons who lined the roads, Mrs. O'Sullivan gave a sad shake of the head and said, "They are taking the food to Galway City. It'll be put on ships and taken away to England."

"Are the people starving there too?" Molly had asked.

"No, child. The people there are not starving because we are. The English are starving us to feed themselves. We're nothing but savages in their eyes. Like the red Indians in America."

Potatoes. Sure, there was more to it than that. How can those in charge sleep at night? They've the blood of half of Connaught on their hands. Bastards. A pang of guilt crept into her mind as she surveyed the ornate parlor and dress that she wore. *I'm living a life people in Ireland can only dream of*, she thought. *I have the finest food and the finest clothes in town. The only thing wrong is what I've done to earn it. Now, I have to keep at it until we've found Ellen and I've got enough to set us up somewhere else. Somehow else.*

"Molly?"

Daphne's voice brought her back to the present.

"Sorry," Molly said. "I was distracted."

"Looked like you were a million miles away," Daphne said.

"I suppose I was," Molly said. "Daphne … that army officer that was in here a couple of weeks ago."

"What about him?" Daphne asked.

"Has he been in here before?"

"Yeah," Daphne grunted, "you could say that."

"What do you mean?"

"Nothing," Daphne said. "Just … look, don't go believing any promises he makes you. That's all."

"He didn't promise me nothing," Molly said. "He just talked about

Chicago and his family."

"Well, don't say I didn't warn you," Daphne said as she left the table.

Molly frowned and made her way to the office in the back of the building, where she found Madam Delacroix sitting behind a pile of papers with a thick ledger book open on the desk.

"You girls sure like to eat," the madam said when she saw Molly in the doorway. "The expenditures on food have gone up fifteen percent over the past month."

"We do work up an appetite, ma'am," Molly said.

Madam Delacroix's laugh turned into a hacking cough.

"Damn lungs," she said. "I think it's the humid climate. Turns the lungs into wet paper bags. Can you do figures?"

"You mean add numbers, like?" Molly asked. When Madam Delacroix nodded, Molly said, "Not really. I mean, I can read the numbers. But I can't make sense of what happens when you put them together. Or take some away."

"Do you want to learn? I could use some help with the books from time to time."

Molly thought of her mother's words back on the quayside in Cork. *She'd want me to learn my figures too. It may come in handy one day.*

"I would like that, ma'am," Molly said.

"Good." Madam Delacroix smiled, crooked teeth gleaming in the light of an oil lamp. "You have ambition. I can see it on your face."

"I just want to get by, ma'am," Molly said.

"I think it goes a bit deeper than that. I started out just like you, you know. I worked for Madam Charpentier on Royal Street. I was an orphan. Or at least that is what they told me. She took me in when I was fourteen. Taught me to read and write. She taught me how to comport myself like a lady. I saved up as much as I could for the next ten years. Then, I was able to get my own establishment. Small, at first, but I've built up to this over the past twenty years."

"But I thought you was a French countess or something," Molly said. "That's what Miss Miles in New York told me."

"Sometimes, a woman has to pretend to be something she's not to get what she wants," Madam Delacroix said. "No different than an actress upon the stage. Now, did you need something from me?"

"I'm going to step out and take a walk," Molly said. "I just wanted to let you know."

Madam Delacroix pulled a coin purse out of the desk drawer and tossed it to Molly. Startled, Molly nearly dropped the small brown bag onto the floor.

"Would you mind dropping that at the desk at the precinct house for me?"

"I will, ma'am," Molly said.

An hour later, after dropping off the money and taking a stroll through the neighborhood, Molly walked along Decatur Street. Music drifted from the dim interiors of several saloons. Uniformed men milled about, talking of anything but the war. The air smelled of alcohol and fresh seafood, a mixture which made her stomach growl and turn at the same time. A drunken sailor bumped into her and mumbled an apology as he staggered away. He leaned on a building for support for a moment, and then toppled over, to the delight of those nearby who laughed and applauded. She wondered if the man had been in battle during the war. Unconsciously, Molly's right hand moved up to her neck and clasped the Saint Michael's medal. Her mind ran through the words. *Michael the Archangel, defend us in battle. Be our protection from the wickedness and snares of the devil.*

Outside of a warehouse, several black men sweated as they unloaded sacks of flour from the back of a wagon. They laughed and joked with one another until an elderly white man walked out of the building and yelled at them to be quiet and work faster. Thus chastised, they fell silent and went about their work with renewed vigor. *It must be a terrible thing to have to work with no laughter*, Molly thought as she hurried past them. *Even in a whorehouse, you can always find something to laugh about. If not with the customers, then among ourselves. Or at least you can here. There was precious little to laugh about at Miss Cecilia's.*

A group of soldiers marched up the street in her direction, and Molly quickly stepped out of the way. They wore a uniform she'd not seen before—dark blue frock coats and white trousers that shone in the afternoon sun. She looked around and saw a man nearby watching the men just as she was.

"Excuse me, sir," Molly said, "what kind of uniforms are those? They look different than the other soldiers I've seen."

"They ain't soldiers, miss," the man said. "Them's marines."

"What does that mean?" Molly asked.

"Oh, they's sorta like soldiers, I reckon, but for the navy."

"Thank you," Molly said as she frowned in confusion over how one might be a soldier in the navy. She turned to ask another question, but the man had drifted away.

Sure, the war will be over by the time I get all the uniforms figured out, she thought. As she made her way in the general direction of Madam Delacroix's, a voice called out "Miss Molly!" She turned and saw Major Warlow in the doorway of a saloon.

"Good afternoon, Major," Molly said. "I hope the day finds you well."

"It does indeed now," he said. "How fortunate I am to run into you. Please tell me how you have been these past few weeks."

"Umm," Molly hesitated, Daphne's warning ringing in her ears, "I've been fine, sir. Truly."

What kind of man strikes up a conversation with a whore in the middle of the street, she wondered. *Don't most men act as though they've never laid eyes on us before when they cross our paths in public?*

"I've been meaning to pay you a visit," Major Warlow said.

"Well, you know where to find me," Molly replied with a smile. "I'm easy enough to track down."

"Yes, well"—Major Warlow cleared his throat—"I've been wanting to ask you something. I have acquired tickets to a stage performance of a play. Would you be interested in accompanying me?"

"You mean to take a whore to a play?" Molly asked, her eyes wide. "Have you gone daft? I'd love to see a play, but—"

"I don't care if people laugh or not," Major Warlow said. "If I mean to take you to a play, then I will. Provided you say 'yes,' of course."

"I don't think that's a good idea, Major."

"Very well, then you have to allow me to walk with you for a bit this afternoon."

"If you insist," Molly said in a tone that suggested indifference, though the idea appealed to her.

"I do," Major Warlow said as Molly took his arm. As they walked, he talked again of the war. "The Rebs can't hold out forever. Once we've crushed them beneath our heels, the country can move forward towards a glorious future made secure by the fact that all men are free."

Molly laughed. "You talk just as funny as you did the first time we met."

As they ambled along in the direction of Jackson Square, Major Warlow told her about his law practice in Chicago. When the war began, he had left the firm in the hands of his partner, whose bad lungs prevented his military service. Warlow hoped the army would see fit to give him a field commission, but he found himself assigned as a staff officer instead, first in Washington, DC and then in New Orleans. Despite frequent requests for a transfer, he had resigned himself to never getting to see action.

"Not that I'm in any great hurry to rush off and die," he said as they reached the square and paused in front of the statue of Andrew Jackson on a horse, "but I'd like to see if I have the fortitude to stand in the ranks and face Rebel shot and shell without flinching."

"My brother was a soldier," Molly said. "He told us after he came home from a place called the Crimea that he was terrified in battle, but he did his job anyway."

"Indeed," Major Warlow agreed, "that is what I'd like to find out about myself. Fate has other plans in store for me, I fear. I'll not see my chance in this war."

"Maybe you should consider it lucky then. Your assignment, I mean. No sense dying when you don't have too. I'm afraid it is time for me to get back to the … house."

"Can I escort you there?"

"I can't stop you," Molly said with a shrug. "You being with the occupation government and all."

"That's the spirit." Major Warlow laughed as he patted her hand.

On the walk back to Dauphine Street, Molly told the major a

little about her life in Ireland and the trip to America but left out any mention of Ellen or the circumstances which led Molly into her present occupation.

A block away from the house, the major pointed out two men who lounged against the outside wall of a saloon, hats pulled low across their faces and cigars dangling from the corners of their mouths. "I wonder what they are up to."

"What do you mean?" Molly asked with a frown.

"They are Pinkertons—private detectives. I can spot them from a mile away. I've plenty of experience dealing with them in Chicago before the war, and we've had some pass through here on some mission or another. Very secretive bunch."

Molly froze in her tracks. *Pinkertons*? She'd read of them in the papers and dime novels back in New York. *Surely, they cannot be here after me? It's the peelers what want me, not the Pinkertons. They'd come for me themselves if they knew I was here. They'd not send some secret agents after me. Would they*?

"Is something wrong, Molly?" Major Warlow asked, concern visible on his face. "Did I say something to upset you?"

"No, Major," Molly whispered. "I think it's just the heat what got to me. I'm sorry. Please, let's just get home."

"As you wish," Major Warlow said as they resumed their walk, "but I do wish you'd call me Timothy, or Tim. It's only fair since you permit me to call you Molly."

"That's because I'm a woman of the town and you're a fancy gentleman lawyer what talks like he sits on the throne of England," Molly said with a forced smile.

"A fancy gentleman lawyer that would dearly like to be your friend, Molly."

"Oh, aye, any man can be my friend, or a friend of one of the other girls too, providing they pay the proper rate and don't got the French disease."

"Molly!" Major Warlow exclaimed. "There's no need to be lewd. No, I meant I would like to be your friend outside of working hours. That is, if Madam Delacroix would permit it."

"Gentlemen don't go sparking whores," Molly said. "Madam Delacroix don't care what I do on my off time, but you'd get drummed out of the army if your bosses caught you walking out with a girl like me."

When they reached the house, the major took Molly's hand and lifted it towards his face, his dry lips brushing across the back of it. Molly felt her face flush. *Damn pale skin*, she swore. *But ain't he the most bizarre man I've ever run across inside a whorehouse? It's almost like he's some knight what rides around on a white horse. I ain't no princess though. Maybe … maybe Daphne's wrong about him.*

"I'll be seeing you, Molly." Major Warlow released her hand. "Either inside there or out here, I'll be seeing you again."

"I do enjoy your company," Molly replied. "You are welcome to call around any time. I was wondering if I might ask you for a favor, Major."

"Please, call me Timothy. And yes, you may ask me anything."

"Well … if you find out what them Pinkertons are up to, do you think that maybe you could tell me?"

"I suppose so, but may I ask why?"

"Oh"—Molly's mind raced to come up with a reason that would make sense—"call it my own curiosity. When I was in New York, we had a paper called the *National Police Gazette* that was full of stories about private detectives and the like."

"How could I say no to such a request? Certainly. I'll make a few inquiries, discreet inquiries, mind you, and should I uncover any tales of daring do, I will bring them to your attention at once."

Molly smiled and stepped towards the major. She placed her hands on his shoulders, raised herself upon her toes, and gave him a kiss on the cheek.

"Thank you," she said. When she reached the door, Molly gave him one more smile over her shoulder before going inside.

Chapter Twenty-Three

October yielded to November, and the newspapers told of the reappointment of General Butler to the Army. At breakfast one morning, Molly read a story which described the General in less than flattering terms but didn't reveal why he was so hated. Across the table from her, Daphne busied herself spreading butter on a piece of toast.

"Daphne," Molly said, "who is this general the papers say is like the devil himself? What did he do to get people so worked up?"

"He got his knickers in a twist cause the ladies in town were being mean to the Yankee troops that was here. They'd try and dump their chamber pots on top of the soldiers' heads when they went walking by under the balconies!"

"That's foul," Molly said, though she could not suppress a chuckle. *Then again*, she thought, *wouldn't plenty in Galway do the same to an English lord if they had the chance!*

"Well"—Daphne paused to take a bite of her toast—"one day someone dumped a whole pot full of piss on the head of some Yankee admiral named Farragut. General Butler got downright apoplectic about it. Published this order in the newspaper that said that any women that insulted the soldiers or sailors would get treated like a common street whore. Don't you know that made them society women madder than a hornet's nest. President Davis protested to Lincoln, and Butler got sent home."

"The soldiers treat us well enough," Molly said. "I don't know what those women would be afraid of."

"We only get the officers, Molly," Daphne said. "But here, let me show you something."

Daphne got up from the table and left the room. A few minutes later, she returned with a porcelain chamber pot and thrust it towards Molly.

"Here! Look!"

"I'm not interested in your bodily waste," Molly protested.

"No, no," Daphne said, "it ain't got nothing in it. But look what's painted on the inside."

Molly hesitated, then accepted the pot. She held her breath and peered inside. Benjamin Butler's face peered back at her.

Daphne laughed and said, "Ain't it funny? Now at night, we can show ol' Butler exactly what we think of him!"

Molly joined in the laughter, despite herself. "It's funny enough," she admitted. "I'm surprised the people in the Confederacy don't make them with Lincoln's face inside. Do they not look on him the same as they do that general?"

"Most do, I think," Daphne said. "At least, back home in Alabama people didn't speak to kindly of him at all. Said he was like a baboon or a gorilla or something."

"And what do you think?" Molly asked. "Being as you are from Alabama yourself."

"I don't think about it," Daphne said. "My brothers fight for the Confederacy, but all I want to do is make enough money to set myself up real nice once the war ends. Think I could be like Madam Delacroix?"

"Is that what you want to be?" Molly asked. "The keeper of your own bawdy house?"

"There's worse things to be. Say! Why don't you and I partner up once the war's over? The two of us could run our own place. We'd be the envy of the French Quarter! What do you think?"

"I think I better go upstairs," Molly said. As she walked up the stairs, Molly considered Daphne's proposition. *I guess owning your own house is better than working for someone else, but I'd still be a whore. Daphne's a nice girl, but she can't think beyond these four walls. I've Ellen to consider, and if I'm to provide for her, I need some other occupation besides this one. But what else is there for me to do? She thought about the conversation she'd had with Morris on the voyage to New Orleans. Use my voice, he said. Maybe try to make it as a singer rather than on my back. If only it were that easy.*

That afternoon, during her math lesson, she decided to ask Madam Delacroix for advice. Lifting her pencil from the ledger, where she'd been subtracting expenses, Molly asked, "Do you think there's any place I might could make some extra money singing?"

Madam Delacroix looked up. "Are you looking to get out of this line of work?" Madam Delacroix asked.

"No," Molly said, "well, not right away. But I'd like to start putting away some extra money and everyone says I have a nice voice. I've not sung in front of a lot of people before though."

"I see," Madam Delacroix replied. "I cannot fault a girl for wanting to bring in some extra coin, and you do have a fine voice. I tell you what, Molly, I'll make some inquiries and see if we can't get you something. You'd have to do it on your off days, though."

"Of course," Molly said. "I wouldn't want it no different than that."

"And in exchange for my help," Madam Delacroix said, "you'll pay me ten percent of whatever you make. With the caveat that if you being on stage brings men into the house, then I'll waive the ten percent."

"What is ten percent?" Molly asked. "It sounds like a lot."

"It isn't," Madam Delacroix said. "If we continue with the figures, I will show you. Look here."

The madam was true to her word. Within two weeks, she managed to find Molly a small theater in need of a female vocalist after the previous one came down with syphilis and left the city. Madam Delacroix made the arrangements for Molly to audition and loaned her the money for a new dress.

"You must show up looking like you already own the place, my dear," she said. "I'll have my carriage drop you off. You'll arrive five minutes late. Creates a bit of mystery that way. It'll make them want you that much more."

"But won't they know I'm a ..." Molly hesitated. "You know. A prostitute?"

"Aren't the girls who work on stage little better than that themselves? At least you are an expensive one. Be proud of what you are and confident in your voice, otherwise the nervousness will show, and you'll not get the part. All they are looking for is someone to give a small vocal concert, which you can certainly do. You've done the same in this parlor many times. The only difference will be the size of the crowd. Go on upstairs and get ready. Be sure to let me see you before you leave."

With the help of young Jane, Molly dressed and pinned her hair up. She studied her reflection in the mirror for a moment. *You're a long way from Belclare, Molly. Would ma even recognize me now*?

After a few finishing touches of powder on her face, Molly turned to Jane and asked, "Well, what do you think?"

"You is pretty, Miss Molly," Jane said. "Everyone said that Sarah was pretty. But you prettier."

"The Sarah that ran away cause she fell for a baby?" Molly asked.

"Oh no, she didn't run away," Jane said.

"But that's what everyone says," Molly said. "Are you sure?"

"I ain't supposed to say anything," Jane said. "It's a secret."

Molly leaned down and cupped the child's face in her hand.

"Don't worry, Jane. Your secret is safe with me. I'll say nothing to anyone."

Jane grinned and said, "Thank you, Miss Molly."

Molly smiled as Jane skipped out of the room. *What a happy child*, she thought. *I only wish one day that Ellen can be as happy as that. But if Sarah didn't run away, then where is she*?

Molly walked downstairs to Madam Delacroix's office. She paused in the doorway for a moment before she said, "I'm ready to leave now, ma'am."

The madam looked up from her papers and said, "Good luck, Molly. I'm sure you'll do fine. Remember, be confident."

"I will, ma'am."

Molly gasped as she stepped outside and saw the fine white carriage with a massive pair of horses, also white, harnessed to it. An elderly black man dressed in a top hat and tails climbed down from the driver's seat and said, "You must be Miss Molly."

"I am," Molly said.

"Then allow me," the man said as he opened the door, lowered the step, and extended a hand toward Molly. She took a step forward, bracing herself for a flood of memories of the morning in New York when she'd taken her first carriage ride. When no memories came, Molly breathed a sigh of relief.

She accepted the driver's hand and climbed into the back of the carriage. The interior smelled of perfume and cigar smoke. The two benches on opposite sides of the compartment were topped with velvet-lined cushions. Molly noticed a stain on the floor but decided not to dwell on what might have caused it. The carriage rocked slightly as the driver hauled himself up to his perch behind the reins. With a sudden jolt, the horses got underway and Molly settled into her seat for the short ride over to the theater.

"It ain't like the Bowery Theater," she said to herself once the carriage deposited her in front of a large wood-frame building. Faded advertisements for past performances were plastered all over the front of the building, though the edges of most of them curled away and pointed at the ground. The front door opened, and a short, squat man in his shirtsleeves beckoned to her.

"You the singer?" he asked.

"Yes, my name is—"

"Don't matter what your name is," the man interrupted. "Come on in. You're late."

Molly followed him into the lobby. The smell of unwashed bodies from the crowds who frequented the theater had soaked into the walls over the years. Molly wrinkled her nose as she followed the man into the main room. The floor sloped down toward a small stage. A balcony on the second floor covered the back half of the ground-floor seats. There were a few private boxes on the second floor along the side of the room too. A tall thin man with a gray beard walked up the aisles towards her. His black suit hung from his frame, and he had a cigar clenched in his teeth.

"You must be Miss O'Sullivan," he said without removing the cigar or offering his hand.

"Yes, sir," Molly said. "And I'd like to thank you for the opportunity to—"

"Ain't got time for formalities," he said. "My name's Preston. Mitchell Preston. You Irish, I take it?"

"I am."

"Good. All you Hibernians can sing. I'll get straight to the point. Our house singer ain't employed here anymore. I need someone else. How many songs you know?"

"I don't know," Molly confessed. "Lots, I'd say."

"Good. You have enough to do an eight or ten song set? No musical accompaniment. Just singing on stage by yourself."

"I can, but—"

"That's settled," Preston said. "Next Friday night at seven o'clock. I'll pay you ten dollars in gold. Twelve if your voice is perfect."

"But don't you want to hear me first?" Molly asked.

"Why? You said you could sing. One thing though. We can't use your given name. Too Irish and some folks don't like the Irish. How about we call you . . ." He paused as he mulled over possibilities. "I have it. We'll call you Louisa May. That sounds American enough!"

"But—"

"Be here two hours before your start time, so five o'clock. There's a dressing room in the back you can use. It ain't much, but it's private. Have we got a deal?"

He extended his hand, and Molly shook it.

"Thank you, Mr. Preston. I won't let you down."

"Oh, it don't matter," he said. "We ain't got the best clientele here, as you can probably guess. We've lost quite a bit of money since the war started. I think we'll have to close down soon. Unless you can pack the house for us."

"I'll do my best, sir," Molly promised.

The week before the performance passed more slowly than any she could remember. Molly took every spare moment to rehearse a few of the Irish songs she knew while the house piano player taught her a couple of more popular American tunes. *I know me da would be proud of me*, Molly thought as she worked through the songs, *or rather he'd be proud of me singing. Not the other part.*

Three days before the performance, Jane reported that there were new signs up in front of the theater announcing the event. Molly walked over to check them out.

"Introducing Louisa May! A new talent in the city! With a voice like an angel!"

I could have the voice of a goat for all they know, Molly thought as she smiled. *It ain't like I had to audition. Most of the audience will be drunk anyway, so it isn't like an angel I'd have to sound for them to think I was one.*

On the appointed evening, Madam Delacroix summoned the carriage to take Molly to the theater. Preston met her at the door and ushered her through the maze of hallways, costumes, and sets backstage to a door tucked away in the corner with a sign bearing her stage name dangling from the knob.

"Here you go," Preston said as he turned the door and, with a hand on the small of her back, ushered Molly into the room. "We'll let you know fifteen minutes before time for you to go on. Nervous?"

"Not really," Molly lied. She could feel the moisture on her palms as her heart began to race.

Preston nodded and left the room. It contained a desk with a mirror mounted on the wall above it, a table with two chairs, and a screen she could change behind had she not already put on her new dress before she left Madam Delacroix's. With no windows, the room smelled stale, like an old closet, and a layer of dust covered the furnishings. The table contained a vase with a dozen fresh roses in it. Molly walked over and bent down to sniff them, and noticed a small white card stuck in the middle of the flowers. She opened it and read, "To Molly. Good luck. I'll be seeing you."

Odd, Molly thought as a frown crossed her face. *They must be from the madam. She's the only one what knows what I'm doing and can afford flowers. But why would it say 'I'll be seeing you'? Of course she'll see me.*

Molly sat down at the table and closed her eyes. Breathing deeply, she tried to fill her lungs with air to calm her nerves. Her legs twitched a bit as she tried to visualize herself on stage. *It's no different than the parlor*, she said to herself. *You've done this before.*

She was still trying to calm herself when a knock on the door told her it was time for her to go on stage. The buzz of the crowd stopped when she walked up the steps and moved towards the center of the platform. Every seat in the house was full, with a few hundred sets of eyes on her. There in the front row sat Major Warlow, flanked by a general on one side and a naval officer on the other. He smiled up at her and nodded approvingly.

The crowd stared at her, waiting for her to begin. The room seemed to spin a little in front of her eyes. *Am I to faint?*

She took another deep breath and glanced to her left, where she saw Mr. Preston just off stage. He motioned for her to start. She nodded, cleared her throat, and began to sing her first song, "Kathleen Mavourneen." By the time she finished, several in the audience dabbed at their eyes with handkerchiefs. She moved on to "Aura Lee" and "Lorena," the first of which she'd heard outside the Bowery Theater and the second she'd learned at Madam Delacroix's in the week before the concert. Given the circumstances, the madam told her to shy away from any song which overtly mentioned the war, lest one side or the other take offense. In an occupied city such as New Orleans, the mix of people in the audience could cause trouble if a song favored one side or the other. After a few more Irish tunes, Molly concluded with "Annie Laurie," her favorite.

When she finished, the house erupted into cheers and wild applause as men rose to their feet in excitement. A few went so far as to toss their hats in the air while they stamped their feet. Red crept into Molly's pale cheeks as she gave a curtsey and then turned to walk off stage. She paused for a moment and smiled back over her shoulder, and the applause grew louder. *I felt like the queen of New Orleans there for a moment*, she thought as she entered her dressing room. *A grand feeling, for sure. The crowd seemed to like me. Maybe … maybe there could be a future for me in this. If I'm to perform for men for a living, I'd prefer the stage to the bedroom.*

A few minutes after she reached her dressing room, someone knocked on the door.

"Come in."

Preston walked in, a large grin on his face.

"I have to hand it to you, Molly," he said as he fished a couple of half-eagle gold coins from his pocket and tossed them on the table, "you sure know how to bring the house down. The crowd went wild. Why, next week we can pack even more people in! That's all right with you, isn't it? How about you do a weekly performance?"

"I think I'd like that, sir," Molly said.

"Look," Preston said, "I'm gonna be honest with you. I can't afford to pay you this much for every performance. This is just because it was an emergency. You understand?"

"And how much do you propose to pay me?"

"How about five dollars a week. Payable after the performance."

"Five dollars a week with a dollar bonus for every sold-out performance would be better," Molly countered.

"That's kind of steep," Preston said. "I don't know if that's possible."

"I'm sure it would be possible for one of the other theaters in town," Molly said. "This is New Orleans. There's a theater on every corner. I appreciate the opportunity you gave me, Mr. Preston. I truly do. But surely you understand that I must look to my own financial interests, just as you do."

"You drive a hard bargain, Molly," Preston said. "However, I do see your point. If you aren't singing for me, you'll sing for someone else. You have a deal."

Molly extended her hand and Preston shook it.

Chapter Twenty-Four

Months went by with no word from Frank, but Molly continued to perform to a packed house at the theater. Major Warlow never missed a performance, sitting in the front row alongside military officers and local politicians. After a show in late February, he managed to sneak backstage. Molly nearly bumped into him when she left her dressing room.

"Why, Major Warlow," she exclaimed. "You gave me a bit of a start."

"I'm sorry to startle you, Miss Molly. I was wondering if I might entice you into joining me for a quick stroll. I've some news to discuss with you."

"I … well … I guess so," Molly said. "I can spare a few minutes."

The two ducked out a side door into the alley that ran alongside the building. When they emerged onto the street, Major Warlow offered his arm and Molly took it. She paused long enough to tell the carriage driver that she would walk home.

"A while back you asked me about the Pinkertons," Major Warlow said. "I did make some inquiries, but all I was able to find out is that they are here on the trail of a murderer."

Molly's heart pounded in her chest with such ferocity she feared the major might hear it.

"A murderer," she gasped. "From where?"

"I've no idea," Major Warlow said. "If I had to venture a guess, I'd say Chicago or Washington, DC, as that is where their agents all seem to hail from."

"Not New York City?"

"No," Major Warlow asked as he looked down on her with a puzzled expression on his face. "Why do you ask?"

"Oh," Molly said. "It's just that New York had a lot of murders when I was there. Being a big city and all."

As they walked, Major Warlow filled her in on the latest talk around army headquarters. Most of it involved speculations about the upcoming campaign against Rebel troops in Western Louisiana. With the fall of Vicksburg and Port Hudson the previous summer, the Union Army and Navy had effectively cut the Confederacy in two by seizing the last Confederate bastions on the Mississippi River.

"General Franklin is going to command the advance division in the Army of the Gulf," Major Warlow said. "I asked for a transfer to his staff and General Butler approved it. Can you believe that? I'm finally going to get my chance to see some action! I thought it would never happen."

Molly stopped and turned to face him, "That's … well … if you are happy, then I'll be happy for you. Promise me you'll be careful, Major."

Major Warlow laughed and said, "I'll be the soul of caution, Miss Molly. That I can assure you."

Molly thought of what Jane had said earlier about Sarah and how she didn't really run away.

"Major Warlow … Timothy …" She looked up at his face. "Did you know a girl named Sarah that worked out the house?"

Major Warlow stopped as if he had walked into a brick wall. He looked at Molly and frowned. "Why do you ask?"

"I heard she ran away," Molly said, "but then … well, she left some things, personal things, in her room. That doesn't seem to fit with her leaving deliberately, does it?"

"You sure you aren't wanting to be a Pinkerton yourself?" Major Warlow asked. "I do believe they employ some female operatives."

"I'm only curious, that's all."

"I never met her," Major Warlow said as he looked away. "Come on, let's get you home."

The major was silent as they walked the rest of the way back to Madam Delacroix's. *Odd behavior, that,* Molly thought. *But maybe it's true. Maybe she didn't work long enough here for him to know her. It ain't like he comes in every night. But … didn't Daphne said that he used to come in all the time?*

As they reached the side entrance, Major Warlow stopped and took both of Molly's hands in his.

"I may not get a chance to see you before I sally forth to fight the rebel horde," he said, "but I will be back. You can be assured of that."

Molly nodded.

"And when I get back," he continued, "I've something I'd like to talk to you about. Something regarding the future."

"The future?" Molly asked.

"Farewell, Miss Molly," Major Warlow said as he released her hands, stepped back, and gave her a slight bow. "May we meet again when this cruel war is over."

Now what is he going on about, Molly wondered as she watched him disappear around the corner. *The future? Whose future? Mine? His? Surely, he is not after marrying me. No man such as himself would want a girl what does what I do. But … there's Frank Lynch and he seems fond enough of me. Daphne said not to believe anything Major Warlow says. What did she mean?*

When she got back to her room, Molly placed the week's pay from the theater inside a small wooden box. With her pay at Madam Delacroix's and the theater pay, Molly was quickly amassing a sum of money that would allow her to take care of Ellen and, perhaps, move out west, maybe even California, as soon as Frank turned up the child's exact whereabouts. Several times over the past few months, Molly considered writing to Frank to ask for more information, but she feared that the letter might be intercepted and her whereabouts made known to the police. Instead, every night she said a silent prayer that the girl might be found before some unspeakable horror befell her.

As Molly slid the box under her bed, someone knocked on the door.

"Come in," Molly said.

Daphne walked in and dropped into a chair as Molly sat down on the bed.

"How was the performance?" she asked.

"Grand," Molly said. "It's funny, you know. Standing up there on stage with all them eyes on you. Makes me feel like I'm Queen Victoria herself."

Daphne laughed and said, "Ain't that a funny thing for an Irish girl to say."

"Daphne, can I ask you something serious?"

"Yes." Daphne moved across the room and sat down on the bed next to Molly. "What is it?"

"It's about Major Warlow."

"He hasn't been making a bunch of promises to you, has he?"

"Why do you say that?" Molly asked.

Daphne looked around the room as if to make sure they were alone, then she leaned close to Molly and whispered, "You have to swear that you won't say anything to Madam Delacroix."

"I swear," Molly said. "Tell me. What is it?"

"Sarah didn't run away," Daphne said. "She cut her wrists in the bathtub. Little Jane is the one that found her. Cold as the clay. Madam D knows that much. She's the one that came up with the story about her having run off to avoid bringing a scandal down on the house."

"But what does that have to do with Major Warlow?" Molly asked. "He told me he didn't know Sarah at all."

"That's horseshit!" Daphne exclaimed. She lowered her voice before she continued. "No, your major knew Sarah very well. They never came upstairs together, so they didn't know each other like that, but he'd walk out with her when she had an afternoon off, and he would pay the missus just to have Sarah sit and talk to him in the parlor."

"What's the harm in that?" Molly asked. "I'd rather a man pay for my company downstairs than up."

"It ain't that," Daphne said. "Sarah thought he aimed to marry her. She told me that he'd proposed to her. Before she got the baby inside her. It weren't his, since they never came upstairs. But she thought that he would take her in no matter what since. But when she told him, he refused to so much as look at her again. That's why she done herself in. And the baby insider her too."

"That's quite a secret to keep," Molly said.

Daphne shrugged. "New Orleans is full of secrets. I think it's cause of all the voodoo and the Frenchies. But say, Molly, he hasn't been telling you he wants to marry you, has he?"

"Not in so many words," Molly said. *The future is what he wanted to discuss*, she thought. *And I can only take that to mean one thing. But what kind of man goes along making promises to whores he don't intend to keep? Does it make him feel … powerful somehow? He's an attorney and an army officer. That's important enough, is it not?*

"Remember," Daphne said as she walked to the door, "you promised not to say anything."

"I won't," Molly said.

Daphne disappeared back to her room, and Molly sat in front of the mirror on her dresser. She unpinned her hair and shook out her curls. *Is the Major just Charles Ellsworth in a uniform?* Her stomach tightened as the image of the man's face floated through her mind. *And his female accomplice*, she thought. *Susannah. What kind of woman would do that to another woman? Forced me into this life without no thought at all for what it'd be like for me. Or for young Ellen. Though I've not done murder before, despite what the newspapers said, I'd kill them both if I got the chance. I only stabbed that man because he attacked me. That ain't murder. And I didn't kill Miss Cecilia either. But God help me, I'd kill Ellsworth and Susannah if I could. All this talk about the laws, but the laws protect people like that. Just like they protect the people that abuse young girls like Ellen.*

A bell rang which indicated there were customers in the parlor. When she got downstairs, Molly circulated among a group of well-dressed businessmen as they discussed the cotton trade.

"I say," said a round man in a dark brown suit, "the war will end this spring."

"How?" asked another. "Lee still has his army and Lincoln can't find a general that can beat him on his own ground. It'll go on forever. Or at least until the election in November. Maybe with a different president in the White House, they can reach a peace settlement. Is an independent Confederacy such a bad thing? The two sections of the country will still have to do business with one another. There's plenty of room for mutual profit."

"Good evening, sirs," Molly said. "How are you this fine night?"

"Well enough," said the portly man. "And what might your name be?"

"It's Molly, your honor."

"You look familiar," the man said. "Have we met before?"

"We have not," Molly said. "Have you been here before? Maybe you saw me then?"

"No, this is my first visit. I must say, this is a fine establishment. Prettiest girls I think I think I've ever seen. But no, I think I've seen you elsewhere."

"The theater," his companion said. "She's a singer. Isn't that right?"

"It is," Molly said.

"That's right! I've seen you a few times," the portly man said. "You've a voice like a Greek goddess."

"Have you ever heard a Greek goddess sing before?" Molly asked.

"Well, no, but well, just … come here. Let's sit down and you can tell me all about how you came to be such a fine mistress of the song."

Molly allowed the man to lead her over the sofa. She sat next to him and listened as he rambled on about his business dealings, the war, and his wife back home in Baltimore. At appropriate times, she made enough small exclamations to convince him that she hung on every word he uttered. *The life of a whore is like that of an actress*, she thought as he began to talk about his preferred military strategy for winning the war. *Or a singer. I perform here on the couch just like I do on the stage. Only one is preferable to the other.*

"And that's what we need to do," the man finished with gusto.

"I'm just a girl and I don't know much about war," Molly said with a smile, "but it seems as though you've a sound plan. Have you considered writing a letter to Lincoln and telling him your suggestions? Surely he would welcome assistance from such a brilliant man as yourself."

"Ha!" the man laughed. "You aren't putting me on, are you?"

"Oh, no, sir," Molly said, her eyes wide as she shook her head. "I'd never seek to deceive such a distinguished man. Why, I bet if you wrote that letter, Old Abe might even commission you a general and let you be the one to make it work. And then, here I'd sit having once entertained the man what won the war! You'd make me famous too, I bet."

"Yes, well," the man said, "I suppose I should leave military strategy to those who really know what they are doing. I'm a mere businessman. A successful one, mind, but a not a soldier. I do not seek glory on the battlefield, but rather to aid my country through supplying uniforms for the army. That's why we, my partner and I, are in New Orleans. We've come to purchase a large supply of cotton."

"Oh sure," his companion called out from across the room, where Daphne stood with her arm linked through his. The man raised his glass in salute and continued, "You make it sound like we are some kind of patriots when, in truth, we serve the dollar, not the Union."

"Somebody has to do it," the round man said. "Soldiers need shirts to wear and if we weren't providing them, and cheaply at that, then some other soul would. And where would that leave us?"

"I'm sure the government appreciates all your hard work, your honor," Molly said. "Would you care to go upstairs? We could further discuss your business. It'd be a bit more private."

"I have been thinking about branching out and getting into women's fashion," the man said. "Perhaps you might like to show me some of your dresses and … other garments. It might be the inspiration that I need."

"I'd be delighted to, your honor," Molly said. She stood and extended her hand. The man took it and stood, his knees crackling as they straightened.

"A touch of the rheumatism," he explained as they started toward the stairs. "The doctor says it is on account of my girth, but I think that's just his way of trying to get me to give up the drink. He and my wife have conspired against me for several years. Don't drink so much. Go for a walk in the evening. Give up cigars. In fact—"

"Shhh …" Molly interrupted. "How about you don't talk no more?"

Chapter Twenty-Five

One morning in early April, Molly walked downstairs to the kitchen, where she found Daphne sitting in a chair, a newspaper spread out on the table in front of her.

"Big fight near Mansfield," she said.

"Where is that?" Molly asked.

"I don't know," Daphne replied. "Over by Texas, I think. Sounds like the Rebs gave Banks's boys the what for."

I do hope Major Warlow is safe, she thought as Daphne folded the paper and got up from the table. *No matter what he is or may be. He wanted to see a battle and now, I guess he has.*

"This came for you, Miss Molly," Jane said as she walked into the room with an envelope in her hand.

"Thank you," Molly said as she took the envelope. She assumed it was from Major Warlow, who had written to her on a weekly basis since marching off to fight. The letters contained little more than a description of the weather and the route of march.

But when she glanced down at the envelope in her hand, her heart froze. *Frank*! *That's Frank's handwriting or my name ain't Molly O'Sullivan*!

Molly tore the envelope open and pulled out the letter. In a few short lines, Frank informed her that he had not yet located Ellen, but he had a promising lead that he intended to check out. He made a vague reference to being busy with work related to the war and he closed by telling Molly to be careful, as rumors reached him of a possible plan to send some NYPD detectives down to New Orleans as somehow they'd caught wind of her whereabouts.

Jesus, she swore to herself. *That's just what I need. Peelers all the way from New York poking their nose into things here. Right when I have a managed to make something for myself.*

With many soldiers gone on campaign, Molly's performances at the theater had not drawn crowds quite as large as when she'd first started, but Mr. Preston still paid her a regular wage. He seemed happy enough that there were any visitors at all. *What will I do if they show up*? *For Christ's sake, why did I have to use my own name when I got here? I could've made up another one like what Mr. Preston uses for me at the theater.*

"Bad news, Miss Molly?" Jane asked, her eyes narrowed with concern.

"Oh, not too bad, Jane," Molly said. "It could always be worse. But thank you for asking. Thank you very much."

Jane flashed her a smile and hurried out of the room.

What a sweet child, Molly thought as she made her way upstairs to select a dress for the performance scheduled at the theater that evening. As she whistled the tune of the popular Union Army song "The Battle Cry of Freedom," Molly opened her wardrobe and studied her options. *The green one*, she thought. *That'll look the best.*

Her thoughts turned to the letter from Frank and of the news of the battle in western Louisiana. *If Frank can spirit Ellen away*, she thought, *I have enough money for her to come here. I have just enough money now that I could find us a place, somewhere small, to stay. As long as I can sing, I can make more.*

She frowned as she closed the wardrobe. *Is it true what Miss Miles said? That Frank Lynch just has an eye for the whores? He's been kinder to me than I could ever have a right to expect. There he is chasing after Ellen like she's his own child. For a moment, Molly thought of herself as a peeler's housewife. Frank sat in a rocking chair near the fire and smoked a pipe as Molly told Ellen all the legends of old Ireland.* In a flash, the image vanished. *No*, she told herself. *It's not me that he's after. He's helping me because he is a policeman and that's his job. It goes no further than that. Does it? I think he's a good man. Certainly, a good man for a peeler. If the Royal Irish Constabulary had more men like him, then maybe they wouldn't be so hated back at home.*

Molly sat at her desk and pulled out some stationery and an envelope to draft a letter to Frank to update him on what had transpired since she arrived in New Orleans. She closed by asking him to wire her the minute he found Ellen and that she would send money to purchase passage to New Orleans for the girl. She signed her initials rather than her name. On the envelope, she used her stage name, Louisa May.

Molly bounded down the stairs and gave the letter to Jane, with instructions to hurry to the post office and place it in the mail. A few coins for postage and a few extra for the girl, and Jane ran out of the door. Molly laughed as she watched the child disappear around the corner. *Wouldn't it be grand to face the world with that much enthusiasm*, Molly thought. *What with the hunger and all, I had no real childhood. And neither has Ellen in the clutches of those devils.*

The afternoon passed quickly, with few visitors. Molly spent the time sitting in the parlor listening to the piano music, though she did not sing as she needed to rest her voice. Around three in the afternoon, Molly asked Jane to fill the tub upstairs. After a twenty-minute soak, Jane came in and helped Molly wash her hair.

"You got pretty hair, Miss Molly," Jane said as she dipped her hands in the tub to rinse the soap away. "Wish I could have red curls like you."

"You are beautiful just like you are," Molly said. "You don't need red curls for that. Why, I think you are the prettiest child I've ever seen."

"Really?" Jane asked as a smile stretched across her face. "You ain't just messing with me?"

"No, of course not," Molly insisted. "I'd not lie to a child."

"Thank you, Miss Molly!" Jane said. She held up a towel for Molly as she stepped out of the tub. "Need anything else?"

"No, thank you," Molly said. "You're a big help. I don't think Madam Delacroix could manage without you."

Jane darted out of the room, and Molly dried herself off and got into a robe for the short walk down the hallway to her bedroom. After she dressed, Molly sat at the desk and applied a bit of cosmetic. Daphne walked in just as she finished and said, "The carriage is waiting outside, but Madam Delacroix wants a word before you leave."

"How do I look?" Molly asked as she stood up and twirled around.

"Like you are a fine lady," Daphne said, "fresh from the Garden District."

Molly laughed and said, "Anyone who thinks that would be sorely disappointed to know the truth. Why don't you come tonight? I'm sure the madam would let you have the time. I can get you in free of charge."

"I'd like to, honest," Daphne said, "but one of my regulars is supposed to be stopping by tonight and he's a big spender. I'd hate to miss him."

"I'll leave word with Mr. Preston to let you in," Molly said. "In case you finish early enough to make it by."

Daphne nodded and Molly made her way downstairs to Madam Delacroix's office. The older woman looked up from her ledgers and motioned Molly to sit down.

"You look ready for the big night," Madam Delacroix said.

"Thank you for letting me do this, Madam," Molly said. "It's been grand. I'm … I'm starting to feel … to feel like … like I'm at home when I'm up there singing."

"Just make sure that you keep track of the money owed you by the theater. Managers can be untrustworthy at times. Especially with you being a young woman."

"You wanted to see me before I went, Madam?" Molly asked.

"Yes. I think you've more than held up your end of the bargain, so I'll no longer take a ten percent cut."

"Thank you, ma'am," Molly said.

"I realize you've made a good amount of money," Madam Delacroix said.

"I have, ma'am," Molly said.

"Are you planning on leaving us soon? Be honest. I won't hold it against you."

"Not right away, ma'am," Molly said. "There's some … business in New York that a friend is tending to for me. I don't know how long that will take. And I can't, or won't, leave until it is settled."

"That's good to hear," Madam Delacroix said. "Truth be told, I'd be sorry to see you go. You've done right by me since you arrived. The customers all speak highly of you. Are you planning on pursuing a career on the stage?"

"Do you think I could do that?" Molly asked. "Be a singer full time?"

"You have the talent for it. And you've built up quite a following here. Maybe when the war ends, you could go on tour. You came here from New York. I'd start there."

Molly frowned at the mention of New York City.

"What's wrong?" Madam Delacroix asked.

"It's nothing," Molly said as she forced a smile to drive away the frown. "I'd love to go on tour one day. Maybe even go back to Ireland. But with a bit more money than I had when I left."

"Good luck tonight," Madam Delacroix said, dismissing Molly with a nod.

Molly walked out the front door and paused for a moment to take in the white carriage. It never ceased to amaze her that the madam allowed her to ride down to the theater in such style. *No one in Belclare would believe this,* she thought. *Molly O'Sullivan riding through the streets of New Orleans in a carriage fit for some grand emperor. I bet even Napoleon himself didn't ride in something so nice.*

The coachman opened the door for her, dropped the step, and extended his hand. Molly smiled at him as she climbed into the passenger compartment. As the horses lurched their way down the street, she closed her eyes and envisioned herself on the stage looking out at a packed house. She felt the light on her face and heard the applause from the crowd. *All that attention for an Irish whore,* she thought. *New Orleans surely is a strange city.*

When she arrived at the theater and got out of the carriage, Molly told the driver that she would prefer to walk back from the performance.

"You sure, miss?" he asked. "It'll be dark."

"Oh, I'll be fine," Molly said. "It won't be late, and the streets will be full. It's a lovely evening for a stroll, I think."

A few patrons outside called out greetings to her as she approached the door. Molly made a point to smile and thank each of them. Mr. Preston met her outside her dressing room and told her that this would be her first sold out show in several months. Molly made sure to mention to him that Daphne might come with a companion. He promised to let the doorman know.

She went into her dressing room and poured a cup of water from the pitcher on the table. Before each show, Molly liked to drink a bit of lukewarm water to relax her vocal cords. Mentally, she ran through the words of the songs she had chosen to sing tonight. After a few of her own favorites, Molly added a few new songs to her list. Tonight, she planned to sing "I'll Twine 'Mid the Ringlets" and "The Irish Jaunting Car" for the first time. With all her performances, it seemed as though the men in the crowd most appreciated the songs that talked about loved ones left behind at home. *It's like that in every war in history, I bet,* Molly thought. *Men rush off to war and then when they get there, they miss the one's they've left behind.*

She thought about Major Warlow, off somewhere fighting the rebels. And of Patrick. And Frank as he haunted the back alleys of the city looking for Ellen. Somewhere amid that mass of humanity, the young girl awaited rescue. *No,* she told herself. *Now is not the time to dwell on that. You've a performance to give. There'll be time for that later.*

The crowd roared as Molly finished her last number. She tried to say thank you, but the shouts and cheers drowned out her words. Backstage, Mr. Preston saw her and shook his head.

"I do believe that's your finest one yet," he said.

"Thank you, Mr. Preston."

He handed her some coins in a small purse. "I think you've managed to put this theater back on the map. You know, the Opera House closed when the Yanks took over the city. But people here still like their entertainment. When the war's over, we'll be making so much money we might very well have to add seats. Tonight, there were even people standing out in the street. I had them open the front doors. Couldn't hear much from the street, but it was enough to maybe get some of them inside next time."

"I hope so," Molly said. "Now, if you'll excuse me?"

"Certainly," Mr. Preston said with a bow.

Molly smiled as she slipped out the side door. A full moon shone down over the streets. Lights flickered inside some of the buildings as she made her way back towards Madam Delacroix's. Well-dressed men and women strolled by in both directions and the occasional carriage passed, the hooves from the horses sounding like Morse Code on the streets. Men tipped their hats to her as she walked by, sometimes earning them an angry look from their female companions.

I could almost get used to this, she thought. *It's not so much the attention as it is people treating me as though I'm a human rather than a brood mare or a piece of Irish trash what ain't got no feelings of her own. Is this what Lord Sanderson and his kind feel like whenever they strut about the estate? Except I'm not after acting like I'm better than the people around me. But if they knew my true occupation, not that this one is much better in their eyes, they certainly wouldn't be as friendly. Not in public, anyway.*

To her left, Molly saw a dark coach along the street, curtains drawn over the windows. Two black horses pawed and snorted at the ground as the coach driver spoke soothingly to them in a Scottish accent. As she walked by it, Molly heard the coach door open, but thought little of it. Two children chased one another around in circles and laughed as a street musician scraped out a tune on a fiddle.

For a moment, the scene reminded her of her last night in Belclare. The music. The dancing. She smiled. *I think I'm happy*, she thought, *and I've not had much cause for any of that since I got to America.*

Suddenly, her world went black as a rough burlap sack dropped over her head. Something inside the bag made it smell sweet. Strong arms encircled her waist and lifted her off the ground. She heard a woman scream on the street and several men called out in alarm.

Molly felt herself being carried backwards. She tried to scream, to call for help, to fight, but her voice and limbs did not respond, as if the signals from her brain couldn't reach them. Her eyelids grew heavier as the person carrying her placed her gently on the floor of a coach. As Molly drifted off to sleep, she had a vague sensation of being rolled onto her stomach and ropes pulled tight around her wrists and ankles. *What … what … what's happening?* Her last conscious thought was *Pinkertons!*

Chapter Twenty-Six

The first thing Molly felt, before she opened her eyes, was a slow rocking motion. Her eyelids felt glued to her face, but she managed to force them open. A wave of nausea overtook her, and she rolled onto her side and vomited onto the floor. Her head pounded and she wrapped her arms around her stomach and groaned. *A ship*, she thought, feeling the familiar rolling motion. *I must be on a ship. How did I get here?* Through the fog in her brain, Molly had a vague recollection of someone grabbing her and throwing her into a carriage. *But why? If it was the peelers in New York City, they wouldn't have needed to kidnap me. Jesus! My head hurts.* It took her five minutes to push herself out of the bed. Legs unsteady, she wobbled her way to the door and tried the knob. *Locked! I'm locked in here!* She collapsed back onto the bed and fell asleep.

When she awoke, Molly did not know how much time had passed. It could have been days, or just a few minutes. Her stomach and head felt a bit better, though a thin mist still hung over her mind. She jumped when she heard a key in the door. It opened and the man with a scar on his face came into the room. He grabbed a chair from the corner and sat down while Molly drew herself up in the bed, shrinking away from him.

"Calm down," the man said. "I've no designs on hurting you."

"Who are you," Molly asked.

"Name's Barnabus," he said. "No need for you to know my last name. I do apologize for the circumstances that have led us to meet. Kinda unfortunate."

"Where am I?"

"We are on a ship bound for New York City," Barnabus said.

"You are a Pinkerton," Molly said.

Barnabus let out a low whistle. "They wasn't lying when they said you was a smart one. Since you already know, I reckon there's no harm in admitting it. Yes, I'm a Pinkerton."

"Why would the police need to hire Pinkertons? If they were after me, couldn't they have just come for me themselves?"

"It ain't the police that sent us," Barnabus said. "Though I imagine they'll be happy enough to get their hands on you when we arrive. That's who we are to turn you over to."

"Then who?" Molly asked. "Who sent you?"

"We keep all matters involving our clients strictly confidential," Barnabus said. "I am not at liberty to say. But a smart girl like you can figure it out, I'm sure. Now. Listen here. They warned me you was a hellcat too. But you are on a boat. There's nowhere for you to run off to. If you promise to behave yourself, I'll leave the door unlocked. One false move, and you'll find yourself chained to the bed for the duration. Understand?"

"I do," Molly said. "I won't cause any trouble. You've my word."

"It pains me to take the word of a whore." Barnabus scratched his cheek near the scar. "But I reckon I ain't got no choice."

"And you are to deliver me to the police, Mr. Barnabus?" Molly asked.

"That's what they are paying me for. You are wanted on a charge of arson and for the murder of one Miss Cecilia Pearl. No doubt you'll swing for it."

"I'll what?"

"Heard they got solid evidence of your criminal nature. They'll hang you just as sure as my name's Barnabus. So be a good girl and enjoy the time you have left. You must be hungry. I'll have some food sent down for you. And just in case you are thinking about enticing any of the crew to help you, they've been warned you are a dangerous murderess and will steer clear. There's no other passengers on board neither."

The gallows? Molly thought. *But I didn't do nothing wrong! I murdered no one. It was an accident, as was the fire. Surely someone will believe me. They'll have to believe me.* She watched Barnabus as he walked out of the room. He closed the door behind him but did not lock it.

A few minutes later, the door opened and a boy in his early teens walked in carrying a tray with some food and a small pitcher of water. Molly waited for him to speak, but he kept his eyes focused on the floor.

"Here," Molly said. "Just set it on the bed."

The boy did as Molly said, though his eyes never moved.

"Thank you," she called after him as he ducked out of the room.

My God! The boy was either terrified or shy. What exactly did Barnabus tell them? That I'm some mad ax murderer?

As she scooped up some soggy peas with a spoon, her mind drifted back to that last afternoon at Miss Cecilia's. The attack. The knife. The blood. And the fire. *That's who done it,* she realized. *They must've found out I fled to New Orleans, but how? And they sent the Pinkertons after me. They only want me for Miss Cecilia's death, so the family will let the law punish me for that.*

She forced herself to eat a stale ship's biscuit, though it was so hard she had to soak it in a bit of water first to soften it up. As much as she wanted to stay in the room, to shut the door and await the ship's arrival in New York, Molly decided to go up on deck. *I'll appreciate the fresh air once I'm languishing in the cells awaiting the hangman.*

With two seagoing trips to her credit, Molly quickly regained her sea legs and walked with the rolling gait of an experienced sailor. She made her way to the stern and watched as the sun set. It looked as though the sun was sinking beneath the waves. When she looked down at the dark waters of the Gulf of Mexico, Molly thought of Hannah. *She found her escape here. The ocean saved her from her fate.*

Molly reached out and took hold of the rail with her right hand, before her mind even had time to process what she was doing. She took a step closer.

A hand shot out and closed around her wrist. It jerked her away from the rail. She turned to see Barnabus grinning at her.

"Figured you might try that," he said. "That's my only worry about letting you roam around the ship."

"Try what?" Molly asked.

"Try to jump overboard. But I wager you can't swim, so you'd be trying to drown yourself."

"No," Molly said. "I wouldn't …"

"It wouldn't be fair to cheat the client out of watching you dangle from the noose now, would it? If'n they want to watch, that is. Come on, let's get back to the cabin."

Molly jerked her wrist away and put her hands on her hips.

"You listen to me, Mr. Barnabus," she said. "I have no design on harming myself. There was a girl … on the trip to New Orleans … she jumped over the side of the ship. I was just thinking about her. That's all. And you seem very convinced of my guilt. And that I'll be convicted. Do you know that I am innocent?"

Barnabus shrugged and said, "Honestly, miss, it makes no difference to me if you are innocent or not. I just got paid to bring you back and give you to the police. They say they got plenty of evidence and a witness or two. What would you think if you were me?"

"I think I'd find a different occupation," Molly said. "One that doesn't require you to go around snatching innocent young women off the street and carting them off to their doom. You are no better than a slave trader. Tell me, Mr. Barnabus, can you sleep at night?"

"Like a baby," Barnabus said. "Come on, let's go below. I'll have to lock you in your cabin for the night, but you'll be allowed out tomorrow at daybreak."

With a sweep of his arm, Barnabus indicated that he wanted Molly to walk ahead of him. She hesitated for a moment but did as he wished. When she reached the room, Molly noticed right away that someone had cleaned the vomit from the floor. Probably the young man what brought me food, she thought. A small lamp cast shadows on the wall.

"Can I get you anything?" Barnabus asked.

"No," Molly said. "I would like to send some letters, but I'll wait until we get to the city."

"Until tomorrow, then," Barnabus said as he closed the door and turned the key.

Will they let me write letters from the jail? Surely, they will. She debated whether she should write to her mother, in care of the priest, and explain what tragedies had befallen her in America. *No*, she decided. *I cannot do that. She sent me off to America as an innocent girl. I can't write her and tell her that I'm a whore and an accused murderess now. The shock of it would kill her. And Father Byrne too.*

Sleep came slowly that night. When she finally drifted off, Molly dreamed of New York City. She saw herself cold and hungry, making her way through the streets with Ellen in her arms. She felt the warmth of the whiskey provided by Ellsworth and his companion as it settled into her stomach and made her warm. Then her dream took her back to the room at the boarding house. Terror gripped her as a dark shape entered the room. She heard Ellen's scream and felt hands pulling at her. Her heartbeat accelerated and she began to scream.

The door was flung open, and Barnabus stormed in. Molly's eyes opened and she looked around in confusion. Her breath came in ragged gasps and sweat poured from her face..

"What in the hell is going on?" he demanded.

"What do you mean?" Molly asked.

"You were screaming bloody murder," Barnabus said. "Is something wrong?"

"No," Molly said. "No … I … it was a bad dream, that's all."

"You sure?"

"I'm sorry," Molly said. "I didn't mean to disturb anyone."

"You woke up half the Confederacy," Barnabus said with a growl. "Keep it down the rest of the night, will you? For that matter, keep it down the rest of the trip."

"I will, sir," Molly said. "I truly am sorry."

Barnabus slammed the door and locked it. Molly swore under her breath. *I can't believe that was only a dream*, she thought. *For a moment … for a moment I thought I was back in that room and it was happening to me all over again. I don't want to ever relive that again. Jesus! Once was bad enough.*

She poured herself a small cup of water and rinsed her mouth out, as it had gone dry during the night. She lay back on the bed but as tired as she felt, her brain fought against sleep. When Barnabus arrived to unlock the door the next morning, she was still awake. When he pushed the door open, instead of coming in himself, he stepped aside and the boy from the day before brought in another tray. Like before, he kept his eyes downward. Molly nibbled a piece of toast and drank a mug of strong chicory coffee. She tried to remember how long it had taken her to reach New Orleans from New York, so that she might know how much time remained on this voyage, but since she did not know how long she'd been on the ship before she awoke in the cabin with the ship underway, Molly couldn't piece it together and she did not want to ask Barnabus.

For the remainder of the voyage, Molly settled into a predictable routine. She rose each morning, tried to eat as much as her stomach would accept, and then took a stroll around the main deck. For the most part, the sailors ignored her other than to touch a knuckle to their foreheads and say "Ma'am." Barnabus secured a couple of books from the ship's captain and gave them to Molly to pass the time. In the afternoons, she sat in a chair at the stern of the ship and tried to read. She worked her way through the first volume of *The Decline and Fall of the Roman Empire* by Gibbon, though at various points she was tempted to chunk it into the sea. She found a Dickens novel, *Hard Times*, more to her liking. She finished reading it during her last full day on board. *Hard Times, Mr. Dickens*, she thought as she closed the book. *I could tell you all about hard times.*

"Please give my thanks to the captain," Molly said as she returned the books to Barnabus. "It was most kind of him to loan them to me."

"I will," Barnabus said. "We'll be in the harbor tomorrow. I'll have to turn you over to the police. Thank you for not causing me any trouble on this trip. Was kinda scared you might try to kill me or something at first."

"Why would you think that?" Molly asked.

"Well, from what I was told about you, it sounded like you was some kind of fiend that would try to murder me and whole crew in our sleep and take over the ship for herself."

Ain't that what Queen Maeve would've done, Molly thought. *And sailed off into the unknown to be a pirate like Grace O'Malley. If only I had that much bravery, maybe I would've done just that.*

"Don't believe everything you hear about someone, Mr. Barnabus," Molly said. "Meet them first and form your own opinion. People can say anything they want. It don't make it true."

That night, Molly again found herself unable to sleep. Her stomach churned in nervous anticipation of what the next day might bring. As she'd only spent seven months in New York, Molly knew little of the criminal justice process, other than from the often-suspect stories she read in the newspapers. Everyone in the city knew about the Tombs, Molly included, but that special circle of hell seemed reserved for those hauled in for minor transgressions. For those accused of serious crimes, Molly did not know where they might be taken to await trial. Though part of her feared being locked in a cell for months more than she feared gallows, she told herself that a barred cell was no different than her life at Madam Delacroix's or Miss Cecilia's. *Isn't the world just a prison without walls anyway*, she thought. *I can no more escape a prison in New York City than I can escape my life as a whore. No! That's not true. I was making my way out. Slow enough, for sure. But I was doing it. I'll not give up hope now. I can't.*

When the sun rose the next morning, Barnabus told Molly that he'd managed to secure permission for her to have a bath. At first, she hesitated, but he assured her it would be private.

"Besides," he said, "don't you want to look your best for the police? And you don't know when you'll get the chance to wash again. I doubt they have a bathing day in the prison."

Molly laughed and said, "I suppose you are right, Mr. Barnabus. Other than the circumstances in which we met, I think you are a kind man underneath it all. Perhaps you could find something else to do with your life."

"Being a private detective suits me. I think I'll stick with it."

In the hold of the ship, Barnabus had rigged a curtain around a barrel filled with lukewarm water. Molly quickly removed her dress and stepped into the barrel. She got as clean as she could with the greasy bar of soup he'd provided. As she tried to scrub her hair, Molly thought of the day she'd left Ireland. *If I'd have known then where I'd end up, taking a bath in a barrel of water before I'm marched off to the prison, would I have still come to America? Or would I have stayed behind and taken my chances with Lord Sanderson's son with the roaming hands? No, this is fate. If I'd have stayed behind, I'd have taken a knife to him for thinking he owned me and then I'd be tossed in jail and awaiting the noose just like I am to be here. We cannot escape what fate has dictated our lot to be.*

Molly climbed out of the tub and dried herself as best she could before she put her clothes back on. She wished she would have had time to wash them as well. The ship had eased into the slip at the docks when Molly walked up to the main deck. It's in almost the exact spot where the *Dublin Rose* landed, she thought as she looked out over the docks. The workers and the warehouses had not changed much in her absence. The air had turned chilly during their trip up the East Coast. *I won't miss the heat*, Molly thought. *New York is the better in that regard.*

She scanned the faces of the people standing around the pier and spotted two men off to the side, hats pulled low over their faces as they studied the ship. *Detectives*, she thought. *They carry themselves just as Frank does. They'll be my escort to the cells, I imagine.*

"I guess this is it, Miss Molly," Barnabus said. "I would wish you luck, but …"

"Thank you, Mr. Barnabus," Molly said. "I understand. It's not luck that I would need to escape my fate. I'd need something more akin to a miracle."

A sailor moved over to the rail and lowered a gangway. Barnabus looked at Molly and said, "Well, shall we?"

Molly took a deep breath and nodded.

Chapter Twenty-Seven

Molly squared her shoulders, lifted her chin, and, gathering her skirt in one hand, walked down the gangway toward the detectives. The taller of the two pushed his brown bowler back on his head and appraised her with cold, dark eyes. Molly smiled when she reached them.

"Good afternoon, gentlemen," she said. They did not respond.

"Can one of you sign for her?" Barnabus asked as he pulled a piece of paper out of his pocket. "All it says is that you are taking receipt of her. We need it for our files."

"You need it to get paid," the taller detective said as he took the paper, signed it, and passed it back. "If you ever get tired of solving rich people's problems and want to do some real police work, I'm sure we could find something for you to do."

Barnabus ignored the comment and turned to Molly. He hesitated for a moment and then extended his hand. "So long, Miss Molly."

"So long," Molly replied. As Barnabus walked away, Molly faced the detectives and said, "Well, gentlemen, lead on."

"We've got a coach for you," the shorter of the two said. "Figured that'll give you a bit more privacy. Not that we have far to go. Promise you won't try any funny business and we won't clap you in irons for the trip."

"I promise to behave," Molly said. "It ain't like I'd get very far if I ran off."

"I wouldn't say that," the taller man said. "You ran off to New Orleans, didn't you? Where you plan on going next? Shanghai?"

The shorter detective laughed and said, "My name's Christopher O'Hara and my partner here is Langley. He ain't Irish, but that's not his fault. Come on, let's get going."

Molly followed them down the pier to the street, where a young black boy stood holding the bridle of a horse attached to a hackney carriage. The horse snorted and pawed at the ground as the boy whispered to him. The smell of the city reached Molly's nose and she swallowed hard. *I'd forgotten the odor of the place*, she thought. *New Orleans smelled like a sewer, but I swear New York is worse.* Rotting garbage, manure, offal, and the smell of teeming masses of unwashed humanity all mingled together to produce an overpowering stench that clung to the clothing and the inside of the nose of anyone who set foot in the city. *Still*, she thought, *to some it is the smell of home*. Molly smiled as she thought of the smell of the damp fields around Belclare after a spring rain, and the smell of the cottage when her mother prepared a pot of stew. *I'd give anything to be smelling that now instead of this shite hole*, she thought. *Maybe when I die my spirit can return to Ireland to stay.*

"Here, allow me, Miss O'Sullivan," Christopher said as he held out his hand to help her up into the coach. "I'm riding with you and Langley's gonna sit up top with the driver."

That's a relief, Molly thought as she took his hand and climbed inside. He seems a bit nicer than his partner. *There's something about authority that can turn a man into a petty tyrant quick if he isn't careful.* She remembered the way the English landlords and the merchant class in Ireland looked on her people with utter disdain bordering on outright disgust. It was as if they looked through rather than at the impoverished Irish all around them. *It is the reason they want us gone. It don't matter to them if it's hunger, immigration, or them executing us for every pretended slight. Just as long as we are gone. We don't exist to them except to serve as a barrier to what they call progress. Sure, but weren't we doing just fine before they showed up.*

As the carriage started up the street, Christopher suddenly leaned close to Molly and whispered, "Frank knows you are here."

Molly's eyes widened and she started to speak, but Christopher put a finger to his lips.

"Shhh, Langley doesn't know that I talked to Frank," he whispered. "It's better that way. We, I mean, Frank and I, we know what evidence they are planning to present at your trial, and we are trying to find a way to counter it. I admit, it don't look good for you, but we'll figure out a way."

"Thank you," Molly said as she felt a wave of relief wash over her for the first time since she'd be taken from the street in New Orleans.

"Frank'll try to come and visit you if he can, but you gotta understand that no one knows about his friendship with you. That could cause problems for him if it got out. So, if he don't visit, he wanted me to tell you that he's still working on your case."

"I thought my case was pretty much closed," Molly said. "They've all the evidence they need."

"Oh, no, not you," Christopher said. "He meant the girl. I can't remember her name. But it's the child he has been helping you look for."

"Ellen," Molly said. "Her name is Ellen."

"Yeah, that one. Anyway, he's still trying."

"Can you get a message to him from me?"

"I don't have any paper to write on."

Molly reached over and took hold of his arm. "Swear to me that you'll tell him this. Tell him that if I am to die on the gallows, to keep looking for Ellen. When he finds her, he is to telegraph Madam Delacroix in New Orleans. She probably has the money that I'd been keeping in my room there. Use the money to send the child to me mother back in Belclare. Understand?"

"Yeah … I think so," Christopher said.

"Swear that you will tell him exactly what I said," Molly said as her grip tightened. "Swear."

"All right, all right," Christopher said. "Go easy on the arm, would ya? Of course, I'll tell him."

"Thank you," Molly said.

"Tell me about New Orleans. I've heard it is nice."

As the boy behind the reigns deftly maneuvered the coach around and through pedestrian traffic and the occasional wagon, Molly described New Orleans to Christopher. She told him of the ever-present heat and humidity that sapped energy from everyone. He asked about the people, and Molly described the never-ending parade of characters the city offered.

"It could have been Dublin," Molly said. "Or, what Dublin must be like. I never went there myself. I'm from the west. Galway."

"I'm from Kerry," Christopher said. "At least that's what my mother said."

"But you—"

"I know," Christopher said with a laugh. "I don't sound Irish. Reason is that I was only a year old when we came to New York. I have no memories of Ireland at all. Only what my mother told me. She died when I was six and I got packed off to an orphanage."

"I'm sorry," Molly said. "That must have been very hard on you."

"Oh, I got by all right," Christopher said with a shrug. "They tried to beat me into submission. Gave up when I was twelve and kicked me out. I lived on the street for a while until a police captain's wife took me in. That's how come I joined the coppers."

"Do you like it?" Molly asked. "Being a peeler?"

"Truth is," Christopher said, "I'd rather be a fire laddie. Looks like a lot more fun. Can't make a living at that though. Rumor is that we are about to drop the volunteer companies and have us a paid department like they got in Boston. If that happens, I'd ask for a transfer, but they'll say no since they'll hire all the boys that are volunteers now."

Patrick, Molly thought. Her eyes watered as she thought of the young fireman, as eager to talk to her as he was to tackle a blaze. *He was so kind to me. And him dying during the conscription riots. Doing his duty for people that don't appreciate it.*

"Are you feeling poorly, Miss Molly?"

Molly sniffed and wiped the back of her hand across her eyes, "No. No, I'm fine. I was just thinking of someone. An old friend that I had here in the city."

"I can take a message to him," Christopher said. "Or her. Whichever. I'd be happy to do it."

"I'd let you, but that won't work unless you can carry the message across the River Styx," Molly said. "My friend is among the departed now. Killed during the riots."

"God what a nasty business that was!" Christopher exclaimed. "I damn near got my head stove in by some gigantic paddy with fists the size and weight of a twenty-four-pound cannonball."

"If you two are finished talking like a couple out for a stroll at Battery Park," Langley called down, "you might be interested to know we are almost there."

Molly looked around and asked, "Are we not going to the Tombs?"

"No," Christopher said. "It's because you are charged with felonies instead of misdemeanors. You'll get a trial with a jury if you want, and the Tombs only houses the Police Court. I mean, we've had felons housed there in the past, but at least for now, you'll be at the prison by City Hall. It'll be better for you that way. Frank managed to discreetly slip some jack to the superintendent and so you'll have a cell to yourself. Beats what you'd get at the Tombs by a long margin."

"Please give him my thanks for that, and for everything," Molly said.

Christopher nodded as the coach turned off the street and passed under a stone archway. The coach jerked to a halt and shook as the driver and Langley climbed down. Christopher jumped out and helped Molly to the ground. They were in the middle of a courtyard, bordered on three sides by a dark stone building of three stories. The fourth side contained the archway, protected by two massive doors. Molly flinched as they swung closed, the sound echoing through the courtyard like a cannon shot. When she turned to her left, away from the arch, Molly froze. Her stomach twisted like an icy hand had grabbed ahold of her intestines. A wood gallows stood watch over the yard. A lone noose dangled from the crossbeam and swung gently in the breeze.

"Is that"—she paused and swallowed—"is that for … me?"

"No," Christopher said as he followed her gaze, "there's a murderer set to hang later today for killing his missus and their children. He might get a reprieve though. It was the drink that made him do it."

"It ain't for you today," Langley added. "But it will be soon enough. Don't worry."

"Shut the fuck up, Langley," Christopher said. "Leave her alone. Christ! I should've done this by myself."

Langley turned to the boy who'd driven them to the prison and paid him. The boy looked down at the coins in his hand and scowled at Langley.

"Give him a gratuity, you cheap bastard," Christopher said. "You can put it on your expense report for the month."

Langley grumbled something unintelligible but passed the boy another coin. The boy smiled and nodded his thanks before he took hold of the horse's bridle and led him to the gate.

"Come on," Langley said as he grabbed hold of Molly's arm, "let's get inside."

"I know how to walk, Detective," Molly said.

"You'll walk how and where I tell you to walk," Langley said. "You ain't some fancy whore now. You are a ward of the state, accused of heinous crimes. If it was my decision, we'd have hauled you here in the paddy wagon. Whores shouldn't get special treatment, if you ask me."

"No one did," Christopher said.

Molly walked toward a heavy wooden door with a detective on either side of her and Langley keeping a firm grip on her arm. Christopher gave a sharp rap on the door with his knuckles. A panel near the top slid open, and two eyes peered out at them.

"Detectives O'Hara and Langley," Christopher said. "We've orders to deliver a prisoner here."

"Prisoner's name?"

Langley squeezed Molly's arm and said, "Tell him your name."

"Molly. Molly O'Sullivan."

"Just a moment," the voice said. The panel slid shut and Molly looked at Christopher, who shrugged as if to indicate he did not know any more about what was going than she did.

Several minutes went by before the door opened. A small man with a pallid complexion and spectacles perched on the tip of his nose beckoned them to enter. He closed the door behind them and said, "I expected you here yesterday."

"Don't know nothing about that," Langley said.

Molly looked around. The anteroom was dark, with minimal light provided by oil lamps that hung on the walls. Doors made of iron bars led to corridors to her left and right. Ahead, another thick wooden door had a sign over it that read "Superintendent." She heard a jangle of keys as a burly man in a uniform like those worn by the police opened one of the iron doors and walked into the room.

"Get the boss, would you Fitz?" the spectacled man said.

The man nodded and walked over to the wooden door. He unlocked it and disappeared behind it for a moment. When he returned, a squat older man with graying hair around his temples accompanied him.

"I see our prisoner is here," the man said. "I'm the superintendent of this prison. You must be Miss O'Sullivan."

"I am, your honor," Molly said.

"You'll be furnished with a list of prison rules," he said. "I expect you to abide by them. To the letter. Understand? If you cause trouble for me, I promise you that I will cause trouble for you. We've had to go through considerable inconvenience to house you here, as we don't find many women inside these walls accused of such serious crimes."

"I understand, your honor," Molly said.

"Right, well, I am to read you this." The superintendent pulled out a piece of paper from his coat pocket. "Molly O'Sullivan, late of Ireland and formerly a resident of this city, is hereby charged with the murder of Miss Cecilia Pearl, of Mott Street, and with a charge of arson for burning the property of the aforementioned Miss Pearl, said property located on the corner of Mott and Bayard Streets. Do you understand?"

"I'm innocent of it all," Molly said. "I swear to you. I murdered no one. And I did not set a fire either."

"Save your entreaties," the superintendent said. "You'll be given a chance to enter a plea of not guilty in court, if that is what you desire. I am merely required to tell you by what reason we are holding you here. Fitz will take you to your cell."

Langley released her arm and Molly turned to face Christopher.

"Thank you for your kindness," she said. "Perhaps one day some of it will rub off on your partner."

Christopher laughed as Langley sputtered, his face red.

"I'll be sure to get a front row seat when they pull the lever on the trap door," Langley said, once he recovered his voice. "We'll see how much sass you've got when you're dancing at the end of the rope."

"I hope I don't disappoint you then," Molly said. She looked at Fitz and said, "I'm ready, sir. Lead on."

Fitz brought her through one set of iron doors and down a long corridor. They turned right, passed through another iron door, and then walked up three flights of stairs. From there, Molly lost track of the twists and turns down various hallways until, finally, Fitz halted outside a heavy wooden door.

"This is it, ma'am," he said. "This cell is special, like. We usually use it for important people we have to lock up, or for the dangerous ones what might cause trouble if we put them in with the rest of the lot."

"I see," Molly said.

"You'll be fed three times a day. Food ain't much, but it will be hot. You'll be allowed out to take in fresh air in the courtyard for an hour each day, but I don't know what time it will be. There's a bookshelf with some books and newspapers in there for you. I was asked to put them in there by the boss. Sheets on the bed are clean. You need anything, there's a rope you can pull which will ring a bell and we'll send someone up."

"Are visitors allowed?" Molly asked. *Now why did I ask that*, she wondered. *It ain't like I got many friends left in this city. Only Frank and he must be careful not to let on a connection between the two of us.*

"I believe so, miss," Fitz said. "I imagine you'll be wanting an attorney. They can come by and talk to prisoners whenever they like.

As far as others go, we have visiting hours but I'm not sure exactly when they are. Folks here don't seem to get many visitors, if you take my drift."

"I do, sir," Molly said.

Fitz unlocked the door and pushed it open. Molly hesitated for a moment, then smiled at him before she walked into the cell. The coolness of the stones seeped into her and the air smelled stale, like desperation mingled with fear. She flinched as the door slammed shut. Molly's eyes watered, and after a moment, she felt the tears start to run down her face.

Chapter Twenty-Eight

Molly had a few days to adjust to her surroundings, spartan as they were, before she received her first visitor. The cell contained a narrow, iron cot with a lumpy mattress, a small table with a wash basin and chair, and a bookcase filled with mostly religious texts and two novels. A stack of newspapers, a month or so old, were stacked on the table next to the wash basin. The stone walls of the cell made it cool enough that Molly wrapped the wool blanket from the bed around her shoulders as she sat at the table and tried to make her way through the papers. After two days, she'd finished the newspapers, the most recent of which spoke of the start of a great offensive against the Confederate Army in Virginia, and turned her attention to the books.

With no clock, she measured time by her meals. Though the food was always warm, the meager provisions left her in a constant state of hunger. *I thought I'd left all that behind in Ireland*, she thought as she chewed on a stale roll. *But I've felt plenty of hunger here in the land of plenty, just like back home. Ironic, that.*

She'd been provided with writing materials, and Molly composed a letter to Madam Delacroix explaining the circumstances of her absence. She asked the madam to forward her money to Frank. *Maybe he can use it for Ellen*, she thought. *If he finds her.*

A knock on the door interrupted her thoughts. After a moment, she heard keys in the lock. The door swung open and Fitz stuck his head in.

"Begging your pardon, Miss Molly," he said, "but you've a visitor."

Frank's come, she thought. Fitz stepped aside and a middle-aged man with slumped shoulders and a permanent frown etched onto his face walked into the cell. He carried a leather satchel in his left hand.

"Thank you," the man said to Fitz, "I'll ring for you when I've finished my business."

The door closed and the man studied Molly for a minute before he spoke. "My name is Silas Chadwick. I've been retained as your counsel."

"My what?" Molly asked.

"Your attorney."

"I'm sorry, sir," Molly said. "I don't see how that is possible. I left what money I had back in New Orleans. I've no means to pay you. This must be some kind of mistake."

"The fee has been paid," Chadwick said, "so put your mind at ease on that point. But we've a lot of work ahead of us."

"They are not," Molly said. "but who paid you? Frank?"

"Who is Frank?" Chadwick asked. He hesitated and said, "There is a certain doctor in the Sixth Ward whom you know from your time there. He heard of your return to the city, and the circumstances of that return, and sought my assistance. I was instructed to do the best I could to keep you away from the gallows. Beyond that, there are no guarantees."

"Dr. Howard!" Molly said. "He was always good to me. Is he well?"

"He is," Chadwick said, "but I assure you that his health and well-being are not what we should be discussing. My time is short, and I have other cases, so would you be so good as to let me sit at the desk so I might discuss your case with you and take notes as appropriate."

"Please," Molly said as she stood up and moved over to sit on the bed.

Chadwick sat down and withdrew a notepad and a pencil from his briefcase. "Now, start from the beginning. I will let you tell your story without interruption and save my questions for the end."

Molly told him about the day of the attack, of her flight through the city during the draft riots, her escape from the boarding house, her trip to New Orleans, and her return to New York at the hands of the Pinkertons. Chadwick filled two pages with notes as she spoke.

When she finished, Chadwick was silent for a moment. "The Pinkertons most certainly kidnapped you. The warrant for your arrest did not extend beyond this state, and it was directed to the police. You could prefer charges against them in Louisiana, should you choose, but I would not bother if I were you. As you have surmised, I believe the family of the man who attacked you wishes to see you punished for his death, but they also wish to keep those circumstances a secret. This led them to hire the private detectives to bring you back here so that you might face justice for the death of Cecilia Pearl and, by proxy, be punished for the man's death as well."

"Yes, sir," Molly said. "Do you think that a jury will believe me? It is all the truth that I told you."

"I don't think they will," Chadwick said. "I mean no offense when I say this, but the word of a prostitute in court carries little weight. And, though you may be telling the truth, you did admit to shoving Miss Cecilia down during the fire."

"Only after she attacked me," Molly protested. "It was self-defense! I swear!"

Chadwick held up a hand to stop her. When Molly fell silent, he said, "I think the best chance to save your life is to have you plead guilty. I think I can guarantee that if you did that, you'll avoid the noose. A prison sentence of ten or twenty years would be likely, but I assure you that I can get that reduced. You'll be a free woman inside of five years."

"What?" Molly exclaimed. "Are you telling me to admit to a crime that I didn't do? And spend five years locked away n exchange for that? What kind of attorney are you?"

"A good one," Chadwick said. "And a realistic one. Come now, if we take your case to trial, there'll be a jury full of upstanding men who don't visit brothels, or at least don't admit to it. There'll be a latent prejudice against you due to your Irish birth. Once a witness points a finger at you and says you committed the act, you are as good as dead."

"But won't that witness be a whore too?" Molly said. "If I'm not to be trusted because of that, then why should she?"

"I have not seen a list of proposed witnesses yet," Chadwick said, "but you are correct. The accuser will be one of your former ... one of Miss Cecilia's girls. And to answer your question, the jury will assume that you are lying because it is you on trial, not the witness. Though I could savage them on cross-examination, it won't do any good. I'm telling you, Miss O'Sullivan, if you value your life, the only thing we can do is plead guilty and throw yourself upon the mercy of the court."

"Mr. Chadwick," Molly said, "one thing that I've learned in this world is how little value my life actually has."

For a moment, she thought about Ellen. *If I go away to prison for a while, could I still find her when I got out? No, my only chance is to win the trial and secure my release. In five or ten years, Ellen might very well be dead, or, God forbid, worse! As bad as what happened to me in this city was, at least I was older. Ellen is a child. Even if the odds are against it, going to trial at least gives me something of an opportunity to go free now, or whenever the trial is.*

"I'm sorry to have to press you," Chadwick said, "but the trial is scheduled to begin in three weeks. We'll be picking the jury early next week. I need to know now what you wish to do. But think about what I told you. To go to trial is to march headlong into certain death."

"Isn't death certain for everyone as it is?" Molly asked. Chadwick scowled and she said, "I wish to go to trial, Mr. Chadwick. I won't pretend that it will be easy for you, or for me, but I've got my reasons. I'll not admit to something I did not do. Surely you can understand that?"

"No, Miss O'Sullivan," Chadwick said, "I cannot understand that. However, you are the client and I will respect your wishes. We'll mount the best defense we can. I'll need to speak with you again once I see the list of witnesses for anything you can tell me about who they may be. But the prosecutor doesn't play fair. He's not above bribing or intimidating witnesses into saying exactly what he wants them to say. It's hard for me, as a criminal defense attorney, to counter that. But on your head be it. It'll truly be a pity to see you climb the steps of the gallows. Are you sure that's what you want?"

"I am," Molly said. 'The day that man attacked me in my room at Miss Cecilia's, I thought he meant to kill me. I decided that if I were to die, I would do so fighting. The same applies here. If I am to hang for what they've falsely accused me of, I'll not go down without a fight. And like the prosecutor, I also do not fight fair."

"I'll be in touch before the trial," Chadwick said as he swept his notebook into his satchel and rang the bell. "Is there anyone who might be able to help you? Anyone I could talk to?"

"Frank Lynch," Molly said. "He's a detective. You gotta be careful though, because his bosses don't know that he knows me. If you talk to him, make sure it is secret like, so they don't get suspicious. I don't want to get him into trouble."

"Very well, then," Chadwick said as the cell door opened, "have a good day, Miss O'Sullivan. I'll be back as soon as I can."

"And, sir?" Molly held the envelope out to him. "Can you post this to New Orleans for me? Please?"

"I suppose," Chadwick said. "I'll bill Dr. Howard for the cost of postage."

When the door closed, Molly buried her face in her hands for a moment as sobs wracked her body. *A choice like that is no choice at all,* she thought. *I can't believe it's all come down to this. He's right. No jury will believe the word of a whore accused of murder. I'm as good as dead already. If only I'd had the courage to hurl myself overboard from the ship and join poor Hannah down there in the depths of the ocean.*

She stopped crying long enough to yawn, and stretched out on the bed. In a few minutes, Molly drifted off to sleep until another knock at the door startled her awake.

"Yes?" she called out. It must be Mr. Chadwick come back to ask me more questions, she thought. Molly rubbed at her eyes and tried to wipe away any traces of tears as the door opened.

"Another visitor, miss," Fitz said. "You are a popular one today. I can give you ten minutes, but I'll try to stretch it to fifteen."

"Who is it?" Molly asked.

Fitz stepped back and a man appeared in the doorway. Molly stared at him for a minute, not believing her eyes.

"Don't ya recognize me?"

"Patrick!" Molly exclaimed. She jumped from the bed and hurled herself into his arms with such speed that he nearly toppled over. "They said you were dead!"

"I very nearly was," he said. "A beam came down on me head during the riots. Knocked me senseless. I got carted away to a hospital and when I woke up, I didn't know who or where I was. Took about a week for everything to start coming back to me. The boys what saw me carried off just assumed I'd died and, given how hectic everything was at the time, there was no way for them to check up on me."

"I would've written to you if I'd known you were alive."

"Oh, I know that," Patrick said. "I asked Dr. Howard where you'd gone. Dr. Howard didn't know and so he asked a peeler named Lynch who said he couldn't say, outta concern for your protection. Makes sense given what happened to you."

"I'm so sorry, Patrick," Molly said. "I'm afraid I treated you terribly."

"You did no such thing," Patrick said. "I was proud to have you as a friend. I still consider you as such, that is, if you still want to be."

"Of course," Molly said as she sat down on the bed. He sat in the chair and she reached over and took hold of his hand. "So much has happened to me since I left here. I wouldn't even begin to know where to start. What of you? Are you still with your fire company?"

"Not quite," Patrick said. "The doctors said given the blow I took to the head, it might not be safe for me to keep fighting fires. Chief Decker gave me a job working in his office as sort of a clerk, though I deliver messages for him too. It keeps me busy, and it's close enough to the fires to make me happy."

"I'm glad he was able to give you a job," Molly said. "It would've been terrible for you to have to give the whole department up. Tell me the truth. Have you been well?"

"I have," Patrick said. "And I've big news of me own. I met a girl what worked in a shop across the street from Chief Decker's office. Her name is Elisabeth. She's German, not Irish. We got married. We'll be having a baby here in a few months."

"Why that's … that's … wonderful," Molly said after a moment as she mentally calculated the speed at which their courtship, not to mention pregnancy, must have progressed. "I'm happy for you both. Truly I am. I'd love to meet her, though not in my present circumstances. I'm sure she's quite special."

"I think she is," Patrick said. "As special as you are."

"Oh stop," Molly said as she heard keys in the lock on the door. "Thank you so much for coming to visit me. I admit it was a bit of a shock seeing you standing there. You nearly gave me a heart attack. Like a spirit, you were!"

Patrick stood up as the door opened. "I'll come back and see you again."

"Patrick," Molly began, "it might be best if you didn't. Not while I'm locked up here. I'd rather you remember me how you used to know me rather than now, with me dirty and wearing the same dress every day. When I get out, then we, your wife, you, and I, we'll … we'll … go somewhere special to celebrate."

He nodded and walked to the door. Then he turned and said, "When my younger brother and me mother died, it was just Seamus and me. Then he got himself killed. I feel like maybe, maybe you are the only family I got left. I know that sounds odd."

"I know, Patrick. And I was, am, a lucky girl to have known you. If things don't go well for me, and the attorney insists that they won't, I want you to know that you were always very special to me. I carried your memory to New Orleans and back. I'll always cherish our friendship, Patrick. Truly, I will."

"If it is all the same, Molly, I'd rather not think about things not going well for you. There's no joy to be found in that."

"Go on," Molly said. "Raise your child to be as brave as you were when you faced the mobs during the riots. But please don't forget me. Please."

"I can't do that, Molly. Forget you, I mean."

With that, Patrick walked out of the cell and closed the door behind him. Molly sat back on the bed stunned. *Was he real or just a ghost? I'll have to ask Fitz if he saw him too. Or am I to be haunted by the spirits of people I hurt in my life as I wait here for my own to end? I'm glad he's alive. And glad he's found happiness with someone. This city has been kind to someone, at least.*

Her mind drifted back over the days before the attack and the fire, when, despite her circumstances, she at least felt some happiness in life. *Or was that all because I was planning on making my way to California as soon as I could? Too bad I'll never get there now.* She thought of her small chest filled with her savings left behind at Madam Delacroix's. *What's become of it? Did one of the other girls pocket the money for herself? I hope the letter gets to her before the money disappears.*

Molly crossed over to the bookshelf and picked up a copy of *Pilgrim's Progress*. After two pages, she chucked it across the room and started reading the newspapers over again. Eventually, Molly fell asleep, and when she did, she dreamed she was climbing Knockma Hill with Patrick by her side, as a light mist fell on the green fields below the summit. At the top of the hill, Queen Maeve herself waited for her with a fine sword in one hand and a shield in the other.

Queen Maeve, what shall I do? Molly asked.

You must not give up hope, child, Queen Maeve said. *No matter how dark the world around you may seem, the sun is always shining somewhere. You must find it, grab hold of it, and never let it go.*

I won't let go, Queen Maeve, Molly promised. *Not now. Not ever.*

Chapter Twenty-Nine

Three weeks passed in a blur as May yielded to June. Chadwick visited a few times and reported that he had spoken with Frank, who was looking to secure witnesses on her behalf, though the attorney did not think it would come to anything. The night before the trial began, the superintendent permitted Molly to take a bath, her first since the voyage from New Orleans. Fitz carried a large cast iron tub into the cell and returned with buckets of hot water. A package had arrived earlier that day with a new dress, though it contained no return address. *Dr. Howard, maybe*, Molly thought as she lowered herself into the water, *or maybe Frank. But I'd lay money on it being the good doctor*. The water soon turned gray from the dirt and grime as Molly scrubbed her arms and legs. During his last visit, Chadwick told her what to expect in the courtroom.

"You'll have to testify," he said. "There's no way around it. That's our only chance to tell your side of the story. It won't be easy. The prosecutor will go after you hard. Don't get angry. Don't get upset. Just stay calm and repeat your story. Understand?"

"I do, sir," Molly said.

Molly could not sleep the night before the trial. Dawn found her sitting in a chair and staring at the stone walls of the cell. *I just want to get it over with*, Molly thought. *Win or lose, it is the suspense that is eating away at my insides.* She dressed quickly and sat for over an hour before Fitz knocked on the door.

"It's time to go, miss."

"Where is the courtroom?" Molly asked.

"Across the courtyard," Fitz said. "Judge Ward is a mean one, so mind yer manners in front of him. Give him any sass and he'll clap you in irons for the duration."

As they walked into the courtyard, Molly paused for a moment and looked up at the morning sun, wondering how many more mornings she had left. *It feels grand*, she thought. *I want to remember what it's like.* She nodded to Fitz and they continued across the yard, with Molly carefully avoiding a glance in the direction of the gallows. Chadwick met them just inside the door.

"Are you ready, Miss O'Sullivan?" he asked.

"I suppose so," she said. "Let's get on with it."

The courtroom contained of several wooden benches for spectators. A rail separated them from the two tables for opposing council. Twelve chairs for jurors faced the tables from the left. A second rail ran in front of an imposing wooden desk, elevated on a platform, where the judge could observe the proceedings. The witness chair sat beside the judge, on the same side of the room as the jury. A few reporters sat on the benches, notepads on their laps, and a sketch artist sat in the front row. A young man with a slim build and an erect posture stood next to the table closest to the jury.

"That's the prosecutor," Chadwick whispered. He led her to the other table and held out the chair for her to sit down. No sooner had she settled into the chair than a loud voice yelled, "All Rise!" Molly stood as Judge Ward swept into the room with all the pomp of a general on the battlefield. She suppressed a smile as she thought, don't he carry himself just like the captain on the *Dublin Rose. Like he's God almighty come down to earth to consort with us mere mortals.*

"Stay on your feet for the jury," Ward barked, though he sat down and pulled a cigar from underneath his black robe. As he struck a match, a uniformed man opened a side door and twelve men filed in and took their places. Molly tried to make eye contact with them, as Chadwick had previously instructed her to do, but all of them avoided her eyes.

"Sit down," Ward ordered. "We are here to decide the State of New York versus Molly O'Sullivan. Both of you tend to be verbose. I want this case off my docket today, so restrain yourselves. I have a dinner engagement with the mayor this evening. Do not make me late for it. Is counsel ready?"

"Yes, your honor," Chadwick and the prosecutor said in unison.

"Very well," Ward said. "Mr. Morris, you may make your opening statement."

The prosecutor stood and picked up a single sheet of paper. He nodded to the judge and turned to the jury, "If it please the court, good morning gentlemen. You are here to decide a very simple matter. It is my intention to prove to you that on or about July 13th, 1863, the accused, a notorious scarlet woman of this city—"

"Objection!" Chadwick said as he jumped to his feet.

"Overruled," Ward said. "Sit down."

"Thank you," Morris said. "As I was saying, it is my intention to prove to you that on or about July 13th, the accused, Molly O'Sullivan, a notorious scarlet woman then residing in this city, did, with malice aforethought, commit a murder upon the person of Miss Cecilia Pearl of Mulberry Street as an attempt to cover up her, the accused's, act of arson upon the property of said victim, Miss Pearl. It is a very simple case. Did she or didn't she engage in these heinous acts? I submit to you, gentlemen, that she did indeed, and that is what I shall prove to you."

Morris sat down and Judge Ward turned to Chadwick. "The defense may now present its opening."

Chadwick stood and said, "Thank you, your honor."

He moved in front of the table and turned to face the jury.

"Gentlemen of the jury. My learned colleague at the prosecutor's table has stated that this is a simple case. In that, we agree. The simple fact is that the only evidence he has is the word of a woman of equal reputation to the defendant. He will ask you to disbelieve Miss O'Sullivan due to her … occupation. Yet at the same time, he will ask you to believe his witness of like occupation. We intend to show that the unfortunate events of July 13th were a mere accident and nothing more. I say this because my learned colleague for the prosecution cannot prove anything else. At the end of the day, you will have no choice but to find my client not guilty. Thank you."

Chadwick returned to his seat. The judge gestured to Morris. "The state can call its first witness."

Morris stood and turned to the door in the back of the courtroom. "The state calls Miss Elizabeth Randolph."

The door swung open. Molly gasped when she saw Liza, resplendent in a blue gown more suitable for a ball than a courtroom. She glided down the aisle and smiled at the jury, who looked on with rapt attention, as Morris took her hand and helped her step up onto the platform with the witness chair.

After the judge swore her in and Morris established her name, occupation, and residence, he asked, "How long have you known the defendant?"

"We met in … I think it was December. Around six months before the fire."

"And can you describe her personality?"

"She was moody," Liza said as she looked at the jury. "Kinda bitchy, if I may say so. Kept to herself for the most part. But always seemed like she was up to something. Planning something, I mean."

"That's a lie," Molly exclaimed.

"Mr. Chadwick," Ward yelled, "control your client!"

"Shhh," Chadwick said as he leaned over and whispered in Molly's ear. "Let her say her piece. Do not yell out like that again. I beg you!"

"Did she have cause to harbor any animosity towards the victim?" Morris asked.

"Any what?"

"Any … resentment. Anger?"

"Oh, yeah," Liza said. "One of the other girls, named Katie, owed Miss Cecilia some money. She ran off, right before the riots. Molly was hiding the money for her so Miss Cecilia wouldn't know about it. Since Katie owed her. Anyway, Molly got real angry and tried to hit Miss Cecilia and she had to slap Molly to protect herself."

Molly started to say something but instead clenched her fists. *That lying bitch*, she swore to herself. *Miss Cecilia attacked me! How can she lie like that? How? Is it because of the money she says I cost her? Or is it just jealousy?*

"Now tell us about the day of the crime," Morris said.

"I was in my room and heard a commotion outside. I opened the door and saw Molly standing next to an oil lamp. She picked it up and smashed it on the floor. The oil started to burn on the floor and wall. There's was smoke. I thought I might perish in the flames."

Molly looked on, incredulous, as Liza stifled a sob.

"Please," Morris said, "take as much time as you need. I know this is difficult for you."

"Yes, thank you. I'm fine," Liza said. "Anyway, I went back into my room to try and grab some personal items. I didn't want them to get burned up. When I went back into the hallway, everyone was trying to run out the door. I saw Molly standing there with a devilish smile on her face. Miss Cecilia, she had come upstairs. I saw her yell at Molly."

"What did she yell?" Morris asked.

"I can't remember exactly, but something like 'Why did you set my house on fire?'"

"Go on," Morris said. "What happened next?"

"I was trying to get down the stairs," Liza said. "I looked over my shoulder and saw Molly push Miss Cecilia to the floor and kick her. Miss Cecilia, she tried to get up, but Molly hit her again. And then a piece of the ceiling came down on her. Miss Cecilia, I mean. Her dress caught on fire. She screamed at Molly to help her, but Molly just stood and there and laughed.

"Did she, Miss O'Sullivan, say anything?" Morris asked.

"Yeah," Liza said as she nodded her head. "She said, 'Just shut up and burn.' It was horrible! I've never seen the like of it."

Liza began to cry. Molly shook her head and frowned. *Has she taken acting lessons while I've been away? She belongs on a stage with those tears.*

"Now," Morris said, "one more thing. Can you please, just so we all know, point to the person you worked with and the person you saw standing over Miss Cecilia's body as it was consumed with flames?"

"That's her." Liza pointed a finger at Molly, though she kept her gaze on the jurors. "With the red hair. Sitting right there at that table."

"Thank you, Miss Randolph," Morris said. He looked at the judge. "I pass the witness, your honor."

"You may cross examine, Mr. Chadwick," Judge Ward said.

"Miss Randolph," Chadwick said as he stood up, "I must commend you. It would appear that you are possessed of remarkable vision and hearing. Why, even amid a fire you are able to observe everything around you. Truly remarkable."

"Objection!" Morris said as he stood up. "That's a statement, not a question."

"Sustained," Ward said. "Ask a question or sit down, counselor."

"Yes, well," Chadwick said, "Miss Randolph, in the course of your … duties … at Miss Cecilia's, did you ever have cause to lie, or perhaps stretch the truth, when talking with customers?"

"No," Liza said.

"So, you are the only honest whore in New York City?"

Several of the reporters chuckled, and Judge Ward banged his gavel on his desk.

"Objection!" yelled Morris.

"I withdraw the question," Chadwick said.

"The jury will disregard that statement," Ward said. "I'm warning you, counselor."

"Sorry, your honor," Chadwick said. "Miss Randolph, you testified that you were in your room and then came out into the hallway and saw Miss O'Sullivan smashing a lamp?"

"Yes."

"And you went out into the hallway because you heard a commotion?"

"Yes."

"Who else was in the hallway?"

"No one, sir. Just Molly."

"I see," Chadwick said. "A one-woman commotion then? Can you describe exactly what you heard in the hallway before you opened your door?"

"Noise. It was just noise."

"Describe the noise, please."

"I don't know. Voices, maybe. And thumping sounds."

"Hmmm," Chadwick said. "But you said she was there alone? So how did you hear voices if there was only one voice?"

"Like I said," Liza said. "I heard noises, opened the door, and saw her. Ain't she the one on trial here? Not me?"

"Do you know what perjury is, Miss Randolph?"

"Objection!" Morris yelled. "Your honor, he's badgering the witness."

"Sustained," Judge Ward said. "One more such question and I'll toss you out on your ear. Understand?"

"Forgive me, your honor," Chadwick said. "Now, Miss Randolph, you returned to your room and gathered valuables?"

"I tried to, sir."

"And as you made your daring escape down the stairs, that's when you saw the confrontation between Miss Cecilia and Molly?"

"Yes, sir."

"As you fled for your life, you took the time to stop and observe a confrontation, and note everything that happened, and everything that was said. Is that your testimony?"

"It's the truth, sir."

"And what of the valuables that you grabbed? What did you do with them?"

"I don't know what you mean," Liza said.

"You said you took valuables with you," Chadwick said. "I'd like to know what you did with them."

"I took them with me, of course."

"Did you now?" Chadwick asked. "Remember, Miss Randolph,

you were seen on the street by many witnesses. They'd certainly notice if you were carrying anything."

"I put them down when I got outside," Liza said.

"So you would have us believe that these personal items, so valuable to you that you risk a fiery death to retrieve them, were simply sat on the ground in the middle of a crowd on the street?"

"You can believe what you want," Liza said. "I'm telling the truth."

"That remains to be seen," Chadwick said. "I have nothing further, your honor."

"Do you wish to re-examine, Mr. Morris?" Judge Ward ask.

"The state has nothing further for this witness," Morris said.

"The witness may step down," Judge Ward said.

Liza smiled at the jury as she exited the witness box. The men grinned back at her and their eyes followed her as she left the courtroom. When she passed the defense table, she smirked at Molly.

"I think that went as well as can be expected," Chadwick whispered to Molly. "It was obvious to everyone that she was lying."

"Was it?" Molly asked. "Them jury men were so focused on her they didn't hear a word she said. Look at them! They are struck dumb."

"Yes, well, there's still your testimony to give," Chadwick said.

"Call your next witness, Mr. Morris," Judge Ward said. "Let's keep this trial on a steady pace."

Morris stood and said, "The state calls Detective Taggert of the Metropolitan Police of the City of New York."

"If it please the court, your honor," Chadwick said as he stood up. "It is my understanding that this witness will testify to the recovery of the remains of Miss Cecilia Pearl."

"That is correct," Morris said.

"The defense will stipulate that Miss Cecilia died in the fire," Chadwick said, "if my learned colleague will stipulate that there were no signs of foul play upon the person of Miss Cecilia, other than burns."

"Well, Mr. Morris?" Judge Ward asked.

Morris appeared to ponder this question for a minute before he nodded and said, "That is reasonable. The prosecution will so stipulate, provided the defense will also stipulate that no signs of foul play could be found due to the condition of the corpse."

"Fair enough," Chadwick said. "The defense agrees."

"Gentlemen of the jury," the judge said, "you are hereby instructed that Miss Cecilia Pearl died in the fire which occurred on the date in question. Thus, a death occurred, but there were no signs of damage to the body beyond the fire itself. And no further signs of damage could be found because of the burns suffered by the deceased. You are ordered not to read anymore into it than that. Understand?"

The jurors nodded their heads at the judge's instruction.

"Now," Judge Ward said, "what else do you have, Mr. Morris?"

"I do believe the state will rest, your honor."

"If it please the court," Chadwick said as he rose to his feet, "the defense moves for a directed verdict of not guilty. The state has not come near the burden of proof required by law. Their case is merely innuendo and speculation from a witness who wouldn't know the truth if it snuck up and bit her."

"Mr. Morris?" Judge Ward asked. "Your reply?"

"With the utmost respect to my learned colleague," Mr. Morris said as he looked at Chadwick, "I have presented a witness who described seeing the defendant in the act of committing an arson. Furthermore, she watched the defendant commit a bodily assault upon the person of Miss Cecilia, which was the proximate cause of her death in the fire set by said defendant. My learned colleague has stipulated that a death occurred. I respectfully argue that we have met our burden of proof, and any question as to the veracity of my witness should properly be left in the hands of the learned gentlemen on the jury."

"Have you anything else, Mr. Chadwick?" Judge Ward asked.

"No, your honor," Chadwick said as he looked down at the floor.

"Very well," Judge Ward said. "Your motion for a directed verdict of not guilty is denied. As the state has rested their case, we will pass over to you. Call your first witness, Mr. Chadwick."

"Your honor," Chadwick said as he glanced down at Molly, who looked up at him, eyes wide, "the defense calls Miss Molly O'Sullivan."

Chapter Thirty

Molly took the stand and duly swore to tell the truth. When she sat down, Chadwick smiled at her and said, "Please tell the jury your full name and where you are from."

"I'm Molly O'Sullivan," she said as she looked at the jurors. "I'm from County Galway, near a village called Belclare."

"And when did you arrive in America?"

"A few weeks before Christmas," Molly said. "Not last Christmas. The one before that."

"1862?" Chadwick asked.

"I … I think so," Molly said.

"And how have you been employed during this time?"

Molly lifted her chin and stared at the twelve men in the jury box. "I've been a prostitute," she said, "though I know there are more colorful terms for it."

She heard Judge Ward chuckle and even Mr. Morris smiled.

"Yes, well," Chadwick said, "perhaps you could tell us how you came to be so employed."

Molly swallowed hard and recounted the story of the day she arrived in New York City. She told them about Ellen, and how she found her family's apartment burned. Though she left out the names, Molly told the jury about the man and woman who met her and offered assistance, only to lure her into a trap. When she reached the part of the story where the door opened and two men entered the room, Molly paused and bit her lip.

"Please go on," Chadwick urged. "Though I know it is hard on you. It's important for the jury to hear what happened."

"Two men came into my room. One of them grabbed young Ellen and carried her away. And the other …"

"Yes?" Chadwick asked.

"He … attacked me."

"How so?"

"I was … I was …" Molly stopped talking and looked down at the floor. "I was raped, Mr. Chadwick. That's what happened. The next day, two girls came to the room and took me to Miss Cecilia's. One of them was Liza. She's the one what sat up here and lied today."

"Your honor!" Mr. Morris said. "Please instruct the witness to answer the questions and not comment on the veracity of any other witness."

"Just answer the questions without additional commentary, miss," the judge warned.

"Sorry, sir," Molly said.

"Now," Mr. Chadwick said, "tell us about the day of the fire."

"I had a customer in my room," Molly began. "After we … well … after we finished, he decided he wanted another go for free. I said no and I knocked on the floor. That was our signal to the bouncers for help. They didn't hear me. He slapped me and I fell over the bed. I managed to get out into the hallway, but he grabbed me from behind."

"Excuse me for a moment, Miss O'Sullivan," Mr. Chadwick said. "But did this man have a name?"

"Not one that I knew," Molly said. "We don't usually ask the customers for their names. When he grabbed me, I thought he meant to choke me. I managed to pull my knife out of my boot and stuck him in the leg. He let me go but bumped into the oil lamp and knocked it onto the floor. That's how the fire started."

"And, during any of this time, did you see Liza?"

"No, sir," Molly said. "I didn't see her until I knocked on her door to warn her of the fire."

"I see," Mr. Chadwick said. "To be clear, what did you do after the fire started?"

"I knocked on all the doors that I could to warn everyone to get out," Molly said. "The fire was spreading very quick like."

"Which staircase?"

"The one that ran from the second floor down to the street. Not the main one. I got halfway there, and someone grabbed me. I turned around and it was Miss Cecilia. I told her we had to get out or else we'd burn alive, but she wouldn't let go of me. I … I … pushed her away, and that is when part of the ceiling came down on her. It was an accident … I didn't mean to … I didn't want her to … die."

Molly sniffed as tears welled up in her eyes. "I didn't want anyone to get hurt. That's why I was trying to get everyone to go outside."

"Tell me a little about Miss Cecilia," Mr. Chadwick said. "Is it true that you had a confrontation with her over one of the girls running away?"

"That weren't nothing serious," Molly said. "She just thought that I'd been hiding money for Katie so she could get away. But I didn't. It was my money. Katie took my money and ran off."

"Did Miss Cecilia strike you about the face?"

"She did slap me, sir," Molly admitted. "But I've been hit harder than that."

"Did you face any other discipline?"

"She said that I had to work to pay off the money Katie owed her, in addition to what I owed. But there weren't no hard feelings over it. She even let Liza and I go to watch the boxing match between a fireman and that copper what stands as tall as a mountain."

"I will ask one last question, Miss O'Sullivan," Mr. Chadwick said. "Did you purposely set fire to Miss Cecilia's place, and did you, with evil intent, seek to murder the same."

"No, sir," Molly said. She turned to the jury and said, "The fire was an accident and I was only trying to get outside when Miss Cecilia grabbed me."

Chadwick turned to Mr. Morris and said, "Your witness."

Morris sat for a long moment before he got up and approached the witness box. "Well, Miss O'Sullivan," he said, "you've given us quite a story."

"It's the truth, sir," Molly said.

"Let's see ..." Morris said, "you were criminally attacked on your first night in the city. And then you were assaulted in your room by a customer, and again by the victim in the hallway. Is that right?"

"It is, sir," Molly said.

"That's quite a bit of assaulting," Morris said.

Laughter echoed around the courtroom. To her dismay, Molly saw the jurors join in. "Women being assaulted is a joking matter now, sir?" Molly asked. "I ain't laughing."

Morris frowned and began his cross examination.

"Did you report that first incident, when the men attacked you in the boarding house, to the police?"

"No, sir," Molly said.

"Why?"

"I ... I don't know ..." Molly said. "I didn't get a look at their faces. And I was only just arrived in the city. I didn't know what to do. That's why I went with Katie and Liza when they came to my room. I had nowhere else to go."

"And when you were attacked at Miss Cecilia's and you say you stabbed the man," Morris said, "did you report that incident to the police?"

"No, sir."

"In fact, Miss O'Sullivan, isn't it true that you fled from the scene of the crime?"

"It wasn't a crime," Molly said. "And I did run away. But only because I thought the peelers meant to arrest me."

"But if it were really self-defense, as you seem to be claiming,"

Morris said, "then you would have nothing to fear from the law. Isn't that right?"

"It was self-defense," Molly said. "And I'm here, anyway, aren't I?"

"Are you familiar with the proverb that says the wicked man flees when none pursueth?"

"I'm not, sir," Molly said.

"Tell us the truth, Miss O'Sullivan," Morris said, raising his voice. "You intentionally started that fire to destroy the property of the woman who took you in off the streets. And then, not content to merely cause her financial ruin, you took it upon yourself to shove her into the flames."

"No!" Molly exclaimed.

"You then fled the scene, in guilt over your heinous acts. Not only did you escape the fire, you escaped the city itself. Ran all the way to New Orleans, didn't you? All in an attempt to distance yourself from your crimes. Isn't that true? Answer me!"

"It's not true," Molly insisted. "I did nothing wrong but try to protect myself."

"So you say," Mr. Morris replied. "But your actions speak otherwise. Tell me something—did you hear Miss Cecilia screaming as she roasted alive?"

"Objection!" Mr. Chadwick shouted as he jumped from his chair.

"I withdraw that last question," Mr. Morris said. "I have nothing further for the witness."

"Anything else, Mr. Chadwick?" the judge asked.

"Just one thing, your honor," Chadwick said. "Miss O'Sullivan, when you were forced to defend yourself from Miss Cecilia, did you have cause to see Miss Randolph anywhere around?"

"I saw her," Molly said. "Just after Miss Cecilia fell. It was dark from the smoke, but I remember seeing her."

Chadwick frowned and said, "I have nothing else for the witness, your honor."

Molly stepped down from the witness stand and returned to her seat.

"Call your next witness, Mr. Chadwick," the judge said.

"The defense rests, your honor," Chadwick said. He then leaned over to Molly and whispered, "I've no witnesses to call on your behalf, but that is all right. I think we've cast enough suspicion on Miss Randolph's testimony."

Molly felt a growing sense of unease, but she smiled at him and said, "I agree, Mr. Chadwick."

"Very well," the judge said. "This is proceeding much faster than I dared hope. You may present your closing argument, Mr. Morris."

The prosecutor stood and said, "If it pleases your honor, the state wishes to waive its closing and reserve the right for a rebuttal."

"That's your right," the judge said. "Mr. Chadwick, you may give your closing now."

"Your honor and gentlemen of the jury," Chadwick began, "my learned colleague for the state began this trial by saying it was a simple case. It is. The case is quite simple. This is the story of a young woman who traveled two thousand miles across the ocean for a chance at a better life in this country. Upon the streets of our city, she was cruelly used by the kind of characters that I know you've read about in the newspapers."

Molly looked over at the jurors. One consulted his pocket watch. Another man dozed in the back row. The rest watched Chadwick speak, but they leaned back in their chairs, legs crossed.

"Men little better than wild animals that lie in wait to prey on innocent girls like Miss O'Sullivan. Taken in by a madam, she had no choice but to work as a prostitute. Why? Gentlemen, I respectfully submit to you that society judges the prostitute and will always hold that against a woman forced into it so that she may never escape. We judge them as sinners, as scarlet women, as harlots, yet who among you would marry one? Allow one to serve your meals? Or watch your children? The prosecution wants you to find Miss O'Sullivan guilty of arson and murder simply because she holds an occupation which the law permits. She's a prostitute and therefore a liar, according to Mr. Morris, when his own case is built entirely upon the words of another prostitute. Why is one automatically truthful and the other not? Miss O'Sullivan sought to protect herself from an assailant, and a fire started by accident. During that fire, Miss Cecilia accosted her, and in her attempt to get away, Miss Cecilia was tragically, but accidentally, killed. Keep this in mind, gentlemen, this is a young woman who took in a child who was not her own. And, upon noticing the fire, sought to warn others to avoid a loss of life. Are those the actions of a heartless murderess? Of course not! Miss O'Sullivan is a victim, just as surely as Miss Cecilia is a victim. Miss O'Sullivan is a victim of the evils of our society that we wink at and ignore, unless they affect us directly."

A juror yawned. Molly frowned at him as he covered his mouth with his hand and glanced around to see if anyone else had noticed.

"The only thing that prosecution has given you is the word of Miss Randolph, a person who cannot be trusted to be truthful, and even then, her testimony does match Miss O'Sullivan's in some aspect. Miss Randolph says she heard a commotion in the hallway, which strengthens Miss O'Sullivan's story. Conveniently, however, Miss Randolph seems to have forgotten just what that noise was. I need not remind you how ludicrous her statement about setting her valuables down on the ground outside was. Would you send a young woman to the gallows or a long prison term based on that shaky testimony? What if it were your own wife or sister or daughter in this chair? What would you do then? I respectfully submit to you, gentlemen, that you must take the same action now, for Miss O'Sullivan. You have no option but to find her not guilty of the charges. Thank you."

"Mr. Morris, you may proceed," the judge said as he rubbed the bridge of his nose.

As the prosecutor rose to speak, the jurors sat up in their chairs. A few leaned forward to listen as he walked close to the jury box.

"Gentlemen of the jury, I will ask you the same question I asked the defendant. Why would you run if you committed no crime? Why would you say nothing to the police if you were so cruelly attacked? What we see here is a pattern of behavior. Do not let this Jezebel fool you. She's certainly a comely young woman, but there's steel beneath the attractive exterior. The deadly steel of a knife's blade. Did she not sit right there in that chair and say she carried a knife in her boot? Did she not sit right there and admit that she did, in fact, lay hands upon Miss

Cecilia? Did she not admit that she saw Miss Randolph in the hallway at that time? And doesn't that support the testimony of Miss Randolph? Do not let yourself be fooled. I pray you. Miss O'Sullivan is a criminal of the worst kind. She uses her looks and pleasant disposition to lull us into danger, just like the Sirens tempted Odysseus. Look beyond her words, look at her actions. Judge her according to what she did, not what she says. If you do so, you'll have no choice but to find her guilty. *Guilty!* Thank you."

Molly's heart beat so loud that she was not able to hear the judge's instructions to the jury. They filed out of the courtroom, and she turned to Mr. Chadwick. "What happens now?"

"They'll deliberate and return with a verdict."

"How long will that take?"

"There's no way to know," Mr. Chadwick said. "While a quick verdict usually favors the prosecution, that is not always true."

"Do you think our odds are good?"

"I do," Mr. Chadwick said, but Molly noticed he broke eye contact when he said it.

It seems all I've done the last three weeks is wait, Molly said. *Waiting for a visitor. Waiting for a trial. And now waiting for a verdict. If it don't go my way, I'll be waiting for the hangman too.* She thought of the lone noose from the gallows in the courtyard and the stories her grandfather told of the Irish heroes hanged by the British. *Will I be as brave as bold Robert Emmet when my time comes? No, no, it won't come to that. I know we will win. We have to win.*

Thirty minutes passed, and the uniformed man who escorted the jury out of the courtroom returned and announced they had a verdict. Everyone stood as the twelve men filed into the room. The judge motioned all to be seated.

"Have you reached a verdict?" he asked.

"Um, we have, your honor," one juror said as he stood up.

"Very well," the judge said, "hand your paper to my man."

The uniformed man took a folded paper from the juror and passed it across to the judge. He glanced at it, looked at Molly, and then passed it back to the juror. Molly felt a sinking feeling in her stomach.

Her hands began to shake, and her knees trembled. *None of them would look at me when they walked into the room,* she thought. *That can't be a good sign.*

"The defendant will rise and face the jury," the judge said.

Chadwick stood, reached down, and took hold of Molly's arm. He pulled her to her feet and then slipped his arm around her waist to steady her.

"In the case of the People of the State of New York versus Molly O'Sullivan, on the count of arson, how find you?"

"Guilty," the juror said.

"And as to the second count, of murder, how find you?"

"Also guilty, your honor," the juror said.

Molly felt as though two sharp knives had been plunged into her chest. She bit her lip to hold back tears. Mr. Chadwick whispered, "We can always appeal, you know. All is not lost."

"The court will now pronounce sentence," the judge said. "Mr. Chadwick, have you anything to say in that regard?"

"I only ask the court to take the youth of my client into account, along with her circumstances. She poses no danger to others, your honor."

"Mr. Morris?" the judge asked.

"Poses no danger to others?" Morris said with a laugh. "She's just been convicted of murder! Your honor, there's only one sentence appropriate in this case. The defendant has willingly engaged in harlotry, which led to arson and murder. As you well know, a prison sentence will see her back on the streets in a few short years, no matter how stiff a term you give her. And then? Why, you must think to the continued safety of our citizens!"

"I'm afraid I have to agree with you, Mr. Morris," the judge said.

Molly's knees shook as the judge peered down at her. "Miss O'Sullivan, it gives me no pleasure to do this. Quite the opposite. It pains me greatly as I do have some sympathy for those unfortunates like yourself who find themselves compelled into a life they do not want. However, the law is clear on this matter, and I do not have much leeway in assessing a sentence. So, Molly O'Sullivan, having been found guilty of the crimes of murder and arson, I hereby sentence you to be remanded into the custody of the prison to be held until such date which will be set by the court, and then to be delivered over to be hanged by the neck until you are dead. May God have mercy on your soul, Miss O'Sullivan."

The judge banged his gavel and disappeared out of the courtroom so fast that the guard did not have time to order everyone to rise. Molly did not notice, for as soon as the judge spoke his words, blackness enveloped her and she sank back into the chair, oblivious to the room around her.

Chapter Thirty-One

A week and then another passed in a blur. Molly spent her days staring at the stone walls of the cell as they seemed to press in on her. It was as if the cell got smaller every day. Fitz reported to her that the judge had set an execution date of July 1st. Dr. Howard stopped by to visit during the second week after the trial. He apologized profusely for not visiting earlier and expressed regret that the attorney he hired did not seem up to the task.

"It's my fault, Miss Molly," he said. "I should've found you a better attorney."

"The blame isn't yours, Doctor," Molly said. "The men on the jury made their minds up when they heard Liza up there lying and carrying on."

"Still," the doctor said, "I feel responsible. I ran into young Patrick McMahon the other day. He asked after you and said he'd like to come and see you again, but given the circumstances, he is afraid he'd …"

"'Tis no bother," Molly said. "Truly. Please give him my love when you see him again."

"I've not seen Detective Lynch since before your trial," Dr. Howard said. "I know he's been working on finding the child for you. And he was attempting to find witnesses on your behalf, but I guess he couldn't. Maybe he's too ashamed to admit it to you."

Molly smiled and said, "He's done more than I had a right to expect. Or, at least, I think he has. There's still time for him to stop by. The … well … the … it's not for a few days yet. There's still time."

"I've news of my own to tell you," Dr. Howard said. "I'll be leaving New York in the morning. I joined the army."

"You what?" Molly asked.

"There's been a fearful slaughter in Virginia over the past six weeks. They are swamped with injured men. Doctors are in short supply. So, I got myself a commission as an assistant surgeon. With the regular army too, not a volunteer regiment."

"But don't you like your work here?" Molly asked.

"I do," Dr. Howard said. "More than anything. I do. But now, with what is happening to you, I don't think I can stand to see this city chew up any more innocents like yourself."

"Like I was, you mean," Molly said. "That ain't exactly the case now."

Dr. Howard stood to leave. He looked down at Molly, who sat on the edge of the cot, and said, "I guess this is … goodbye."

"You've always been kind to me, Doctor," Molly said. "You were the first person to befriend me in this city, other than Frank Lynch. You'll always have my thanks for that. You are a good man with a kind spirit. Promise you'll be careful."

"You are a special girl, Miss Molly," Dr. Howard said. "Don't give up hope. Miracles do happen in this world."

They do, Molly thought, *but not to me*. The doctor left without another word, and Molly thought back to the first day she met him. *I was in a bit of shock over what had happened*, she thought. *I was hardly able to even understand what had happened. And there he was, with a job to do, and yet kind at the same time.*

The next day, Molly was full of restless energy, despite being unable to sleep the night before. After breakfast, Fitz opened the cell door without knocking and stepped aside as a man with a hat low across his face darted in. He looked up as the door closed behind him.

"Frank!" Molly exclaimed as she recognized him. "Where the hell have you been?"

"I'm sorry, Molly," he said as he pulled his coat off and leaned against the wall. "I'd say that you are looking well. Or as well as you could be under the circumstances."

"What news do you have of Ellen?"

"That's what I've come to tell you," he said. "I think I know where she is."

"Where?" Molly asked.

"I found out there's a place just off Washington Square. A woman runs it and takes in children like Ellen. When they are old enough, she sells them. I've been on her trail for a while now but didn't know exactly where she was until today."

"How did you find out?" Molly asked, her own situation forgotten.

"Let's just say I persuaded someone to tell me," Frank said.

"Are you going to get her out?" Molly asked.

"I will," Frank said. "In a couple of days. I got the message you sent. Are you sure you want the girl to go back to Ireland? Surely there's a nice family here that could take her in."

"I don't want her to end up like me," Molly said. "If she stays here, well, there's no telling what will happen when she gets older."

"Fair enough," Frank said. "And I've other news as well. I don't … well, I don't want you to get your hopes up, but …"

"What?" Molly asked as she crossed the room and took hold of Frank's hand.

"I managed to find a couple of men to sign an affidavit saying they was in the building when the fire started, and it was as you described. And I got a third to swear out a statement saying he was in the parlor and heard Miss Cecilia say she was going to go up there and take care of you once and for all after the fire started."

"How?" Molly asked. "That's not true. No one was there."

"Yeah, well, since when are trials really about the truth? The men are local vagrants, but the court won't know that. I turned everything over to the judge. I've got people looking for Liza too. She seems to have skipped town right after the trial, but the day after she testified, two shopkeepers saw her flashing plenty of money around. And one of them overheard her saying how grateful the prosecutor was for what she said."

"What does all this mean?" Molly asked as she walked back over to the bed and sat down.

"Right now? Not much," Frank admitted. "The judge has taken it all under advisement. If he wants, he can set aside the verdict. Or at least delay the execution until he looks into it. There's one last chance after that."

"What?" Molly asked.

"One of my sources says the good judge likes to visit a certain molly house over on Chatham Street."

"A what?" Molly asked.

"A molly house," Frank said. "It's kinda like the place where you worked, except all the employees are boys, usually young. And the visitors are men."

"Oh ..." Molly said. "But what does that have to do with me?"

"Simple," Frank said. "I've got some reliable detectives who are willing to help. One of them, O'Hara, you remember him? Anyway, he's tailing his honor as we speak. If he'll pay a visit to one between now and ... you know when ... we are going to raid it along with a friendly reporter from the *National Police Gazette*. When we catch him in the middle of forbidden acts, I'll give him a choice. Grant you a stay of execution to examine the true facts of the case, or his name gets plastered all over the front page with a very detailed article about how this symbol of law and order in the city is a pederast. I admit, I'm quite proud of this plan I've devised. It's too bad I didn't know this before the trial."

"And you think it will work?" Molly asked as, for the first time since the trial, she felt a faint glimmer of hope. "Any of it?"

Frank dragged a chair over to the bed and sat down. He said, "I don't see why it wouldn't. The only problem, and one we can't anticipate, is whether or not he will visit this place before Friday. But, even if he doesn't, he still has the other information I've provided him. Is it a bit dishonest? It is, but you didn't get a fair shake at the trial. This is New York City, Molly. Justice is for sale here to the highest bidder, or the one willing to play dirty. I tried, I *really* tried to do what I could before you were in court. I hope you believe that. It's why I couldn't come and see you. I was busy with it all."

"I know, Frank," Molly said. "The important thing to me is that you've located Ellen. No matter what happens to me, I just want to know that she is safe."

"She will be soon," Frank said. "I can assure you of that. I took the liberty of sending a telegram to Madam Delacroix down there in New Orleans. I told her what happened to you and asked about your money. I got a reply that said the money was safely locked away there and that she'd hold it until you sent word of what to do with it."

"I sent her a letter. Right after I got here. I told her to forward the money to you. That way, you can use it for Ellen."

"Molly …" Frank reached out his hand and then paused as if to draw it back. "If things don't go right for us, I want you to know that your girl will be taken care of. I won't let anything happen to her or my name ain't Frank Lynch."

"Thank you." Molly took hold of his hand. "Will you be there on the … the … day?"

"If you want me to be there," Frank said. "I will. Though I'll take no pleasure in it."

"I would hope not," Molly said. They burst into laughter and then fell silent. A moment passed. She looked down at the floor and said, "It would be a relief to see the face of a friend when … when …"

Frank squeezed her hand and Molly's eyes found his. *He's a good man*, she thought. *No doubt he's broken enough heads with the peelers, but it's a good heart Frank Lynch has. Miss Miles was right about that. I know he will do right by young Ellen, no matter what happens to me.*

"I've got to go," Frank said. "There's still work to be done. Don't give up hope, Molly."

"I won't," she whispered.

Her promise was easier to make than to keep. When the next morning arrived with no more word, Molly resigned herself to her fate. A man dressed entirely in black stopped in that morning and introduced himself as the hangman. Molly almost laughed as she shook his hand. *Is it ordinary to shake hands with the man that will send you to eternity*, she wondered?

The man did not give his name, but instead asked a few questions in a brisk manner. Before he left, he instructed Molly to pin her hair up lest it interfere with the placement of the noose. That evening, Fitz brought the iron tub into the cell. As much as Molly wanted to tell him to take it away, she decided to use it. *I'm hardly the first Irish person to climb the steps of the scaffold*, she thought. *If I'm to die, at least I can look somewhat presentable instead of like a street urchin what hasn't seen water in a month.*

Shortly after dawn on the appointed date, a priest stopped in to speak with Molly. She gasped when she recognized him as the same man that had turned her away her first night in the city.

"Child," he said, "now is the time for you to confess your sins to God. All can be forgiven. Your debauchery and criminal conduct need not bar your admission to heaven, provided you clear your conscience now while you still can."

"Don't you remember me, Father?" Molly asked.

"No, child. Should I?"

"I came to your church scared and hungry on my first night in New York. I had a child with me. You tossed us out into the street where we fell victim to a most horrid attack. The child was stolen from me. Snatched out of my very arms. And I was forced into prostitution. Had you done the Christian thing and taken us in, I would not be here now."

"The church is not a shelter for every poor soul on the streets," he said. "And though you claim you were forced into prostitution, I remind you that we all have a choice. There's many a girl like you in such establishments, and, as a priest, I know all too well that it is the love of the carnal act itself which makes women behave in such a shocking manner. Now, will you confess or not?"

"The only thing I have to confess is that if you don't get out of my sight within the next ten seconds, I'll take that Bible from your hands and shove it up your hole. Is that clear enough for you, Father?"

"You … you … Jezebel!" the priest sputtered. "I hope you burn in hell for all eternity for your harlotry and your blasphemy. You wicked, wicked girl!"

"Your ten seconds are up, Father," Molly said as she took a step in his direction. She laughed as he fled the cell. *Vulture*, she swore, *preying on the unfortunate and taking what little money they have while he holds eternity over their heads*. She fingered the Saint Michael's medal around her neck. *If the Archangel is truly what they say he is, he'd smite the lot of them and give us priests what care about us.*

Fitz stuck his head in after the priest left and said, "They'll come for you in about thirty minutes, Miss Molly. The boss says I can offer you some laudanum or some absinthe. It might make things … easier for you."

Molly considered it for a moment and said, "No, thank you. If is to the devil I must go, it will be as a whore alone, and not a whore in the arms of the green fairy."

"Miss Molly," Fitz said, "you may have worked in an unfortunate occupation, but you ain't really a whore. Anyone that meets you can see that."

Molly smiled and said, "Everybody but Liza Randolph it would appear."

"Oh, her," Fitz said. "She's a lying, scheming bitch what told those stories cause she's jealous of you. That's all."

"And now I'm to die because of it," Molly said. "Don't that seem a steep price to pay?"

"Justice ain't never blind, Miss Molly," Fitz said. "I've seen men as guilty as Lucifer walk out of here free cause they or their family knew the judge, or the police captain, or some politician. And that's if they got arrested in the first place. It's no different here than back home in Ireland, where we get locked up on the slightest pretense while the landlords strut around with their fancy clothes and take their liberties with the whole country."

"You are right about that," Molly said. She reached up and unfastened the Saint Michael's medal around her neck. "Fitz, will you please see that Frank Lynch gets this? Tell him to give it to Ellen when he finds her. Tell her … tell her … tell her she's strong enough to get through anything. Will you do that?"

"I will," Fitz said.

Fitz gave her a sad smile and closed the door. *What do you do with your last thirty minutes*, Molly wondered. *Scream? Cry? Beg? No! I won't give any of them bastards the satisfaction. I'll be as brave as me own brother was when he marched off to fight the Russians in the Crimea. As brave as Queen Maeve herself.* She rose and paced the cell, as her thoughts turned to home and Ireland. *What's me ma doing right now? And will she ever know what became of me? Is she thinking of me now? Or does she even notice I'm gone?*

Despite her resolve, she jumped when the cell door opened. The superintendent walked in, dressed in a black suit with a gray vest, followed by two men in uniforms of dark blue wool. One of the men crossed the cell to Molly, grabbed her shoulder, and spun her around. He shoved her into the wall before she had time to react. Her wrists were pulled behind her and she gasped as the man looped a thin, rough rope around them and pulled it. Tight. Then he spun her back around.

"It's time to pay for your dark deeds," the superintendent said.

The priest walked in and began to recite a scripture.

"Man that is born of woman is of few days, and full of trouble …"

"Get that man out of my sight," Molly snapped.

The superintendent looked surprised, but nodded at the priest, who closed his Bible and left the room. Each of the two uniformed men took hold of one of Molly's arms, and they led her out of the cell behind the superintendent. Molly's legs moved as though they were guided by some force outside her own body. Her mind raced as she fought to keep herself calm. The words of a song came to her in a sudden flash and she began to sing softly.

Maxwelton's braes are bonnie when early fa's the dew
And it was there my Annie Laurie gave me her promise true

"Shut up," the man holding her right arm growled. "It's not a concert that you are going to."

Molly raised her voice and sang a bit louder.

Gave me her promise true which ne'er forgot shall be
And for bonnie Annie Laurie, I'd lay me doon and dee

When they got downstairs, the superintendent pushed open the doors that led to the courtyard. Molly blinked as the bright sunlight penetrated her eyes. She turned her face upward to feel the sun. For the last time, she thought.

Atop the gallows, Molly saw the executioner standing beside the noose, his hands clasped in front of him and a somber expression on his face. A few reporters stared at her as they jotted down notes. Several police officers lounged around the yard, trying to look busy as they kept an eye on the proceedings. And then she noticed Frank alongside one of the reporters. Frank smiled at her and gave her a wink.

What's the meaning of that? He's winking at me like we just crossed paths in Paradise Square. She hesitated for a moment as they neared the gallows and then lifted her right foot to the first step.

"Stop at once!"

A voice echoed around the courtyard and brought everyone to a halt. Molly turned and saw the prison clerk she met when she first arrived running across the courtyard. He thrust a piece of paper into the hands of the superintendent, who glanced at it and frowned.

"By order of Judge Ward," the superintendent declared, "the scheduled execution of one Molly O'Sullivan, is hereby ordered to halt, pending further judicial proceedings."

"What?" Molly said, unbelieving as one of the uniformed men untied her hands. She rubbed the red welts on her wrists as Frank walked over to her with a smile on his face.

"Told you not to lose hope," he said. "It's all taken care of. You'll be set free later today."

"Jesus Christ, Frank!" Molly exclaimed. "You waited until the last minute!"

"No, that wasn't me," Frank said. "The judge made his decision last night after a consultation with me and a reporter at a certain infamous establishment. He's setting aside the verdict based on the statements I gave him. But he wanted to draw it out as long as he could"

"And I'm not to go to prison instead?" Molly asked.

"No, you'll be as free as a bird in four hours' time. I'll be here to collect you when you get out. We've work to do, Molly."

"Frank … I …" Molly tried to speak, but no words came as the guards pulled her toward the prison door.

Chapter Thirty-Two

True to his word, Frank was waiting outside the door that afternoon when Molly walked out, a free woman. The world swirled around her like a dream. Molly had a difficult time processing it all. When Frank saw her, he moved to take her arm.

"Forgive me, Molly," he said, "but you look like you need a bit of help."

"Thank you," Molly said. "Everything is … just … unreal to me now."

"You are a brave girl, Molly," Frank said, "but I've need of you to be braver still. I hesitate to say this, but the family of the man you stabbed knows about the judge setting you free. They were looking forward to you swinging on the gallows, though they couldn't be here to see it. Word is, they've again set someone on your trail with the intent to kill you."

"My God," Molly said. "Will I ever be able to escape it?"

"It was a risk we had to take, Molly," Frank said. "In exchange for your life, you also put your life at risk. But better free with a chance to fight back than a date with the hangman."

"You are right," Molly said. "And fight back I will."

"That's the spirit," Frank said. "And we've your Ellen to think of too."

"Have you retrieved her?"

"No," Frank said. "Not yet. I had you to think of first. But I've a plan in place and I'll need your help. If you are up for it."

"Of course, I am," Molly said as they reached the street. "I'll do whatever it takes to get her back!"

"That's grand," Frank said. "Come along. I've a place where you can stay since I know you are a bit short of jack, arriving here in the custody of the Pinkertons and all that."

Frank led her to the small room he kept in Paradise Square, the same room he brought her on the night he found her on the streets and secured her escape to New Orleans. Molly sat in a chair as Frank lit a lamp at the table.

"The place is yours as long as you need it, Molly," Frank said. "It might make a nice spot for you and Ellen to live while you decide what you are going to do."

"Frank …you've done so much for me, even when I was here before. I fear I'll not be able to repay you."

"I wouldn't expect you to," Frank said. "Now, listen, we've got to talk about how we are going to get Ellen back. Or would you rather rest for a bit first?"

As exhausted as she felt, Molly insisted they discuss the plan.

He told her that Ellen slept in a room on the third floor of a large house. To gain entry, they could not walk in through the front door. Frank suggested the roof might be the best way, as there was access to the third floor via a hatch.

"O'Hara is going to help us," Frank said.

"And what is my part?"

"I need you with us. Hopefully the child will remember you, though it's been quite a bit of time since you last saw her. And you alone know what she looks like, or rather what she did look like. But my source tells me they did not cut or dye her hair. I need you to be the one that goes into the room and gets her. So, do you fancy a dash across the rooftops of our fair city?"

"And what happens when we get her? Won't they try to get her back?"

"No, I'd say not. They'll simply snatch another child to take her place."

Molly frowned. "So, if we rescue young Ellen, we are condemning another child to take her place? What a terrible choice. I want Ellen, but I do not want another innocent to suffer in her place."

"Look, Molly," Frank said with a shrug, his face serious, "this city is full of evil. You of all people know that. We can't stop it all. We can only stop what we can. I assure you there is a day coming when all vice and corruption in this city will be swept away, but it isn't our place to worry about that. Do you want Ellen back or not?"

"I do," Molly said.

"Fine," Frank said. "Forget the rest and let's focus on what we need to do."

Frank told her that O'Hara would cause a distraction in the street to draw the men who guarded the first floor outside. This would lessen the chances of Frank and Molly being discovered. Frank assured her that his contacts told him that no one actually guarded the rooms upstairs, though the doors were locked at night.

"So how will we get in?" Molly asked.

"There's not a lock in the world that can keep me out," Frank said with a grin.

"Jesus, are you a peeler or a burglar?"

"Truth is, we are all a bit of both here."

"You warned of that very thing the day I met you," Molly said. "When you wore a uniform and patrolled the streets."

"Did I?" Frank asked. "Well, it's the truth after all. I remember most of that day. Just not the exact words we exchanged."

"You were kind to me, Frank," Molly said. "And now, you are doing me a grand favor by helping me retrieve Ellen. It'll be dangerous enough, I reckon. But with all that's happened to me since I stepped off that boat, I think I'm ready for it. God in Heaven! It seems like a million years ago I walked down that gangway and set foot in New York for the first time. I cannot believe all that has happened to me since. Like a story from a dime novel, it is."

Frank rose. "I have to leave for a bit. But I'll return for you after dark. Can I get you anything before I go?"

"No," Molly said. "I can manage."

"Here"—Frank reached into his coat and withdrew a pocket revolver—"keep this with you at all times. There's no reason to think anyone can track you here, but if you find yourself in need of it, don't hesitate to pull the trigger. Just be sure to thumb the hammer back first. But you only got one shot. If you have to use it, make sure you hit what you aim at."

"Here I am hours out of prison for murder and you wish me to get sent back?" Molly took the revolver, which felt cold and heavy in her hand.

Frank laughed. "No, the family what wants you dead wouldn't want it known they hired someone to come after you. Too embarrassing for them, I think."

Frank slipped out the door and Molly sat back for a moment, letting all the tension from the past month leave her body. *All this time,* she thought, *I've focused on finding Ellen. I've not thought of much I can do once I have her. But I know I can make money with my voice. I can provide for her that way. Can't I?*

Molly stood and paced the room as she thought. *New York City won't be safe for us ever, so long as that family is after me. Besides, no one will hire a convicted murderess, not even to sing, no matter if I did cheat the gallows by the slimmest margin. It's a new start that I need. That we need. Perhaps California. I could say I was a war widow and young Ellen is my own child. But how to get there? That is the question.*

Molly considered going out for a walk but decided against it. *Someone might recognize me. Either from the trial or from Miss Cecilia's. I'd love to run into Liza. But if I did? What? Would I hit her? No, let it go. She'll receive her just reward one day.* Molly thought of what it must have taken for someone to lie with no sign of remorse. *She's a whore like me. We have to lie to survive. And I know nothing of what brought her to Miss Cecilia's. It could be she was a young innocent, just as I was. In that case, pity is what she deserves, not punishment.*

Molly decided to take a nap. She did not undress, but she did remove her shoes before she stretched out on the bed. She lay on her back, with the revolver clutched in her right hand. The cold steel barrel rested on her stomach as she closed her eyes and took several deep breaths. Her mind replayed the events of the morning, but this time with a different outcome. She saw herself plunging through the trap door, only to be jerked to a halt by the rope, her body twisting and turning as the assembled crowd applauded with as much enthusiasm as the crowds that saw her perform in New Orleans.

For God's sake, Molly thought as she opened her eyes. *Why am I doing this to myself? It didn't happen. I'm alive.* She groaned as she rubbed her face with her left hand. *Am I to be tormented by these memories for all eternity?* As an answer to her question, a second memory, of the boarding house that first night in the city tugged at the edges of her brain. Molly felt as though a heavy weight pressed down upon her chest. Her heart accelerated and her lungs felt as though they could not get enough air. She sat up and leaned over the side of the bed, her mouth open like a fish out of the water. *My God! What's wrong with me? Why am I stuck on things in the past that I cannot change? It's as if I've given those fiends what attacked me power over my sanity forever. Is this why so many of the girls at Miss Cecilia's or at Madam Delacroix's turn to the laudanum? Is that the only thing that can dull these horrible visions?*

Not wanting to risk more memories, Molly got out of bed. Gradually her heartbeat slowed and her regular breathing resumed. She sat down in the chair for a few minutes, then got up again, restless with a nervous energy. *Tonight will be the final chapter,* she thought. *Once we get Ellen, I'll be able to put it all behind me. Should we go back to Ireland instead of out west? No,* she thought. *There's nothing for either of us there. You cannot have a fresh start in a place you left to begin with.*

Eventually, darkness descended upon the city and Molly heard a knock on the door. She froze for a second, then reached for the revolver. *Should I open the door? Or bid them enter?*

"Molly! It's me!"

Molly let out a sigh of relief when she heard Frank's voice. The door opened and Frank walked in, a bundle of clothes draped over his arm. He caught sight of the revolver in her hand and said, "It's a good thing I announced myself. You'd have filled me full of lead sure as I'm standing here."

"You told me to be careful, did you not?" Molly said as she placed the gun back on the table.

"I did," Frank said.

Molly gestured to the clothing. "What's that for?"

"You'll draw less notice dressed as a man. It'll be easier to move around. Easier to hide the revolver too. I pray we have no need for it tonight, but you never know."

"And you?" Molly asked. "What do you carry?"

"Oh, I've a Colt Navy, a pair of brass knuckles, a pocket revolver like the one I gave you, and a short truncheon."

"Jesus," Molly exclaimed. "Are we going to retrieve a child or are you planning on invading the Confederacy all by yourself?"

"Present company excluded," Frank said, "it's not like I deal with any of the city's better elements."

"I wouldn't place myself among the better elements," Molly said, "but thank you all the same."

"Are you ready, Molly?" Frank asked as he handed her the clothing. "I'll step out while you get dressed. Here, take my hat too. Tuck your hair under it."

"And what will you wear?"

"I'll grab one off a drunk in the street. Don't worry."

Frank left the room and Molly quickly shed her dress and undergarments. She pulled on a pair of white cotton drawers, as she tried not to think about the stains on the legs. He'd given her a blue checkered shirt with dark brown wool trousers and a faded plaid striped coat. Molly stepped into the pants and slipped the suspenders over her shoulders. Then she put on the coat, buttoned it, stuck the revolver in her pocket, and put on the hat. Finally, Molly sat in the chair and pulled her own leather ankle boots onto her feet and tied the leather laces. The weight of the gun made her feel slightly off balance as she made her way to the door.

She found Frank leaning against a building across the street, smoking a cigar. On his head, he wore a black bowler hat.

"You almost look like an uptown fancy man with that hat," Molly said.

"Perish the thought," Frank said. "We've a bit of a walk ahead of us. Stay beside me so we don't get separated."

"I will," Molly said.

They made their way north, up Bowery Boulevard. When they passed by the theater, Molly felt a pang of longing for the simple stage in New Orleans. Sure, it's nothing like the Bowery Theater, but it was still grand to be on stage in front of an audience.

When they reached Canal Street, Frank and Molly turned left, making their way several blocks to Broadway. They followed the main thoroughfare north into the heart of the city. The crowds on the street were as she remembered them. Throngs of people went about their business. She heard the cry of hot corn girls peddling their wares on the corners, and the happy sounds that spilled out of saloons and concert halls. *You'd hardly believe there was a war on*, Molly thought. *Men fight and die a few hundred miles away and here; life goes on as it always has.*

Over an hour had passed by the time they reached Washington Square. Frank stopped and pointed to an imposing three-story building made of gray stone.

"That's our destination," he said. "Look, there's O'Hara."

Molly searched but could not find him in the darkness.

"He's there," Frank said as he nodded his head toward the shadows alongside the building. "You can't see him?"

"No," Molly said. "You've the eyes of a detective. I don't. But, Frank, are we to carry Ellen all that way back to the Five Points after we get her? That's a long walk for a child."

"No," Frank said. "I secured a wagon to meet us here. The driver will take you back to my place, well, your place I guess it is now. O'Hara and I will split up and follow at a safe distance, and then I will meet you back there. There'll be some food for you both in the wagon to take with you and I took the liberty of getting a doll for the girl."

"That's kind of you," Molly said.

Frank shrugged. "I just figured she'd be wanting something to play with. Come on, if we are to do it, we gotta go now."

Frank led Molly around to the back of the building, sticking to the shadows as they crept along. He pointed to a ladder which ran from the ground up to the roof.

"Here's where we go up," he said.

Molly gasped. "And I'm to climb that?"

"Now ain't the time for second thoughts."

"No," Molly said, "it's not that. It's just that it seems a very long way up."

"It's only a long way if you fall," Frank said, "which you won't so long as you hang on tight and look up, not down. Whatever you do, don't look down at the ground. Come on. You go first and I'll follow along behind. And for God's sake, don't fall or you'll take me down with you."

Molly reached out and took hold of the ladder. Rung by rung, she made her way up. When she reached the level of the second floor, Molly paused for a second and collected her wits.

"Come on," Frank urged in a whisper. "Keep moving, Molly. You can't stop now. You are almost there."

Molly bit her lip and nodded. With her eyes fixed on the roof, she began to climb again. When she reached the ledge, Molly scrambled off the ladder and fell to her knees for a moment, breathing hard. She rubbed the moisture from her palms on the front of her trousers while Frank moved alongside her.

"See?" he said. "It wasn't that bad. And you are halfway done."

"Halfway?" Molly asked.

"We've still got climb down once we get Ellen," Frank said. "Unless of course you plan on sprouting wings and flying off into the night."

"Let's just get on with it," Molly said.

"The roof hatch is just over there," Frank said.

Molly followed the direction of his finger and saw a square hatch with a handle on it near the part of the roof closest to the street. Frank casually walked over to the ledge, removed his hat, and tossed it over the edge. It floated lazily on the air as it made its way earthward.

"What did you do that for?" Molly asked, her voice low.

"That's the signal for O'Hara to kick up a fuss. Once we hear the noise, I'll open the hatch and in we go. I'll go first. You follow behind me but leave the hatch open. Follow me to the room, get the girl, and then we'll get the fuck outta here. I'll let you climb up first, and I'll follow. Then you pass the child to me and go down the ladder. I'll bring Ellen down. Then hop in the wagon, cover up with the blanket, and don't so much as move until you get back to the room. Understand?"

"Frank …" Molly took a deep breath. "If something goes wrong, just know that I…"

Shouts from the street below interrupted her as O'Hara's demonstration began.

Chapter Thirty-Three

The sound of loud singing and bottles smashing against the pavement drifted up to the roof where Molly crouched alongside Frank. He waited for a few moments to allow the noise to reach a crescendo, then he lifted the hatch. Molly peered down and saw a short ladder led to a hallway. In a flash, Frank moved down the ladder and beckoned for Molly to follow him. She turned around and felt with her foot until it contacted a rung and made her way into the building. Frank put his hands on her hips to help steady her as she reached the floor. When she got off the ladder, Molly turned to face him and whispered, "Now what?"

Frank held a finger to his lips and motioned her to follow behind him. They crept down the hallway, making sure to stay in contact with one of the walls. A lamp halfway down the corridor provided scant light, and the shadows provided them with cover. When they reached a door, Frank dropped to a knee and pulled Molly down beside him. He fished around in his coat pocket and pulled out a tool though, in the dark, Molly couldn't make out the exact type.

"When I get this lock popped," he said, "get in there and grab her. I'll stay here in the corridor in case there is trouble. If you hear any gunplay while you are in there, stay put."

"Jesus, are you planning to have a dustup here in the hall?" Molly said. "I thought you said this would be easy."

Frank motioned her to be quiet as he focused on the lock. "Almost got it. Come on, you bastard. There! Got it!"

The locked gave way with an audible click. Frank turned the doorknob and eased the wooden door open.

"Get in there," he whispered as Molly crawled past him into the room.

She got to her feet and scanned her surroundings, her eyes taking time to adjust to the blackness inside the room. Molly made out a table and a desk but saw nothing resembling a bed until she moved further into the room. A shape beneath a blanket indicated that there was someone, a small someone in the bed. Molly held her breath as she crept toward the bed. Her heart nearly froze when the shape stirred for a second. *Just do it,* Molly told herself. *Just see if it is her and if it is, take her and get out. What are you afraid of?*

"Molly hurry the fuck up," Frank whispered from the doorway. "We gotta get out of here, now!"

His words pushed her to act. Molly covered the distance between herself and the bed in two big steps. She squinted her eyes as she looked down at the child. Her hand shook as she gently pulled the covers back. *It's her—it's Ellen*! Tears sprang to her eyes as she thought of all that had transpired since the time she last held the girl in her arms.

"God damn it, Molly," Frank said. "Get moving or I'll leave you here!"

What if she doesn't recognize me, Molly thought. She pulled the hat from her head and let her hair fall down. When Molly reached down to pick Ellen up, the child opened her eyes and smiled. "Molly," she said. "Your name is Molly."

"It is, Ellen," she said as she picked the girl up. Ellen nestled her head on Molly's shoulder. "Shhh. You just go on back to sleep. I've come to take you to live with me."

"Finally," Frank said when Molly walked out of the room. "Get her up to the roof. I'll be right behind you. Where's my hat?"

"I took it off," Molly whispered.

"Damn," Frank said. "That was my favorite hat. Go on. Get moving."

Molly heard a sudden noise from the down the hallway as she reached Frank's side. Ellen cried out in alarm as light from a lamp flickered to life. Though her brain urged her forward, Molly could not help turning to look over her shoulder. She froze. A woman walked towards them, holding a lamp out in front of her. The light reflected off her face. No! Molly thought. It can't be!

"What's going on here?" Susannah called out. "Charles! Get up here now! We've a pair of burglars!"

Blind raged seized her. Molly wanted to thrust the child into Frank's arms and tear the woman to pieces. *I'll kill her*, Molly swore. *So help me God, I'll not let her escape punishment. Her and her man too. The bastards.* Her free hand moved towards her pocket, where the revolver pressed into her side.

"Go!" Frank yelled.

His voice shook her from her trance, and she scrambled up the ladder to the roof, her arms aching from carrying Ellen's weight along with her own. Frank moved up behind her and knelt down to close the hatch. He pulled a small chain from his pocket and wrapped it around the handle along with a large padlock.

"That'll keep anyone from following us this way," he said. "Now, give me the girl and get down to the ground."

Molly looked at Ellen and said, "Mr. Frank is going to carry you for a bit. But Molly will be waiting for you on the ground. Is that okay?"

Ellen nodded, her eyes still full of sleep, and Molly handed her to Frank and ran to the edge of the roof. Down below, illuminated by a streetlight, a wagon halted beside the ladder. Molly turned around and started to back down the ladder. She kept her eyes focused upward on Frank, as he came down behind her with Ellen tucked tightly under his arm. From somewhere inside the house, Molly heard a shout as her feet touched the ground. Frank turned and thrust Ellen into Molly's arms. He stuck his hand in his pocket and removed his Colt Navy.

"Quick," he said. "Get in the back of the wagon!"

The man in the driver's seat reached back into the wagon bed and folded a canvas tarp back.

"Come on, Ellen," Molly said. "We are going to go for a little ride."

"Don't make a sound," Frank said as he covered them with the tarp. "I'll see you later."

Molly heard him speak a few words to the driver, but she could not make out what they were. The wagon lurched forward, and she felt it turn onto the street. Keeping her voice as soft as she could, Molly sang the words of "Mo Ghile Mear" as the wagon rocked and creaked its way south down Broadway. The girl soon fell asleep, using a burlap sack as a pillow. Molly allowed herself to breathe for the first time since they reached the building. The revolver in her pocket dug into her hip, and she shifted a bit to try and make herself more comfortable.

Thank God it did not come down to that, she thought. *I'd not want to put Ellen in danger by having to shoot our way out. But I'd have done it if need be. For the sake of the girl.*

"I'm so sorry," she said to Ellen as the child slept. "I'm so sorry I lost you. We'll get Dr. Howard to look you over. No, it'll have to be someone else. He's gone now. If those bastards hurt you, I'll go back there and pull them apart with my own two hands."

The slow, steady movements of the wagon nearly lulled Molly to sleep as well. When it finally stopped, Molly felt the weight shift as the driver got down. She blinked as he pulled the tarp back.

"Here you go, miss," he said. "Got you home safe and sound."

"Thank you, sir," Molly said as she climbed out of the wagon with Ellen. The driver handed her a sack and Molly shifted the child to her right arm and took hold of the sack with her left. It wasn't heavy, but the combined weight of the girl, the revolver, and the sack staggered her a bit.

"Just some food and a toy for the girl in there," the driver said. "Look here, let me help you."

"I can manage myself, sir," Molly said as she walked toward the door to her room. "But thank you all the same. And I know Frank is grateful as well."

"Ma'am," the driver tipped his hat and hopped back on the wagon.

"Let's get inside," Molly said. "Are you hungry, Ellen? There's a bit of food and a nice little surprise for you too. Do you like surprises?"

"Molly," the girl said. "Where are we, Molly?"

"This is our new home," Molly said as she pushed the door open. "Or rather, it's our home for now. I'll try to find us something nicer just as soon as I can. Here, let's sit you on the bed."

Molly placed the child on the bed and placed the sack on the table. After she lit the lamp, Molly pulled out a loaf of bread, two apples, a bottle of spring water, and a small doll. There was a small coin pouch inside as well. Molly took the revolver out of her pocket and placed it on the table, then she opened the coin pouch. Inside, she found her Saint Michael's medal.

"Look here!" Molly said as she turned and handed the doll to the child. "I've a new friend for you!"

Ellen smiled sleepily and took the doll. She held it up and studied it for a minute, and then placed it in her lap.

"Let's get you some food," Molly said. She broke off a piece of bread and handed it to Ellen, along with an apple. Ellen sat the bread down and bit into the apple while Molly opened the bottle of spring water. She took a small sip and passed it to the girl. For the first time Molly was able to study the child in the light. Ellen had grown over the past year and a half but didn't weigh much more than she had when Molly carried her through the city before. Still, Ellen did not appear malnourished in the least. If anything, she looked even healthier than Molly remembered. *So at least they fed her*, she thought. *I guess they weren't entirely savages. No, they are savages, the lot of them.*

After they finished eating, Molly tucked the child into bed. Though weary herself, Molly decided to wait for Frank to return. As she sat in the chair, Molly fought a war with her eyelids to keep them open. Eventually she lost and drifted to sleep. A soft knock on the door woke her up. Startled, she looked around the room. Ellen slept beneath a wool blanket. Molly blinked and tried to figure out how long she'd been asleep and if the knock had just been a dream. Though the room lacked windows, Molly could tell it was still dark outside. *It must have only been a few minutes*, she thought with a yawn. Another knock, soft, but insistent came from the door. Molly stood up and walked toward the sound. She placed her hand on the lock and said, "Who is it?"

"Frank Lynch sent me," a male voice said. "I've a message to give you from him."

"What is the message?" Molly asked.

"Don't know," the man said. "He wrote it down."

"Then read it to me," Molly said.

"I can't read it to you. It's dark out here and besides, I don't know my letters that good. He said I was to hand it to you personally."

Is it safe, Molly asked herself. It has to be. *Nobody knows I'm here except Frank. Maybe there was some trouble and he's trying to warn me.* She glanced back at the table.

"Just a minute," she said as she walked over and picked up the revolver. Holding it in her right hand, facing the door, Molly unlocked it and pulled it open.

A stocky man with his hat pulled low across his brow looked up at her. His eyes widened for a moment when he saw the barrel of the revolver, then he glanced over his shoulders.

"I'll take the note now," Molly said.

"Easy with that thing," the man said. "I'm going to put my hand in the inside pocket of my coat to get it. Okay? Don't shoot."

"I won't," Molly said. "Just hand me the note. Slow like."

With his left hand, the man pulled his coat open and slipped his right hand inside. He fumbled around for a second as he said, "It's in here somewhere. Just let me dig it out."

"Hurry up," Molly said. "I've a child sleeping inside, and I don't want her to wake up."

"A child?" the man asked.

Warning bells sounded in Molly's head. *If Frank sent him, surely, he would know about the child. Yet he seems surprised by it. What is going on?* As she tried to thumb the hammer back on the revolver, the man stepped close, as his left hand shot forward and grabbed her wrist. He twisted it to the side and the revolver dropped from her hand and slid along the floor. Molly tried to scream, but the man grabbed her around the throat with his right hand and shoved her back into the room, kicking the door closed behind him.

"Who is the girl?" the man asked.

Molly tried to answer but his grip prevented it.

"All right," the man said. "I'm going to let go of your throat. But if you scream, I'll cut the child into pieces right in front of you. Understand?"

Molly nodded and the man released her. She backed up and sat down in the chair. Her eyes searched for the revolver and she spotted it a few feet away.

"Who is the child?" the man asked again. "Answer me."

"She's in my charge," Molly said.

The man frowned and said, "They didn't say nothing about a child. Just you."

"Who are you talking about?" Molly asked.

"The people that paid me," he said as he pulled his own revolver from his pocket.

"How did you find me?" Molly asked. *I've got to keep him talking until Frank gets back. It's my only chance.*

"It was simple," he said. "They told me you was friends with Frank Lynch. He's easy enough to find." He came closer and peered into her face. "You're a pretty thing," the man said. "Guess it's worth what they are paying me. Too bad the little one is here. Otherwise, I might be tempted to take some payment from you too."

"I beg you, sir," Molly said. "You may do as you wish to me, but please don't hurt the child."

"I won't," the man said. "They didn't pay me for that. And I don't work for nothing. But we do have a problem here."

"Sir?" Molly asked.

"I intended to shoot you, but that might make too much noise. Might wake the child up too, and if she sees me, well, I'd have no choice but to kill her too. So, I have to kill you quiet like."

Molly mentally calculated the distance to the revolver. The man saw the direction of her gaze. "Don't. If you make a move for that, I'll have no choice but to shoot you dead."

As he spoke, the man shifted his revolver to his left hand and reached around behind his back, under his coat, and withdrew a knife. Molly gasped as the light from the lamp reflected from the blade.

"I'll have to slit your throat. It's the quietest way I can think of, so don't you make a sound. Understand?"

This is it, Molly thought. *After everything I've been through, I'm to die here, when I've gotten Ellen back. I hope she'll forgive me.*

The man grinned at her and gestured with the knife. "Best you just stay sitting there. I'm going to walk around behind you. It'll be over in a flash. You won't feel much of anything. It'll be like going to sleep. Or so they say."

He advanced on her with the knife. Molly closed her eyes.

The door flew open. The man whirled around in time to see Frank barge into the room, gun in hand.

The man fired first. His bullet caught Frank high in the chest. Frank's gun dropped from his hand as he staggered back into the wall and slid down to the floor, a look of confusion on his face.

Now, Molly's brain screamed. She flung herself into the man's back, sending him sprawling forward as she dropped to the floor and grabbed her revolver. The man swore and started to turn around.

Ellen sat up in the bed and screamed. Molly thumbed the hammer back and, from her knees, she fired at the man's chest. The bullet hit him in the side of his neck.

He tried to scream, but it came out as a gurgling croak as blood began to spurt from the bullet hole. Despite his wounds, the man tried to raise his gun. With her one shot expended, Molly tossed her revolver across the room and lunged for Frank's Colt.

With jerky movements, the man tried to find which direction she went. Molly's hand closed on the wooden grip and she fired a wild shot which struck the man in the kneecap. His legs flew out from under him and he crashed to the floor. With his right hand pressed to the wound in his neck, the man tried to sit up. Molly got up and stepped on his left wrist, pinning his gun to the floor.

"Close your eyes, Ellen," she called out over her shoulder, then she looked down at the man who stared back at her with eyes glazed, yet full of fear.

"By God, you are the last man who will ever lay a hand on me," Molly said as she pulled the trigger.

Then she turned her attention to Frank. "Are you badly hurt?" she asked as she knelt beside him.

Frank smiled at her. Blood trickled from the corner of his mouth as he said, "Molly. Ask … ask … O'Hara … to give … you … my … address."

"I will, Frank," she said. Outside she heard someone yelling for a doctor. "The doctor is coming to help you. Don't die, Frank. Please. Don't leave me now, Frank. Please!"

Frank shook his head and groaned. "Look … in … desk."

"Frank!" Molly exclaimed as she clutched his bloodstained hands against her chest. "Please, Frank. Stay with me."

"I … love … you … Molly," Frank said.

"I know, Frank. I know!"

She raised his hands to her lips and kissed them, tasting the coppery blood. He smiled at her again and then his breath left him in a ragged gasp as his eyes glazed over.

"What's going on?" O'Hara shouted as he burst through the door, gun in hand. "Jesus! It smells like a slaughterhouse in here."

Molly rose to her feet and turned to O'Hara.

"Frank's dead," she said as she walked across the room and picked up Ellen, who began to cry when she saw the blood on Molly's hands.

"Shhh," Molly said. "I promise you I'll not let you come to harm ever again."

Chapter Thirty-Four

Before she left the room that night, Molly searched the pockets of the man sent to kill her. She found a pouch with fifty dollars in gold. *Now I know what my life is worth*, she thought as she pushed the money into her trouser pocket. *More than I thought, I must admit.* A doctor arrived, an older man who reeked of brandy and cheap tobacco. He took one look at both men on the floor and declared them dead. Molly asked him to look over Ellen and he pronounced her fit.

"Detective O'Hara," Molly said. "Frank said I was to ask you to take me to his house."

O'Hara nodded, "I can do that, Miss Molly. Come on, let's go now."

He walked over and knelt beside Frank's body. O'Hara opened Frank's coat and pulled a bloody key out of his inside pocket. He wiped the blood on his trousers and stood up. Molly grabbed her Saint Michael's medal off the table and slipped it into her pocket, then picked up the small revolver Frank had given her and gathered up her dress and undergarments.

"I'll carry the girl," O'Hara said.

Molly nodded. When the trio walked outside, over a dozen uniformed police officers were gathered in the street. She felt a moment of panic. *Are they here to haul me to the cells again*, she wondered. But a few of them nodded at her or touched a finger to the brim of their caps.

"Will they be wanting to talk to me about what happened tonight?" Molly asked after they passed through the officers.

"No," O'Hara said. "I'll tell 'em what they need to know. And besides, it's obvious what happened inside the room."

Frank lived a short six blocks from the room he kept in the Five Points. When they arrived at the house, O'Hara handed Ellen to Molly and unlocked the door. He followed her inside and watched as Molly placed Ellen on the couch.

"Stay as long as you like," he said. "It's what Frank would've wanted."

Molly nodded as she searched until she found an oil lamp on the wall.

"Do you have a lucifer?" Molly asked.

O'Hara pulled a box of matches out of his pocket and passed them to Molly, who lit the lamp.

"What are you going to do now?" O'Hara asked. "I mean, not right now. But in the future."

"I don't know," Molly confessed. "I know one thing. I can't stay in the city. The family what sent that creature after me might do it again. Before all this, I only wanted to find Ellen. Now we have. When I got to this country, I thought I might like to see California. Maybe we'll go there."

"I don't think they'll send someone else," O'Hara said. "But just in case, why don't you stay inside for the next couple of days. I'll drop off some provisions for you in a few hours."

"Thank you, Detective O'Hara," Molly said. "Before you leave, could you fetch us a pail of water? I want to wash the blood off me hands."

O'Hara nodded and went out back. A few minutes later, he returned with a pail. He bid them good night, though it would soon be dawn. Molly scrubbed the dried blood from her hands as the child slept. Once she'd finished, Molly explored the house. There was a bedroom just off the parlor with a narrow wooden bed. She picked up Ellen and carried her to the bed. Before she tucked the child under the covers, Molly pulled the Saint Michael's medal from her pocket and fastened it around Ellen's neck.

"My father gave me this," she said. "When I was about your age. I want you to have it now."

Ellen lifted the medal and studied it.

"Thank you, Molly," she said.

"It's Saint Michael," Molly said. "He's the saint what protects you when times are hard."

Ellen smiled and Molly helped her get under the covers. Molly stayed in the room until the child was asleep, and then she went in search of the desk. She found a telegram on top of a stack of other papers. Molly glanced at it and noticed it was from New Orleans. Madam Delacroix had replied to Frank's telegram and said that Molly's money was safe and on deposit with a bank in the city. *She must not have gotten my letter yet when she sent this,* Molly thought. *But that makes sense. I'll have to collect the money somehow. Even if that means going back for a while. Besides, it was there that I got my start singing. But I'll not stay long. I'll have to send her another telegram and tell her to ignore my letter when it arrives.*

Molly opened the drawer and found a wooden box. Opening it up, she gasped when she saw the pile of gold coins inside. When she counted it out, it came to two hundred dollars. There was another hundred dollars in Yankee greenbacks, but Molly knew those to not be worth as much as one might think. *How did Frank come to have this? With him on a peeler's salary? He couldn't have made all this at work. Not by legal means.* She considered asking O'Hara if he knew where Frank had come by the money, but quickly dismissed the thought. *No, he may not know about it. What if Frank was up to something other than just policing the streets? After all, didn't he say that some of them was dangerous?*

Molly dozed for a few hours on the couch and awoke when she heard a knock at the door. She first went to check in on Ellen, who was still asleep, and then picked up the revolver and crept to the door.

"Who is there?"

"It's me, Miss Molly," O'Hara said.

Molly lowered the gun, unlocked the door, and opened it. He carried a burlap sack in his right hand and had a leather-bound book and a couple of newspapers tucked under his right arm.

"Morning," he said as he walked into the kitchen and placed the sack on a table. He returned and handed her the book and newspapers. "Frank told me you liked to read. I got you some of today's papers. And a book. It's by a guy named Dickens. Something about two cities. Thought you might like it."

"Thank you," Molly said.

O'Hara hesitated for a moment and said, "I ain't sure if you are interested or not. But Frank's funeral is the day after tomorrow. Mass will be at Saint Patrick's on Mulberry Street by the police headquarters. The boys took up a collection. We were able to get a plot for him at a cemetery too. Not the one right there at the church. But it's close enough. Won't have a fancy marble headstone or anything. But it's something at least."

"I'm sure he'd appreciate that," Molly said.

"You are welcome to be there, of course," O'Hara said. "It'll be safe enough for you, with half the department being there and all."

"Thank you. I'll do my best to be there. With Ellen, of course."

"There's a boy named Anderson that lives next door," O'Hara said. "You can trust him. If you need to get a message to me or if you need any errands run, he'll do it. I've already had a talk with him. Well, I gotta get back to work. Maybe I'll see you in a couple of days. At the funeral."

Molly nodded and thanked him again as O'Hara slipped out the door. *We're better off the sooner we are out of the city*, Molly thought. *Less of a chance that someone might spot us and do us harm, even if O'Hara thinks it is safe*. From her time at Miss Cecilia's, Molly remembered that the clippers which sailed from New York City bound for San Francisco generally took around four months to arrive if you went around the tip of South America. It took less time, fifty days or so, if you sailed to Panama and crossed over land to the Pacific side and booked passage from there. *I'll not subject the girl to a trip of four months on the ocean,* Molly determined. *But I won't march her through a jungle either.*

She got up and looked around the house. Finally, she found a faded map in a cabinet. In the bedroom, Ellen began to stir. Molly walked into the room and sat down on the bed.

"Come, Ellen," she said. "Let's figure out how to get to California. Look, I know we can take a train, though not all the way."

Molly took hold of Ellen's hand and folded three fingers into her palm, leaving the index finger extended. She guided the child's finger from New York to Philadelphia to Cincinnati to Saint Louis.

"From there we might go on a steamboat down to New Orleans for a bit," Molly said. "It wouldn't be a long trip. Just a couple of days. Does that sound fun?"

Ellen nodded.

"Then back up to St. Louis and west from there. We are going to end up here!"

She guided Ellen's finger across the plains to California.

"When, Molly?" Ellen asked.

"Just as soon as we can," Molly said. "We'll need to purchase tickets to Philadelphia first and then try to find us some clothes and suitcases. Let's get you cleaned up and then go see what we can find in a shop. We'll try and go as far as St. Louis, then I'll see if there's a theater in need of a singer. And then, we'll go down to New Orleans to pick up my money. And maybe do a concert or two. And then … California. It'll be a long trip, but we'll make it."

The next few days passed in a blur. Molly took Ellen to some shops and found enough of what they needed. She felt a few pangs of worry as she considered taking a child across the Great Plains, but she told herself that the land had to be safer than the ocean since people can't sink on land. While they busied themselves getting ready, Molly sent Anderson to find out about the cost of tickets and to the telegraph office to send a message to New Orleans. When he returned, Molly gave him the money, with a small tip, and sent him off to secure their spots on the train.

The night before they left, Molly read to Ellen from *A Tale of Two Cities* before she put her to bed. When the girl's eyes closed, Molly kissed her forehead and slipped out of the room. *The best of times and the worst of times,* she thought. *For some of us, even the best of times are still tough enough.*

It's a shame you can't go with us Frank, she thought as she sat down at the desk and picked up a sheet of stationery. It took her several attempts before she managed to draft a letter to her mother. Rather than delve into the entirety of her story, Molly simply let her know her aunt and uncle were dead, and Molly was taking care of a child whose parents died on the trip to America. To explain the lack of a letter written up to this point, Molly said that she had been so busy providing for the child that there was not time, though she knew that excuse did not sound believable. *She's probably given up on me by now anyway,* Molly thought. *Maybe she thinks I died on the ocean or died in the city. That's near enough to the truth.*

Molly found sleep difficult to come by that night. As she lay in the dark, she thought of Frank, standing there in the middle of a crowded street in his blue uniform on the day she met him. That image was replaced by one of him standing in the prison cell as he told her not to lose hope. She could feel his hand in hers. *Jesus, Frank,* she swore softly, *you were kind to me and look at the result. I got you killed for your trouble.* Eventually exhaustion overtook her, and her eyes closed.

It seemed like she'd only been asleep for an hour before the gray light of morning crept through the windows. She rose and lit the fire in the stove in the kitchen to make breakfast and to heat up water for a bath. They ate, then Molly helped Ellen bathe first. When it was Molly's turn, she leaned back for a moment in the tub and thought, this must be what freedom feels like in America. It's a moment to remember, for sure.

Their belongings fit into two suitcases, neither that big, but Molly sent Anderson to the train station with them so that she would not have to carry them to the funeral.

A light drizzle fell as they left the church following the funeral mass. A horse-drawn hearse carried Frank's coffin; a small contingent of uniformed police officers and a few firefighters marched behind it. When they reached the cemetery, Superintendent Kennedy stood at the grave and spoke of Frank's devotion to duty and how he'd given his life in the service of the city. Molly smiled despite herself. *He was helping me, not the city*, she thought. *Still, he died in service of another. And for a peeler, there's nothing grander than that I suppose.*

As a priest read a scripture, Molly looked down at Ellen, who stood beside her, holding her hand. Ellen smiled up at her. The graveside service ended, and the officers began to drift away. O'Hara came over and shook Molly's hand.

"If there's ever anything you two need," he said, "just send word to me."

"Thank you," Molly said. "Take care of yourself, Detective O'Hara."

He smiled and walked away. Molly waited until the cemetery emptied except for the gravediggers. She watched as they lowered the casket into the ground and began to shovel dirt on top of it. The misty rain fell heavier as they finished and walked away, shovels trailing behind them. Molly led Ellen over to grave.

"I owe you more than … more than … Jesus, Frank! I owe you my life," Molly said. She choked back a sob and continued, "And so does young Ellen. We'll always be in your debt. We will never forget you. I give you my word, Francis Lynch. We will never forget you."

She started to walk away but paused. She turned and faced the grave. Softly, she began to sing.

Maxwelton's braes are bonnie when early fa's the dew
And it was there that Annie Laurie gave me her promise true
Gave me her promise true which ne'er forgot shall be
And for bonnie Annie Laurie, I'd lay me doon and dee

When she finished, Molly looked down at Ellen and said, "Come along, Ellen. We've a train to catch. Philadelphia and then St. Louis are waiting for us."

Author's Note

I learned quite a bit during and after the publication of my first novel, *So Others May Live*. One thing I gleaned was that readers frequently ask where authors get their ideas from. It is tempting to say something like "I get mine on aisle three at Kroger." I shall, however, resist that temptation and address the matter head on here. My wife got me a book called *Working Girls* by Robert Flynn Johnson in May 2019. The book consists of previously unpublished photos of sex workers in a house of ill fame in Reading, Pennsylvania circa 1892. The photographer, who had a studio nearby, had his favorites among the working girls, and several of them have numerous photos included in the book. It was the photo on page seventy-three that caught my eye. A young woman is sitting in a chair in front of a dresser. She is looking at a photograph in her hand and she has a locket around her neck. I found myself drawn in, nay, captivated, by the photograph. Who was she? Where did she come from? Who was in the picture she was looking at? Who gave her the locket? It was obviously important to her since she had it on in the numerous other photos of her in the book. She became my Molly. As I gazed at the photograph, the lyrics to Soul Asylum's 1993 hit "Runaway Train" came to mind. That, in and of itself, was kind of odd since, though I went to high school and college in the '90s and love the decade's music, that song was never a favorite of mine. On a whim, I decided to watch the music video, which I had not seen before. Imagine my surprise when I learned the video featured missing children. Later that day, when I got in my truck to run some errands, the first song that came on PopRocks on SiriusXM was—you guessed it—"Runaway Train." And that, dear reader, is where the idea to write *Molly's Song* originated.

I made the decision to set the novel during the American Civil War rather than during the time period in which the photos in the book were taken for a few reasons. First of all, the Civil War is the American

Iliad. You can argue that the war and the attempts at reconstruction that followed are the defining events in our nation's history. I knew that the upheaval brought about by the war would make a more compelling background for the novel. I would not call this a Civil War novel, but rather a novel set during the Civil War, as it is far removed from the battlefields of Virginia, though events there do impact the story.

Second, prostitution has long been associated with times of armed conflict, and the Civil War was no different. Though we tend to look at the nineteenth century through rose-tinted glasses, the truth was quite different. Prostitution was legal, or at least tolerated, in much of the country. It was widespread as well. The Union Army waged a war against venereal disease just as they fought the Confederates. Union troops who occupied Nashville took 20 percent casualties, not from the Rebels, but from the ladies who worked the area known as Smoky Row. In an attempt to combat the spread of disease, the US Army did, in fact, license prostitutes in areas under their control, as referenced in the novel. While armies battled back and forth across the land, Sons of Mars frequently found succor in the arms of Daughters of Venus. For those who are tempted to look at the Victorian era as being prim and proper, with no carnal relations taking place outside the marital bed, I will only point out that in the 1860s, one could buy a ten-year-old virgin on a street corner in New York City. Now, as in the nineteenth century, there are those who blame the prostitute for her profession. Truthfully, many young women were forced into this environment due to economic reasons, or were, to use a modern word, trafficked. Once engaged in the life, they found it hard to escape. It is easy to sit in moral judgment of others if you have not experienced life in their shoes.

For those of you who are devotees of legal dramas on television or the legal thriller genre in fiction, you probably noticed that the courtroom scenes in this novel were a bit different than what you would find in a modern courtroom. The mid-nineteenth-century court was, indeed, a different place. Juries were all male. There was no exclusionary rule applied to the states through the Fourteenth Amendment. The novel is set before *Weeks v. US* applied such a rule to the federal government either. In a way, trials were a bit more wide open when it came to questioning witnesses than we see today. Lest you think that nineteenth century gender norms would have meant there was no way that a young woman like Molly would ever have been sentenced to the gallows, I point you to the case of twenty-two-year-old Irish immigrant Bridget Durgan. It only took the jury twenty minutes to find her guilty of murder, and spectators in the courtroom burst into wild applause when they heard the verdict. Ms. Durgan was hanged in New Jersey on August 30, 1867. Given Molly's ethnicity, immigrant status, the victim's political connections, and the fact that Molly was a prostitute, the sentence in her case would, in all probability, have been given if this were real life and not fiction.

Though I did not include a firefighter as a main character in this novel, as I did in *So Others May Live*, I did work one into the story to give the reader a glimpse of nineteenth-century firefighting. Hibernia Engine Company 14 on Elizabeth Street is a figment of my imagination. In the 1850s, Hose Company 14 was based at that location, but they were no longer there by the time of the Civil War. Other companies, such as Engine Company 6 were, however, real. Chief Decker really did face down a mob at the Colored Orphan Asylum in July of 1863 during the Riots and his statement to them, which saved his life, was as I described it in the novel. The city finally replaced the volunteer companies with a paid department in June of 1865. Chief Decker was asked to stay on as the first chief of the new department. He declined.

I suppose it was a natural enough thing that one day I would set out to write a novel set during the Civil War. One of my great-grandmothers was born in 1898 and lived well into her nineties. When I was a kid, she told me stories about her grandfathers, both Irish immigrants and Civil War veterans, along with sundry uncles and cousins who also served. It is kind of odd to be in my forties and yet able to say that I talked to someone who talked to Civil War veterans. Later, when I was in college, I decided to become a Civil War re-enactor. It was then that I met Robert, one of the people to whom this book is dedicated. Over the next sixteen years, we traveled all over the country attending events. We logged thousands of miles in his truck. Our conversations ranged from music to women, but they always circled back to the War. Robert was a virtual encyclopedia of all things Civil War, particularly the naval aspects of the conflict. He never met a stranger and would not hesitate to help a person in need. Particularly adept at reaching children with his love of history, I have no doubt that he ignited a fire in some young student which led them to become a history teacher. He went on to that big reenactment in the sky in 2014. His loss still stings, and I swear I feel it more with each passing year, especially when I start to cover the Civil War each semester in my 1301 courses. I miss him but I know we will meet again in Valhalla and once again lift a jug of grog.

Likewise, I have a supportive group of readers both here in the United States and, indeed, throughout the world. To all of them I say, "Sorry that it took so long for a second book to come out." Hopefully, my third novel will not take as much time. My friends and family have traveled along this road with me as well, and they have my gratitude. As always, that caliph of the comma splice, potentate of plot, and mogul of the manuscript, my editor Kristen, at The Blue Garret, has my thanks. Her input on an earlier draft of *Molly's Song* made this a better book. She has been with me for two books now and is not yet threatening to retire every time she sees a manuscript from me, so that is a good sign. Right? I also would like to thank Mary Lou, Jacqueline, and the staff at Fireship Press for believing in this book and its author. Naturally, any factual errors, whether intentional, accidental or by omission are the fault of myself alone and none of the individuals thanked in this Author's Note.

I would also like to thank an amazing group of people. Several years ago, I discovered a podcast called All Bad Things. As you can imagine from the title, it covers various disasters from around the world and throughout the centuries. The intrepid hosts Rachel and David, aided by their feline companions Jesse Pinkman and Demetrius, put out a new episode every Monday. Through the podcast's Facebook group, I have met some wonderful people who have followed along on my writing journey. They are among the finest humans I have ever encountered and are a breath of fresh air among the usual divisiveness that plagues social media platforms. We come from all different backgrounds and are brought together by our interest in disasters and their aftermaths.

Anastasia won't forgive me if I fail to include here that she has a crush on Demetrius and sends her affection.

Writing is a labor of love, yet sometimes it seems to be an exercise in futility. It is a profession full of rejection, self-doubt, and times where you wonder if all the blood, sweat, and tears are worth it. Then one day you get a kind note or email from a reader who tells you how much they enjoyed your book. I think I can speak for most authors when I say that those are the days we live for. Signing books is a pure joy. At the end of the day, I write because it is one of the only things, apart from firefighting, that I have ever been good at doing, though I suppose my skill at either is debatable, depending upon who you ask. It is the only thing that gives me that same sense of excitement too. When starting the day in front of a blank screen, my heart races with the same energy as it did when we would get dispatched to a box alarm for a house fire in the wee hours of the morning. To receive kind notes from readers helps keep me, helps keep us, going. It fortifies us for those long nights when we stare at the wall contemplating giving up. So, to you, dear reader, I give my most heartfelt thanks.

Feel free to follow my adventures at http://leehutchauthor.com. In case you are wondering, my "little" princess Anastasia Colleen helped with this manuscript too, as did my wife Elizabeth, who makes all things worthwhile.

Stay tuned, for Molly O'Sullivan still has plenty of stories left to tell.

L.H.

About the Author

Lee grew up on the Texas/Louisiana border. As a child, he enjoyed playing football, reading, and hanging around fire stations. He entered the fire service as a young man and spent 15 years as a firefighter and arson investigator before an injury forced his retirement. Along the way, Lee picked up a BA and an MA in History along with an MS in Criminal Justice. Presently, he teaches history at a community college in Southeast Texas. A lover of cats, Lee is also a boxing fan and he is obsessed with Russian Literature. His first novel, *So Others May Live*, was published in 2019. *Molly's Song* is the first in a projected three book series.

Instagram: @leehutch_author
Facebook: https://www.facebook.com/leehutchauthor/
Website: https://leehutchauthor.com/

Other Books by Fireship Press

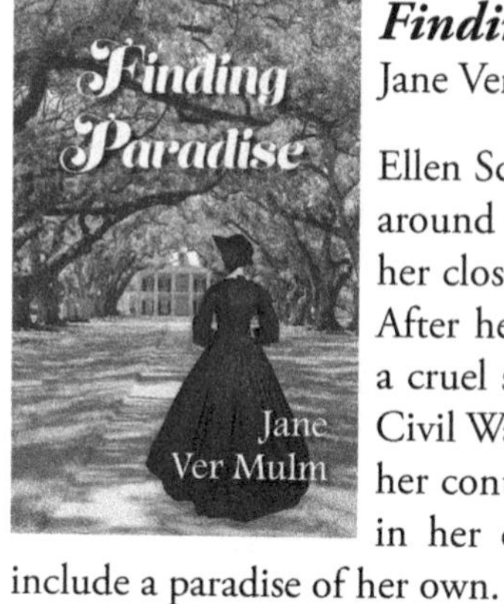

Finding Paradise

Jane Ver Mulm

Ellen Schmidt finds herself out of step with the world around her. Considered a spinster in her community, her closest friends are the slaves that her family owns. After her father arranges her marriage, she must face a cruel set of circumstances and the beginning of the Civil War, setting her on a path that seems to be out of her control. Strong and independent, Ellen continues in her own unique way to forge a future that can include a paradise of her own.

"If you enjoy reading about the Civil War era, this book [*Finding Paradise*] should be placed on top of your reading list."

—Trudi LoPreto, *Readers' Favorite*

The Prophet of Cobb Hollow

Mingo Kane

When a New York novelist finds the dusty journal of a lost American legend, he can scarcely believe what he is reading. The story tells of a man having been rescued and raised by a Cherokee shaman named Three Crows, of riding with known gunslingers and a young Teddy Roosevelt, as a Confederate spy working for Mosby's Rangers during The Civil War, and the horrific conditions he experienced in the deadly trenches of World War I.

As the War Between the States ends and our country begins to heal, this American legend returns home to find the remains of his murdered family, swearing an oath of vengeance against everyone responsible.

He is the only man to have walked through the portals of our national history. He is the oldest living human on earth and now his oral collections are told as it was lived. His name is Reuben Shadrack Judah, and he is: *The Prophet of Cobb Hollow.*

CPSIA information can be obtained
at www.ICGtesting.com
Printed in the USA
LVHW030155081221
705559LV00001B/99